Diane Chamberlain

'Emotional, complex and laced with suspense, this
fascinating story is a brilliant read.'
-*Closer*

'An excellent read'
—*The Sun*

'This complex tale will stick with you forever.'
—*Now*

'A hugely addictive twist in the tale makes this a sizzling sofa
read…a deeply compelling and moving new novel.'
—*Heat*

'This exquisite novel about love and friendship is written like
a thriller…you won't want to put it down.'
—*Bella*

'A bittersweet story about regret and hope'
—*Publishers Weekly*

'A brilliantly told thriller'
—*Woman*

'An engaging and absorbing story that'll have
you racing through pages to finish'
—*People's Friend*

'This compelling mystery will have you
on the edge of your seat.'
—*Inside Soap*

'A fabulous thriller with plenty of surprises'
—*Star*

'Essential reading for Jodi Picoult fans'
—*Daily Mail*

Kiss River

Diane Chamberlain

GETS TO THE **HEART** OF THE STORY

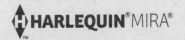

Published in Great Britain 2013
Harlequin MIRA, an imprint of Harlequin (UK) Limited,
Eton House, 18-24 Paradise Road,
Richmond, Surrey, TW9 1SR

© Diane Chamberlain 2003

ISBN 978 1 848 45209 1

59-0113

Harlequin's policy is to use papers that are natural, renewable and recyclable products and made from wood grown in sustainable forests. The logging and manufacturing processes conform to the legal environmental regulations of the country of origin.

Printed and bound
by CPI Group (UK) Ltd, Croydon, CR0 4YY

For Haseena and all the other waiting children

The bond that links your true family is not one of blood, but of respect and joy in each other's life. Rarely do members of one family grow up under the same roof.

—Richard Bach

Chapter One

THE AIR CONDITIONER IN HER AGING CAR WAS giving out, blowing warm, breath-stealing air into Gina's face. If she could have torn her concentration away from her mission for even a moment, she would have felt a pang of fear over what the repair of the air conditioner would cost her. Instead, she merely opened the car windows and let the hot, thick, salt breeze fill the interior. She took deep breaths, smelling the unfamiliar brininess in the air, so different from the scent of the Pacific. The humidity worked its way into her long hair, lifting it, tangling it, forming fine dark tendrils on her forehead. Another woman might have run her hands over her hair to smooth the flyaway strands. Gina did not care. After six days of driving, six nights of sleeping in the cramped quarters of the car, several quick showers stolen from fitness clubs to which she did not belong and eighteen cheap, fast-food meals, she was almost there. She was close enough to Kiss River to taste it in the air.

The bridge she was crossing was very long and straight and clogged with traffic. She should have expected that. After all, it was a Friday evening in late June and she was headed toward the Outer Banks of North Carolina, an area she supposed was now quite a tourist attraction. She might have trouble finding a room for the night. She hadn't thought of that. She was used to the Pacific Northwest, where the coastline was craggy and the water too cold for swimming, and where finding a room for the night was not ordinarily an impossible chore.

The cars were moving slowly enough to allow her to study the map she held flat against the steering wheel. Once she left the bridge, the traffic crawled for a mile or so past a school and a couple of strip malls, and then perhaps two-thirds of the cars turned right onto Highway 12. She turned left and entered an area the map identified as Southern Shores.

Through the open car windows, she could hear, but not see, the ocean on her right. The waves pounded the beach behind the eclectic mix of flat-topped houses, larger, newer homes and old beach cottages. In spite of the slow-moving stream of cars, the Outer Banks seemed open and wide and empty here. Not what she had expected from reading the diary. But the diary had not been about Southern Shores, and as she continued driving, live oaks and wild vegetation she did not recognize began to cradle the curving road. She was approaching the village of Duck, which sounded quaint and was probably expensive, and interested her not in the least. After Duck, she would pass through a place called Sanderling, and then through a wildlife sanctuary, and soon after that, she should see a sign marking the road to the Kiss River lighthouse. Although she knew she was miles from the lighthouse, she couldn't help but glance to the sky again and again, hoping to see the tower in the distance through the trees. Even though it was the tallest lighthouse in the country, she knew she could not possibly see it from where she was. That didn't stop her from looking, though.

She had more time to study the little shopping areas of Duck than she wanted, since the cars and SUVs crept along the road at a near standstill. If the traffic didn't clear soon, it would be dark by the time she reached Kiss River. She'd hoped to get there no later than five. It was now nearly seven, and the sun was already sinking toward the horizon. Would the lighthouse be closed for the evening? For that matter, would it be open to the public at all? What time did they turn on the light? Maybe they no longer did. That would disappoint her. She wanted to see how it illuminated Kiss River, once every four and a half seconds. If people *were* allowed to climb the lighthouse, she doubted they would be permitted to visit the lantern room, but she would have to get into that room, one way or another. Only recently, she'd discovered that she was a pretty good liar. She'd lived her entire life valuing honesty and integrity. Suddenly, she'd become manipulative, a master at deceit. She could, when pressed, travel far outside the law. The first time she'd snuck into a fitness club to use the shower on this trip east, she'd trembled with fear, not only at the possibility of being caught, but at the sheer dishonesty of the act. By the time she sauntered into the club in Norfolk, though, she'd almost forgotten she didn't have a membership at the place. The end justified the means, she told herself.

So, if visiting the lantern room of the lighthouse was not allowed, she would find another way to get up there. That was the entire purpose of this trip. She would talk with someone, one of the guides or docents or whatever they were, and make up a reason for needing to see that room. Research, she would say. She was writing about lighthouses. Or taking pictures. She touched the borrowed camera hanging around her neck. It was heavy, impressive looking. She'd make up something that would sound plausible. One way or another, she needed to see the lantern room and its enormous globe of glass prisms, the Fresnel lens.

The drive through the wildlife reserve seemed to go on forever, but at least the traffic had thinned out, as cars turned onto roads leading to the houses near the beach. The remaining traffic moved briskly and the road was, for the most part, straight. Gina could examine the map easily as she drove. The sign indicating the location of the lighthouse should be somewhere along here, she thought. The road to Kiss River would run off to the right, cutting through the red oaks and loblolly pines, although it was possible that the landscape had changed since the days of the diary. Given the size and newness of many of the houses she had passed, it was possible the trees were completely gone by now and the road lined by more of the touristy homes.

Finally, she spotted a narrow road heading east into the trees. She pulled to the side of the main road, as close to the trees as she dared, and studied her map. There was no street sign, no hint at all that anything special lay down that road, but this had to be it. On the map she could see the way the land jutted out from the road. There was no river at Kiss River. It was little more than a promontory with a whimsical name and a towering lighthouse. Surely that lighthouse was a tourist attraction. So why was there no sign?

She wondered if she should continue driving up the main road to look for another, more promising, turn, but shook her head. The sign must have blown over or been struck by a car. Trusting her map, she turned right onto the road.

Instantly, the road jogged to the left, surrounding her by trees. The macadam was rutted and poorly maintained, and the road twisted its way into near darkness. The air was dusky, the trees so thick that little light could cut through them. Through the open windows, she heard the buzzing of crickets or frogs or some other critter, and the sound grew louder the deeper she drove into the forest.

The road ended abruptly at a small cul-de-sac in the woods. Stopping the car, she turned on the overhead light. The map clearly showed the cul-de-sac, with a smaller road leading from it out to the lighthouse. Looking to her left, she spotted a narrow gravel lane with a heavy, rusty chain strung across its entrance. A sign hanging from the chain read in bold red letters, NO TRESPASSING.

This could not be right, she thought. Even if the lighthouse itself was not open to the public, the grounds surrounding it and the keeper's house certainly should be.

She checked the map again. There were no other roads like this one, ending in a cul-de-sac. This was it, whether she wanted it to be or not. She looked up at the gravel lane beyond the chain again. The path was foreboding, dark and shrouded by trees.

She did not consider herself a brave person, although these last few months she had found courage in herself she'd had no idea she possessed. Getting slowly out of the car, she locked the door behind her. She did have a flashlight in the trunk, but the batteries had died somewhere in Kentucky, so she carried only her map and the camera around her neck as she walked across the cul-de-sac. One end of the chain was attached to a tree, the other padlocked to a post. Skirting the post, she started walking down the gravel lane.

Even if this was the wrong road, she told herself, what harm could she come to by walking down it? True, she could break an ankle in one of the many ruts or trip over one of the tree roots that raised the gravel in a disorderly veinlike pattern. More likely, though, the worst that could happen was that she'd come to someone's tucked-away home. She would apologize, ask for directions to the lighthouse. But then she remembered the horses. There were wild horses out here. And wild boars. They could be dangerous, she remembered reading in the diary. She imagined trying to climb one of the stubby trees to escape them. Her heart pounding, she listened hard for the sound of horse hooves or breaking twigs and realized that, this deep into the woods, she could not even hear the traffic. Only the thick, strange buzz of those crickets or whatever they were. It occurred to her that she would have to walk back through these woods again, and it would be even darker by then.

How far had she walked? It couldn't have been more than a quarter of a mile. Stopping on the road, she peered hard through the trees. The road had looked quite short on the map, and surely she should be able to see the top of the lighthouse by now. She walked a bit farther and heard a whooshing, pounding sound that took her a minute to recognize as the ocean. It sounded close. Very close.

Ahead of her, the road turned slightly to the right. The vegetation was thinner and she could see light between the branches of the trees. Quickening her step, she suddenly broke free of the forest and found herself in a small, sand-swept parking lot. Had this been the visitors' parking lot for the lighthouse? One thing she knew for certain by now: for whatever reason, the Kiss River light was no longer open to the public.

Through the trees and shrubs surrounding the parking lot, she saw the curved white brick wall of what had to be the lighthouse, and she knew immediately that something was wrong. There was a narrow path cutting through the trees, and branches scratched against her bare arms as she followed it. A few steps later, she stopped, staring in horror at what stood in front of her.

"No," she said aloud. *"Oh, no."*

The lighthouse rose high above her, but the top portion of it was missing. The lantern room was gone, and the entire tower could not have been more than three-quarters of its original height. Craning her neck, she could make out several steps of the steel staircase jutting a few yards above the jagged opening at the top of the tower.

She stood numbly, consumed by a distress that went far beyond disappointment. No wonder no one else was out here. It must have been the sea that destroyed the lighthouse, because even now the breaking waves swirled around the base of the tower, and it was apparent from the packed, damp sand beneath her feet that it was not yet high tide. *A storm,* she thought. *This was the work of a damn storm.*

Panic rose up inside her. She'd driven all this way. *All this way.* For nothing. For dashed hopes. Shutting her eyes, she felt dizzy. The sound of the waves cracking against the base of the lighthouse filled her ears, and a spray of salt water stung her face.

As she took a few steps toward the tower, a house came into view thirty or so yards to her left. The keeper's house. Long ago abandoned, most likely, although she noted the windows were not boarded up and two white Adirondack chairs graced the broad porch. Odd.

She looked up at the tower again, then took off her sandals. Dangling them from her fingertips, she stepped into the shallow water. It was colder than she'd expected, and she caught her breath at the unanticipated chill. The sand sucked at her feet and the water rose nearly to her knees one moment, only to fall to her ankles the next.

She climbed the three concrete stairs leading to the foyer beneath the tower. Despite her disappointment over finding the lighthouse damaged beyond repair, she still felt a thrill at finding herself inside it. She knew this place. Oh, how she knew it! She knew, for example, that there had once been a door at the foyer entrance, although there was no sign of one now. She knew there might be birds inside the tower, and indeed, when she took another step deeper into the foyer, she heard the flapping of wings above her.

She was in the cool air of a circular room. The floor was covered with octagonal black and white tiles, and on the white brick wall across from her, the steel stairs rose at a diagonal. Walking across the room, she dropped her sandals on the floor near the first step and began to climb.

The stairs had a woven texture and she could see straight through them to the purply-gray sky high above her and, as she climbed higher, to the dimly lit floor below. The spiral of stairs gradually narrowed and she quickly grew breathless. She'd never been great with heights, and she hugged the cold, white brick wall as she rested on the landings. Through the wavy glass of the tall, narrow windows at each landing, she could see the keeper's house. Then she'd return to the stairs, clutching the railing, no longer daring to look down as she climbed higher.

The stairs rose several yards above the opening of the lighthouse, right up into the evening sky. Gina leaned against the brick wall, her heart beating more from fear than from exertion as she contemplated climbing those last few unprotected steps. She could sit on that top step, she thought, and look out at the ocean. Maybe she'd discover the lens was directly below her in the shallow water near the base of the lighthouse.

She forced herself up another step, then another, holding on to the railing with both hands, and when she reached the top step, she turned and gingerly sat down on it. She was above the world here. The ocean was spread out in front of her like a huge, deep-purple rug fringed with white. The thick wall of the lighthouse looked as if it had been chewed off by some huge monster, leaving the jagged edges of the brick behind.

What was she going to do now?

Afraid of losing her balance, she carefully leaned a bit to the left and pulled the small photograph from the rear pocket of her shorts. Pressing it against her knee, she studied the image. A little girl. Much smaller than she should have been for being one year old, her age when the picture was taken. Skin the color of wheat. Very short, jet-black hair. The hugest, darkest eyes. Sad, hopeful eyes.

Gina shut her own eyes, feeling the sting of tears behind the lids. "I'll find a way, sweetheart," she said out loud. "I promise."

She sat very still for a long time, watching the last traces of daylight disappear in the sky, her mind only on the child in the picture. She did not think about how she would manage to climb down the spiral staircase in the dusky light, or walk back to her car through those darkening woods, or find a room on a Friday night in a place overrun by tourists.

She must have moved her head just a fraction of an inch to the left, because something caught her eye and made her turn around. And what she saw then stopped her breath in her throat. Every window of the keeper's house glowed with stained glass.

Chapter Two

CLAY O'NEILL STOPPED HIS JEEP DIRECTLY IN front of the chain. Removing the key he kept attached to his visor, he got out of the car, unlocked the padlock, then dragged the chain to one side of the road. He tried to remember if his sister would be home yet. It was Friday, and Lacey usually attended an Al-Anon meeting on Friday evenings. He would leave the chain open, then. Save her the effort of unlocking it.

Once back in the Jeep, he noticed a car parked on the opposite side of the cul-de-sac. Strange. Someone must have left it there, then hiked through the woods to the beach. He forgot about the car as he turned onto the gravel road, avoiding the familiar ruts and driving very slowly, since he had nearly broken an axle on one of the tree roots a few weeks earlier. He would need to trim some of the branches back one day soon; they scraped the roof of the Jeep as he drove through the tunnel they formed above him.

Emerging from the woods, he could see the keeper's house, its windows aglow with stained glass. Seeing the house so alive

with color in the gray dusk of evening, he understood why
Lacey insisted on setting the lights on a timer. She usually beat
him home after work and she'd told him she hated coming
home to a dark house, but he knew her real reasoning: she
loved to see her handiwork glowing from all the windows.
He'd argued that it was a huge waste of electricity, but he
didn't argue hard or long. Lacey had done too much for him.
He would let her have her lights. He supposed the stained glass
comforted her in a way, and although he would never admit it
to her, it comforted him as well. Their mother had also been
a stained-glass artist. Coming home to those windows was
like hearing an old lullaby.

He parked in the inch of sand that covered the corner of
the parking lot nearest the house, then got out and opened the
rear of the Jeep to retrieve the groceries. It had been his turn
to do the shopping, and he had bought thick, mauve-colored
tuna steaks to grill for a late dinner, along with a week's worth
of milk and cereal and fruit and some cleaning supplies. The
grocery bags were heavy, but he managed to carry all four of
them as he made his way across the sand to the house.

Setting the groceries down on the new wooden countertop
in the kitchen, he heard Sasha bounding down the stairs. The
black Lab ran into the room to greet him, and Clay leaned
over to give him a hug.

"Hi, boy," he said, scratching the dog's broad chest. "Bet
you'd like to go for a walk, huh?"

Sasha took two steps toward the door and looked back at
his master. *Poor neglected dog,* Clay thought as he opened the
refrigerator door. "Just let me get this stuff put away and I'll
be right with you," he said.

The small kitchen was the first room he and Lacey had
helped refurbish when they moved into the house six months
earlier, right after the first of the year. The room was a small

square, with pine cabinets and wood flooring. The original porcelain-topped table sat in the center of the room, surrounded by four oak chairs. The room was inelegant but functional. Elegance was not their goal in this house. Historical accuracy was far more important.

He had finished putting away the groceries and was nearly to the door with Sasha when he happened to look through the kitchen's rear window. Beneath the wide panel of stained glass hanging from the sash, he could see the lighthouse. The sun was down, the sky a milky gray, but he could still make out the silhouette of the tower, and he looked hard at it. Something was different. Squinting, he leaned closer to the glass. He knew how the tower should look from here. He knew the ragged shape of the rim and the way the spiral staircase rose above it. The line of that staircase was blurred now, and it took him a moment to realize that someone was sitting up there, on the top step, the place he thought of as his own private roost.

Was it Lacey? But no, her car was not in the parking lot. It was a stranger, then. It was so rare to see anyone out here. Tourists had long ago forgotten Kiss River, and the road had been chained off ever since the storm destroyed the lighthouse ten years ago. It was possible to get to the lighthouse by the beach, but difficult, since the water had eroded so much of the sand. By boat, perhaps? His eyes scanned the area in front of the lighthouse for a boat. He didn't see one, but it was too dark to be sure. Then he remembered the car parked in the cul-de-sac.

"Come on, boy," he said, opening the door and stepping onto the porch. He kicked off his sandals, picked up the flashlight from the seat of one of the Adirondack chairs and headed toward the tower. Sasha ran full speed toward the trees at the side of the yard, where he liked to do his business.

It was a woman sitting on the lighthouse stairs, that much he knew for certain. Her long hair rose and fell with the breeze, and she was facing the sea. *And looking to break her neck,* he thought. Those stairs could be treacherous in the dark if you weren't used to them. The waves swirling around the base of the lighthouse shone white with froth, and Clay stepped into the chill water, keeping enough distance between himself and the tower that he could still see the woman when he craned his neck to look up.

"Hello!" he shouted, just as a wave crashed onto the beach.

The woman didn't turn her head, and he guessed she could not hear him over the sound of the sea.

He cupped his hands around his mouth. "Yo!" he hollered. "Hello!"

Sasha came running at the sound of his call, and this time the woman peered over the edge of the tower at him. So high above him, she was very small, her features invisible. If she answered him, he didn't hear her.

"It's dangerous up there," he called. "You'd better come down."

The woman stood up, but Clay instantly changed his mind. It would be too dark inside the tower. "Wait there!" He held up a hand to tell her to stay. "I'll come up and get you. I have a flashlight."

He told Sasha to stay on the beach, then waded through the water to climb the concrete steps into the foyer. Turning on the flashlight, he saw the familiar, eerie, nighttime look of the stairs and railing against the curved white brick wall. He was used to the stairs and took them easily, without a hint of breathlessness. He made the climb nearly every day, sometimes more than once. The tower was a wonderful escape.

The salt breeze washed across his face as he stepped above the broad, jagged-edged cylinder of bricks. The woman stood up again, backing away a bit, and he thought she might be afraid of him. Understandable. It was dark; she had nowhere to run.

"You could trip going down the stairs in the dark," he said quickly, showing her his flashlight.

"Oh. Thanks." Her dark hair blew across her face, and she brushed it away with her hand.

She was extraordinarily beautiful. Very slender—too slender, perhaps—with long dark hair and large eyes that looked nearly black in the dim light. There was a fragility about her, as if a good gust of wind could easily blow her from the top of the tower.

As though reading his mind, she lurched a bit, grabbing the railing. He knew how she felt. The stairs held you suspended in the air above the tower, and it was easy to experience vertigo. The first few times he came up here with Terri, he'd actually felt sick. The stairs were solid and sturdy, though. It simply took the inner ear a while to get used to that fact.

"Sit down again," he said. "We'll wait till you feel steady on your feet before we go down."

The woman sat down without a word, moving to the edge of the step closest to the railing, which she quickly circled with both her hands. Clay sat one step below her.

"What brings you up here?" He tipped his head back slightly to look at her, hoping he didn't sound as if he was accusing her of something. Behind her windblown hair, the sky had turned a thick gray-black. There were no stars. No moon.

"Just...I..." Her gaze was somewhere above his head, out toward the dark horizon. "What happened here?" she asked, letting go of the railing with one of her hands, waving it through the air to take in the lighthouse and all of Kiss River. "What happened to the lighthouse?"

"Hurricane," Clay said. "More than ten years ago."

"Ten years." The woman shook her head. She stared out to sea, and Clay thought her eyes were glistening. She didn't speak.

"I'm Clay O'Neill," he said.

The woman acknowledged him with a brief smile. "Gina Higgins." She pointed behind her to the keeper's house. "Has that become a museum or something?" she asked.

"No." From where he sat, the house looked like a church, its windows filled with color. "It was abandoned for many years," he said. "Then a conservation group I'm part of took it over. My sister and I are living in it while it's being restored. We help with the work and act as general contractors, for the most part." The restoration was progressing very slowly, and that was fine with him. There was no target date, no reason to rush.

Gina looked over her shoulder at the house. "The stained glass…"

"It's my sister's," he said. "She just hung it in the windows while we're living here. It's not part of the restoration."

"Your sister made it?"

"Yes."

"What a talent," Gina said. "It's beautiful."

He nodded, glancing at the house again. "She's pretty good at it."

"And what are the plans for the house when it's refurbished?"

"Actually, none, so far," he said. Holding tight to the railing, he stood up to peer over the edge of the tower, hunting for Sasha. He spotted the dog nosing at a pile of seaweed and took his seat again. "Possibly a little museum," he said. "Possibly a B and B. Maybe even a private residence. The situation is unusual, since the lighthouse is off limits. They aren't sure they want to draw people out here. I was surprised to see you here, actually. How did you get in?"

"I walked in from the road, where that chain is. I ignored the No Trespassing sign." She looked beautifully sheepish. "Sorry," she said.

"It's off limits because it's dangerous out here, as you can probably tell," he said. "But you haven't gotten yourself killed, so no big deal. Were you hiking? Exploring? Most people don't even realize this lighthouse is here anymore."

"Oh, I'm an amateur lighthouse historian," Gina said. She touched the camera hanging around her neck. "So I was curious to see the Kiss River light and get some pictures of it. Where is the rest of it? Where is the Fresnel lens?"

She pronounced the word *FREZnal* instead of *FraNELL*. Odd for a lighthouse historian. But she'd said she was an amateur; she had probably seen the word in writing but had never heard it spoken before.

"The Fresnel lens is somewhere at the bottom of the ocean," he said, diplomatically using the correct pronunciation, and even in the darkness, he could see coins of color form on her cheeks.

"Why didn't they raise it?" she asked. "It's very valuable, isn't it?"

He nodded. "Yes, but there was a lot of opposition to raising the lens," he said. His own father, once an advocate for saving the lighthouse, had led the fight against finding the lens. "The travel bureau and the lighthouse society wanted it raised, but the locals tend to think that things should remain right where nature puts them. And, as you can imagine, they're also not keen on bringing even more tourists to the area as it is. Besides, who knows? The lens could be in a thousand pieces down there."

"But it also could be in one piece, or in just a few pieces

that could be put back together," she argued, and he knew she had a feisty side to her. "I think it's a crime to leave something that's historically valuable on the bottom of the sea. It should be displayed in a museum somewhere."

He shrugged. He didn't really care about the lens. Never thought about it, actually. In the great scheme of things, it did not seem worth getting upset over.

"It was a first-order lens, wasn't it?" Gina asked.

"Yes. It's three tons, at least. Whether it's in one piece or a hundred, it would be a job to bring it out. Once they got the thing up, it would probably have to spend months in an electrolyte bath so the metal parts didn't disintegrate in the air."

"No, it wouldn't," she said. "The metal parts are brass, aren't they? Brass wouldn't need an electrolyte bath."

She was right, and he was wrong. And also a little impressed.

"And if it's three tons," she continued, "it couldn't have drifted too far from the lighthouse, then, could it?"

He looked out toward the black cavern of the sea. Long ago, he and Terri would drive up here to Kiss River and sit on these stairs at low tide, trying to spot the lens, expecting to see it jutting out of the water. They never were able to spot it. "It was an unbelievable storm," he said. "And there have been a few just as bad since then. The coastline's really changed here. Before that storm, the water was never up this high. It's washed away the beach. By now the lens could be just about any—"

"Hey!"

The shout came from the beach, slipping past Clay's ears on the breeze. Leaning over, he saw a flashlight far below them.

"Hey, Lace!" he called back. "We'll be down in a sec."

Turning to Gina, he stood up. "That's my sister," he said. "Are you ready to go down?"

She nodded. He held his hand out to her as she stood up, but she didn't take it. Leading the way down the staircase, he kept his flashlight turned backward a bit to light the stairs for her. "Watch your step," he warned. "It's not as easy in the dark."

He moved slowly, aware that Gina had a death grip on the railing behind him, and it was a while before they exited through the tiled foyer. The waves washed over their feet and legs once they'd descended the three concrete steps into the water. Sasha bounded toward them, splashing their arms and faces as they waded to the dry sand where Lacey stood.

Gina nearly ignored Lacey as she squatted low to the ground to pet Sasha, and Clay's opinion of the woman instantly rose a few notches. Sasha rolled in the sand, exposing his stomach to the stranger, and Gina obliged by rubbing his belly.

"That's Sasha," Clay said. "And this is my sister, Lacey. Lacey, this is Gina…?" He couldn't recall her last name.

"Higgins." Gina stood up, wiping her sandy hand on her shorts before extending it to Lacey.

"Are you a friend of Clay's?" Lacey asked as she shook Gina's hand, and Clay heard the hope in her voice. His sister would love nothing better than for him to have a new woman in his life.

Gina smiled at her. "No," she said with a slight laugh. "I'm a trespasser, actually. I was up on the lighthouse when it got dark and your brother rescued me. That's all."

"Really?" Lacey raised her eyebrows at him.

"She came in from the road," he explained.

"I walked around the chain," Gina said. "I'm sorry. I just wanted to see—"

"No big deal," Lacey said, waving her unlit flashlight through the air. Her long red hair was tied back against the breeze, and her fair skin glowed white in the darkness. "We don't own this place." She glanced from Gina to Clay and back again, and he could almost see what she was thinking. *Right age, very attractive, perfect for Clay.* "Are you here on vacation with your family?" she asked. "Or with a bunch of girlfriends?" Clay nearly groaned at her transparent probing. Why didn't she just come right out and ask the woman if she was available to be fixed up with her pathetic brother?

"I'm alone," Gina said. "Just here for a few days."

"She's a lighthouse historian," Clay said.

"Amateur," Gina added, glancing away from him. She was probably still embarrassed over her pronunciation of Fresnel.

"Well, listen." Lacey swatted a mosquito that had landed on her bare shoulder. "Have you eaten? Would you like to stay for dinner?"

"Oh, no," Gina protested.

"We know absolutely every minute detail there is to know about the lighthouse," Lacey coaxed. "We can tell you everything." He knew his sister would not take no for an answer. He understood how her mind worked. It wasn't so much that she was hoping to fix Gina up with him, or that she was eager to tell her stories about the lighthouse. It was that she couldn't bear to think of anyone being alone.

"I bought plenty of fresh tuna for dinner, so you might as well stay," Clay said, surprising himself as well as Lacey. "Then one of us can drive you back out to your car." The truth was, he didn't want her to go, either. He wanted to see her in the good light of the kitchen. He wanted to find flaws in that perfect face.

Gina looked down at Sasha, who was leaning against her thigh. She scratched the dog behind his ears.

"All right," she said. "That's so nice of you. I have to admit, I was a little nervous about walking back through those woods, with the wild horses and pigs and all."

He and Lacey stared at her, then started to laugh.

"Wild pigs?" Lacey asked.

"I'd heard there were wild pigs," Gina said. "Boars, I mean."

"A long, long time ago," Clay said, wondering where she'd received that piece of information. Whatever lighthouse source she was using had to be ancient. She hadn't known the Kiss River had been destroyed. And wild pigs?

"The horses were moved way up past Corolla and fenced in," Lacey explained. "Too many were getting killed because of the traffic. And it used to be open range here, long ago. Full of cows and hogs, and some of them did run wild. Mary Poor, who used to be the keeper, told me about them. I think there's still some wild boar up in the wildlife refuge."

"You know Mary Poor?" Gina asked. The name was obviously familiar to her.

"I did," Lacey said. "She died a few years ago, but I used to visit her in the nursing home where she was living."

"I'd love to hear more about her," Gina said.

"Sure," Lacey said, motioning in the direction of the house. "Let's get dinner started and I'll tell you all about her."

The three of them began walking toward the house, sand sticking to their damp feet. Gina was tall and long-legged, and she carried her sandals dangling from her fingertips. Watching her, Clay nearly forgot about the charcoal.

"I'll fire up the grill," he said, breaking away from the women to make his way to the shed where he kept the charcoal. He was only half-surprised when Sasha elected to stay at Gina's side rather than walk with him. His dog could be as manipulative as his sister.

★ ★ ★

When he brought the grilled tuna steaks into the kitchen, he found Lacey and Gina making salad and boiling cobs of corn. They were deep in conversation, deep in that world of women that was so natural for them and so elusive to men like him. They were talking about the history of the light station, Lacey entertaining Gina with tales of the keepers, Mary and Caleb Poor. She knew far more than he did, due to both her interest in the subject and her relationship with Mary, and Gina kept her eyes on his sister while she tore apart the leaves of romaine, clearly enraptured.

In the light of the kitchen, Lacey and Gina looked like two women in a painting, one a redhead, the other raven-haired. Both beautiful. Both slender, fair-skinned. His twenty-four-year-old sister looked tougher than Gina, though. The muscles in Lacey's arms and legs were tight and defined. Her face was fuller. She not only had her mother's vivid hair and artistic talent, but her dimples as well, along with that pale, freckled skin that needed serious protection from the sun. Although she was also fair, Gina looked as though she might be able to tan well, but he doubted her skin had seen the sun in years. She was older than he'd thought, a couple of years older than himself. Thirty maybe. The damp sea air had found its way into her hair, which had taken on the same windblown, wild look that would mark Lacey's hair if she were to let it loose.

He put the plate of tuna steaks on the porcelain-topped table and Gina brought over the salad, while Lacey carried the platter of corn.

"Where do you live?" Clay asked, taking his seat at the table. He passed Gina the tuna steaks, motioning to her to help herself.

"Bellingham, Washington," Gina said. "It's north of Seattle."

"Washington!" Lacey said. "What are you doing out here?"

"I had time off," Gina said, reaching for the salad, and, Clay thought, measuring her words. "I teach school, so I have summer vacation, same as the students. I'm familiar with the lighthouses in the Pacific Northwest, and I wanted to visit some in the East. I thought I'd start here."

Clay laughed as he transferred one of the steaks to his plate. "Well, you picked the wrong one to start with," he said. "To-morrow you can drive up to the Currituck Light. That one's in great shape and open to the public."

"Bodie's not that far," Lacey added. "And Hatteras is only a couple of hours from here. You probably know that they moved the Hatteras lighthouse a few years ago because it was going to fall into the sea, just like this one did—" Lacey nodded toward the beach "—so you might find that really intriguing. They have a video there you can watch."

Gina nodded. "Thanks," she said, poking corn holders into the ends of the cob on her plate. "I'll be sure to see them all. But right now I'm a bit distressed over the fact that the Kiss River lighthouse is crumbling away. And I don't understand why no one has tried to see if the lens is still in one piece."

"I agree with you," Lacey surprised him by saying. "I think they should have at least salvaged the lens."

"You'll have to fight Dad on that one," Clay said.

"Why your father?" Gina looked from him to Lacey.

"He's got OCD," Lacey said with a flash of her dimples. "Obsessive-compulsive disorder. He used to be obsessed with saving the lighthouse. He led the Save the Lighthouse com-mittee. After the hurricane, he became obsessed with keeping it the way it is and leaving the lens in the ocean." She held up a hand to ward off the obvious question. "Don't ask me to explain why my dad is the way he is, because I can't."

"Is he...does he...have some say in what happens to the lighthouse and the lens?" Gina asked.

"Not officially," Lacey said. "But when it comes to the locals, everyone follows his lead."

There was silence at the table for a moment, filled only by the crunch of corn and the chink of forks against the plates. Gina took a swallow of iced tea.

"This is the first time I've eaten fresh tuna," she said, putting down her glass. "It's wonderful."

"My favorite," Lacey agreed.

"You must get a lot of salmon where you live," Clay said.

"Tons." Gina nodded. She cut another piece of the fish with the side of her fork, but didn't bring it to her mouth. "If I wanted to look into getting the lens raised," she said, returning to the more difficult topic, "is your father the person I should talk to?"

Clay didn't understand her apparent interest in the lens, but after growing up with his father, he was accustomed to an unexplained fixation on the Kiss River light. He nodded. "If you don't have his backing, you can forget about getting anyone else's," he said. "But...and don't take offense at this, please...you have to keep in mind that you're an outsider here. People won't much care what you want. The fact that you're a lighthouse historian, though, might give you a little credibility."

Gina's huge, dark eyes were on him as she set down her fork. "Where would I find him?" she asked. "Your father?"

"He's a vet," Lacey said. "He works at Beacon Animal Hospital in Nag's Head."

"Is that far from here?"

"Half an hour," Clay said. He pictured Gina walking unannounced into the animal hospital, and his father's response when he realized the purpose of her intrusion. "If you want to contact him, though, I'd call him first. And don't get your hopes up."

"I won't." Gina smiled at him, but it was a quick smile that seemed somehow false. "So," she said, "what sort of work do the two of you do? I assume you're in construction?"

Lacey shook her head. "I'm a part-time vet tech at the animal hospital," she said. "And a full-time stained-glass artist."

She sold herself short, Clay thought. Vet tech and stained-glass artist just scratched the surface of who his sister was. She also volunteered on a crisis hot line, tutored kids at the local elementary school, read to residents in the nursing home where Mary Poor used to live and attended Al-Anon meetings in support of her biological father, Tom Nestor, who was also her stained-glass mentor and—at long last—a recovering alcoholic. She gave blood regularly and had donated her bone marrow the year before. She had, in short, turned herself into their mother, who the locals used to call Saint Anne. Lacey's gradual metamorphosis into Annie O'Neill made Clay uncomfortable.

"And how about you?" Gina was looking at him.

He finished chewing a mouthful of salad. "Architect," he said.

"Really?" Gina asked. "What sort of architecture?"

"Residential," Clay said. "I have an office in Duck."

For the first time that evening, he felt the too-familiar dark cloud slip over his shoulders. It used to be that, even before Clay would say he was an architect, he'd say that he trained dogs and their owners for search and rescue work. That had been his avocation and his passion, but he hadn't put Sasha through his paces once since Terri's death, and he no longer bothered to return the calls from people looking for training. Lacey had nagged him about it at first but quickly learned that approach could only backfire. It made him angry. It made him wonder if she'd loved Terri at all. She used to say that Terri felt more like a sister than a sister-in-law. Then why didn't she understand that he just didn't feel like doing a damn thing that reminded him of his wife?

"What grade do you teach?" Lacey asked their guest.

"Junior high," Gina said. "Science."

That explained her knowledge of brass and the electrolyte bath, Clay thought.

"Rough age," Lacey said, and Clay had to smile to himself. Lacey had been one of the roughest fourteen-year-olds imaginable.

"I love it," Gina said. "I love the kids."

"Do you have any of your own?" Lacey asked.

Gina didn't answer right away. She toyed with her salad for a moment, pushing a cherry tomato around with her fork. "No," she said. "Someday, I hope."

"Are you married?" Lacey asked. God, Clay thought. His sister could be so damn nosy. But his eyes fell to Gina's hands, searching for a wedding ring. She wore two rings, actually: on her right hand, a small ruby in a white-gold or platinum setting, and on her left hand, an onyx set in silver. Her fingers were long and slim, like the rest of her, and her nails were unpainted, pink and rounded, cared for but not pampered.

Gina shook her head. "Not married," she said.

Clay stood up and lifted his plate from the table to carry it to the sink. He had never been very good at sitting still for long, especially not for after-dinner small talk. He was just like their father that way, filled with a nervous sort of energy that had driven Terri crazy and was now doing the same to his sister. Lacey had long ago given up on asking him to stay seated for a while after dinner.

"Well." Gina looked at her watch as if he'd given her the

cue that it was time to leave. "I'd better be going," she said. "I still have to find a room for tonight."

"You're kidding, right?" Clay asked from the sink. It was a Friday night at the end of June. She would never find a room.

"No." She looked guileless. "I didn't think about making a reservation. After I saw the traffic coming over the bridge this afternoon, I knew I should have, but..." Her voice faded away as she shrugged. "It's not a problem for me, though. I slept in my car the entire trip out here. I can certainly do it one more night."

"That's crazy," Lacey said. "You stay with us tonight, Gina. Tomorrow you can look for a room. No way we're letting you sleep in your car." Lacey didn't look at him as she spoke. He knew she didn't want to see any disapproval in his eyes.

"Oh, I couldn't," Gina said. She looked genuinely cha-grined by the invitation. "You've already been so kind. And after I trespassed on your property and took over your evening."

"You're staying here," Lacey insisted. "The spare bedrooms haven't been redone yet, but you're welcome to take one of them as is, if you like. We have clean sheets for the bed. So you have no excuse not to stay."

He knew he should speak up himself. He should tell her it was okay, that he'd like her to stay, but for some reason the words were stuck in his throat.

Gina played with her crumpled napkin where it rested on the table. "Well, thank you so much," she said, glancing from Lacey to him. "I can't believe how nice you two are being to a perfect stranger."

"Let's go move your car," Lacey stood up.

"May I use your bathroom first?" Gina asked, and Clay pointed the way. Once she was out of hearing range, Lacey dared to look at him.

"I hope you don't mind," she said.

"No," he said. "It's fine." But he couldn't explain the apprehension he felt at the thought of sharing the house with this stranger, a lighthouse enthusiast who couldn't pronounce Fresnel, if even for just one night.

Chapter Three

GINA KNEW THIS ROOM. SHE HAD NEVER BEEN in it before, but she knew it all the same. She stood in the doorway in the darkness, breathing hard, although the small, soft-sided suitcase she'd carried up the stairs, along with her backpack and camera, was not heavy. Without turning on the light, she walked to the window and, with a little work, managed to open it. A soft breeze blew through the screen. The sky had changed since she'd first walked into the house earlier that evening, and now it was filled with stars, more stars than she'd seen before in her life. She could make out the tower, a gray ghost against the night sky, fifty or so yards away from her.

In all her fantasies of what this day might bring, she had not expected to find herself in this room, this house. She had not expected to eat dinner at that old kitchen table, running her fingers over the smooth porcelain, knowing things about it her host and hostess could not know.

The last thing she'd expected was to be taken in, however temporarily, by two strangers. How quickly they had felt like friends! Lacey, primarily. She reminded Gina of one of her students, a red-haired girl with an expansive nature, the sort of person who could talk to anyone as if she'd known them all her life. But Gina was not here to make friends. She was not generally an introvert, but she would have to keep to herself on this trip. Lying to strangers to get what she needed was one thing; lying to friends, another. And already she had lied to Clay and Lacey.

Fresnel. She squeezed her eyes shut, still embarrassed by her faux pas. *A lighthouse historian, my foot.* But Lacey and Clay seemed to buy it, or at least to accept it. Tomorrow she would find herself a room, then see if she could talk with their father about raising the lens. And if he said to forget it? She wasn't certain what she would do then. One bridge to cross at a time.

The lens was so close. Through the window, she could hear the sound of the sea, the breaking of the waves. White foam swirled around the base of the lighthouse under the night sky. The lens was out there, just below the surface of the water. There had to be a way.

She switched on the lamp on the night table. From her suitcase, she pulled the T-shirt she would sleep in and her toiletries bag, which held only her toothbrush, toothpaste, floss and sunscreen. She wore a bit of makeup when she taught, but lately, her looks had been the last thing on her mind.

The small pink diary with its broken lock and tattered corners rested on the clothing in her suitcase, and she took it out and set it on the bed Lacey had already made up for her. She knew the diary's contents by heart.

Pulling off her shorts, she extracted the picture of the little girl from her pocket and propped it up against the lamp. She finished undressing and climbed beneath the covers, then picked up the picture to study it in the lamplight. She had wanted things in her life. She'd wanted her mother to get well. She had at one time wanted a husband and a good marriage, but that was not to be. But never had she wanted anything so much as to hold this child in her arms again.

She set the picture back on the night table, then turned out the light. Lying in the old, full-size sleigh bed in the dark, she could still see the stars. Years ago, the light from the lens would have shot through this small bedroom once every four and a half seconds, illuminating the walls and the ceiling and the covers on the bed.

Yes, she knew without a doubt whose room she was in.

Chapter Four

Saturday, March 7, 1942

THE LIGHTS WENT OUT AGAIN TONIGHT. I'M
sitting on my bed, writing by the glow of the hurricane lantern, just like I used to do when I was younger, before the
electric came to Kiss River. Daddy's put the lighthouse on the
emergency generator—he won't let *that* light go out no matter what. But here in the house, we have no backup. Mama
says "You've gotten spoiled and soft, Elizabeth." Maybe she's
right. She argues with me no matter what I say these days. Or
maybe I argue with her. I don't know. We're not getting along
well, is all I can say about that. All I know is, even though it's
not unusual for the lights to go out, tonight I feel scared by
the sudden darkness. And I have to add that nothing much
usually scares me. Not the storms that wash clear across this
island or even the wild boar that kill chickens and sometimes
a dog or cat and once that I heard of, but don't know for a
fact, an old woman hanging out her wash on the line behind

her house. I'm not even sure now why I feel scared. Maybe because the adults are. They don't say it, of course, but I can feel fear everywhere I go. Everybody's talking about the war. People sit around at Trager's Store and talk about it, not laughing much or telling jokes like they used to. In my own living room, my parents sit right next to the radio, listening. Always listening. There's still music. I am sick of hearing that song, "Let's Remember Pearl Harbor," and especially "Perfidia." What does Perfidia mean, anyhow? Is that supposed to be someone's name? If it's not Glenn Miller music, it's Gabriel Heater and his "Up to the Minute World News!" and none of that news is good. Lines I never noticed before are on Mama's forehead. Although I am angry with her and all her rules for me, I want to take my hand and smooth it over her forehead to erase those lines. When I feel like that, I know I still love her and Daddy. Sometimes I have to remind myself of that!

We're not in any real danger up here in the northern beaches, Daddy said to me just yesterday, even though some ships have been sunk not far from here. Most of the ships that have been torpedoed by the Germans were down around Hatteras. After today, though, I bet Daddy's thinking he might have to eat his words.

This morning, I was up in the lantern room, cleaning the lens. We are not needed here the way we used to be before the electric came, when we had to keep the lighthouse lantern lit all night long, winding the clockworks and toting oil up them two hundred and seventy steps. The keepers of other lights have been let go, but somehow Daddy's been allowed to stay on as a "civilian keeper," as long as he does all the maintenance work around here. So I help by cleaning the lens. At least, the lower part of the lens. I can't reach much higher than that, and Daddy won't let me use the ladder near all that glass, and secretly I'm glad he won't, because it's much harder work than I guessed. All these years, I've been watching him clean the smooth glass prisms with his soft chammy and jeweler's rouge, wishing I could do it myself. A year ago, when I turned fourteen, he finally let me, and now I wonder why I begged him to do it. You have to be so careful not to scratch the glass. I wasn't supposed to ever touch it. "Eighteen panels of crown glass prisms, manufactured and polished in Paree, France," Daddy says to anyone who will listen and even some people who won't. Fingerprints can dull the light, he always says, but I used to touch the prisms when he wasn't looking, because I loved the slick, cold feel of them. The lens is more than twice his height and I never realized how truly huge around it was until I had to clean it myself. I think it would take up half this room (my bedroom).

It's funny that I'm writing in this diary now. Toria (my cousin) gave it to me for my fourteenth birthday and I couldn't have cared less then. I had too many other things to do, like fishing and crabbing and riding my bicycle and playing with the dogs. Now, fishing bores me all of a sudden. That's all anyone ever does around here. Fishing, crabbing, clamming, oystering. The time I used to spend fishing, I now seem to spend thinking, and I know that's not a very useful way to pass the time, but I can't seem to help it. Anyhow, I put this diary in my dresser drawer after I got it, beneath my underthings, and pretty much forgot about it. About a week ago, I was reaching into that drawer and my hand brushed something hard. It was the key, stuck in the keyhole of the diary, and I pulled the book out of the drawer and stared at it and words started coming to me. I want to write down what I'm thinking, and put them thoughts somewhere safe, where no one can see them except me. There is no other place I can say what I think. Mrs. Cady (my teacher) doesn't want to hear it. And Mama and Daddy are right critical of every word out of my mouth, like those words might burn them and they have to protect themselves from them. So suddenly I am grateful to Toria for giving me this book. I still keep it in my underwear drawer, only now, after I lock the diary, I hide the key between the mattress and box spring of my bed.

So, the light is still burning in the lantern room tonight, and when it swirls around I can see the white tower of the lighthouse outside my window, even though I can't see the light itself unless I move closer to the window and bend my head over, but I like how from my bed, the white tower is smack in the center of my window. My whole room fills up with the light. When Toria stays over, she can't sleep at all. I don't think I could sleep without it, I'm so accustomed to it.

But here's what happened this morning that's got me full of jitters. While I was in the lantern room doing my cleaning, something out to sea caught my eye. I knew what it was right away—smoke, a big black bubble of it, expanding from a spot straight out from Kiss River, not quite to the horizon. And I knew where it was coming from, too.

Daddy keeps binoculars up there and I looked through them, but I couldn't see the ship itself, just the smoke. There were orange flames coming out of the water, and I guessed it must've been an oil tanker. This was the closest one. The first one I've seen with my own eyes, although I know it's not the first to go down. Not by a long shot. The sign at the post office says, Loose Lips Might Sink Ships. That means we should be quiet about anything we know about the merchant ships traveling along the coastline, because you never know who might be spying right next to you. That seems silly to me, because I know nearly everyone around here. A stranger would stand out, especially a German stranger. Krauts, some people call them. I heard Daddy call them that once, when he didn't think I was listening. It shocked me to hear him say that, because he and Mama are always after me not to see my-self as any better than anyone else. When Mama heard one of the boys at Trager's call Mr. Sato "slant-eyes," she threatened to wash his mouth out with soap.

None of us ever saw a Japanese person before Mr. Sato came here a year or so ago. His son was married to a girl from here and they lived with Mr. Sato in Chicago. When the son died a year ago, the girl, whose name I don't remember, wanted to move back here, and she brought Mr. Sato with her, since he's crippled in a wheelchair and couldn't live alone. They live in a house on the sound, across the island from me. I have to go right past his house on my way to school, and I used to see him out fishing. He would sit in his wheelchair on the deck that hangs right out over the water from their house, with the fishing pole in his hand. I used to wave to him because I felt sorry for him, and he'd always wave back. Everyone calls him slant-eyes behind his back and the kids make fun of him. No one is very friendly to him, and after Pearl Harbor, I'd be surprised if anyone talks to him at all. I never see him outside these days. He might be scared to go out and I don't really blame him. He looks like a harmless old man, though, tiny, gray-haired and sort of shriveled up in his wheelchair. I wouldn't know he still lives in that house if I didn't hear other people whispering about him, saying how they don't like having a Jap for a neighbor.

Anyhow, I got off my topic again. Mrs. Cady is always after me about that. She says, "You write real well, but you jump around too much." Glad she's not reading this!

Back to the burning ship. So those Germans are killing us right outside our back door now. Their sneaky U-boats come up from under the water and attack, just like a shark. When I watched that black smudge growing out to sea, I wondered if someone's loose lips might have gotten word to the U-boats out there somehow.

I have not seen a U-boat myself, although I keep looking for one. When I'm cleaning up in the lantern room, or after school when I come home, I go up there and stare at the water with the binoculars, looking for one of the German subs. I'm not sure what to look for, exactly. Would a periscope be too small for me to see? That sounds like it would be fun to have. A periscope. To see what was happening someplace you weren't. You could see people, but they couldn't see you. Without a doubt, that's what happened out there this morning. Some American ship filled with hardworking men got spied with a U-boat's periscope, and then *bam!* The Germans torpedoed them. This is the first I've seen this close up, and I don't want to see another. It was as if, when I saw that smoke, all the fun went out of me. I was suddenly as sour and dead inside as some of the grown-ups I know, and I didn't like the feeling.

There is one good thing and one thing only that I like about this war: it's brung the Coast Guard boys to the Outer Banks. They've taken over the lifesaving stations, and each one of them is more handsome than the next. They are from all parts of the country, and hearing all their different accents makes me want to get out of North Carolina and see the world. I've been to Elizabeth City and Manteo and even once to Norfolk, but that's it. Mama keeps an eye on me when they're around. I can feel her watching every move I make, and so I pretend not to even notice those boys. But I do. And some of them notice me right back.

Tonight, Mr. Bud Hewitt (he's the chief warrant officer for the Coast Guard up here) came to dinner like he does sometimes. He and Mama and Daddy have become friends. He told us they fished a bunch of the sailors from the torpedoed ship out of the sea, but fifty-some were lost, and already a few bodies had washed up on shore. "It's getting worse, isn't it?" Daddy asked Mr. Hewitt, and Mr. Hewitt looked serious and sad, and said, "Yes, we just aren't prepared for this. We're so used to being spared fighting right here in the United States that no one expected this bombardment. And nobody thinks much about North Carolina. All eyes are on the West Coast. But they better start thinking, or it'll be too late."

Mr. Hewitt said we need a blackout, but one hasn't been ordered, and I can tell he's mad about that. He explained how the U-boats can see our ships clear as day out there, silhouetted against the lights from shore. Mr. Hewitt actually got tears in his eyes as he talked about it. I could see how frustrated he is about the whole thing.

I told Mr. Hewitt how I was looking for periscopes out on the water, and my parents laughed at me, making me feel foolish. Mr. Hewitt saved me though. He said he was glad I was doing that, he wished more people would take their duty seriously, but it was more likely I'd see the conning tower—that's the raised-up part of the deck—rise up out of the water. The periscope would be too hard to see, he said. And if I ever did see something, I should go to him immediately. I promised him I would. The station is only a half mile from my house, but I wish I could just call him on a telephone. Down where Toria lives, they have them crank phones. There aren't any phones yet in Kiss River, even though people are getting them on the other side of the island. I've heard that Mr. Sato's daughter-in-law was one of the first to get one. It won't be long till we have them here, too, Daddy keeps telling me.

I asked Mr. Hewitt if it had been an oil tanker and he smiled at me and said I was right, how did I know? I explained about the orange flames I saw, that I knew it must be oil burning on the water. He said I was smart. I like him.

He always treats me like I'm an adult, even in front of Daddy and Mama. He said something about the boys at the Coast Guard station thinking I'm a good-looking girl, and I thought Daddy was going to clobber him. But both Mama and Daddy like Mr. Hewitt. "He's on God's side," Daddy says, which is something he says about all the Allies. Even Mrs. Cady says that, and when I asked her if the Japanese and the Germans and the Italians tell their children that God is on *their* side, she accused me of being unpatriotic. That is not true. I love my country and I know we're right. But I bet the Germans think they're right, too. I don't think God picks sides. And when I see what God lets happen to them merchant ships, I'm sure of it.

I've learned a lot about the war from Dennis Kittering. He's a teacher in High Point who comes here almost every single weekend, winter and summer, to camp on the beach near Kiss River. Since January when the U-boats started sinking ships, he's had to have a special pass to be able to camp out there, but they gave him one without any trouble. I like him, even though he can aggravate me to no end with his know-it-all attitude. He is very young for a teacher, only out of college one year, with dark hair combed straight back and glasses with wire frames, like Mrs. Cady's, and he walks with a limp because he was born with one leg a little shorter than the other. He treats me like Mr. Hewitt does, like my thoughts are worth something. I've learned more from him about what's going on in the world than I have from anybody. It's Dennis who explained to me why this war is happening, and about the internment camps that are starting up for the Japanese people. He said they are innocent people who are suffering and struggling just to survive. The way he explained it put tears in my eyes. I asked him how come Mr. Sato isn't going to one of them internment camps, too, and he said because it's only on the West Coast, so I guess Mr. Sato is lucky to be living here even if people pick on him.

Dennis is the one who told me I should read *The Heart Is a Lonely Hunter*. I am the library's best customer. I read more than anyone I know. I am the top reader in my school, although I guess since there are only twenty-three students in my whole school, and most of them are younger than me, that's not saying much. But I read even better than the older ones. I'd finished all the Nancy Drews, and then Mrs. Cady told my parents I should be allowed to read whatever I want. They said it was all right with them. So I am now reading *The Heart Is a Lonely Hunter* and a book of stories by Eudora Welty, and I discuss them with Dennis on the weekends. I was reading at the kitchen table yesterday, taking notes with my pencil right on the tabletop, because I didn't have any paper right there and the table is porcelain and the notes will wash right off, but Mama yelled at me anyhow.

Mama says I'm not allowed to call Dennis by his first name. I'm supposed to call him Mr. Kittering, like I do with other adults. But Dennis laughs at me when I call him that. So around him, I call him Dennis. When I talk to Mama, though, I call him Mr. Kittering.

The lantern's getting low on oil, so I am going to turn it off now and go to bed. I'm afraid of having nightmares tonight after seeing that ship burn, but at least if I wake up afraid, I'll be able to see the light fill up my room and know I'm safe.

Chapter Five

GINA WAS TOUCHING HIM. CLAY FELT THE HEAT of her body next to him in his bed, and he held his breath as she slipped her hand beneath the sheet, over his chest, lower. Lower. Touching him, teasing him. *This is a dream,* he told himself. *He wasn't responsible if it was only a dream.* She smiled at him with those lovely white teeth before tossing the sheet aside and lowering her head, her mouth, to where he wanted it to be. He waited to feel her lips and her tongue on him, but instead, he was jolted awake by the touch of something cold and damp against his arm. Opening his eyes, he turned to find the bed empty next to him and Sasha nudging his arm with his nose. Clay groaned and rolled onto his back.

He hated the weekend because he had no real need to go into his office, no way to lose himself in his work. During the week, he'd go in early and stay late, and that seemed to keep his mind occupied well enough to save him from too many disturbing thoughts. But the weekends were different. There was plenty of work to keep him busy around the keeper's house, of course, but it was solitary work, for the most part, and gave him too much time to think. Some weekends, he went diving with his long-time buddy, Kenny Gallo, but Kenny had to work today. Clay decided he would replace the rotting boards in the cover of the old cistern on the south side of the house. That would take him most of the day and he would wear his Walkman and listen to jazz. Terri had hated jazz, so he would hear nothing that would remind him of her. A decent plan. He did this every day before he got out of bed: planned the day so that every minute was filled and safe from thoughts of Terri and any guilt that might accompany them. Maybe later, when he was done with the cistern and Kenny got out of work, they could meet at Shorty's Grill and just hang out for a while. He relished spending time with Kenny these days. Kenny didn't expect—or even want—him to talk about anything heavier than the results of the latest ball game.

Sasha nudged his arm again, and he patted the bed, inviting him up. Sasha was another source of guilt. Poor dog. He had to miss the old days, when he and Terri's dog, Raven, were constantly on the go, being challenged and rewarded and the center of the universe. Back then, Clay and Terri had lived in Manteo, on a large, treed lot with a huge pile of rubble in the backyard. Clay had dragged other people's castoffs into the woods behind their house: old appliances, huge chunks of concrete, narrow boards suspended between sawhorses, even an abandoned, totaled Mustang. That was where he'd trained dogs for search and rescue work. Not only Sasha and Raven, but dogs from other search and rescue teams who traveled to see him. Because he was the best. Or at least, he had been, once. Sometimes he missed Raven nearly as much as he did Terri. A shepherd-Lab mix, Raven had been the finest, keen-est rescue dog Clay had ever worked with, and she'd been a bit wasted on Terri. Terri had been an interior designer, and she had never truly enjoyed the work with the dogs. Clay didn't like to think about that fact. He'd ignored Terri's lack of interest in search and rescue, because he didn't want to see it.

He still owned the house in Manteo, although he hadn't really lived there since late November, shortly after Terri died. He'd tried staying there for a while, but he couldn't tolerate the loneliness, and he'd quickly retreated to the spare room in the cottage Lacey used to rent in Kill Devil Hills. Then Lacey arranged for both of them to live here in the keeper's house. Leave it to Lacey. She could find a solution to anyone's problems—except, perhaps, her own. For once, he was grateful for his sister's ability to play the role of savior.

So, the old Manteo house stood empty. He could probably rent it, if he could find someone who didn't mind a pile of trash in their backyard, but he didn't have the motivation to fix up the house on the inside to get it ready for a tenant. He'd always been known for his energy, his need to constantly be on the go, but the truth was, he didn't feel like doing much of anything these days. He knew he was not well. Not in his head or his heart. But that was another thing he didn't want to think about.

So strange, living with Lacey. It reminded him of when he was a kid, living with his mother. Feed the hungry, clothe the poor. Did you inherit that sort of thing? It was almost spooky. And she *always* had something to feed him. He could look in the pantry and see nothing. She could take that nothing and turn it into something delicious. She was taking care of him, and he was letting her. His little sister.

He heard voices in the hall outside his room. Lacey's and the deeper voice, the voice of the woman who had been about to give him a blow job before Sasha had ruined it. He wouldn't be able to look her in the eye this morning. *It was a dream, Terri,* he thought to himself. *Out of my control.*

He would wait awhile before getting up. Maybe Gina would be gone by then and he wouldn't have to look at her long hair and dark eyes and faintly pointed chin across the table from him over his bowl of cold cereal.

Sasha, though, was not going to cooperate. He jumped from the bed and began whining at the door, which was colored green and blue from sunlight pouring through the stained-glass panel in the window. Sasha's handsome brown eyes pleaded with his master. No choice now. Clay had to get up and let him out.

"Hold on just a minute, boy," he said as he dressed. Sasha sat down by the door, eyeing him patiently, his tail thumping against the old wooden floor.

He made Sasha wait another minute while he used the bathroom and brushed his teeth, then he followed the dog downstairs.

The kitchen smelled of good coffee, homemade waffles and the yeasty aroma of rising bread. He could see the bowl of dough on the counter, covered with a dish towel. Lacey made whole wheat bread every other week, just as their mother had. Right now, she was seated at the table across from Gina, the steaming waffle iron next to her plate.

"Huckleberry waffles," Lacey said, looking at him, and he knew she had been up early, picking the huckleberries from the bushes at the edge of the woods and kneading her bread dough.

Gina glanced up at him. "They're delicious," she said, reaching for the syrup with the slender ruby-ringed hand that had touched him in his sleep. She had the phone book open on the table next to her plate, her finger marking her place on one of the yellow pages. The portable phone rested next to the book, and her large, heavy camera hung around her neck.

He merely nodded at the women as he walked outside with Sasha. Standing on the porch, he breathed in the already hot morning air as the Lab ran off to the woods. Sasha reappeared, running across the sandy yard, then leaping up the porch steps with one wild jump before stopping short in front of the screen door. He sat down, as he'd been trained to do, turning his head to look at his master, waiting for him to enter the kitchen first. Sasha knew very well the pecking order in this house.

Lacey already had Sasha's food in the bowl, and the dog dived into it with gusto.

Gina laughed. "I've never seen a dog eat like that," she said.

"Do you have a dog?" Clay poured himself a cup of coffee and sat down across from her. He reached for the handle on the waffle iron and looked at his sister. "Is this ready yet?" he asked.

"Wait till the steam stops." Lacey put a plate in front of him and sat down again herself.

"When I was a kid," Gina said. "I don't have one now. I work long hours, so it wouldn't be fair."

Clay opened the waffle iron and used his fork to extract the berry-marbled waffle from the grill. "What are you looking for in the phone book?" he asked.

"A room," she said. "I tried a couple of places already, but no luck. I thought I'd try this place next." She looked down at the book. "Suiter's Inn."

"No, not that one," Clay said.

"Is that the one near Shorty's Grill?" Lacey asked him, and he nodded. "It's a bit seedy, Gina. You shouldn't stay there."

"I can't pay a lot," Gina said, her finger still on the page in the phone book. "I might have to settle for something a little less luxurious than the Ritz."

"What area do you want to be in?" Clay asked.

Gina shrugged. "Near Kiss River, I guess. But anyplace on the northern part of the Outer Banks would do."

"Maybe there's a cottage available," Clay said. "Maybe someone had to cancel their reservation at the last minute. That happens. Then you'd have something for a week or two. How long were you planning to stay?"

"No more than that," she said.

"I'll try Nola," Lacey said, reaching across the table for the phone.

"Who's Nola?" Gina asked.

"An old family friend," Lacey said, dialing. "She's also a Realtor and she'd be able to find out what's available."

Gina and Clay ate quietly while Lacey spoke with Nola. She pulled the phone book toward her to write a few notes in the margin of the page, but from the conversation, Clay could tell that the news was not good. Lacey hung up the phone and wrinkled her freckled nose at their guest.

"She could only find one cottage available," she said, reading from her notes. "It's soundside in Duck and it's sixteen hundred dollars a week."

Gina shook her head. "I can't do it, then," she said. "But if I can't find something here, maybe there'd be a room available on the other side of that long bridge. That would be close enough, and—"

"Stay here," Clay said, the words surprising him as they slipped out of his mouth. He didn't need to look at Lacey to know she was astonished by the invitation, but he also knew she wouldn't mind. She'd probably been thinking the same thing herself, but had been afraid to suggest it because of how he might react. "You can rent the room you're in for a hundred a week," he said.

"I...I..." Gina stammered. "That's so nice of you." She

looked at Lacey. "Are you sure that's all right with you? Do you two want to talk it over in private, or—"

"It's great with me," Lacey interrupted her.

"You have to charge more than that, though," Gina said. "I'm not *that* broke. I can—"

"It's a token amount," Clay said. "We'll put it into the keeper's house conservation fund." He was aware he was not acting rationally, but he hadn't felt rational in a long, long time.

"Well, thanks," Gina said. Her hand shook a bit as she lifted her glass of orange juice to her lips. She took a sip, then set it down again. "That's a huge relief to me. I really appreciate it."

"No problem," Clay said. He extracted another waffle from the iron and offered it to Gina, but she shook her head again. He put it on his own plate, then poured more batter into the grill.

"Do you mind a check from my bank in Bellingham?" Gina asked. "Or I could get some money from an ATM and—"

"A check is fine," Clay said.

Gina sat back from the table, finished with her breakfast but not with conversation. "I thought I would call your father today, and see if I could talk to him about raising the lens." She looked at him, then Lacey. "It's been ten years, right? Maybe he and the other people who objected to raising it ten years ago have mellowed about the idea by now."

"You're talking about our father," Clay said with a half-hearted laugh. "Mellow, he ain't."

"You're a fine one to talk," Lacey said. "You're exactly like him."

He couldn't argue with her. As much as Lacey looked like their mother, he resembled Alec O'Neill. So much so, that when one of the old-timers spotted him and Lacey together in the grocery store a few weeks ago, he'd thought they were Alec and Annie. It had taken them quite a while to convince him of the truth. And although Clay didn't like to admit it, he was no more mellow than their father. He had both Alec's wiry build and the bundled, hyper sort of energy that accompanied it.

"Dad's off this afternoon," Lacey said. "I think you should just go to his house and talk to him."

"Call first, though," Clay said.

"I don't think she should call," Lacey said, her tone more pondering than argumentative. "He might just blow her off if she calls."

"He can blow her off just as easily at his front door," Clay argued. His father would be kind about it, but it was doubtful he'd have any interest in talking to anyone about the Kiss River light.

Gina followed their conversation as if watching a Ping-Pong match.

"Well, *we* can call him, then," Lacey said.

"No, no." Gina held up a hand. "You two have done too much already. Let me take care of this on my own. Okay?" She looked at each of them in turn, and they nodded. "Can you give me his address and phone number?" she asked.

Lacey stood and walked over to one of the kitchen drawers, then returned to the table with a notepad. In her seat again, she jotted down the address. "I'd go with you," she said, "but today I have two kids to tutor, a three-hour shift on the crisis hot line and an appointment to donate blood at two-thirty. Not to mention bread to bake."

Gina stared at her. "I thought today was your day off?"

Lacey dismissed her question with a wave of her hand. "It's all fun for me," she said.

"Where do you do your stained glass?" Gina asked.

"I share a studio in Kill Devil Hills," she said. "But I do some work here, too, in the sunroom." She pushed the pad across the table to Gina. "His house is on the sound in Sanderling." Pointing to the camera hanging around Gina's neck, she added, "You know, he used to take pictures constantly of the lighthouse. He'll have a thousand for you to look at if you ask him."

"What sort of pictures?" Gina looked intrigued.

"You name it, he has it. It used to be all he ever did. Drove me nuts." Lacey shuddered at the memory.

"He's still consumed with photography," Clay said.

"Yeah, but now he just takes pictures of his kids," Lacey said. "At least that's normal."

"His kids?" Gina asked. "You mean, you two?"

"No. He's remarried." Lacey hopped up again and reached for her purse where it sat on the counter by the door. Clay knew she was going after her wallet and the pictures of Jack and Maggie. She held them out for Gina to see. "He started over again. This is Jack. He's ten. And that's Maggie. She's eight."

"What beautiful children," Gina seemed genuinely interested. It was, Clay knew, a womanly skill. She looked up at him. "They both look like you, Clay."

Clay and Lacey laughed. "They both look like Olivia, our stepmom, actually," Lacey said. "Jack isn't even my dad's son."

And Lacey was not even her dad's daughter, Clay thought. Lacey didn't share that little detail with people quickly or easily, though, and he thought he knew the reason why: it made their mother look bad.

"Jack's from Olivia's first marriage," Lacey continued. "But my dad adopted him."

"Ah," Gina said, touching the pictures with the tip of her finger. "Do you see them much?"

"We do things with them all the time," Lacey said. "They're the cutest kids."

Clay felt antsy. The last thing he wanted was to get into a conversation about marriage and relationships. He stood up, and Sasha immediately ran to the door.

"Taking Sasha for a walk," he said. "Then I'm going to work on the cistern. Gina, holler if you need anything."

Chapter Six

ALEC O'NEILL PULLED THE BEDROOM SHADES against the midday view of the sound and lit the five jasmine-scented candles Olivia had set on the dresser. From the corners of the room, Bocelli sang in wistful Italian, and Alec was pleased he'd finally had the speakers repaired. He and Olivia had sold their separate homes and moved into the house on the sound when they were married nine years earlier, and the bedroom speakers had never worked. Clay fixed them just last month after Alec had mentioned their useless existence, and now he knew what he and Olivia had been missing. If they'd had Bocelli singing in their bedroom all these years, who knows how often they would have gotten around to making love?

He could feel Olivia's presence behind him as he lit the last of the candles in the stained-glass holders Lacey had given them years ago. Olivia was already in their bed, already na-ked, having nearly torn her clothes off as she walked from the living room to the bedroom. She'd made him laugh, as she often did. An impatient lover. He could barely remember a time she'd held off long enough to actually let him be the one to undress her. Her eagerness this afternoon only made him take his time with the candle, pretending he could not get it lit, because he liked teasing her.

"Alec, don't worry about the candle," she said from the bed.

"Got it," he said, blowing out the match.

It had been, what? Two weeks? Maybe longer. When you had kids, it was sometimes impossible to carve out time together. That's why he had rushed home after his morning appointments at the animal hospital and why Olivia had swapped her day off with one of the other docs at the E.R. Jack and Maggie were at day camp, and now he and Olivia had a couple of hours free for lovemaking.

He walked toward her, pulling off his T-shirt. Olivia's arms were folded beneath her head and her eyes were on his, a small smile on her lips. She was the sort of woman who became more beautiful with the years. He liked the laugh lines at the corners of her eyes. Her hair was still the same soft brown it had been when he first met her, although now the color came from a bottle. He would have been equally as happy if she'd let it go gray, but at nearly fifty and with two young kids, she feared looking more like their grandmother than their mother, so he understood. His own hair was more gray than black now, and he still felt an occasional jolt when he looked in the mirror, expecting to see the dark hair he'd once possessed. He still felt like that younger man inside. Most of the time, anyway.

He began to unbuckle the belt on his jeans, but Olivia stretched an arm toward him.

"Come here," she said. "Let me do that."

He lay down next to her, and she kissed him, her hand freeing the end of his belt from the buckle just as the doorbell rang. Olivia's fingers froze, and she groaned, burying her head in his shoulder with a laugh.

"Let's ignore it." He pressed his hand over hers where it rested on the snap of his jeans.

Olivia nodded in agreement, then unsnapped his jeans and curled her fingers beneath the waistband. The bell rang again.

"What if it has something to do with the kids?" she asked, leaning away from him. Her pretty, green eyes were wide open, the desire that had been in them only a moment earlier already gone. She was mother now, all of a sudden. Not wife. Not lover. She would not be able to ignore the bell.

He nodded and sat up, pulling on his shirt. He knew she was right. Their house stood alone, at the tail end of a small, out-of-the-way road that ended at the edge of the water. No one came out here unless they had a real purpose.

He bent over to kiss Olivia's temple, then walked out of the room, buckling his pants. The bell was ringing again by the time he reached the living room, and he opened the door to find a young woman standing on the wooden front porch.

"Yes?" He tried to place her. Some of his patients occasionally brought their sick pets to him when he was off, and he didn't always recognize them out of the context of his office, but he doubted he'd ever seen this woman before. He would remember her if he had. She was in her late twenties or early thirties, with long, very dark hair, milky-white skin and eyes the color of charcoal. In short, the sort of woman you could not see once and then forget.

"Are you Dr. O'Neill?" she asked. She was wearing dark-blue shorts and a light-blue shirt, open, over a white top of some sort.

"Yes," he said.

"I'm Gina Higgins, a friend of your son and daughter's."

With his mind already on Jack and Maggie, his heart did

a nervous little dance in his chest until he realized she was probably not talking about his two youngest children. "Oh," he said. "Do you mean Clay and Lacey?"

She nodded. "That's right," she said with a smile. "I should have made that clear. I forgot you have younger children."

He felt awkward, if not downright rude, standing in the doorway without inviting her in, but this did not appear to be an emergency, and he was anxious to get back to Olivia. "What can I do for you?" he asked.

"I was wondering… May I come in for a moment?" She looked past him into the living room. "Is this a good time?"

"Actually, it's not," Alec said, but Olivia walked into the room in her khaki shorts and white shirt, and he figured there was nothing to get back to, at least not at that moment. He opened the door wider. "It's fine," he relented, stepping back to let her walk past him into the living room. She was wearing a green backpack. "Olivia," he said, "this is Gina Higgins. Right?" He looked at Gina to check his memory.

"Right." She held out her hand to Olivia, who shook it, smiling her usual gracious smile.

"Gina's a friend of Lacey and Clay's," Alec explained.

"It feels so good in here," Gina said, taking in a deep breath and smoothing her dark hair back from her damp forehead. "The air conditioner's broken in my car."

"Have a seat, Gina." Olivia motioned toward the sofa. "Can I get you something to drink?"

Gina sat down, slipping her backpack from her shoulders to her lap. "No, thank you. I don't want to take that much of your time." She looked up at Alec, who was still standing in the middle of the room. "Lacey and Clay suggested I talk to you," she said. "I'm a lighthouse historian in the Pacific Northwest. I came to the Outer Banks to do some exploration of the Kiss River light. I hadn't realized that it had been demolished."

Alec felt his smile freeze at the mention of the lighthouse. Out of the corner of his eye, he saw Olivia lower herself to the other side of the sofa, and he knew she was watching him, waiting for his reaction to this news. He rarely thought about the lighthouse anymore. His long-ago fight to save it had been misguided and had sapped far too much of his time and energy. It had been part of his crazy grieving process after Annie died. "All grieving seems crazy," Olivia had comforted him, but he knew he'd gone a bit over the edge.

He sat down on the arm of the upholstered chair near the door and studied their guest. It seemed odd that a lighthouse historian would not have known that the Kiss River light was no longer standing. "I'm surprised you didn't know it had been damaged," he said.

"Well—" Gina smiled "—my focus has been on the West Coast. And I'm just an amateur at this. I'm really a school-teacher, and I only get to pursue my lighthouse passion in the summer. I admit I didn't do my research very well, did I?" She was clearly nervous. Her hands clutched the backpack in her lap as she leaned forward on the sofa, and her smile had a shiver to it. He felt some sympathy for her. "I was using an older lighthouse guide because it's a favorite of mine," she continued, "and I popped out here, expecting the light to be just as it was described in the book."

"That must have been upsetting," Olivia said.

"There are several other lighthouses here for you to explore," Alec suggested.

She shook her head quickly. "I'm into preservation," she said. "And I was very upset to realize that not only had the lighthouse been destroyed, but that no one has ever tried to retrieve the Fresnel lens from the ocean."

"That's an issue that was put to rest a long time ago," Alec said, wishing he could put it to rest in this room as well.

"I know." She rubbed her palms over her backpack. "I wanted to see if I might be able to do something about that."

"About raising the lens?" Olivia asked.

Gina nodded. "Yes. I'd like to see it on display somewhere."

Alec did not understand why someone from the Pacific Northwest would give a hoot about the Kiss River light, and her intrusion into something that really did not concern her annoyed him. As a lighthouse historian, though, amateur or not, she had to know that the lens was very rare. Only two of them still existed in North Carolina, and they were valued at over a million dollars apiece. He was suddenly suspicious of her motives.

He folded his arms across his chest. "The first thing for you to realize is that it's unlikely the lens is still in one piece."

"I know that," she said.

"And second, the lens would be government property, no matter who salvaged it. You wouldn't get any money out of raising it."

She looked stricken, and he knew he had offended her.

"I'm not after money," she said. "I just want to see it displayed appropriately for the public to enjoy. I was hoping you might be able to help me make that happen."

"I'm not the right person to help you with this, Gina," he said, shaking his head. Again, he was aware of his wife's eyes on him. She was a quiet, but hardly disinterested, observer.

"Lacey and Clay said you used to be the head of the Save the Lighthouse committee," she said.

"That's true, but that was a long time ago and I've since changed my allegiance. Now I just want to let things stay the way they are." The eldest of their three cats, a Persian named

Sylvie, stole into the room and hopped up on Olivia's lap. Gina reached over to scratch the cat's head.

"Are there other people who were on the committee with you who might still want to see the lens salvaged?" she asked, her eyes on Sylvie.

Alec sighed. He wanted her to go. Wanted to get back to bed with his wife. But there *were* other people who might be willing to help her, and in the interest of fair play, he thought she should have those names. He could see the determination in her eyes and knew she would dig them up anyway, with or without his help. "There's Nola Dillard," he said.

"Oh. The real estate agent, right?" Gina pulled a pad and pen from her backpack and wrote down the name.

"Yes."

"Where can I find her?"

"She has her own company now," Olivia said. "It's on Croatan Highway in Kitty Hawk around milepost four."

"What's the name of the highway again?" Gina asked.

Olivia spelled the word for her. Croatan was the common name for Highway 12, the main road through the Outer Banks. Gina was showing her outsider status in more ways than one.

"And who else?" She looked across the room at him.

"Walter Liscott and Brian Cass are the other two," he said. "They're getting up there in years, though, and spend their days playing chess at Shorty's Grill and not doing much else."

"That's on the beach road in Kitty Hawk," Olivia volunteered.

"They're not going to be up for much of a fight these days," Alec said, although he knew both men would probably love to raise that lens as their final tribute to the Kiss River light.

"Well, I can talk to them about it," Gina said, writing on her notepad.

"The only other person on the committee was another woman, Sondra Clarke," Alec said, "but she got married and moved away a few years ago." There *had* been one other person on the committee—Olivia's first husband, Paul—but his work for the committee had not been born of a sincere effort to save the lighthouse. Besides, he lived in Maryland.

Gina nodded. "Well, I'm grateful to you for giving me the names," she said.

"You know—" Alec shifted his weight on the arm of the chair "—I hate to see you waste your time with this. It'd be better spent on some other project."

"This particular project is important to me," Gina said. Something in her voice reminded him of himself back when he'd fought to save the lighthouse, and he wondered if she, too, was being driven by more than the mere salvage of bricks and glass.

"How do you know Clay and Lacey?" Olivia asked her. She had her legs tucked under her on the sofa now, as if expecting Gina's visit to last a long time.

"I was looking at the lighthouse, and Clay came out of the keeper's house and we started talking. He and Lacey offered to let me rent one of the rooms in the house for a little while. It was so kind of them."

Lacey had been the one to invite her to stay, almost certainly. His daughter would take in any stray she could find, while Clay would barely notice his or her existence. It had bothered Alec when Clay and Lacey moved into the keeper's house in January. He hadn't been back there in nearly a decade, and he'd had a sick feeling in the pit of his stomach the first time he'd driven to Kiss River to visit them. That storm should have taken the entire Kiss River promontory, in his opinion.

"How long are you staying?" Olivia asked their visitor.

"I'm not sure yet," Gina said. "At least a week. Maybe longer."

"Do you know that Monday is Lacey's birthday?" Olivia asked, and Alec knew the question was as much to remind him as it was to inform Gina. He didn't need the reminder, though. He had forgotten Lacey's birthday once, long ago. He would never make that mistake again.

"I didn't know that," Gina said. "Thanks for the heads-up." She stood, and so did he and Olivia. "And thanks for the help," she said to Alec. "It was nice of you, especially since I know you'd rather I didn't pursue this."

Alec shrugged as he opened the front door for her. "You know there are other first-order lenses already on display, don't you?" he asked.

"But they're not the Kiss River lens," she said with a smile. She stopped short as she walked through the doorway, and he followed her gaze to the small, oval-shaped stained-glass window to the left of the doorjamb.

"Oh, this must be Lacey's," she said, touching the glass image of a woman walking a greyhound.

"No, actually," Alec said, "it was made by my first wife." The oval window had been one of ten in the house he'd shared with Annie. When he and Olivia sold their separate homes to buy this one, it was Olivia who'd insisted he not leave all of Annie's work behind. "You'll regret it someday," she'd said. He'd let her pick which oval window they should bring with them, not really caring at the time. But over the years, he'd been grateful to her for knowing he needed that little reminder of the good times with Annie.

"Oh," Gina said. "I can see where Lacey got her talent." She nodded to him. "Thanks again," she said, then looked past him toward Olivia. "Nice meeting you both."

"Nice meeting you, Gina," Olivia said from behind him.

After closing the door, Alec walked over to where his wife was sitting on the sofa and leaned down to kiss her, but he knew the mood had long ago been broken. Bocelli was no longer singing, and most likely Olivia had blown out the candles when she left the bedroom. She returned his kiss, but then pulled away to look at him.

"The money is there to salvage the lens," she said. "You know it is."

He shook his head. "Olivia…"

"You could help her," Olivia said. "No one knows the history of that lighthouse as well as you do."

"No," he said, letting go of her, standing up straight. "And please, don't talk to me about it again." He bent over again to kiss her lightly on the forehead, then turned to walk toward the kitchen, and if he hadn't disliked the stranger the moment he'd opened his front door to her, he certainly did now. She had ruined his entire afternoon.

Chapter Seven

Saturday, March 14, 1942

MAMA AND I BAKED ALL MORNING, AS WE DO often on the weekend. Today was very cold for the middle of March and I was glad to have the oven heat up the house. I am so tired of going out to use the privy in the cold! This seems like the longest winter ever. First warm day we have, I'm taking off my shoes and not putting them on again until next fall.

Even though I spent all morning with Mama, we hardly talked at all. It is so hard for me to spend time with her. There is a wall between us. I want to hug her and tell her how much I love her and instead, ugly things come out of my mouth. Or nothing at all. We used to sing sometimes when we baked or cleaned together in the house. I can't imagine that now. It's not the war or anything like that. It's ME. I feel like I have a mean guard up and can't let it down for a minute around her. Can't be soft. I don't know why. Except that I am almost fifteen years old. I overheard Mama complaining about me to a friend at Trager's Store when she didn't think I was listening, and the friend said, "Oh, it's just that she's a teenager, Mary. She'll grow out of it." I hated being lumped together with all the teens in the world, but maybe she's right. Though I can't imagine growing out of this. Sometimes I miss having Mama's arms around me, but when she touches me, I stiffen up, so who can blame her for not trying anymore? I can't help it, though. Everything she ever says to me is "Don't do this" and "Don't do that." There's nothing much else to talk about.

Anyhow, we baked four pies and ten dozen cookies. It being so cold out, I didn't want to leave that warm kitchen, but then I thought about the choice I had. Stay in the house with Mama, or take the pies to the Coast Guard boys. I didn't have to think about that too long! I loaded the pies and cookies into the big wooden wagon we keep in the storage shed near the privy, hooked it up to my bicycle and took off down the Pole Road. None of the roads are paved around here. Even the Pole Road, the one used by the electric people to bring in equipment, is just a mess of sand and ruts and crazy curves and turns, but it's the smoothest road there is for bicycle riding and carrying pies. If I was going to the Coast Guard building by foot, I would have just walked along the beach, although earlier this week we were told not to go out there because the bodies were washing up from that ship that sank last week. Most cars use the beach, too. They just follow each other's tire tracks and go real slow, but one has to be dug out every once in a while. Ever since the U-boats started attacking us, the sandpounders (that's what they call the Coast Guard boys) patrol the beach, watching for ships in distress and keeping a lookout for spies and for submarines letting Nazis off on the beach. The drivers of the cars have to give the patrollers a password to be able to go on. The patroller gives the driver a new password for him to use at the next stop, in another three miles, and people make their way up the beach like that. I wanted to have a password, too, when I go walking along the beach, but everybody knows me and they just say, "You go on ahead, now, Bess."

I had to pedal real carefully because of the ditches and tree roots in the road, and I didn't want to spill anything out of the wagon. It was so cold, I put my scarf right across my face to keep the wind out. Once I got there, though, I knew the trip had been worth it.

About half the boys were at the Coast Guard station, the other half out patrolling the beaches or maybe training their dogs or working at some other thing. When I walked in the door and took off my coat, I could see every head turn in my direction and smiles come to their faces, and I know it wasn't just that I was pulling a wagonful of sweets. This is a new experience for me, having boys stare. My body feels different around them. My breasts are not all that big, but those boys stare at them all the same, even though I sure don't dress to show them off. (I still had a sweater over my shirt, for Pete's sake!) I could feel how my hips moved beneath my dungarees and how long my legs were. I'm nearly five foot eight now, the tallest girl in my school, although I guess with only thirteen girls from seven years old to seventeen, that's not saying much. I'm taller than most of the boys at school, too. That's why these older boys (men, really) from the Coast Guard look so good to me. Most of them are taller than me, some by quite a bit. My hair is brown, and up until last year I always wore it in braids, but lately I've been leaving it loose. It's long and wavy and I can tell the boys like it that way.

So, some of the boys come up to me and started talking. Some of them talk so funny it takes me a minute or two to start understanding them, like last year when Mrs. Cady had us read a Shakespeare play out loud. My favorite accent is the one the Boston boys have. Teddy Pearson, who is from near there, said that Hitler should be "tod and fethahd." I didn't understand what he'd said until I was home in my bed that night, and I laughed out loud when I figured it out. Anyhow, they were all talking to me at once, asking me how I was, what kind of pie I'd brought, did I want to go out with them that night. You'd think they hadn't seen a girl in months! If Mama could see how them boys act when I walk in the door of the Coast Guard station without her or Daddy, she would never let me go there alone again.

Jimmy Brown, another of the Boston boys, is my favorite of all of them at the station and not just because he's the sandpounder who patrols the beach near Kiss River. Today, like always, he pretty much ignored me. That's probably why I like him—he's a challenge! Doesn't drool over me and my pies when I walk in. He sat in the corner whittling something out of a piece of driftwood, looking up with those dreamy blue eyes every once in a while, smiling just a bit, though more at how crazy the boys were acting than at me, I think. So I chatted with all the boys, and with Mr. Bud Hewitt who came out to see what the racket was about, and all the while I had one eye on Jimmy Brown (he looks like Frank Sinatra!) whittling in the corner.

I would like the work they do. I wish they took women into the Coast Guard. I know the beach better than any of them, and would love to be out there at night, watching for danger. Mr. Hewitt told me that if I was a boy, I'd be the first person he'd recruit for the beach patrol. After all, some of those boys had never even seen the ocean before, much less know the beaches and the woods around them! I mentioned this to my parents one time and Mama just laughed at me, but I heard that she used to actually work with the lifesaving crew. She says that's only a rumor, but even my father told me it was the truth and said that she doesn't want me to know about it because it might give me ideas.

On the way home from the Coast Guard station, I bumped into Dennis Kittering. I was surprised to see him. He's usually on the beach, not on the Pole Road, but he said he was just exploring a bit. I told him where I'd been and he said, "Why didn't you bring *me* any pies?" I said, "I bring pies to the men who are fighting for our country. What exactly are you doing for the country?" Right away, I could have kicked myself. I forgot about his bum leg. He couldn't go into the service because he has that one leg shorter than the other. I apologized and he smiled at me and said not to worry about it. He said he was *teaching* for his country, that's what he was doing. Educating the next generation. Teaching them why the war was happening, helping them see why we should never let things get so bad again. I felt doubly awful when he said that. We stood there for a few minutes, with my bicycle and wagon between us, talking about *The Heart Is a Lonely Hunter* and that was fun. The truth is, there aren't many people around here who understand much about the books I'm reading. Dennis thinks I'm real smart and that I should be a teacher when I grow up. That's actually my plan. He says I need to get a better education than I'm getting here, though, if I want to be a teacher. I don't know what it is about Dennis. He is nice and smart and mostly kind, but he irritates me to no end when he acts like he knows everything and I sometimes end up in a tiff with him. He corrects my grammar all the time, and when he criticizes my education, saying I can't be getting a good one here with just twenty-three students of all grades and ages jumbled up together in one classroom out in the middle of nowhere, I get mad. I don't like that he comes here all the time, saying how much he loves it and all, and then puts us Bankers down.

I made a stupid mistake and told him how I'd like to be a sandpounder and he laughed at that and said, "The sand-pounders are men who have little else to offer the world. They are just a bunch of trigger-happy hooligans with guns, ready to shoot at anything that moves." That *really* made me mad, although I've heard other people say the same thing about the patrollers. They just don't know those boys and how serious they take their duty. Anyhow, see what I mean about some-times getting into a tiff with Dennis?

He asked me if I want to go to church with him tomorrow. He goes all the way up to Corolla for church, where they have a Catholic service. I told him no, thanks. I always go with my parents to the Methodist church down in Duck. I don't understand much about Catholics. Last summer, Dennis was wearing a short-sleeved shirt that was open a little at the neck and I could see he was wearing a necklace made of brown cord. I asked him about it, and he pulled it out and showed it to me. It had these two rectangles of wool attached to the cord, one that goes on his back and one on his chest, and they have pictures of Jesus and Mary on them. I don't remember what the necklace is called, but he said he wears it all the time, that it makes him feel closer to God. Anyhow, when I said yesterday that I was going to the Methodist church, I was afraid he was going to start mocking my religion like he does my education, so I told him that I had to go home, I was late (which was true). I'll take him a pie next weekend, to make up for being so rude to him.

I just realized that I'm starting to feel uncomfortable around Dennis. It's not just the way he criticizes us Bankers, but it's also that I know he looks at me different this year. He tells me I've gotten real pretty and actually said if I was a bit older, he would ask me to marry him! "You have potential," he said. "I'd like to marry you and take you to High Point, where you could get a real education." I admit I am flattered by all he says, but also I feel creepy, like I don't want to be close enough to him for him to touch me. I think that's why I wanted to keep my bicycle between us on the Pole Road. There was no one else around and it made me a little nervous. He's not bad-looking. He wears glasses he looks nice in, and I like his dark hair. But he is ancient, eight years older than me, and I am definitely not interested in him as a boyfriend. Besides, I don't like how "Bess Kittering" sounds. (I love how "Bess Brown" sounds, though!)

Mama scolded me when I got home. I stayed too long at the Coast Guard station, she said. I am supposed to just drop the pies off and leave, not stay and expect those boys to entertain me. I told her I was late because I met Mr. Kittering on the way home and we got to talking, and that made her even angrier. She thinks Dennis is strange to come out here every weekend. She's never even met him, only seen him from a distance, and I told her how nice he is, how I like to talk about books with him, but she just kept yelling at me. I think Mama must have been born an old lady.

Chapter Eight

THE SUN WAS STILL HIGH IN THE SKY WHEN CLAY pulled into the short gravel driveway of the small cottage, which, like many other soundside cottages, was set on stilts above the water. Getting out of his car, he could see that the front gutter was a bit askew and a section of the deck railing was missing. He would have to spend a day over here soon working on those repairs and the other inevitable problems with this house that were not immediately visible. The old cottage took a great deal of his time—much like the old man living inside it. But these days, he loved nothing better than to fill up his time to the mind-numbing brim.

Standing on the front porch, he rapped his knuckles against the frame of the flimsy screen door, leaning close to peer inside the small living room of the cottage. Henry quickly appeared in the living room, obviously champing at the bit to get out of there. Clay pulled the screen door open, and the dapper old man stood in front of him, dressed in his usual white shirt and dark tie. He had to be the only Outer Banks resident who wore a tie every single day, Clay thought. With the exception of Henry's three-day hospital stay after having his appendix removed, Clay couldn't remember ever seeing him without one. Or without his hat.

"Hey, Henry," he said, resting his hand on the man's shoulder. "How are you doing?"

"Got ants in my pants." Henry placed his straw fedora on his head and stepped onto the porch. He flexed his knobby, arthritic hands. "Need a good game of chess at Shorty's," he said, and Clay knew he'd been waiting all day for this outing. He wished now that he'd stopped his work on the cistern to pick him up earlier.

"What happened to the railing there?" Clay pointed to the spot where the two-by-four was missing.

"Woke up one morning and it was gone." Henry shrugged his shoulders. "'Twas the day after I caught twenty-two crabs, so I think their pals must've up and took it to get back at me." He chuckled. Henry could crab without even leaving his house. All he needed to do was walk around the deck and scrape the crabs off the pilings with a net. Even at seventy-nine, Henry could make some of the best crab cakes Clay had ever tasted.

"You be careful there," Clay said, pointing to the railing again. "I'll come over soon to fix it."

Henry liked to boast that he lived in a house as old as he was. In theory, he was right. The house had been built sometime in the twenties. But it had suffered a massive fire in the forties, and flooding off and on over the years, with a bit of the house being replaced here, another bit there, until very little of the original structure still stood.

The old man still had a bounce in his step, and he walked ahead of Clay toward the car. He was lively and sharp-witted—and he was now Clay's responsibility entirely.

Henry Hazelwood was Terri's grandfather, and she had

taken on his care as he'd aged. Her father, Henry's son, had died four years ago, and her mother lived in California, so she had been the only relative nearby. She'd adored Henry, though, and had never complained about that obligation falling on her shoulders. Clay liked Henry, too, but at the age of twenty-nine, he had expected to be creating a family of little rugrats, not caring for an old man. He was all Henry had, though, and letting him down was not part of his nature. Henry's eyesight was going, and he'd been wise enough to give up driving a couple of years ago. That meant that Clay frequently had to take time off from work to drive him to doctor's appointments, the grocery store, and most important to the old man, Shorty's Grill, where he could play chess and visit with his old friends, Walter Liscott and Brian Cass.

The one thing about Henry that Clay simultaneously loved and hated was that he reminded him of Terri. Both Terri and her father had had a slant to their eyebrows above steel-gray eyes, and those features were mirrored in Henry's face. Clay saw his wife there every time he looked at his grandfather-in-law.

"What did you do this morning?" Clay asked once they were in his car and crossing the island to the beach road.

"What do you think?" Henry asked him.

"Crabbed?"

"What else?" Henry chuckled again. "Snared my dinner. And how about you?"

"Oh." Clay sighed. He was always caught off guard when Henry asked him about himself. "I worked on the cistern."

"Sounds like a better use of time than catching crabs," Henry said.

Clay smiled. "Can't eat a cistern, though."

Henry chuckled, and they both grew quiet. Henry was a man of few words. Any conversation between them was usually short and to the point, and that was fine. They had never, not once, talked about Terri. That was fine, too. Clay didn't talk to anyone about Terri.

He had rejected his father's suggestion that he see a therapist after Terri died. What could a therapist do? He—or she—couldn't bring her back. Clay kept his dark thoughts and deepest feelings under wraps, throwing himself into his work, killing time more than filling it. The world thought he was doing fine. He stayed active and he made sure his spirits seemed up around his friends. Lacey was probably the only person who knew he wasn't the jovial sport he pretended to be. He was around her too much to keep up the act, and he knew she was struggling to find a way to save him, the way she would save a stray kitten. Or a wandering lighthouse historian.

At breakfast that morning, he could see his sister looking from Gina to him and back again, hope in her conniving blue eyes that he would find the newcomer attractive. Well, he did find her attractive, but that only added to his problems, and he hoped Lacey wouldn't try to push him too hard. He supposed she needed to focus on some new deficiency in him since she'd failed at getting him back into search and rescue work. He felt sick at the mention of those words: *search and rescue.* Literally sick. The other night, he'd had to turn off the television when a newscaster mentioned a search and rescue team involved in an earthquake in some other part of the world, the wave of nausea sending him to bed. Lacey had been in the room at the time, and she'd said nothing when he turned off the TV and went upstairs. A few months ago, she would have followed him up, trying to get him to talk. But she was learning. She no longer badgered him to open up about his feelings. One of these days, she would give up trying to save him. He was destined to be her one failure.

"Looky there!" Henry pointed in the direction of a new fish market on Croatan Highway. "We'll have to try that one."

"Looks like a good one," Clay said.

Henry had lived on the Outer Banks forever, since being stationed there during the Second World War. He'd fallen in love with a Banks girl and married her, a union that produced one child, Terri's father. The Outer Banks had grown up around him, but he never complained the way a lot of the old-timers did. He never talked about what things had been like in the old days, or grew crotchety over how crowded it was in the summer or griped about the tourists who acted as if they owned the place. He actually seemed to like the over-growth of buildings and stores and restaurants that disturbed many of the natives. He'd spend hours in the supermarket, still amazed by all the choices, reading the labels on the frozen foods, which he loved. Clay had learned to bring a book with him when he took Henry shopping; otherwise, he would go out of his tree with boredom. Henry loved his TV dinners, but he had to have fresh seafood as well, so Clay took him to the fish market a couple of times a week. Now that Henry had spotted this new store, he knew it wouldn't be long before he found himself leaning against the interior walls, reading his book, while Henry took his time sniffing the fish.

Clay had learned of Terri's death on a Tuesday in late November, and his own shock and horror had been compounded by his need to tell Henry. Henry had already lost his wife and only son. To lose his beloved granddaughter as well seemed a cruel injustice. And Clay couldn't tell him. It had been Lacey who went over to the rickety soundside cottage to give Henry the news. Clay never asked his sister how the old man took it; he didn't want to know. All he knew was that, for the next few weeks, every time he picked up Henry to take him someplace, the elderly man's eyes would be as red as Clay's own.

They pulled into Shorty's crowded parking lot. Shorty's was a dive—there was no other word for it—and somehow the tourists knew to stay away. A few ventured in, those people who thought they'd find a taste of the old Outer Banks in the ramshackle building, but most of them were there only a few minutes before realizing they would never truly fit in. Especially not in the back room.

The back room, which was in reality on the side of the building, was a hangout for fishermen, weathered old-timers and young men with too much time on their hands. There was a battered pool table on one side of the room and chess and checker boards and decks of cards scattered across the tables. Two dartboards hung on the walls. The windows were filmed with years of smoke. An occasional woman or two could be found in the back room. They usually hung around the younger men, playing pool, displaying varying degrees of cleavage as they leaned low over the table and maybe a tattoo of a rose on one shoulder. It was those women, their skin tanned to the color and texture of leather, who were often the smokers.

Kenny Gallo, whom Clay was to meet for a beer, was not yet in the restaurant, so he walked with Henry into the back room to deliver the old man to his friends. A couple of women were playing pool with a guy who had only recently become a regular, a dark-haired young man of about twenty who was elaborately tattooed all the way from his knuckles to the place where his arms disappeared beneath the sleeves of his black Grateful Dead T-shirt. The women looked up when Clay entered the room. He felt their eyes stay on him as he and Henry moved toward Walter Liscott and Brian Cass and the chessboard. He was as indifferent to their attention as he was accustomed to it.

"You're late." Brian looked up at Henry, his rheumy blue

eyes annoyed. Brian could be as prickly as a sandspur. His thick white hair stuck up on one side of his head as though he'd slept on it, and he tapped the chessboard with a long, bony finger.

"Oh, shut up," Walter said to his friend. "He's here now, so what does it matter?"

"My fault," Clay said, even though Henry had not been expected at any particular time. He pulled one of the chairs from a neighboring table and set it adjacent to the chessboard so Henry could sit down. "I was late picking him up," he said.

"Sit down yourself, Clay," Walter said, as he always did. The wheelchair he sat in was pulled up tight against the table. Walter had used the chair for the past four years. Something about his legs and diabetes. When it was apparent the chess-loving old man could no longer get around without the chair, Clay and Kenny had built a ramp up to Shorty's back door so he could get in. Walter's meticulously carved and painted decoys provided much of Shorty's decor, so it seemed only fitting that the restaurant should remain accessible to him, of all people. The decoy on which he was currently working now rested on the table, next to the chessboard.

Clay glanced back toward the main room. Still no sign of Kenny. "Just for a minute," he said, dragging another chair to the table.

"Do ya see that asshole?" Brian nodded toward the guy with the tattoos, speaking far too loudly.

Clay didn't shift his gaze from Brian's face. "What about him?" he asked, trying to whisper.

"He's got a new one Brian can't get his mind off." Walter laughed.

"It's on his back," Brian said. "He held up his shirt when them girls came in."

"Don't talk so loud," Henry said.

Brian leaned toward Henry. "I'm talking loud so you can hear me, old man," he said.

"I hear you fine," Henry shot back. "And so can everyone in the next room."

"It's a mermaid," Walter said.

"What is?" Henry asked. He was studying the board. He would be playing the winner.

"The new tattoo," Brian said. "A mermaid with the biggest jugs you ever seen."

Clay had to laugh.

"Ah, you and your jugs," Walter scoffed.

The conversation continued that way, three old widowers baiting and badgering each other as they had for years. It was clear they loved each other deeply, yet they never spoke of anything weightier than the shifting of the tides. Three old men who had fought and fished and lost loved ones together. Brian's wife of half a century had died only a couple of years ago, and his eleven children and twenty-seven grandchildren were scattered around the country. Walter had been widowed for a decade. His two children badgered him regularly to move to Colorado where they lived, but he could not bring himself to leave the Outer Banks. Women were supposed to outlive men, Clay thought, but the old regulars in Shorty's back room hadn't gotten the word. Must be something in the salt air that kept men alive out here. It was only when Clay left their table to walk back into the main room that the realization hit him: there had actually been *four* widowers sitting around that chessboard.

He found Kenny waiting for him at one of the small tables, and he sat down across from his old friend. The waitress brought them beers without even waiting for them to order. They were well known here.

"How was work?" he asked Kenny, taking a swallow of beer.

"Good, but man, I'm losing more hearing in this ear every day," Kenny said, rubbing his left ear with his hand.

"Well, you know the cure for that," Clay said. Kenny did much of the diving for the marine repair business he owned, and hearing loss was part of the job. He'd be deaf in another ten years, but Clay knew that wouldn't stop him. Kenny was happier underwater than he was on land.

"I'd rather go deaf and have my cock fall off than give up diving," Kenny said.

Clay laughed. "You have a way with words, Ken."

He spent more time with Kenny these days than any of his other buddies. Most of his friends were married, and he felt their pity when they were with him. He saw them glance at each other when one of them committed a faux pas by talking about getting in trouble with his wife if he got home late or whatever. They treated Clay as if he was fragile. The worst part of it was, they were right. He *did* wince, if only inside, when they talked about their wives. He was jealous, resentful, angry and hurt, all those things they thought him to be, but he let none of it show. Being with Kenny was much easier. Kenny was not ready to give up bachelorhood. He could talk to Clay about diving or windsurfing the way they always had, with no mention of a wife at home who might try to put a damper on their fun. Still, Kenny liked women, and they liked him. He was a notorious flirt, burly, bearded and blond. It could be disconcerting talking to him, since he so rarely looked Clay in the eye. He was too busy following the movement of every woman within sight.

Now that he was done with the cistern repair and had delivered Henry to his friends, now that he was just sitting and relaxing, one particular woman crept back into Clay's

mind. For a moment, he thought of telling Kenny about Gina.
About how beautiful she was, how he was both drawn to and
repelled by her at the same time. But he couldn't do that. It
would break one of the unspoken rules of his current relationship with Kenny: talk about sports or diving or fishing—anything but women.

They had been friends in high school, but had taken different paths when it came to careers. Kenny, reluctant to leave
the Outer Banks, took over his father's marine repair business
after graduation from high school, while Clay went to Duke
to study architecture. It would have been logical for their
educational differences to separate them, but they remained
friends. Kenny was not educated, not in books or in life—he
still called women "girls," for example, and he would probably
get off on the jugs on tattooed guy's back—but he had brains
that Clay respected, and he was a better, smarter diver than
Clay would ever be.

The young man with the tattoos left the back room and
started walking through the main restaurant, probably on his
way to the rest room, but he stopped short as he passed their
table, his eyes on Clay.

"Hey, you're Clay O'Neill, right?" he asked. He wore a
diamond stud in his left ear, and his dark hair was very short.

Clay nodded. "Yes."

"I'm Brock Jensen," the man said, holding out his hand.

Clay shook his hand, and for the first time got a good look
at his arms. The tattoos were designs rather than drawings,
swirls and curlicues and arrows and waves, and they covered
so much of his skin that it made Clay's arms burn just to look
at them.

"I know your sister," Brock said.

"Lacey?" Clay asked, as if he might possibly mean Maggie.
Lacey rarely came to Shorty's.

"Yeah. I met her at an Al-Anon meeting. She said she might be able to help me find a job."

"What kind of work are you looking for?" Kenny asked.

"Construction."

Construction jobs were a dime a dozen here, especially for someone who looked like this guy. He was slim, but powerfully built. The dark swirling lines on his biceps shifted with the slightest movement of his arms.

"Shouldn't be hard to find a construction job," Clay said. There were people he could put him in touch with, but he frankly didn't feel like helping him out.

"Try this place." Kenny pulled a pen from his T-shirt pocket and wrote something down on a napkin. He handed it to Brock, who glanced at it, then nodded.

"Hey, thanks, dude, I will," he said, then looked at Clay. "And tell your sister I said 'hey.'"

"Sure," Clay said. Neither he nor Kenny spoke again until the man had left the main room and was out of earshot.

"Brock?" Kenny laughed. "Give me a break."

Clay laughed as well, but he felt uneasy. Houses and stores were being built and remodeled up and down the Outer Banks. That guy could walk onto any construction site and be working within two minutes. He didn't need anyone's help. Clay had a feeling that help in finding a job was not all this guy wanted from his good-hearted sister.

Chapter Nine

GINA SAT IN THE HIGH-CEILINGED WAITING room of Dillard Realty, with its faux sea-worn paneling and beach motif. She was nervous, on the verge of panic, and sitting still was a challenge. She'd told Mrs. King, a woman she had never met but had come to despise nevertheless, that she would be in touch with her no later than today. She'd thought that surely by now, three days after her arrival in Kiss River, she would have things figured out, but she was no closer to resolving her dilemma than she had been before this trip east. She had completely lost Sunday because she'd spent the day crampy and nauseated, most likely from the fast-food hamburger she'd eaten after leaving Alec O'Neill's house on Saturday. A fitting ending to that most unproductive visit. It was ironic that Alec suspected her of hoping to make an easy million by raising the lens. It *was* money she was after, but she knew she would not get that money from ownership of Kiss River's Fresnel lens.

She wondered if Alec and Lacey would talk about her today at the animal hospital. Might Lacey have any influence over him? Gina doubted it. He'd been stubborn, his mind made up. Whether because of his suspicions about her or some other reason she couldn't fathom, he had been no help at all, and now her hopes were pinned on the real estate agent, Nola Dillard.

She'd simply walked into this office and requested to see Mrs. Dillard. She probably should have called first, but she was too afraid of hearing the woman say she wasn't interested in helping her, and over the phone, Gina would stand little chance of persuading her. Persuasion was not her forte, anyway. Yes, she could talk a bunch of seventh-graders into sitting down and paying attention, not a skill to be taken lightly, but that was about the limit of her influence.

She'd been waiting nearly half an hour when a woman stepped into the reception area and marched directly over to Gina, holding her hand out toward her like a spear.

"Are you Gina Higgins?" she asked. She was a tall woman in her mid-fifties, with white-blond hair held back with a clasp and tanned skin so smooth and tight it could only have come from the gifted hands of a plastic surgeon.

Gina stood to shake her hand. "Yes," she said. "Would you have a moment to give me?"

Nola Dillard looked at her watch. "About fifteen minutes," she said. "I have to show a house in South Nag's Head at four."

Gina followed her down a hallway to a large office with a huge mahogany desk, expensively upholstered chairs and the same silvery paneling as the reception area. Several plaques and award statues graced the walls and bookcase behind the desk. Nola Dillard was an obvious success as a Realtor. There was also a photograph of a young woman with glimmering blond hair holding a little girl of about three on her lap. The woman had her chin pressed lightly to the top of the child's head, and mother and daughter, for that was what Gina supposed them to be, wore broad smiles. The picture made Gina ache with longing to hold her own daughter.

"Are you interested in a house?" Nola said as she took a seat behind her massive desk.

"No, actually." Gina pulled her gaze away from the photograph to look at the Realtor. She sat on the edge of her chair, her damp palms cupping her bare knees. "I'm interested in the Kiss River lighthouse."

"Kiss River?" Nola looked surprised, her gray eyes wide. "Interested in it in what way?"

"I'd like to see the lens rescued from the bottom of the ocean and displayed someplace where the public could enjoy it," Gina said.

"Ah." Nola leaned back in her chair, nodding. "Are you the friend Lacey was trying to find a rental for?"

Gina nodded. "Yes. I'm staying at the keeper's house for now."

"I see. I guess Lacey told you that I had been on the Save the Lighthouse committee long ago. Before the storm."

"Her father…Dr. O'Neill, told me, actually."

"Really?" Nola looked surprised by that. "I didn't think he cared about Kiss River anymore."

"Well, I don't think he does," Gina said. "That's why he told me to contact you." Not quite the truth, but not exactly a lie, either.

Nola swiveled her chair back and forth, her eyes on Gina. "I happen to be one of the few Outer Banks natives who would love to see the lens raised," she said, then smiled. "Of course, I have a vested interest in attracting more tourists and keeping them happy."

"Will you help me then?" Gina tightened her hands on her knees. "I know I need to find someone to fund the project, but I'm an outsider and I really need the support of someone who isn't."

"Where are you from, hon?"

"Washington State. I'm an amateur lighthouse historian there, and I wanted to see some of the lighthouses in the East. I was shocked to discover that no one had bothered to raise the Kiss River lens."

"I agree with you one hundred percent," Nola said.

Gina let out her breath in relief. Nola Dillard seemed the type of woman who could get things done.

"I could contact the travel bureau for you," Nola continued. "Put you in touch with someone there. If you're willing to take on the administrative work involved, they would probably help you out with the money."

"That would be wonderful!" Gina smiled. Finally, she was getting somewhere. "Alec O'Neill was so adamant about not getting involved, I had just about given—"

"I thought you said Alec told you to get in touch with me," Nola interrupted her.

Gina knew by the tone of the Realtor's voice that she had suddenly stepped onto thin ice. "He gave me your name," she said.

"Does he want the lens to be salvaged?"

Gina hesitated. "No," she said in a rush of honesty. "But I think it's just that he—"

"I can't help you then, hon," Nola interrupted her again, folding her arms across her chest.

"Why?" Gina's voice was a near wail.

"Oh, I think Alec is probably right," Nola said. "The lens should stay where it is. That's what most people want. I just got caught up in the idea for a moment."

"Please, Mrs. Dillard," Gina said, disturbed by the emotion

in her own voice, but Nola didn't seem to notice. She was already standing up, looking at her watch again.

She smiled at Gina with real sympathy. "Alec's a friend," she said. "I've never completely understood his change of heart about the lighthouse, but I'm not going to go against his wishes. I'm sorry."

Gina was slow to get to her feet, and Nola put a gentle arm around her shoulders as they walked out of the office and down the hall.

"How's Lacey doing?" she asked. "I haven't seen her in a while."

"Well, I've only known her a few days," Gina said, aware of the flat tone of disappointment in her voice, "but she's one of the nicest people I've ever met." Lacey had nursed her and her upset stomach the day before, buying her ginger ale and crackers, making her chicken soup from scratch for dinner. "Today's her birthday."

"The first of July," Nola mused. "That's right. A couple of weeks after my daughter's birthday. Lacey was my daughter Jessica's best friend when they were growing up."

Gina thought back to the picture on the bookcase of the young woman and little girl. She knew exactly how that child's hair would feel against the woman's chin.

They had reached the waiting room, and Nola turned to face her. "I'm sorry about the lens," she said.

"What should I do?" Gina asked her.

"Have you talked to Walter Liscott or Brian Cass?"

"Not yet," she said. "Alec said they were very old, though, and—"

"They're getting up there in years, but they're not dead," Nola said with a laugh. "And age has its benefits. They have a lifetime's worth of contacts."

Gina nodded. "I'll talk to them," she said without much hope. "And if you change your mind, you know where I am."

There was a new rattling coming from the underbelly of her car as she drove back to Kiss River. The rutted lane to the keeper's house had probably shaken something loose. Between that and the broken air conditioner, she wondered if the car would ever be able to take her back to Washington.

She parked in the sand-covered parking lot near the keeper's house, then opened the car door but didn't move from her seat, not quite sure what to do next. She had the house to herself this evening. Lacey and Clay and even Sasha were at Alec O'Neill's tonight, celebrating Lacey's birthday. She had not been invited, and certainly hadn't expected to be. Frankly, the last person she felt like spending more time with was Alec O'Neill. She'd looked forward to the evening alone, yet now she found herself missing Lacey's caring company, and that worried her. The closer she got to Lacey, the harder it would be to lie to her. She had to remember to keep some distance from her hosts. She had no room in her for the responsibilities that came with friendship. There was no one she could talk to about her plight anymore, no one she could open up to. They would think she was crazy. And maybe she was, if only just a little. Desperation could make you that way.

At breakfast, she had given Lacey a birthday card with a note inside promising her a massage whenever she wanted one. It was the one gift she could give that would cost her nothing.

"I'm a good masseuse," she said after Lacey had thanked her. It was true. She had taken a few courses several years ago, because massage was the one thing that had eased her mother's pain during the last few months of her life.

"I'm so sorry you can't come with us tonight," Lacey had said. She had been standing in the middle of the kitchen after breakfast, the card and note in her hands while Clay opened the back door, ready to leave for his office. Gina could tell that Lacey felt guilty about leaving her alone.

Gina had put her hands on the younger woman's arms and looked her firmly in the eye. "You've barely known me three days, Lacey," she said. "I'm just your boarder, not part of your family, and that's fine. You and Clay go and have a great time tonight. You're going to have an ulcer, worrying so much about people."

Lacey gave her a hug. Clay, who was halfway out the door, turned to add his usual succinct two cents. "Ulcers are caused by bacteria, not worry," he said. He walked outside, Sasha running ahead of him, and Lacey followed the two of them, leaving Gina hugged, chastened and deserted all at once.

She knew that Clay was a widower. Lacey had told her his interior-designer wife had died in an accident in November and that he was still not over it. They'd had a fantastic marriage, she'd said. Gina was not a believer in fantastic marriages, but she was not about to argue the point with Lacey, who obviously missed her sister-in-law. And Clay, although quiet and understandably humorless, was nevertheless treating her very kindly. He'd even let her use his computer to check her e-mail, something she had been anxious to do since leaving Bellingham, and he told her she could use the computer anytime she liked.

Sitting in her car in the parking lot, she thought about using it now to check her e-mail again, although she had done so just before noon. She glanced toward the broken lighthouse, and noticed that the ocean sounded calmer and quieter than she'd heard it since her arrival. There were a few more hours until sunset, she thought. She would go for a walk. Maybe she could find the Coast Guard station from Bess's diary.

She left her sandals in the car and walked along the short

path through the shrubs until she came to the lighthouse. Wading through the shallow water past the tower, she turned right onto the beach. The coastline was obviously quite different from the days of Bess's diary and not at all easy to walk on. Now, the beach was very narrow, even disappearing in some places where the waves chewed at the green groundcover instead of sand, and Gina had to walk through water. The waves were little more than ripples slipping toward shore.

In the pages of the diary, the Coast Guard station seemed to be no more than a half a mile from the lighthouse, but Gina walked at least a mile without seeing a trace of it. She had seen *no* buildings, as a matter of fact. The slender thread of beach butted up against hardy-looking trees and shrubs. She'd seen no people, either, and the solitude was eerie, the only sound the lapping of the nearly flat waves against the shore and the occasional breaking of twigs in the woods to her right. She was glad she'd learned that the horses and hogs were gone.

Dead bodies had washed up on this beach, she thought as she walked. *And a man had been murdered here.*

Her gaze was drawn to the water a distance ahead of her. Someone was swimming in the ocean. As Gina grew closer, she saw it was an older woman, who was now coming out of the water onto the beach, wringing the sea out of her long gray hair.

The woman waved at her, reaching down to pick up a towel from the sand.

"Hi," Gina called as she neared her. "How's the water?"

"Glorious," the woman said. "It's so calm. I think I swam about two miles today." The woman looked like a swimmer, with broad shoulders and powerful thighs. She tilted her head at Gina. "I come here almost every day and you're just about the first person I've seen out here," she said.

"I was looking for the Coast Guard station."

"Coast Guard station?" the woman said. "You mean a life-saving station?"

Gina recalled that the Coast Guard stations had originally been home to the life-saving crews. "Yes," she said.

"The nearest are up in Ocean Sands or down in Sanderling," the woman said, toweling off her arms.

Gina was confused. "I thought there was one right about here."

The woman shook her head, then a spark came to her eyes. "Oh," she said. "I know the one you mean. I've read about it, and it *was* along here, you're right. But it was lost in a storm in the sixties, I think. That was before I moved here, so I'm not sure exactly when. A lot of erosion along here since then." She waved her hand to take in the beach. "It's changed a lot even since I moved here."

"Ah, that figures," Gina said, disappointed. Storms, storms, storms. She was coming to realize that weather was the source of devastation around here. "Well, thanks," she said with a wry smile. "I guess I can stop looking now."

"Sorry," the woman said. She bent over to pick up her beach bag. Straightening again, she looked at Gina.

"You have a nice evening," she said, then waved as she walked toward a path leading into the vegetation near the beach.

"You, too," Gina said.

She watched the woman disappear into the trees, then turned and headed back toward Kiss River.

She walked along the beach, her feet slapping in and out of the shallow waves, feeling alone. When she reached the lighthouse again, she stood in knee-high water, staring out at the sea. She thought of that woman on the beach, walking out of the water. Gina could swim, but she had never before been in the ocean. The Pacific off the coast of Washington was far too cold to swim in. Her eyes searched the water in front of her. What if the lens was just below the surface? Maybe it would not even need to be raised to suit her purpose.

She'd brought no bathing suit with her, since swimming had certainly not been part of her plan when she drove east from Washington. But she had on shorts and a T-shirt and no one was around to see her make a fool of herself. Slowly, she started walking into the water. It was nearly high tide, probably not the best time for a search, but the sea was rarely this calm. She would do this methodically, she told herself. She'd walk in an arc around the ocean side of the lighthouse, expanding the arc each time she changed direction. The idea suddenly seemed amazingly simple. The lens weighed three tons. Even if it had broken apart when it fell into the sea, the pieces should still be large enough for her to find.

She walked quickly at first, whisking her hands through the water in all directions, hoping to feel something hard and smooth. Then she had to slow down as the water grew deeper. Occasionally, her feet stumbled over chunks of brick and mortar, but nothing resembling glass. Finally, she was deep enough that she was half swimming, half treading water, trying not to think about sharks and riptides. She'd never experienced either of them, but had certainly heard enough about both hazards. A couple of times, she held her breath and dipped her head below the surface of the water, opening her eyes to look around her, but she couldn't see more than a couple of feet away from her in any direction and the salt burned her eyes.

She'd been in the water a long time when she turned to look behind her and was stunned to see how small the lighthouse had become. A little jolt of fear shot through her. She was far out into the sea, but still, it was not that deep here, perhaps only a couple of feet above her head, and she calmed herself with that thought as she swam toward shore, a heavy aching in her chest. She had covered a lot of territory out here. She had touched every speck of the sea bottom with her feet and found nothing. The lens, with its tie to both her past and her future, had simply disappeared.

Chapter Ten

Thursday, March 19, 1942

THE MOST SHOCKING AND HORRIBLE THING happened to me today. I am not even sure I can write about it because words just can't tell how awful it was, but I think it might make me feel better if I write it down, so I will try. It's midnight now and I can't sleep, anyway. I'm afraid if I go to sleep, I'll have nightmares.

I like to climb trees. I always have. Mama scolds me about it, saying that I think I'm so grown-up and all, but I am still just a little kid who climbs trees. Well, I don't know if I'll ever outgrow that, or even if I want to. I plan to climb trees with my own children someday. Anyhow, I like sitting up in the trees above the beach just south of Kiss River. There is a wonderful tree there, not very tall, with its branches spread out almost like a platform about ten feet above the ground, and I usually sit up there after school, eating an apple or something and sometimes reading. And to tell the truth, I sometimes sneak out of the house and sit up there at night, because that is the stretch of beach that Jimmy Brown patrols and I like watching him. I would die if he ever knew I was there, but the trees are thick and I am sure he can't see me at night, even if he turned his flashlight on me.

So today, after school, it was really warm out and not as windy as usual and I couldn't wait to get up in my tree. So I took the book I'm reading now (*The Grapes of Wrath*) and went up in the tree. On the beach below me were pieces of wood, nearly covering every inch of sand, and I knew they were probably from one of the ships that had been sunk out to sea. I knew that bodies sometimes washed up with that salvage, though I'd never seen any. Just as I was thinking how glad I was about that fact, I saw some blue and white cloth off to the side of the wreckage. I stared at it, and soon I could make out that it was someone's shirt, and that someone was still in it!

My first thought was to get Daddy, but I thought I'd better check on the person before I ran off, just on the off chance he might still be alive and need help. I was so scared my knees were actually shaking, but I climbed down the tree and walked out to the beach, trying to find places to put my feet amongst the pieces of wreckage from the ship. The man was lying facedown in the sand and a distance from the wreckage. His shirt was blue and white stripes and his pants were brown. And he had on shoes and socks. I will remember every detail about him until the day I die. I knew he was dead. I knew it. Yet there was this little part of me that thought I had to make absolute sure. So I carefully tucked my foot underneath his ribs and rolled him over. And then! Oh my God! His throat had been cut! The blood was brown and it was all over his shirt and in a wide, revolting gash across his throat. His head had nearly been cut off, I think. I screamed, and then I started running. Not toward home and Daddy, but toward the Coast

Guard station. I had to stop once because I thought I was going to retch, but I managed not to. I couldn't get that man's face out of my mind.

At the Coast Guard station, I immediately found Mr. Hewitt and told him what I'd discovered. We (me, him and Ralph Salmon, who is another one of the Boston boys and nice, but no Jimmy Brown) climbed in the Coast Guard jeep and headed back down the beach. There was wreckage all along the beach. It looked so different from usual that it took me a minute to figure out when we reached the right spot. While we were bouncing over the sand, I kept asking Mr. Hewitt the question that was driving me crazy. If the Germans torpedoed the ship, which they would have done from a distance away, how did they also manage to cut the man's throat? Mr. Hewitt didn't answer me. He was driving, just looking straight ahead of him at the beach, a frown on his face and his lips tight, and I guessed he was trying to figure out the same thing.

I sure as heck didn't want to see the man again, and Mr. Hewitt told me I should wait in the jeep. I didn't want to look like a chicken, though, so I said I was going with him. We had to climb over all sorts of boards and things and Ralph got a nail through his shoe, but lucky for him, it didn't quite reach his foot.

Once we got to the man, I had to force myself to look at him, and Ralph actually *did* retch, going off in the woods (too close to my tree!) to do it. Mr. Hewitt got down on his haunches next to the dead man. "This man was not on the ship," he said to me.

"How can you tell?" I asked. I leaned over, my hands on my legs, like I was trying to get a good look at the man. I didn't want Mr. Hewitt to think I was scared.

"The tide would've washed in the salvage just a couple hours ago," Mr. Hewitt said. "Look how wet it is."

I did look, and saw that the boards were still dripping water. I still wasn't sure of Mr. Hewitt's point, though.

"This fella's clothes are completely dry." Mr. Hewitt pointed at the man's bloody shirt. "Even his shoes are dry. There's no sign he was ever in the water at all. And his body's not bloated the way it would be if it had spent some time in the water."

Ralph came out of the woods then, but didn't seem to want to get too close to us or the dead man. He sat down on the beach a ways away from us, green around the gills.

"This man has nothing to do with a torpedoed ship," Mr. Hewitt reported. He fished around in the man's pockets, coming up with a pack of Chiclets, but no wallet or other identification of any variety. "Take a good look at him, Bess," Mr. Hewitt said to me. "You know everyone around here. Have you ever seen this man before?"

I looked hard at the man's face, not letting my eyes fall to the grisly gash across his throat. I am certain I've never seen him before. He was young, and I know all the young men around here. Most of them are gone, anyhow, fighting in Europe. I shook my head and told Mr. Hewitt the dead man was a stranger to me. Mr. Hewitt stood up and looked at me then.

"You know what, Bess?" he said. "You're quite a gal. You've got guts. Look at ol' Ralph there, white as a sheet." Ralph had gotten up and moved closer to the man, but not close enough to get a good look. When Mr. Hewitt said that, Ralph started blushing. At least he finally had a little color other than green in his face! He laughed, though, and I knew he took Mr. Hewitt's words as teasing, even if there was some truth behind them.

I asked Mr. Hewitt what he was going to do. He said he'd get in touch with the sheriff who would check the missing person's reports and maybe they could find out who this fella was.

"He was killed here," Mr. Hewitt said. "Right here on this beach. Otherwise there wouldn't be all this blood on the sand."

Killed right there! Practically right below my tree. Mr. Hewitt was right. I don't know why I hadn't thought of it, but the sand was soaked with the same brown blood that was on the man's shirt. I did start to feel sick then. I am not sure I'll ever be able to relax in the branches of my tree again.

"He looks German to me," Ralph said suddenly. It was practically the first words he'd said since we left the Coast Guard station.

Mr. Hewitt laughed. "And what does a German look like?" he asked.

Ralph pointed out the man's blond hair and eyebrows. I knew he was thinking the dead man was a German spy. Everyone thinks every stranger around here is spying for the Germans. Otherwise, how would those U-boats be able to know exactly where our merchant ships are nearly every minute of the day? But Mr. Hewitt just laughed.

"You just described yourself, Ralph," he said. "Blond hair and blond eyebrows."

"I'm no Kraut!" Ralph said. He looked really upset.

Mr. Hewitt ignored him. Instead, he said to me, "We'll escort you home now, Bess."

"You don't need to do that. I'm not afraid." Although the thought of walking back through the woods did put a chill up my spine.

We argued about it for a bit, then finally they walked me partway. Mr. Hewitt told me to make sure I tell Daddy about the man, since it happened so close to the light station. "And you be careful," he said. "I don't know how or why this fella met this fate, but one thing's for sure and that's that there is a murderer on the loose out here."

I headed home. It was strange, but I hadn't thought about that until he said it. That there was a murderer on the loose. I guess I'd been so caught up in thinking about the man somehow coming from a torpedoed ship and so surely a victim of the Germans that I hadn't stopped to think. But Mr. Hewitt was right. There's a murderer out here.

For the first time since I can remember, Daddy locked the house up tight before we went to bed. Mama kept hugging me hard, and I knew they'd be keeping an eye on me tonight, and I wouldn't be able to sneak out to watch Jimmy Brown on his patrol. That's all right. I'm not sure I'll ever be able to go out on the beach in the dark again.

Chapter Eleven

THERE WAS SOMETHING ABOUT THIS HOUSE IN the middle of the night that Clay found unsettling. When he'd wake up in the dark, the thunderous pounding of the ocean would be right outside his window, as though the sea had moved closer to the house during the night. But if he got up to use the bathroom or go downstairs for something to drink, he would find the interior of the house eerily still. It was as though someone—or something—was lurking in the dark corners.

Lacey had taken a vacation in April, leaving him alone in the house for a week, and although he would admit it to no one, he'd been glad to have Sasha with him. If he'd had the house entirely to himself, the hushed darkness might have driven him even further around the bend than he already was. Too much history in this house, and the ghosts all came out at night.

On Tuesday night, he woke up at one in the morning, needing to use the bathroom. Shutting his eyes, he tried to drift off again, but knew it was no use.

Sasha stirred in the corner of the room as he got out of bed, but the dog only uttered one of his low, doggie moans, and went back to sleep. Clay stumbled into the hallway, expecting the house's nighttime silence to envelop him, but instead, he heard a sound coming from his sister's room. He stopped for just a moment, worried that she was sick, but then quickly identified the murmured cries of passion and the rhythmic creaking of her bed. He hurried past her room to the bathroom.

Who was she with? In the bathroom, which was adjacent to her bedroom, he could still hear the lovers. He felt intrusive— not for the first time since moving into the keeper's house with Lacey—and he ran the water in the sink so he wouldn't have to hear. Maybe, he told himself, you're just jealous that she has someone and you don't. But that wasn't it, and he almost wished it was. What troubled him about Lacey and her lovers was that she did not seem to discriminate. He didn't know who was with her right now, but most likely, it was not the same man who had been with her the week before.

The following morning, he found his sister and Gina in the color-washed sunroom. Lacey was at her worktable, glass cutter in hand and a piece of cobalt-blue glass on the table. She was often up early like this, trying to get some work done on her glass before going to her job at the animal hospital. Gina leaned against the narrow wall between two of the windows, eating a peach and watching Lacey slip the cutter cleanly across the glass. Gina's hair was sleek and straight this morning, although that would certainly change the moment she walked into the damp air outside. She was bathed in red and gold from one of the stained-glass panels hanging in the windows, and Clay had to tear his gaze away from her to look at his sister. He wanted to question her about the man in her room the night before, but he hated to do that with Gina there in case it led to a confrontation.

"Gina tried to find the lens last night while we were at Dad's," Lacey said before he could think of a way to broach the subject.

"I think someone might have already gotten to it," Gina said. "I couldn't find it."

"How did you try to find it?" he asked.

"I went into the water." She sounded proud of herself.

Clay laughed and leaned against the doorjamb, arms folded across his chest. "There's a lot of water out there," he said. "I don't think it would be that easy to find."

"Well, there were a lot of pieces from the lighthouse," she said. "I felt them with my feet. But I checked each one out, and none of them seemed like part of the lens." She must have seen the skepticism in his eyes, because she continued. "I was very methodical about my search," she said, a bit defensively. "I walked or swam in an arc out from the lighthouse, and I kept increasing the radius."

Lacey shook her head, looking up from her work with a dimpled grin. "Does she remind you of anyone?" she asked Clay.

Clay nodded, knowing that both he and Lacey were thinking of their father and his old preoccupation with the lighthouse. "You're obsessed," he said to Gina.

She shrugged, apparently unable to deny it.

"I told you," he said, "it was a hell of a storm. And I am absolutely certain no one else has salvaged that lens. We would know."

Gina finished the last bite of her peach and wrapped the pit in a napkin she pulled from the pocket of her shorts. "Well," she said, "I'm going to talk with the two older guys from the Save the Lighthouse committee today. They're my last hope."

"Who's that?" Lacey asked.

"Walter and Brian, right?" Clay said. "Are you going to Shorty's?"

Gina nodded. "Your father said that would be the best place to find them. Although I don't know exactly where it is."

Lacey leaned back from her worktable to give Gina the simple directions, then she looked at Clay. "Will Henry be there today?" she asked.

Clay nodded. "You'll probably meet my wife's grandfather," he said to Gina. "I'm picking him up on my way into the office and dropping him off there for the day. He hangs out with Walter and Brian."

"Oh, that's nice," Gina said. She seemed a little confused, and Clay wondered if he should say more. How much had Lacey told her in their woman-to-woman chats? Did she know about Terri's death? Instead, though, he shifted his gaze to his sister.

"Who was over last night?" he asked, trying to sound casual.

Lacey looked a little surprised, but made another careful cut in the glass before answering him. "Josh," she said. "And Pirate."

He felt some relief. Lacey had introduced Josh to him a few weeks earlier and he seemed like a decent guy.

"Who or what is Pirate?" Gina asked.

"His yellow Lab. Gorgeous dog." Lacey looked up at her brother. "Josh wanted me to ask if you'd consider evaluating Pirate for search and rescue work," she said.

He was annoyed. "I don't do that anymore," he said, and he could hear the warning in his voice. Lacey knew better than to ask him. He didn't want to get into an argument with Gina there.

"Just an evaluation," Lacey said, as if she knew he wouldn't fight back with their houseguest present. "He'd pay you. Pirate has potential. He's still a gangly little thing, but he's energetic and a quick learner. I think his temperament—"

"What part of 'I don't do that anymore' don't you understand, O'Neill?" Clay asked her.

"Oh, come on, Clay," Lacey pleaded. "You're going to let a perfectly good potential search and rescue dog turn into just another—"

"Aren't there other trainers he could go to?" Gina surprised him by coming to his defense.

"None local," Lacey said. "And none as good as Clay."

Clay's laugh was caustic. "I am less than no good anymore," he said. "Get off my back about it, all right?"

An awkward silence filled the room. He exchanged a quick glance with Gina, but couldn't read whatever was in her face.

"Is it getting serious with Josh?" he asked Lacey, changing to what he hoped was a safer topic.

"Uh-uh," Lacey said, her eyes on her work.

"He seems nice, though. Why don't you find one good guy to go out with and stick with him?"

Lacey rested her glass cutter on the side of the table and raised her head, long red hair slipping over her shoulders. "Because I don't want one guy, nice or otherwise," she said. "You date just one guy, pretty soon he wants to marry you, and then where are you?"

"Isn't that what women want?" he asked. "Marriage? Kids?"

She and Gina both laughed as though they shared some secret.

"Well, the kids part would be okay," Gina said. "But you can keep the marriage."

"Why do all men think women are just dying to get married?" Lacey asked. She looked up at Gina. "Do you know the difference between a man and childbirth?" she asked.

Gina lowered herself into the straight-back chair in front of the windows. "What?"

"One can be excruciatingly painful," Lacey said, "while the other is just having a baby."

Gina laughed. At one time, Clay might have laughed himself, but male-bashing jokes—*any* jokes, for that matter—didn't seem very funny to him these days.

"Why is it so hard to find compassionate, sensitive, handsome men?" Gina asked Lacey.

"Why?"

"Because they all have boyfriends."

Lacey groaned, but was raring to go two seconds later. "Why do men give their penises names?" she asked.

Gina shook her head, the smile already on her lips.

"Soooo," Lacey dragged out the answer, "they can be on a first-name basis with the one who makes all their decisions."

Gina giggled, but Clay was annoyed. "Have you two had enough male bashing for one morning?" he asked.

"We're just making up for centuries of female bashing," Lacey said, but Gina looked genuinely contrite.

She leaned forward in her chair. "Sorry, Clay," she said. "Just remember that women bash men out of fear."

"How so?" he asked.

"It's our defense," she said. "You know, using humor to cover up for all the times we've been hurt. It's just a way of coping with our fear."

"Speak for yourself," Lacey said, but Clay's eyes were on Gina's. For some reason, her words put a lump in his throat. The simplicity in her explanation, perhaps, or just the fact that she was taking responsibility for something that annoyed the hell out of him.

"I don't think I'll ever get married and have kids," Lacey said, returning to the topic that had started the joke-telling.

"Why not?" Gina asked.

"I'll mess them up," Lacey said. She looked up at their boarder. "Or I'll die and desert them."

Whoa. The conversation had suddenly taken much too serious a turn for his comfort level.

"I'm off to work," he said abruptly. "You guys have a good day." He left the room, anxious to pick up Henry and have some good safe conversation about the weather and crabs and home repair while he drove across the island to Shorty's.

But Gina caught up to him in the kitchen. "Clay?" she said, walking quickly into the room.

He turned toward her.

"I was too glib about marriage," she said. She reached out, touched his arm. "I'm very sorry. I wasn't thinking. I was married for a few years and it wasn't very good, that's all, but your marriage was probably great. One of the rare ones. I'm so sorry for your loss."

"Thanks." He rested his hand on hers for a moment, feeling the fine bones beneath the warm skin. He wanted to keep his hand there longer, to curl his fingers into her palm. But he let go, smiling at her, then pushed open the screen door and stepped onto the porch.

That had been kind of her, he thought as he walked through the sandy yard toward the parking lot. But she was wrong about his marriage.

Chapter Twelve

GINA PULLED INTO THE CROWDED PARKING LOT of the ramshackle building. A small, sun-faded sign hung on the gray siding. Shorty's. The sight of the building put a smile on her face and made her feel strangely at home. She'd grown up on the north side of Bellingham, decidedly the wrong side of the tracks, within both sight and smell of the pulp factories on the waterfront. Places like this one had been common.

She got out of her stuffy, rattling car, still rehearsing what she would say to the two men she hoped to find inside. The steps up to the front door of the building looked old and worn, but they felt solid beneath her feet. A man on the top step held the door open for her.

"Thanks," she said, and she caught the scent of fish on his clothes as she walked past him.

Inside the building, she felt momentarily self-conscious as she stood near the cash register, surrounded by the din of a place where people clearly knew one another, but the discomfort quickly passed. The place was loud, filled with voices and the clatter of dishes and unrecognizable piped-in music. In front of her, people—mostly men—sat at a long counter, and tables and booths stretched off from her in either direction. A couple of customers stood to her left, paying their lunch bills at the register. The lighting was dim, the paneled walls dark with grease. The smell of onion rings was strong in the air and made her mouth water.

No one looked up from their food and conversation, and no one came to ask her if she needed a seat. Directly to her left, on the counter near the cash register, there was a huge glass jar filled with five- and ten-dollar bills. A sign taped to the front of the jar read Fifty-Fifty Raffle Drawing Sunday, July 7. Below that the words, *proceeds for Crisis Hot Line. Questions? Contact Lacey O'Neill.* A white index card leaned against the box, with the number $676 crossed out and $780 in its place.

Gina was not a gambler, and she'd never won a thing in her life, but the thought of an easy three hundred and ninety dollars when she was in dire need of money was too seductive to pass up. Lacey's name attached to the jar probably also had something to do with why she leaned toward the cashier to ask, "How much to take a chance on this?" She pointed to the enormous jar.

"Six chances for five dollars," the woman said. She was perhaps forty, sharp-featured and tanned. Her short blond hair looked as if it had been styled by raking her fingers through it after her shower.

Gina dropped a five-dollar bill through the slot cut into the jar's white metal top, and the cashier handed her six raffle tickets. Leaning on the counter, she wrote her name on each one, trying to stand out of the way of customers paying their bills. She didn't know the phone number at the keeper's house, so she simply wrote "Kiss River keeper's house" beneath her name. While she was handing the tickets back to the woman, she noticed another sign, this one on the wall above the cashier's head: Waitress Wanted.

She felt herself smile again. It had been a long time since she'd set foot in a restaurant like this, longer still since she'd waitressed in one. She'd put herself through college waitressing in places no better than this. It hadn't crossed her mind to work while she was here, of course. She hadn't planned to stay that long and still hoped that she would be able to leave North Carolina—armed with cash, or at least the information she would need to get the cash—very soon. But she might as well earn a little money while she was here. If she was going to wait tables, one of the busy upscale restaurants would make more sense. She could make far more in one of them than she could here. But there was comfort in this loud little building. This was where she wanted to be.

She leaned across the counter to the cashier again. "Who do I see about the waitress job?" she asked.

"Me." The woman raised her eyebrows in surprise. "I'm Frankie." She reached past Gina to hand a customer his change.

"I'm Gina Higgins," Gina said. "I've had experience waitress—"

"Can you start today?" Frankie reached for the next customer's check.

"Uh," Gina laughed, surprised. "No, but I could start tomorrow. What hours?"

"You name it," Frankie said, punching keys on the register. "I need somebody either eight to three or the dinner-to-eleven shift. That starts—"

"I'll do the morning," Gina said. "Can I work just four days a week?"

"Five, including weekends. You can pick your days off."

"Okay," Gina said. Hesitating a moment, she thought of

telling Frankie that she would probably be leaving the area very soon, but she doubted the woman would care. She had the feeling Frankie would take whatever help she could get for however long she could get it.

One of the waitresses whisked past Gina, holding a tray of food above her head to prevent it from knocking into anyone. The young woman was dressed in shorts and a T-shirt.

"Anything special I have to wear?" She turned back to Frankie.

"Closed shoes," Frankie said without looking up from the cash register. "That's it. The rest is up to you."

"Thanks," Gina said. "I'll be here at eight tomorrow morning."

Well, that was damn impulsive, she thought as she moved away from the register. She stood in the bustling center of the building again, trying to remember where Lacey had said she would find Walter Liscott and Brian Cass: in "the back room that's actually a side room." She could see an open doorway far to her left, and she walked between the booths and tables to reach it. Once she crossed the threshold, she knew she'd found the "back room."

It was not quite as noisy in the large, open room as it had been in the main restaurant. Sunlight poured in through a wall of windows and caught tendrils of smoke wafting into the air. There was music, something not too loud but heavy and throbbing enough for her to feel it in the soles of her feet on the hardwood floor. Small tables were scattered haphazardly around the room, and a pool table dominated one end. Her eyes fell immediately to one of the pool players, a young, handsome, dark-haired man with tattoos covering every inch of his tightly muscled arms. He looked up when she walked in, as did several of the other men, and she felt some of their gazes linger on her awhile. She was conscious of her appearance. She knew she was exceptionally pretty, and tried to downplay that prettiness with her loose T-shirt and draw-string pants, but these guys seemed adroit at undressing her with their eyes. She ignored them, searching through a vague smoke haze until she spotted three elderly men sitting in the corner of the room, hunched over a chessboard. One of them, who was bespectacled and nearly bald, was in a wheelchair, whittling on a chunk of wood as he watched the other two play. God, they all looked ancient. How could they possibly help her? She walked closer.

One of the chess players, a dapper old fellow wearing a blue-striped tie and white shirt, looked up at her as she approached.

"Hey, there," he said.

"Hi." Gina smiled at him. "I'm looking for Walter Liscott and Brian Cass."

The balding whittler glanced up at her, then started to get to his feet from the wheelchair. "I'm Walter, young lady," he said. "And this is—"

"Please don't get up," she said, holding her hands out to stop him.

He lowered himself slowly into the chair again. "This here is Brian Cass." He waved in the direction of one of the chess players, a gently handsome man with disheveled silver hair and watery blue eyes, who nodded to her. "And this is Henry Hazelwood." He motioned toward the man with the tie.

"Ah," she said to Henry. "You must be Clay's…" She wasn't sure how to describe the relationship. "His grandfather-in-law."

"You know Clay?" he asked.

"Yes. Actually, I'm renting a room from him and Lacey at the keeper's house."

"You don't say," Henry said. "He didn't tell me he had anyone who looked like you living there."

She smiled. "I don't want to interrupt your game," she said. "But I was wondering if I could talk with you—" she looked from Brian to Walter "—just for a minute."

"I'll pull you up a chair," Brian said, getting to his feet. She thought of stopping him and getting the chair for herself, but he seemed perfectly capable. "Do you play chess, girlie?" he asked as she sat down next to him.

"Don't call her girlie," Walter said, and he exchanged a look of amusement with Gina.

"Once or twice," she said. "Not in a long time, though. I was never very good at it."

"It's your turn," Henry said to Brian.

"Hold your blasted horses, will you?" Brian retorted. "We have company."

Gina looked at Walter. "Will you play the winner, Mr. Liscott?" she asked.

"Yes, ma'am." He carved a sliver of wood from the block in his lap, and she saw that he was forming the shape of a duck. "And I'll beat the starch out of him, too. And call me Walter. Don't make me feel so old."

"Is that duck going to be like those?" She pointed to the decoys that lined shelves near the ceiling of the room.

Walter nodded. "Yep," he said. "As a matter of fact, every one of them decoys is mine." There was a touch of pride in his voice.

"Really!" she said, standing up to take a closer look at the masterfully painted ducks.

"Too bad he doesn't play chess as good as he carves decoys," Brian said.

All three of the men had similar accents. You could hear salt and syrup in each of their voices.

"So," Henry said, his attention now on her instead of the chessboard. "Where are you from?"

"Washington." She took her seat again. "I'm just here visiting for a while."

"Washington, D.C.?" Walter asked.

"No, Washington State." She had to remember that here in North Carolina, a few hundred miles from the capital, it was necessary to add that fact.

"I visited there back in…who knows…back a while," Brian said, nodding. "Beautiful place. I went up in that needle thing. Is that where you're from? Seattle?"

"Bellingham," she said. "Not too far."

"Plenty of water out there," Brian said. "You been there?" he asked his cronies, who shook their heads.

"Any place with plenty of water sounds good to me, though," Henry said.

"What do you do there?" Walter asked her.

"I'm a teacher. And a lighthouse historian."

"You don't say," Henry said. He nodded at his friends. "Well, you came to the right fellas. These two know all there is to know about the lighthouses."

"It's Kiss River I'm most interested in," she said. "In particular, I'm interested in trying to raise the Fresnel lens from the ocean."

Brian Cass and Walter Liscott exchanged glances. "You're interested in beating your head against a brick wall, too, I guess," Brian said.

"Now, why'd you say that?" Henry said. "Let the girl say her piece."

"I say that because your grandson's damn father won't ever let that happen," Brian said.

Here we go again, Gina thought. Alec O'Neill was going to be the bane of her existence here on the Outer Banks.

"I've met Dr. O'Neill," she said. "You're right that he's not interested in helping. But he did give me your names."

Walter shifted in his wheelchair and set the decoy on the table. "Look, miss," he said, "Brian, here, and I would like nothing better than to see that lens up out of the ocean. See it on display somewhere."

"Right." She nodded.

"And if that could be done without Alec's support," he continued, "it would have been done a long time ago."

"Walter's right, for once in his life," Brian said. "I don't know as we can be much help to you. Henry's the only one with family ties to Alec, and he doesn't really give a hoot about the lighthouse, do you, Henry?"

"Not when there's crabs to catch and one of them game shows to watch on TV," Henry admitted.

"Well," Walter said with a sigh, "Brian and I are both pushing eighty. I don't—"

"You've already pushed right on past it," Brian interrupted him.

Walter ignored him. "I'm not sure how we can help. But I can tell you this—" he looked across the table at her "—we'd like to see you succeed. That light saw a lot of history."

"Hell of a lot," Brian agreed. "It's a sin to leave it on the ocean bottom."

"I agree," Gina said. "So, tell me what to do." She leaned closer to them, her chin inches from the chessmen on the board. "I'm willing to work hard to make it happen."

"First off," Brian said, "you should try talking to Alec again. We're stubborn old coots and he's sick of talking to us. A pretty girl like you might be able to persuade him."

"I never did understand why Alec got so gung ho about leaving the lens right where it is," Walter said, carving again. "One minute he was willing to spend every second of his waking life to save the lighthouse. The next, he says to just let it be."

"He probably just got frustrated after all the work we did to save it and then we lost it in the storm," Brian said.

"I keep hearing about all the work the committee did," Gina said, "but I don't really know much about it."

Brian and Walter slipped easily into a description of the work the committee had done a decade ago.

"They were going to move it," Walter said, shaking his head. "I didn't approve of that plan back then. I thought for sure they'd destroy it in the process. Now they've moved Hatt'ras, I see they were probably right. I regret not pushing for that solution." Sudden laughter broke out from the other side of the room, and he glanced toward the pool players before continuing. "I cried like a baby when that thing broke in two. I said, the least we can do is see if the lens survived the storm. But Alec said forget it. And what Alec says goes."

"Alec isn't God, though, right?" Gina said, feeling almost blasphemous as the words left her mouth.

The men hesitated, as though none of them wanted to be the first to agree with her.

"No, Alec's not God," Walter said finally. "But truth is, he's respected around here and no one likes to go against him."

"Let's give her Bill Keys's name," Brian said.

"That's an idea," Walter nodded. He took a pen from his pocket and jotted something down on the napkin beneath his coffee cup. He handed it to her. "You call the lighthouse association and ask for him," he said. "He'll be behind you. But persuading Alec should really be your first plan of attack."

"Useless," Brian said. He returned his attention to the chessboard, but looked up at her as she rose to leave.

"You come back sometime, all right, girlie?" he asked.

"I'm planning on it." She smiled. "I start working here tomorrow."

Chapter Thirteen

Thursday, March 26, 1942

LAST NIGHT, I FINALLY FELT BRAVE ENOUGH TO go back out to the beach and climbed my tree so I could spy on Jimmy Brown as he did his patrol. It had been a week since I'd found the dead man, and I finally stopped having nightmares about his face and the terrible gash across his throat. Nobody knows who he is or where he came from or what truly happened to him, and everybody's got the jitters knowing there's a killer on the loose.

So, anyway, I was in for a surprise last night. I snuck out about eleven and I was pretty nervous walking through the woods, I can tell you that! The moon was nearly full, though, so it was pretty light out, which helped put my mind at ease. When I got to the beach, it looked empty, but I was still quiet as I climbed up to my favorite roost in the branches. Then I saw the sandpounder. I knew right away it wasn't Jimmy. He was taller than Jimmy and he had a different way of walking.

I was *so* disappointed! I felt as though everything had changed in the past week and no one had told me about it, not that anyone should have bothered to tell a fourteen-year-old girl what was going on. First I thought the new sandpounder might have been Teddy Pearson, but then I realized it was someone I had never seen before at the Coast Guard station and he must've been new. From where I sat, it looked a little like his uniform was too small for him. The pants were up above his ankles, practically. I watched him walk up the beach until he disappeared behind the trees, then after a while I saw him walk back. He had binoculars around his neck and every once in a while he would put them to his eyes to look out toward one of the few white lights on the horizon.

After watching him for a few minutes and feeling really upset that I wasn't going to see Jimmy, I heard a rustling in the woods to my right. It shook me up at first, because I thought of the murderer, and my imagination immediately started thinking that the murderer might kill the sandpounder and I'd be up in the tree witnessing the whole thing. But then I saw what made the noise. The new sandpounder turned around fast to look in the direction of the sound. A wobbly little foal came out of the woods. I had never seen this foal before, but I knew it was one of the wild mustangs. The sandpounder obviously didn't know it, though. He started walking toward the foal, his hand outstretched. I thought to myself, what a crazy man. My whole body stiffened up, waiting for what I knew was coming. This sandpounder was so ignorant. I thought of calling out a warning to him but I didn't dare. Suddenly, just as I expected, a furious neigh and a pounding of hooves came from the woods and the mare leaped out of the trees, heading straight for the sandpounder. He looked up, and even though I was a fair distance away, I could see the look of terror in his face. I had to laugh when he turned and ran straight into the ocean, tripping over his own two feet and falling into the waves.

I know I wasn't thinking when I jumped out of the tree and ran onto the beach, waving my arms to distract the mare from the sandpounder. Of course, she turned toward me then, running in my direction, but I managed to climb back up my tree right quick. The poor sandpounder, standing up in the waves, trying to keep his balance, must've wondered what hit him. After the mare walked back into the woods with the foal, calm as could be, the sandpounder started out of the water. He didn't make much progress, though. His uniform had to weigh a hundred pounds with all the seawater in it. He stood there in the water, trying to keep standing up. His eyes were right on my tree.

"Come down from there!" he hollered at me. "Who are you, anyway?" He took some more steps onto the beach, and fell right on the sand, his wet uniform like an anchor dragging him down.

I figured I had no choice but to go down to the beach. He was still lying in the sand by the time I got to him but he was struggling to get to his feet and I knew right away it wasn't only the weight of his uniform keeping him down but also that he was trembling all over from being just plain terrified. I asked him if he was all right and he managed to get to his knees and say, "What the hell are you doing out here?"

I told him I was the keeper's daughter, and sometimes I liked to come out and enjoy the evening in my special tree. He looked at me like I was crazy. After all, it wasn't evening, it was the middle of the night. But what could I tell him? That I sat up in the tree at night so I could watch his fellow sandpounder, Jimmy Brown, walk up and down the beach? But he started laughing. He was such a mess, shaking with cold and covered with a thick layer of sand attached to his uniform. I figured he was laughing from relief that he'd been saved from the wild horses and that I did not turn out to be a killer lurking in the forest. I started laughing with him and brushed at his uniform, surprised that I would be that bold.

"Are you all right?" I asked him again. "Can you stand up?"

He got to his feet, but only by leaning on my shoulder, and he tried to brush some of the sand from his uniform but failed terribly. It was stuck to him like it was glued there.

"You're freezing," I said to him.

"No kidding," he said. "And I don't get picked up until three." He pulled back the soaking, sandy sleeve of his uniform to look at his watch. "Damn," he said. "I think my watch's busted from the salt water. So who are you, again?" he asked me for the millionth time. His accent was somewhere from the South, but I couldn't say exactly where. I told him my name, and repeated that I was the daughter of the keeper of the Kiss River lighthouse. He looked me up and down and asked me how old I was. I lied and said sixteen even before I thought about it. I knew I could pass for sixteen, especially in the dark.

I asked him where he was from, and he said, "Vermont," so I said, "What's a Canadian doing in the U.S. Coast Guard?" not having any idea how stupid I must've sounded. Maybe Dennis is right that the education I'm getting here isn't all that good.

He laughed at me. He explained about Vermont being in the United States and I felt like a real dope. Then he said he grew up in Kentucky, but his family just moved to Vermont a year ago. That explains his accent.

I started right off calling him Sandy. There was no other name for him. He must've had five pounds of sand on his uniform, and more inside it. I felt sorry for him. I know how it feels to be in wet, gritty clothes, and it's even worse when it's cold out like it was last night.

"If you're this shook up by a horse and a dip in the ocean, what will you do if some spies come ashore?" I asked him.

"Well, I'm human," he said. "This is my first night out here. My first day at this godforsaken place. They told me I was going to be stationed at a beach resort. Ha! I've never seen the ocean before in my life and had no idea it was so damn cold, and big, and rough, and then I get stationed on a beach where someone's throat was cut a week ago. And then some wild horse comes running out of the bushes, and some girl jumps out of the trees. Do you blame me for not feeling particularly confident at the moment?"

I wished I could take back my words. Sometimes I speak before I think, and I can be mean. And this was his first night? That meant I had missed seeing Jimmy Brown out on the beach by one night! But I was starting not to care. Sandy made Jimmy Brown look like a kid. Sandy has brown hair about my color, and a beard and mustache trimmed close to his face, and blue eyes I could see the moon in. I don't mean to sound so fickle, but I guess that's what I am. I told him I was sorry, that I could imagine how strange it would all seem to somebody who'd never been to the Banks before.

He looked at me different then. "I like a person who can admit when she's wrong," he said.

I knew there was no way he could stay out on the beach until three without catching pneumonia, so I told him he could come back to my house and I would find him some dry clothes to put on. I could tell he hated leaving his patrol, but he really had no choice.

Here is where I made a strange decision. I could have woken up Mama and Daddy and explained to them what was going on, and they would have welcomed Sandy into the house and warmed him up and made him some coffee. But that would mean I'd have to explain about being out on the beach at that hour. They would have a fit, especially when they found out it was the beach where the man was murdered. They would never let me out of their sight again and they'd lock my bedroom door at night. But also, I didn't want to share Sandy with them. I was starting to believe in love at first sight, and Sandy was mine, not theirs.

So I explained to him about how I had snuck out and he laughed at that and said he understood, he'd snuck out of his house once or twice himself. I snuck him through the back door and over to the stairway that leads to the old assistant keeper's quarters. It's empty rooms there now. We haven't had an assistant keeper here since I was eight or nine. That way, there was no way Mama and Daddy could hear him come up. I left him in one of the empty rooms—it wasn't much warmer in there than outside, I'm afraid, but at least he was out of the worst of it. I snuck into one of our extra bedrooms, where Daddy keeps some of his clothes. I took an old pair of pants I thought he might not miss, and a couple of old sweatshirts and a slicker that had holes in it. There wasn't much I could do about his shoes, but I got a pair of my socks out of my own dresser. They were way too small, of course, but better than nothing.

I took the clothes back to Sandy. His teeth were chattering and he looked at those clothes like they were the answer to his prayers. I left him alone while he changed, then we tiptoed downstairs again. I made him stay on the porch while I went back in and got him one of the doughnuts Mama had made that morning. It was a little on the stale side by then, but I doubted Sandy would mind, and I was right. He gobbled it up.

He was anxious to get back to the beach, and I really liked

that about him, that he cared so much about doing his job right. I thought about what Dennis had said about sandpounders being men who had nothing better to offer the world and I felt angry at him. How dare he say something like that about people like Sandy and Jimmy Brown and all the others?

I went back in the house one more time and got a wool blanket out of the hall closet and took it out to him. He didn't tell me to stay behind, so I walked with him back to the beach, me carrying the blanket and him his disgusting, wet, heavy and sand-covered bundle of clothes.

"I don't think you should walk your patrol anymore tonight," I said when we finally got to the beach. "You still have those wet shoes on. You should just wrap up in this blanket and sit on the beach. You can still see quite a bit from here."

To my surprise, he agreed with me. He sat down, shivering even though he had the blanket wrapped tight around him. Then he looked up at me. "You'd better keep me company," he said, "or I'll fall asleep."

Just the invitation I'd been hoping for! I plopped down next to him in the sand. He asked me if I was cold. I really wasn't, although I almost said I was in the hope that he would share that blanket with me and I'd be right next to him.

"What's there to do around here?" he asked.

"Most people fish," I said.

"I meant for fun," he said.

I laughed. "Some people do that for fun," I said, but I knew what he meant. "They show movies some nights at the schoolhouse." I thought I should probably tell him about the dances at the schoolhouse, but I didn't want to, because I knew he'd find the older girls there, the ones who danced real close to the Coast Guard boys and gave them anything they wanted. The boys from this area had all left to fight in Europe, and the girls were left behind and dying for some company. The dances at the schoolhouse were where most of the Coast Guard boys spent their free time. Sandy would find out about the dances at the schoolhouse soon enough without me telling him, I figured.

"I was the one who found that dead man on the beach," I said.

He looked at me, then seemed to know who I was all of a sudden. "You're *that* Bess," he said. "I've heard about you. You bring cookies and pie to the Coast Guard station on the weekends, right?"

"Right," I said, wondering what the boys there said about me.

"You're not sixteen," he said. "They said you were fourteen."

I felt exasperated at being found out. "Nearly fifteen," I said.

He laughed, more to himself than to me, and I knew he was thinking I was terribly young. "What would your parents do if they knew you were out here right now?"

"I don't want to think about it," I said. And I didn't.

"You don't look fourteen, though," he said, and he was leaning back to stare at my face in the moonlight. "You're very pretty."

"Thanks," I said. I felt like he was looking at my face way too hard and I tried not to giggle like a fourteen-year-old.

"And you're obviously the adventurous sort," he said.

"Yup," I answered him. "I inherited it. My mother was in the lifeguard service." I repeated this rumor as though it was a fact, and I doubt he believed me, but it didn't matter. We started talking. About everything. And I mean *everything*. He wanted to know all about Kiss River and the Outer Banks, and I told him, adding that he needed to give the mustangs all the room they wanted, though some of the Coast Guard boys have trained them to use on their patrol. He said he didn't plan to ride any horses out here, thank you very much. I said he'd better watch out for the wild boars, too.

"The wild boars?" he asked me. "Hogs, you mean?"

"Right. Livestock used to run wild around here," I said. "Some of the hogs just took off and now they are mean as molasses."

I told him just about everything I know about the Outer Banks, trying to make up for looking stupid when I said that thing about Vermont being part of Canada. I think he was impressed with all I know.

He told me about Vermont, and how he lives in the capital, I forget its name, and how even in Kentucky he lived in the city, where it's "civilized." I'd already figured out he was no country boy.

"It feels slow and empty here," he said. But I did get him to admit that if he was in Vermont this time of year he'd be sitting in three feet of snow instead of on a sandy beach.

He told me about how they were trained in the Coast Guard, how they had to watch for any signs of strange activity on the beach at night, how we should really be dimming the lights on the beach, just like Mr. Hewitt said. But no one was officially telling people to do it, and people just hadn't gotten the message yet. Americans can be selfish, he said. They want to keep their lights and their cars and all and not sacrifice anything, and all the while the German U-boats are attacking our ships, which are lit up from behind by the lights on shore. I argued with him, telling him that my family and my neighbors cared very much what happened, and if someone told us we had to dim our lights, we would do it in a heartbeat. I asked him if he hated the Krauts and the Italians and the Japs. I never use the word *Kraut,* but it slipped out and I know it was because I wanted to sound older and more worldly, but he didn't like it.

"Don't use that word," he said. "They're Germans. Don't use Kraut or Heinie or Wop or slant-eyes or any of those words. It brings us down to their level."

I was glad he couldn't see how my cheeks were burning. "I don't usually use that word," I said. "I'm not sure why it came out."

I told him about Mr. Sato living in the house over on the sound and he looked very interested in the fact that we had a real Japanese man nearby. He asked me if I knew about the internment camps, where we were locking up Japanese people who live in the United States. I was *so glad* Dennis had taught me about the internment camps. I said I thought it was wrong to lock them up, since I know that's what Dennis believes and he's made me believe it, too. But Sandy said it's necessary.

"It seems unfair," he said. "I know most of those people are innocent. But we can't take the chance that they're not. Look at Pearl Harbor."

I thought about Mr. Sato, how I used to see him fishing, looking content in his wheelchair on his deck, how I'd sometimes wave to him and he'd wave back. Even though he's Japanese, I hate the thought of someone coming to take Mr. Sato away from his home and his daughter-in-law and lock him up. The thought actually put tears in my eyes and Sandy noticed that.

"You're a nice girl," he said to me. He touched my forehead, I think to move some hair or sand off it, but I'm not sure. I wanted to tell him I thought he was nice, too, but I couldn't make the words come out, so I just smiled back. He didn't try to kiss me, but I really wanted him to. I would have let him.

Around three, we could hear the jeep coming up the beach

and so I said goodbye and ducked into the woods. I watched him climb into the jeep and heard someone say, "Hey, what happened to you? Where'd you get those clothes?" and I wondered what he would say back, but I couldn't hear his answer. I was sure he would make up something that wouldn't get me in trouble. I watched until the jeep disappeared around the curve in the beach, then I headed home, grinning a silly grin, and thinking how if I'd come out the night before, it would have been Jimmy I'd seen on the beach.

"Jimmy?" I said to myself as I was walking. "Jimmy who?"

Chapter Fourteen

THE LIGHT FADED FROM THE SKY ABOVE THE ocean as Gina sat down on the top step of the lighthouse. This had quickly become her private haven. She'd climbed the spiral staircase every evening since starting to work at Shorty's three days earlier. Although she still held tight to the railing as she ascended those last few steps high above the craggy rim of the tower, she no longer suffered from vertigo up there. Once she was seated and looking out to sea, the small frustrations of the day disappeared and she felt her body begin to relax. It was not peace she found at the top of the lighthouse; there was no peace for her anywhere. But sitting up there, awed by the vastness of sea and sky, she became keenly aware of both her insignificance in the world at large, as well as her importance to one small child.

If it was not peace she found up there, at least it was rest. Working at Shorty's was even more exhausting than teaching, and her feet were on fire by the end of her shift. She'd taken no time off yet, and didn't plan to until Monday, wanting to get into the rhythm of the job and put some money in her pocket. The tips were surprisingly good for such a seedy-looking place. But tips would not be enough to help Rani, the child whose picture was, now and always, in the pocket of her shorts.

As usual, she'd taken off her sandals to walk through the swirling waves toward the tower, and the cool water had felt wonderful on her feet. She'd forgotten to leave the sandals at the bottom of the stairs this evening, however, and now she leaned over to drop them, one at a time, over the side of the railing into the core of the lighthouse. She watched them fall through the spiral of stairs until they disappeared in the darkness, and she listened for the echoing *thunk* as they hit the tile floor far below her.

Although she had the feeling she was wasting precious time, she liked working at Shorty's. Wednesday had been hard, because the other waitresses were too busy to give her much guidance, but now she was starting to feel like a part of the place. The three old men, Henry, Walter and Brian, nursed beers or milky coffee, and they seemed to have taken an instant liking to her, probably because of her love for the lighthouse. Or at least, what they perceived to be her love of the lighthouse. Brian brought in old pictures of the structure, along with newspaper articles from the days of the Save the Lighthouse committee. It amazed her to read those old articles, because Alec O'Neill was the indisputable driving force behind the committee to save the Kiss River light. He was quoted several times in every article. His name was everywhere. And now he was being such a mule about raising the lens.

When Walter and Brian spoke passionately about the lighthouse, Gina couldn't help but get caught up in their zeal about the place. She'd pretended at first, but she felt their passion about the lighthouse, and a little of that couldn't help but rub off on her. Certainly, she had some feelings of attachment to the lighthouse from reading Bess's diary. She liked to imagine Bess climbing these spiral stairs, and she could picture her out on the beach at night with the Coast Guard patroller, Sandy, whose real name the young girl had cut from the one page of her diary where she'd written it, excised carefully as if with a razor.

Gina had called the lighthouse association the day before, asking to speak with the contact given to her by Walter and Brian. The man sounded as old as they were, but he remembered the earlier battle to raise the lens well.

"Has the vet come around?" he'd asked when she explained the reason for her call.

"Excuse me?" she'd asked, wondering if there was some World War II veteran she needed to contact.

"I don't recall his name," the man said. "The veterinarian who didn't want the lens raised."

"Oh." She sighed. She should have guessed. "Alec O'Neill."

"That's right. We'd been all set to fund the salvaging of the lens, but he stood in the way. Both literally and figuratively. He came here in person to stop us."

"Well, I've spoken with him, and he doesn't want to play an active role in raising it," she said carefully. "But I don't know that he—"

"Well, miss." The man sounded suddenly tired as he interrupted her. "We'll help, but only if you can get the vet to come around. Not worth putting our effort and money into something that's doomed to fail again. Without the support of the locals, the cause is hopeless."

She'd gotten off the phone knowing she had no choice but to speak with Alec O'Neill again. No matter who she talked to about the lens, the conversation always circled back to him. So, she'd made a lunch date with Alec for Monday, a bit surprised when he agreed to see her. She'd be better prepared to meet him this time, arming herself with facts about the lens so she would sound as though she knew what she was talking about. If she couldn't persuade him to help her, maybe she could at least get him to agree not to stand in her way.

Stars were appearing in the darkening sky when she heard the sound of footsteps below her on the lighthouse stairs. Peering down into the black hole of the tower, she spotted the beam of a flashlight bouncing off the walls, getting ever nearer, and wondered if she should be afraid. She'd come up when it was still light out and had not thought to bring her own flashlight with her.

"It's just me," a male voice reassured her from the darkness. Clay.

"Hi," she said as he came into view.

He turned off his flashlight, then sat next to her on the top step. "Great night up here," he said. "Are the mosquitoes getting you?"

"Not yet," she said. "I don't think they get up this high."

"They do," he said, and seemed to be about to say more, but grew quiet. Clay was a mystery to her. He worked late hours and she rarely saw him. His sister was a chatterbox and an open book, but Clay kept to himself, and her conversations with him had been limited to the mundane. That was fine. She needed a landlord far more than she needed a friend, and she was grateful to him for allowing her to stay here. But she always felt a bit awkward trying to get a conversation going with him when Lacey wasn't around.

"I think it's nice that you bring Henry to Shorty's every day," she said, testing the waters. "He enjoys it so much. I think he'd probably go crazy if he was stuck at home."

"Well, I don't take him every day," Clay said. "I don't always have the time to pick him up. I feel terrible then. I know he looks forward to it. Brian offers to pick him up sometimes, but I don't think that old man should have a license, frankly."

"Well, let me know the next time you can't get away," she said. "I could get him on my break."

He looked surprised. "That's really nice of you. Thanks."

"The least I could do," she said, meaning it. She felt beholden to her hosts. She'd cooked for them a couple of nights, usually leaving Clay's meal in the refrigerator for him to heat up later, since he was rarely home for dinner. She'd bought some groceries, but other than that, she'd given little back in return for their hospitality. "Is Lacey home yet?" She looked over her shoulder at the keeper's house, with its vibrant night-time windows.

Clay shook his head. "She's at an Al-Anon meeting," he said.

"Ah." She wished he would elaborate, but of course, he didn't, and a silence stretched out between them. She knew Al-Anon was a support group for the families of alcoholics, and she wondered what family member had prompted Lacey to join. Gina's best guess was her stubborn, aggravating father.

"I'm meeting your father for lunch on Monday," she said.

"Are you now?" Clay wore a slight smile.

"I thought I'd give him another chance to tell me he won't help me raise the lens."

Clay laughed. "You're a glutton for punishment."

"Why is he so stubborn about it? If he would just give me the go-ahead, I could find the money and it would all be taken care of."

Clay drew in a long breath, stretching his arms out in front of him. "There's a lot about my dad that I don't understand," he said, lowering his arms to his knees again. "He just doesn't want anything to do with the lighthouse anymore. When it toppled over, that took the wind out of his sails. So to speak."

She felt annoyed. If it had so little meaning to him, why did Alec have to stand in her way?

"Is he the alcoholic?" She blurted out the question before she could stop herself. "I mean, is he the reason Lacey goes to Al-Anon meetings?"

Clay looked utterly stunned, then burst into laughter, and Gina cringed.

"That was too personal a question," she said. "I'm sorry."

"It's okay." He shook his head, still chuckling. "I'm just trying to picture my father as an alcoholic, that's all. No, it's actually Lacey's father—her *biological* father—who's a recovering alcoholic. She goes as a support to him."

She had not expected that answer. "I thought…you don't have the same father?" she asked.

He shook his head. "We thought we did when we were growing up, but the truth came out a long time ago. Lacey's a bit quiet about it, but I really don't think she'd mind you knowing. She got close to Tom, her father, after she learned the truth. Lacey's the one who got him sober. And he's the one who got her doing stained glass. He used to share a studio with our mother."

It took her a moment to absorb all that information. "Lacey's relationship with your father, then… How is it?"

"Oh, it's very good now. They had their ups and downs when Lacey was younger, and she had a rough year when she found out our dad—my dad—wasn't really her father. But they've worked it all out. She's crazy about Tom, though." Clay shook his head with another chuckle. "He's a strange guy, but she adores him. He didn't raise her, so she doesn't have any of the checkered history with him that she has with Dad."

"Well, it seems she turned out okay," Gina said. "I think she's an amazing person."

"Mmm," Clay said, but he sounded noncommittal.

"How about your mother?" Gina asked. "Does she live around here?"

He looked surprised by the question. "My mother's dead," he said. "I thought you knew that."

"Oh, Clay, I'm sorry." She touched his arm, embarrassed. "I didn't know. I assumed your father and mother were divorced." She'd assumed far more than that. She'd figured that Alec had left Clay's mother, most likely to run off with another woman. Olivia, or someone else. That's what men tended to do. She had not thought of him as a widower.

"I think you have my dad figured wrong, Gina," he said. "He's not the divorcing type. He's not the drinking type. He may be stubborn, and he may be giving you a hard time, but you won't meet a better person than my father."

Gina touched his arm. "I'm sorry," she said. "I believe you, and you're right. I've been making him into a monster instead of merely a thorn in my side."

Clay smiled at that.

"How long ago did she die?" Gina asked. "Your mother?"

"Nearly twelve years. She died Christmas Day, 1990." He was staring toward the dark horizon, and she thought there was a glaze of tears in his eyes.

"Had she been ill long?" she asked.

Again, he was quiet. Then he shook his head. "She wasn't sick," he said. "She worked at a shelter for battered women in Manteo, and on Christmas Day, this guy named Zachary Pointer came in looking for his wife, waving a gun. My mother stood in front of the woman to protect her, and he shot her."

Gina's hand rose quickly to her throat, and sudden tears filled her own eyes. "Oh my God, Clay," she said. "How awful. I'm so sorry."

"Lacey was with her," he said. "She saw the whole thing. I honestly don't think she's ever quite recovered from it."

"Why do you say that?"

Clay looked thoughtful a moment, then shook his head. "No reason," he said, evading her.

"Tell me," she prompted.

He shrugged, as though avoiding the question, but then he spoke. "Lacey's just…she's amazing, as you said. She's a lot like my mother that way. Very caring about other people. But she doesn't care enough about herself. My mother was the same way. That's why she risked her life for that woman. I don't want to see Lacey make those kind of sacrifices."

"Have you ever talked to her about it?" she asked.

"Not in so many words."

She wanted to tell him that if he was truly concerned about his sister, he should talk to her, but the conversation had gone so much deeper than she'd ever anticipated that she didn't dare push him further. Instead, she changed the subject. "Your stepmother seems nice," she said, remembering Olivia's graciousness the one time she'd met her—and feeling much better about the woman now that she knew she wasn't a home wrecker. "How do you get along with her?"

"Olivia's terrific," he said. "She's been great for Dad. And Jack and Maggie are a kick." His smile was wide, but disappeared quickly. "Olivia was the doctor on duty in the E.R. when my mother was brought in," he said. "She tried her best to save Mom's life."

"Oh my gosh," Gina said. "You have a very complicated family."

He smiled at her. "Is there any other kind?"

She supposed there was not, but the truth was, she had little experience with families. She'd had her mother, and that had been it. Yet family was what she craved. The mix of personalities, the ups and downs Clay had spoken of, the occasional animosity and disagreements, and the love that was underlying all of it. That's what she had never had and what she wanted more than anything.

She studied Clay's profile, outlined by the light of the moon. His features were straight and sharp, the nearly transparent blue eyes she had thought of as icy cool were now an amazing underwater blue in the moonlight. She rarely noticed men's looks these days, and until this moment, she had not seen the beauty in Clay's face. He had spoken with such warmth about his sister and father and mother, and that touched something deep inside her. She didn't think she had ever met a man so caring about his family. She hadn't thought that sort of man existed. *You don't know him,* she told herself. *They all seem good in the beginning.*

Could she ask him about Terri? About his marriage? She was about to open her mouth to do so when a star suddenly shot across the sky, a short distance above the horizon. They both saw it, both sucked in their breath in wonder.

"It's great up here, isn't it?" he asked. "I love coming here after work."

It suddenly occurred to her that she had stolen his personal refuge. She'd moved in and had made this top step her own, never thinking that perhaps he or Lacey had found the same private haven up here as she had.

"Clay…have I taken your place up here? I mean, is this where you like to come in the evenings for some time alone?"

"It's not a problem," he said, and she knew her suspicion was right. He stood up. "And you can have it to yourself for the rest of the night, if you like," he said. "I've got to go over to the dive shop to get my equipment ready for tomorrow."

"Dive shop?" she asked.

"Scuba." He took a couple of steps down the spiral staircase, then turned to hand her his flashlight.

"Be careful," she said. "Do you want me to shine this down the inside of the stairs for you?"

"I'll be fine, thanks," he said. "Don't get eaten alive up here. Good night."

That was fast, she thought. Suddenly, he couldn't get away from her quickly enough, as if he knew the questions she'd been about to ask. She ached a little for him as she listened to him descending the stairs. He'd lost both his mother and his wife. Rani's picture burned hard in her pocket, and she had to remind herself that she was not the only person hurting in the world.

Chapter Fifteen

THERE WAS SOMETHING ABOUT BEING
underwater that made Clay feel as if he was flying. He had
flown in planes, of course, and in gliders and hang gliders,
but he would take this sense of graceful, slow-motion flight
over those experiences any day.

He and Kenny were exploring the wreck of the *Byron D.
Benson,* a four-hundred-and-sixty-five-foot tanker sunk by a
German U-boat sixty years earlier. The *Benson* was not one of
the more popular wreck dives in the Outer Banks, and today
they had it to themselves. The broken vessel lay on its side one
hundred and ten feet below the water's surface. It had long
ago been stripped of its artifacts, of course, but the marine
life both in and on the ship was enough to make it interesting. The ocean bottom here was like an underwater desert,
an empty expanse of sand. The wreck gave the sea urchins,
anemones, crabs and all variety of fish shelter, something to
attach to, to feed from, and the vessel literally pulsed with life
in the current.

This was Clay's fifty-fourth dive, but compared to Kenny,

he was a novice. Kenny's work in marine construction took him underwater more often than not, and he'd almost certainly lost track of how many dives he'd made over the years. For Clay, diving was pure recreation. He enjoyed swimming in and out of the wreck, watching the fish dart back into the crevices as he floated by, but more than anything, he loved simply flying above the wreckage, from one twisted, decaying end to the other, his hands relaxed at his sides, his legs doing the work of propelling him. There was no better way to slip away from the real world than to sink into this unreal one.

Yet, after they'd been down twenty minutes or so, and they'd seen two tiger sharks and a manta ray and watched a huge, bulky sea turtle swim out from one of the ragged tears in the ship's hull, Clay's mind began to drift back to the night before, when he'd sat on the lighthouse steps with Gina.

God, she was beautiful. She'd been little more than a silhouette in the moonlight when he spotted her there last night, her long hair tossed around her shoulders by the breeze. Yes, she'd been right that she'd stolen his refuge from him; he'd loved the privacy of the lighthouse in the evenings. But he'd felt no resentment when he saw her there. Instead, he'd felt an unexpected longing to be next to her. To be close enough to touch her. He'd been surprised to discover that he wanted to talk to her. *Really* talk. She'd asked him questions, making it easy. He'd been afraid of how much he was saying and had to remind himself that he was a private person, not one to divulge his thoughts and feelings easily.

He could tell that she didn't want to talk about herself. She'd asked questions to keep from revealing her own answers. Who was she, really? A woman who suddenly appeared in their backyard, who lived three thousand miles away and yet seemed consumed with one little part of the Atlantic Ocean, who claimed to be a teacher and a lighthouse historian, who had been married but who described that marriage as "not very good." There were questions he wanted to ask her. Nothing deep. Questions any man would ask any woman he met at a bar, for example, questions tossed out casually, thoughtlessly. But he couldn't bring himself to ask them of her, because he feared her answers would tell him something he didn't want to hear, or worse, pull him even closer to her.

When they had finished their dive, they stored their gear in the back of Kenny's red pickup truck, then drove to Shorty's for lunch. They found a booth near the front door and as they took their seats, Clay searched the restaurant for Gina. Even though Kenny didn't even know of Gina's existence, he spotted her before Clay did. Clay watched his friend's gaze shift from him to the air behind his head, and when he turned to see what he was looking at, he wasn't surprised to see Gina waiting on the next table.

"Hey, Gina," he said across the top of the booth.

She looked surprised, then broke into a smile. "Hi, Clay," she said. "I didn't expect to see you here." She glanced at Kenny. "I'll be with you two in a minute."

Clay turned around to face his incredulous friend.

"You know her?" Kenny leaned across the table to whisper.

"Know her?" Clay whispered back. "I'm living with her."

Kenny's eyes widened. "What the hell are you talking about?" he asked.

"She's a lighthouse historian," he explained. "She showed up one day at the Kiss River light and needed a place to stay for a while. So Lacey and I offered her a room."

"Man, how are you standing it?" Kenny leaned back, talking a bit louder now that Gina had walked away from the next table. "I wouldn't be able to eat. I'd never sleep. I'd walk into walls. I'd—"

"I'm in a different place from you," Clay reminded him.

"Right," Kenny acknowledged. "But maybe this is like God telling you to move on. I mean, could the message be any clearer?"

"It's only been eight months, Kenny."

"Right," Kenny said again, backing off.

"What about you, though?" Clay asked. The thought of hooking Gina up with Kenny gave him a vicarious thrill, and if they hit it off, maybe Clay could stop thinking about her. "She's unattached," he said. "You're an ugly son of a bitch, but maybe she can overlook that."

"I'm in," Kenny said.

Clay gave him the thumbs-up sign as Gina approached their table.

"How was diving?" she asked, her hands holding the pad and pencil on the table. Her hair was up, the long tresses tucked into one another at the back of her head. He wished Kenny could see her hair down, but it hardly mattered. She would be gorgeous bald.

"It was great," Clay said. "Gina, this is Kenny, my diving buddy."

"Hi, Kenny." She smiled at him, and for the first time in his life, Kenny seemed to have nothing to say. Usually wildly flirtatious, Kenny could only nod his greeting.

"We've known each other since kindergarten," Clay said to Gina.

"Really? That's so nice." She sounded sincere. "Nice to live in one place long enough to have friends who've known you forever." She lifted the pad and pencil. "What can I get for you two?" she asked.

Once they'd ordered their burgers and fries, Gina walked away and Kenny let out a long breath.

"Oh, yeah," he said. "I want her."

"You'll have to be able to say at least a few words to her, then," Clay teased.

"Why?" Kenny grinned. "That's not what I want her for."

Clay laughed, but he felt suddenly protective. "You can't have her, then," he said. "She's not that sort of woman." Although the truth was, he didn't know what sort of woman was living with him at Kiss River.

It was ridiculous to think she'd be interested in someone like Kenny, Clay realized. Gina was quiet and cerebral, Kenny a garrulous hedonist. She was far more like him than she was like Kenny, secretive and closed in on herself. Sometimes, he felt like a ghost, unfeeling and invisible, moving through the world without really touching it or being touched by it. And now there were two of them in the keeper's house. It took one ghost to recognize another.

Chapter Sixteen

Sunday, April 5, 1942

LAST NIGHT, MAMA, DADDY AND I WERE IN THE living room, the two of them huddled by the radio and me on the settee, reading. I closed my book, ready to go up to bed, where I would wait until my parents went to sleep before sneaking out to the beach, when there was a sudden terrible BOOM from outside. The windows shook, and three books jumped right out of the bookshelf onto the floor. Mama and I looked at each other, and Daddy got to his feet and walked outside, looking toward the sea. We followed him quickly, climbing up the lighthouse stairs after him, and I guess we'd all been expecting the sight that met our eyes once we stepped out onto the gallery.

There, out in the pitch-black sea, was a vivid red glow. Another ship was burning, this one far too close for comfort. There was no moon, but the glow from the ship spread and spread until it was almost like daylight outside. It reminded me of being up on the gallery toward the end of a brilliant sunset, when the whole world turns scarlet. I started to cry and shake. Really, I couldn't control my body. I felt like my whole world was changing. My safety was gone. I was standing with the two people who had done their best to bring me up and keep me safe all my life, and there wasn't a darn thing they could do to save me or anyone else from what those Germans were doing to us. Mama put her arm around me and I let her. I was too upset to protest. All three of us were real quiet as we watched that ship burn.

"Those men are being incinerated alive," my father said. It occurred to me that the Coast Guard would be going out to help those seamen. My heart started thumping even faster in my chest. I knew Sandy would be on one of those boats and I could tell even from where I was standing how dangerous it would be out there. Not just the tanker, but the ocean all around it was on fire from spilt oil. I remembered something Sandy told me, about how Coast Guardsmen had to go out but there was nothing to say they had to come back.

I have become the best darn liar in North Carolina. Nearly every night in the week and a half since I met him, I have been with Sandy, and no one knows. Not a soul. None of his Coast Guard buddies. Certainly not my parents, although it's their house I sneak out of every night and don't come back to until three in the morning. No one's even said I look tired. I think I'm one of those people who don't need much sleep. I don't feel tired at all. As a matter of fact, I feel wide-awake all day, but my concentration is pretty bad, I have to admit. In school, all I think about is Sandy.

I'm in love. I keep thinking to myself, "So *this* is what it feels like!" Those feelings I'd had for Jimmy Brown seem silly, the longings of a little girl. This is so different. And I knew last night that I really loved Sandy, because the thought of him being in any danger just about made me crazy with worry.

"I'm going to go out and see if I can help," my father said.

Mama looked upset and she put a hand on his arm. "No, Caleb," she said. "Please don't." It was the strangest thing. There were tears in her eyes, glittery red and gold tears from the reflection of the flames, and all of a sudden I understood my mother better. I could see how much she loves Daddy, and now I understand how that feels. You want the person you love to be safe, to not have to face anything hard or dangerous or frightening. I wanted to hug Mama just then, but of course I didn't.

My father looked as though he was rethinking his plan. He is getting pretty old. I thought he should just let the young men take care of this. So I added to Mama's plea and asked him not to go.

"Let's do this, then," he said. "Let's take some food and coffee and blankets over to the Coast Guard station. Those boys are going to need more than they have over there. And the survivors will need that kind of help, too."

We all three of us looked out at that burning ship, and I'm sure they were thinking the same as me, that it was doubtful there would be any survivors at all.

So we put everything we could find into the car, and if Mama wondered why the wool blanket I secretly dragged out to the beach every night was sandy and damp, she said nothing about it. We drove south, following the tracks in the sand along the beach until we reached the Coast Guard station. The smell of fire was in the air. It was chaos there. Men were running back and forth from the station to the cutters, and it seemed like all of them were shouting. Everyone's face was colored an orangey red from the fire, even though the tanker was really farther out to sea than I'd thought. We carried the things we'd brought with us into the station and were jostled left and right by men running past us. I looked for Sandy and for other people I knew, like Jimmy or Teddy Pearson, or Ralph Salmon or Mr. Hewitt, but everyone's face seemed like a blur in that red glow.

Daddy said we should just leave the things we brought and get out of the way. Other neighbors were there as well, with the same idea we'd had of bringing supplies for the survivors, and it was clear we were all in the way. As I turned to leave, I saw Sandy. He ran right past me toward one of the cutters and I know he saw me, but his eyes quickly shifted away from mine. He was right to do that, to not let on that he knew me, yet it was so hard to be that close to him in that moment of tragedy and not give him a hug. He looked determined and brave, but I remembered how scared he had been by a silly old horse on the beach. I knew he must have been really scared and upset right then.

Today, I did not go to church. I told Mama and Daddy I just didn't feel like it and they didn't argue with me one bit. The tanker is still out there. It's called the *Byron D. Benson,* and I'm afraid it's going to float like this for days. Black smoke is still pouring out of it, and the whole sky is a sickening, choking ashy color. I know from the radio that some men were saved last night, but not near as many as were on that ship. I am dying to talk to Sandy.

I'm spending today helping my parents hang some heavy curtains that are supposed to keep the U-boats from seeing the lights in our house and that make me feel like I'm living in a funeral parlor. I helped Daddy put black tape on the headlights of our car. We left just a little slit for the light to come through. As of today, no one's allowed to drive on the beach anymore, except the Coast Guard jeeps. We finally have that dimout the Coast Guard's been wanting all this time.

Mama's back to her usual yelling at me.

"Don't ever peek out from these curtains," she said while we were hanging them. "One peek can cost the lives of hundreds of men."

Teddy Pearson came over to our house this morning and told us not to go out on the beach today. He went to all the houses around here to tell people to stay away, and I know why. They wanted to pick up all the bodies first. I wonder if Sandy will be on his patrol tonight?

Monday, April 6, 1942

Last night, I met Sandy on the beach. Usually, I walk his patrol with him, since he is careful not to let my being there distract him from his job, but tonight he just wanted to sit.

He is wounded. Nobody shot him or cut him or anything, but he is wounded just the same. I think it's even worse when the wound is inside you and you can't bandage it or treat it with medicine. He was real quiet with me at first and when I asked him why, he said he didn't want to tell me about last night. What happened wasn't fit for my ears, he said.

Sandy and I have talked about a lot of things. Our families, how we were brought up and all. He told me how he grew up so poor that sometimes there'd be nothing to eat for two days. He never got presents for Christmas or his birthday. His father is dead and his mama takes in laundry, and that is all the money they had to live on. He has a dream of making a good salary someday, although he's not sure what he will do to earn it. His eyes light up when he talks about having money. I've never felt that way about money myself, but I can understand how, if you've been really poor, it could seem like the answer to all your prayers. Anyway, as I was saying, what Sandy and I do most is talk. We've kissed a couple of times, but nothing more than that, and even though I'd like more than that, that is not what is most important about the two of us being together. It's the talking with him that I love. I like that I can say just about anything to him.

So I told him that, and then I told him I wanted to know what he'd been through last night. I said I cared about him and wanted to know what had happened. I came close to telling him I love him, but I was afraid how he'd react to that. He looked at me for a long time as if he was deciding whether to tell me or not, but then he did.

He said how they went all the way out to the ship in the cutter, how the air was hot and the flames so bright he had to squint to be able to see the ship. New explosions kept getting set off and it was like a fireworks show, he said. There was a slick of oil on the water that was on fire, too, so they couldn't get too close. A couple other ships were there trying to rescue the men, and all around them were the screams of the sailors from the ship.

A lot of men jumped or fell into the burning water. He could see them falling, and he was close enough to see how scared they were. "The men in the water were screaming for us to help them," he said. "And we couldn't do nothing about it." I think that's what hurt him the most, that helplessness.

He told me they circled around the ship in the cutter, trying to get close enough to pick up the survivors, but the burning oil made it impossible. Then he told me the worst thing, the thing he didn't want to say for fear of upsetting me.

"There was this one man who was badly burned and who was clinging to a board," he told me. "He reached an arm up above the water, begging us to save him. There was too much oil on the water there, but we couldn't just leave him. We moved close enough that I could reach over and grab his hand. But the skin on his hand just came off in my hand and he fell under the water. I was left just holding that burned shell of his hand."

Can you imagine? I felt as sick as he did, hearing about it. I put my arm around his shoulders and just hung on to him. He wasn't crying, at least not on the outside, but I knew he was all beat up inside.

There were some survivors and they are at the hospital in Norfolk. Sandy said the FBI is interviewing them, trying to see if one of the crew might have tipped off the Germans. "It's ridiculous," Sandy said. "No one has to tip off the Germans. There're so many boats out there and the lights on the beach just make them sitting ducks."

"The dimout will help, then," I said. I wanted so much to find a way to comfort him.

"It damn well better," he said. "We can't go on this way. Right now, the Germans own this ocean."

We sat there for a long time, then, not saying a word. I rubbed his back the way I see Mama rub Daddy's sometimes, but we didn't talk. And I didn't leave until the sky started getting lighter, when we could see the *Byron Benson* drifting near the horizon, two plumes of black smoke still rising up from amidships to haunt us.

Chapter Seventeen

ON SUNDAY MORNING, GINA FOUND HERSELF
entertaining Henry Hazelwood in Shorty's back room. She
visited with him any chance she got in between waiting on
her customers. The back room was crowded, as usual, but
Walter and Brian had not yet arrived and Henry sat alone at
the chess table, in his white shirt and dark tie, his hat in his
lap. She bought him a paper so he'd have something to do.

"This happens every Sunday," he said to her as she poured
his coffee. "They come late, I come early. And Clay's picking
me up at noon so's we can get my groceries, so I'll probably
miss them altogether today."

He looked so glum at the thought that she leaned over to
give him a hug. She gave him her pencil to use on the cross-
word puzzle and brought him a piece of lemon meringue pie
on the house, and he seemed grateful for her attention.

Clay arrived at noon to pick him up. Gina was balancing a
stack of dirty dishes up the length of one arm when she spotted him, but she managed to catch up to him as he walked
toward the back room.

"He's been alone in there all morning," she said. The scent of fish was strong in the air where they were standing, and Gina wasn't sure if it was coming from the kitchen or the group of fishermen sitting at the counter. "Walter and Brian haven't gotten here yet and he misses seeing them. Any chance you can bring him back later?"

Clay smiled at her. "You're a soft touch," he said.

"If you can't, maybe I could pick him up and bring him back here when I'm done with my shift."

He shook his head. "I'll bring him back after we drop off his groceries and I fix his railing," he said. "Thanks for caring, Gina."

A little more than an hour later, Lacey arrived at Shorty's, and Gina remembered that today was the drawing for the raffle. Lacey disappeared into the kitchen, carrying the huge glass jar that had been gathering bills on the counter next to the cash register. When she appeared again, she was holding a thick envelope and a box filled with the raffle tickets.

Nearly everyone at Shorty's had put money into that jar, and they watched with interest as Lacey and Frankie stood near the cash register, ready to pick a winner from the box of tickets. Gina leaned against the doorway leading into the back room, while Frankie drew a name from the box.

"And the winner is…" Frankie said dramatically as she looked at the ticket. She broke into a smile, her gaze shifting from the ticket to Gina. "Gina Higgins!"

Gina sucked in her breath, then laughed. People applauded, especially those regulars who had gotten to know her in the five days since she'd started working there. She walked toward the center of the room, where Lacey gave her a hug as she handed the fat envelope to her.

"Half the take," Lacey said. "Four hundred and ten dollars."

"Thank you *so* much." Gina slipped the envelope into the

deep front pocket of her apron. She could get the air conditioner in her car fixed and maybe have that rattle looked at. If she had anything left over, she would treat her landlords to dinner out.

She was just finishing her shift when Walter Liscott and Brian Cass arrived, coming in through the kitchen door as they always did, since that was where Clay had built the ramp for Walter's wheelchair. Walter wheeled himself through the crowded main room, declining Gina's offer to push him. The decoy in his lap was finished, and Gina took a moment to admire the realistic paint job.

"Our Gina won the fifty-fifty raffle," Frankie said to the two men as they passed the cash register, and Gina felt herself glow, not over winning the raffle, but over being referred to as "our Gina." She pressed her hand against the overstuffed envelope through the cloth of her apron.

"Hey, that's great!" Walter said, twisting in his chair to look up at her. "Are you going to buy the first round?" he joked.

"Gee, I would," she teased back, "but my shift is over and I'm leaving."

"You can't leave yet, girlie," Brian said, "'cause we got some other good news for you."

"Her name is Gina," Walter said with annoyance. "Is Henry here?"

"He was here this morning, and Clay's bringing him back soon." She looked at Brian. "What good news?" she asked.

"Don't tell her till we get to the back room," Walter said, pumping furiously at the wheels of his chair.

She followed the two men and sat down with them at the chessboard.

"Congratulations!"

She turned to see Brock Jensen at the pool table. He waved

one tattooed arm at her. "I hear you were the big winner," he said.

"Yes, thanks." She smiled, although she never felt completely comfortable around Brock. She didn't understand why anyone would want his body covered in ink.

"Here's the news." Walter set the beautiful decoy next to the chessboard and leaned toward her across the table. "You're meeting with Alec tomorrow, right?"

"That's right." She was nervous about the lunch date with her nemesis.

"So, Brian and I have been thinking how you could persuade him. And Brian made a phone call down to the Graveyard of the Atlantic Museum in Hatt'ras, and they want it. The lens. I know you were hoping to keep it up north here, but we thought it best you find a home for it quick as you could so you'd have some ammunition to use with Alec."

"They'd display it?" she asked.

"Right. Of course, there's nothing in writing or anything yet, but they said they'd be thrilled to have the lens. They have the space for it, too."

"This *is* good news," she said.

"You still probably want to see if there's a place for it up here," Brian said, "but at least now you can tell Alec it has a home."

"And tell him he won't have to do a damn thing," Walter said. "Won't have to lift a finger. You and me and Brian can take care of everything."

"He doesn't even need to know when it's happening if he doesn't want to," Brian said.

"You guys are great," Gina said. "I appreciate your help so much." She stood up, anxious to use the ladies' room before taking off. "I'll let you know how it goes," she said.

She had finished in the ladies' room and was walking back

down the long, narrow hallway toward the restaurant when
Brock Jensen came racing around the corner. Before Gina
could get out of his way, he crashed into her. She fell to the
floor hard with Brock nearly on top of her.

"Oh, shit!" he said, slowly raising his body from hers to sit
with his back against the wall. "Are you all right?"

She wasn't sure she *was* all right. She was lying on the floor
on her side, and she stayed that way for a moment as she tried
out her wrists and elbows and ankles and knees. Her ankle
hurt, but only a bit.

"I think so," she said.

"I'm so sorry." He had his hand on her arm, trying to
help her up. "I had to pee and that was the only thing on my
mind."

She was able to smile at him despite her annoyance. "I
know the feeling." She stood up, leaning against his tattooed
arm. "I'm fine," she said. "Just had the wind knocked out of
me for a minute, I think."

He peered into her face. "You're sure?"

She nodded. "Yeah, I'm okay." She motioned down the
hallway toward the men's room. "Go ahead," she said.

She walked carefully through the restaurant and out to her
car, testing her sore ankle, still amazed that she'd broken nothing in that wild collision. She was absolutely fine. It wasn't
until she had pulled out of the parking lot that she touched
the pocket of her apron again. The money! Swerving to the
side of the beach road, she stopped the car. She took off her
apron and felt in the pocket again, as if she could possibly have
missed that bloated envelope. There were dollar bills in the
pocket, and coins, but they were her tips. The envelope was
gone.

Quickly, she drove back to Shorty's and ran inside to the
hallway where she'd fallen. The wooden floor was hardly

clean, but it was bare. The envelope was not there. In the ladies' room, she searched the stall she'd used and the grimy floor beneath the sink, as well as the small plastic garbage can.

When had she last been aware of the money in her apron pocket? She recalled feeling it there when she'd walked through the main room with Brian and Walter. She retraced her steps through the crowded restaurant, but found no envelope. Frankie was at the cash register, busy with her customers, and Gina couldn't bring herself to ask her if anyone had turned in the money. She couldn't admit that she'd been careless enough to lose it already.

In the back room, she found Walter and Brian deep in a game of chess.

Her gaze fell to the floor beneath the table.

"You lose something?" Brian asked her.

"An envelope," she said. "You didn't happen to see one, did you?"

Walter peered beneath the table. "Don't see anything," he said.

Neither did she. *Damn.* She would have to say something to Frankie. She turned to leave the room, but saw Brock looking at her from the pool table. He held her gaze for a moment, and on his face was an unmistakable smirk. She thought back to his out-of-character offer of congratulations and to the collision in the hallway. How hard he'd smacked into her, how he'd fallen on top of her. How it had taken him a moment to get up. He had planned the whole thing.

She marched over to the pool table.

"Could I see you outside for a moment?" she asked.

"Be right back," Brock said to his pool partner.

She walked outside through the side door of the room, and he followed her. Standing on the pea gravel outside the door, she turned to face him. "I don't think that was an accident in the hallway near the rest rooms," she said.

"What was it, then?" He cocked his head to one side and she wanted to rip that smirk off his face.

"I think you took the raffle money out of my apron pocket," she said.

He held his painted arms out straight from his shoulders. "Why don't you search me?" he asked, raising his eyebrows at her.

She thought she might cry. She was no good at the tough-guy routine. "I need that money, Brock," she said. "Please. Just give it back to me and I won't make an issue out of it."

He leaned toward her, his face close to hers. "I don't have your money," he said. "If you lost it, don't come crying to me."

He turned on his sandaled heel and walked back into Shorty's.

She didn't know what she would say to Lacey, but she sat with her on the couch in the living room later that afternoon, pretending to read, while Lacey opened utility bills that Gina was doing nothing to help her pay.

"I have to tell you something," she said, suddenly getting her courage up. She closed the book in her lap.

Lacey looked up from one of the bills. "What?" she asked.

"I really screwed up, Lacey," she said. "I'm so sorry."

Immediately, Lacey moved the bills from the sofa to the floor and turned to give Gina her full attention. "It's all right, whatever it is," she said, and Gina knew she was lucky to have this incredibly kind woman as her landlord and her friend.

"I lost the money," she said.

Lacey gasped, leaning back from her. "Oh no!"

"I think Brock Jensen might have taken it. He crashed into

me when I was leaving the ladies' room. We both fell down, and I'm not sure, but I think maybe he planned it to happen. I confronted him, but he denied it, of course."

"We'll call the police." Lacey started to get up, but Gina grabbed her arm.

"No," she said. "I don't want to create a huge deal out of it. Maybe Brock *is* innocent. Maybe I did actually lose the envelope. I just don't know." She shook her head. "I'm so sorry, Lacey," she said. "The raffle was a terrific idea. I just wish I hadn't been the one to win it."

Lacey leaned back in the sofa with a sigh. "Well," she said, "maybe whoever has the money needs it more than you do. At least we can hope for that."

Gina nodded, pretending to agree, although she couldn't help but think that no one needed money more than she did.

Chapter Eighteen

GINA HIGGINS WAS WAITING FOR HIM IN THE Sea Tern Inn. Alec spotted her the moment he walked through the heavy double doors. The restaurant was packed with the summer crowd, but she was a woman who stood out. She sat at a table near the windows and lifted one long, bare arm to wave to him. He returned the wave, but spent a moment talking to one of the waitresses, a woman he'd known for years, before walking over to the table and sitting down across from her.

"How are you?" he asked, struck again by the delicate beauty of this young woman. There was no trace of makeup on her fair-skinned face, no noticeable attempt to pretty herself up in any way other than running a comb through her long, dark hair and doing whatever she'd had to do to get those teeth such a sparkling white. Yet, she made a couple of young men turn their heads as they passed the table. She seemed completely indifferent to their interest.

"I'm fine, thanks," she said. "And thanks, also, for agreeing to have lunch with me."

He nodded. "No problem," he said, although he would rather have a root canal than be badgered about raising the lens again, and that was certainly what this meeting was about.

Gina lifted her napkin from the table, and he noticed that her hands had a little tremor to them. She was nervous, as she had been when she'd come to his house to speak to him. "Is your office…your animal hospital near here?" she asked, smoothing the napkin over her lap.

"Just a couple of miles," he said.

A waitress took their drink orders—water for her, iced tea for him—and then they studied the menu for a moment in silence. The menu was familiar to him, and he was anxious to order. The sooner they did, the sooner they would be served. And the sooner he could get out of there.

"So," he said, after the waitress delivered their drinks and took their orders. "Have you decided how long you're staying in the area?"

"I'm not sure," she said. "I have the summer off, so I'm taking it one day at a time, really. As I mentioned to you the last time I saw you, I wanted to explore the lighthouses in this area, but I've gotten a bit sidetracked by Kiss River."

He ignored the mention of Kiss River. "Lacey said you're from Bellingham," he prompted.

"Yes." She played with the napkin beneath her water glass, folding one edge of it, then the other. "Do you know the city?" she asked.

"Not really. My wife and I toured the Pacific Northwest a few years ago, but we didn't get to Bellingham."

"Where did you go?"

"Seattle and then up to Vancouver and Victoria," he said. "It was beautiful. Didn't even rain too much while we were there."

"You were very lucky," she said.

"We did get a good look at Flattery, though."

"Flattery?" She frowned.

"The lighthouse at Cape Flattery," he said.

"Oh! Right."

He recalled his initial suspicions about Gina. He'd wondered how a lighthouse historian, amateur or not, could not know that the tower at Kiss River had been demolished a decade earlier. He'd forgiven her ignorance at the time; after all, she was not that familiar with the lighthouses on the East Coast. But shouldn't she know that Flattery was a lighthouse in the Pacific Northwest?

"You've been there, too, I suppose?" he asked.

She nodded. "Of course."

"You must have a favorite lighthouse," he said.

"Oh." She drew the word out as if thinking through her answer. Her gaze rested on the salt and pepper shakers at the side of the table. Somewhere, he'd heard that if a person looked down and to the left—or was it down and to the right?—when answering a question, they were most likely lying. He had not meant the question to test the veracity of her interest in lighthouses, but he was wondering now if a test might be appropriate.

"I'd have to say New Dungeness," she said, looking at him squarely then.

"Ah," he said with a nod. "We were able to visit there as well. The house was being restored."

She looked surprised. "Did you walk in?" she asked.

"We kayaked." It was impossible for a visitor to drive to that lighthouse. You had to either walk in or arrive by boat. "How about you? You're probably very familiar with it."

"I've visited it several times," she said. "I always walk in. It's more than five miles, but it's worth the walk."

"Is the house still being restored?" he asked.

"I'm not sure," she said. "It might be finished by now."

"There's certainly a colorful history to the lighthouses in that region," he said.

"The history's pretty colorful here, too," she said, gamely trying to shift the topic to the East Coast lighthouses, but he didn't bite.

"Well, our early keepers didn't have hostile American Indians to cope with. And that bit about the smallpox." He shook his head, irked with himself that he was intentionally trying to trip her up now.

"Smallpox?" She looked at him blankly. Her eyes were so dark, they appeared to lack pupils.

"You know, infecting the Native Americans as a way to get rid of the problem."

"Oh, right," she said quickly, then smiled. "That's one little fact I like to block from my mind."

The waitress brought her Caesar salad and his crab cake sandwich. He put his napkin on his lap and lifted the sandwich to his lips.

"How are things at the keeper's house?" he asked before taking a bite.

"Good." Gina tossed her salad a bit with her fork. "Lacey and Clay have been wonderful to me. You have terrific children."

He nodded in humble agreement. "Thanks," he said.

"Neither of them is home much, really," Gina continued. "Lacey's unbelievable, the way she works part-time with you and then runs off to her volunteer jobs and makes all that stained glass, too."

"Yeah," he said. "I wish she'd slow down a bit, actually, and get a social life."

"Oh, she goes out," Gina reassured him, and it bothered him that she seemed to know more about his daughter's life than he did. "When she's not tutoring kids or making stained glass or donating her bone marrow or reading to people at the old folks home, that is." She laughed.

The words had almost slipped by him, but not quite. "What did you say?" He lowered his sandwich to the plate. "What was that about bone marrow?"

"She donated her bone marrow," Gina said between bites of salad. "You didn't know?"

"No," he admitted. "I didn't. When did she do that?"

"I don't know specifically. Sometime last year." Gina looked worried, as though she'd let something slip. She had. "I can't imagine a more generous thing to do," she said.

He was quiet. He could picture Annie on the plane ride home from Chicago after donating her bone marrow, smiling bravely despite the pain in her back. A few years ago, Lacey had told him that she was on the donors' list, and he'd argued against it, probably surprising her with his vehemence. No wonder she hadn't told him she'd actually been called to donate. She was just like Annie. And just like Annie, she was keeping things from him.

"There's such a thing as being too generous," he said, more to himself than to Gina.

She didn't reply, and for a moment they ate their lunches in awkward silence. Then he sighed. Might as well face the inevitable.

"I know you've invited me here to try to persuade me to help you raise the lens," he began. "And I—"

"Dr. O'Neill," she interrupted him. "I'm well aware that I'm an...an interloper," she said with a self-conscious smile that made him like her in spite of himself. "It's hard to explain. I just don't feel as though I can walk away from this. There are a lot of people willing to help me if you would just give me the go-ahead. Brian Cass and Walter Liscott and Nola

Dillard. The lighthouse association. They'd all like to see it salvaged."

"And I'm standing in the way."

She nodded. "Brian Cass spoke with someone at the Graveyard of the Atlantic Museum. They'd like to have the lens there when it's raised."

He suddenly felt very tired. He was done with his sandwich, ready to leave. He pushed his plate away an inch or two. "I know there would be a place for the lens, Gina," he said. "That's not the point."

"Why are you so against it?" She looked justifiably perplexed.

"Why are you so dead-set on doing it?" He turned the tables on her.

Her gaze dropped quickly to the salt and pepper shakers again, and it was a moment before she answered. "Because I care about lighthouses and the preservation of history," she said.

"I was thinking about what shape it's in down there." Alec folded his arms across his chest. "I know you're hoping the light will still be in one piece. But the fact that it has a missing panel makes that even less likely, don't you think?"

"What do you mean, 'a missing panel'?"

If she didn't know what he was talking about, she had not done her homework well at all. "The one destroyed in the storm in the sixties."

She couldn't mask her surprise.

"Did you think the lens was whole?" he asked. The lighthouse guide she was using had to be quite extraordinarily old to have left out that small detail.

"I'd completely forgotten about that," she said. "It doesn't change how I feel about it, though. I'd still like to raise the lens."

He looked at his watch, then at her. "Gina," he said, "I understand all about being obsessed by lighthouses. I truly do. And I actually feel sympathy for you, because I know what it's like to try to save something that isn't easy to save. But..." He wanted to simply say, "I won't help you, and that's final," yet he thought she deserved more of an answer than that. He did not believe she was much of a lighthouse historian, but she sincerely cared about raising this light, for whatever reason. "The lighthouse meant a great deal to my first wife and me," he explained.

"Oh." Gina sat back in her chair. "Clay told me about... how you lost her. I'm so sorry. It must have been terrible for all of you."

He nodded. "I met her at Kiss River," he continued. "I was just twenty-two and I was working construction for the summer. Working on the keeper's house. I helped paint the lighthouse."

"I didn't know that," she said. "No wonder you loved it so much."

"My wife and I would sit up on the gallery and watch the stars at night." *And make love,* he thought. Suddenly, he recalled the times he'd sat up there after Annie died. It had been his escape, his place to grieve. "So, I certainly understand what it means to care deeply about a lighthouse," he said. "But I'm not with Annie—my first wife—anymore, and our...connection with the lighthouse is all in the past. It needs to stay in the past. I don't want anything to do with it now." He knew his obstinancy must still sound strange to her. "My reason for leaving the lens where it is probably sounds as irrational to you as someone from Washington State wanting to raise it sounds to me," he said. "All I can tell you is that you can't count on me for support. I'm sorry. And I have to request that you please don't ask me again. I don't want to talk about it."

She looked apologetic. "All right," she said in a near whisper. "I'm very sorry if it's brought up painful memories for you."

He offered to pick up the tab, but she insisted on paying it herself.

"I invited you," she said. Her voice had become flat, and he knew he had disappointed her greatly. He felt strange around her, drawn in by her beauty and her passion one minute, suspicious of her the next, and irritated by her the entire time. She was making him remember things he didn't want to remember.

They walked together out to the parking lot, neither of them saying a word. Alec felt weighed down by a sudden sense of isolation. He would love to talk to Olivia about this whole situation. Olivia was his rock, his link to sanity. He could talk to her about anything—*anything*—except Annie. He wished that when he got home tonight, he could tell her that Lacey had donated her bone marrow the year before, but he knew how Olivia would react to that. Every time Lacey did something that was Annie-like, he could see his wife flinch. She thought his children should know the not-so-pretty truth about their mother, although she had learned not to argue with him about it. She knew he would never hurt their memory of Annie that way.

He was being stubborn about the lens, and he knew it. It reminded him too much of that crazy time in his life. If there was some compelling reason to raise that lens, if someone's life depended on it, for example, he would certainly agree to it. But an outsider with a questionable role as a lighthouse historian and an irrational desire to raise the lens did not compel him in any way. It made him even more resistant to giving in.

"There's my car," he said, pointing to the second row of cars in the parking lot.

"Okay," she said, starting in the opposite direction. "Thanks for meeting with me."

"Gina?" he called as she started to walk away.

She turned to look at him.

"You obviously have a great deal of energy and passion," he said. "It would be much better spent on something else."

Chapter Nineteen

Friday, April 10, 1942

TODAY I TURNED FIFTEEN, AND I FEEL AS THOUGH I am completely different. Not just my age, but some part of me I didn't know could change. The part that trusted people. The part that always felt safe and secure. The part that thought of Germans as faceless demons out there under the ocean. I know different now, and I don't think I'll ever be the same.

Late last night, just as I was going up to bed (or at least pretending to go to bed, knowing that an hour or so later I would sneak out to the beach to be with Sandy), Daddy came in the house and told Mama and me we needed to come outside with him. I decided I better go so I didn't rouse their suspicions. He took us up to the gallery of the lighthouse to watch the sky because there was a shooting star shower. The lighthouse is dark now. We had to turn it off because of the blackout, and none of us can sleep well, no matter how hard we try. We are all crotchety and irritable. But having it dark makes it easier to see the stars.

Daddy carried the flashlight, but he didn't turn it on as we climbed to the top of the lighthouse. All three of us climb those steps in our dreams. The sight from the gallery was breathtaking. The moon was just a little white sliver, and I've never seen the sky so clear before, since there were no lights anywhere. It was hard even to tell where the ocean ended and the land began. We leaned back against the glass wall of the lantern room and looked up at the sky. I had seen three stars fall when Mama suddenly told us to look out to sea.

She was pointing out in the ocean, a little to the north, and I suddenly saw what had caught her eye: a light was blinking out there. We watched it for a moment, and my father said, "It's an SOS signal!" Sure enough, I began to see the pattern of three long flashes, two short, then three long ones again. My father handed me his flashlight.

"You two stay here," he said, already heading for the stairs. "I'm going out there. I'll need you to shine the flashlight so I can find my way back in."

"I'll go with you," Mama said to him.

"No," he called back over his shoulder. "You make some coffee so there's something hot for whoever's out there when I bring them in."

"I could run down to the Coast Guard station," I said. I could think of nothing I'd rather do, actually.

"No, you cannot," Mama said. "Not on a night dark as this, with that murderer out there."

She followed Daddy down the stairs and I sat down on the gallery, shivering all over. It was cold up there and windy, but it was the turn of events that truly had me nervous. I knew that Sandy was on his patrol, and I wondered if he was able to see the SOS signal from where he was. It might have been a little far north for him.

I peered over the floor of the gallery and could barely make out my father dragging his boat to the water. One thing I *could* see, though, was how rough the waves were. Without the moon, the foam looked gray and it flew up in the air as the waves batted against one another. I felt terrified that Daddy was going out in that.

Even though the water was roaring, I could hear the motor of Daddy's boat chugging through the ocean, and I felt relieved when I knew he was past the breakwater. He'd turned the lights on at the bow and stern, which is strictly against the rules, but I guess he figured he had to let the SOS boat know he was coming. Soon, I heard his motor cut out as he reached the other light. All I could see was two lights bobbing then, moving this way and that, but I had no idea what Daddy and the people in the stranded vessel were doing. Then I heard Daddy's boat start running again, and watched as the two flashlights moved toward shore. First I thought the other boat was just following Daddy's, but then I realized Daddy was towing it.

I pointed the flashlight in their direction to guide my father in. The two lights bobbed like crazy as they passed through the breakwater, sometimes moving completely out of my view, scaring me to pieces, but after a moment I could see them being carried in on the waves. When I knew they were safe on shore, I ran down the stairs.

There were two men in the boat, which was a dinghy, actually. A little thing without a motor, so no wonder they'd been stranded. "Let's get these men into the house," Daddy hollered to me as I neared them.

They were boys, actually. Probably a few years older than me, and they were so shaky and tired they could hardly get themselves out of the dinghy. I let one of them lean on me as he found his land legs.

"Thanks, lass," he said to me in the most beautiful accent.

"They're Brits," my father said to me. "Come inside, boys. The wife will have some coffee to warm you up."

The boys reminded me of the night I first met Sandy and snuck him into the house. They were shivering all over and their faces were white with fear and cold. But they didn't sound a bit like Sandy. I loved listening to them. One of them had almost white hair and was a little odd-looking. His eyebrows and eyelashes were white, too, and his eyes were very strange, sort of a pink color. I tried not to stare, but it was hard. His name was Miles. The other, Winston, was very handsome. He looked a little like Teddy Pearson at the Coast Guard station, only with a British accent. Mama gave them some chicken and collard greens and corn-bread dumplings left over from dinner, and we pushed their chairs close to the fire while they told us what happened.

They said they were on a British trawler called the *Mirage* when it was torpedoed by the Germans. Winston got tears in his eyes when he talked about it, and Miles's lower lip shivered, but he was very quiet and barely spoke at all. I felt sorry for both of them. I could just imagine what it was like to watch your friends dying right before your eyes. There had been three of them in the dinghy, Winston said. The third man jumped overboard to try to save one of his shipmates and never surfaced from the sea. It was a terrible tale.

Mama said that since it was so late, the two men should sleep in the spare room if they didn't mind sharing a double bed, and that in the morning I could run over to the Coast Guard station to tell Bud Hewitt what had happened and report the information on the *Mirage*. The men agreed to this.

Before we all went to bed, though, Mama smiled at me

and said that it was now officially my birthday, since it was nearly one in the morning. Everyone sang "Happy Birthday" to me, or some version of it, at least. I figured they must sing a different birthday song in England, because Miles and Winston were pretty bad with the words. I felt embarrassed by the attention. After a while, they went up to bed and so did we. I was dying to tell everything to Sandy, but I didn't dare sneak out because I knew Mama and Daddy would not be sleeping soundly with the strangers in the house. I hoped Sandy wasn't worrying about me. This would be the first time I missed coming to see him when he's on patrol.

I fell straight to sleep, though. Maybe I needed a good night's sleep after all those nights spent on the cold beach. But I was not going to get one.

This is hard for me to write, to actually put down in words. I started having a dream that I was on the beach, and Sandy was lying next to me, nuzzling my neck and kissing my cheek, and then he slipped his hand under my nightgown and touched my breast, something he has never done in real life to me. I liked the way it felt and I put my arms around him. He was bony. His body had changed, and I remember thinking to myself, "This is a dream and this is the dream Sandy." Then I suddenly woke up and realized it was *not* Sandy lying next to me at all, but Miles, the blond man from the dinghy! My room was so dark. How I miss the light from the lighthouse! I started to scream, but Miles clamped his hand over my mouth, pinning my head to the bed. I tried pushing him away from me, but although he was skinny he was strong, and he held something against my throat. It was cool and smooth, and I knew it was a knife. I have never been so scared in my entire life. Once he'd let me know about the knife, he set it on the bed next to me, then used that hand to reach under my nightgown again, this time stopping between my legs. It was disgusting. I started to cry, out of fear, I guess, but also because I wanted Sandy to touch me there, not this terrible bony white man. I squirmed, and thought about trying to reach the knife, but I didn't dare because I was afraid he would grab it from me and kill me with it. He was lying on my left arm. He took his hand from between my legs then, and I heard the zipper on his pants. The thought of what he was planning to do made me feel so sick and scared. Suddenly, I had the strangest idea, almost like an instinct. His hand was still clamped over my mouth, so I quickly opened my mouth wide. One of his fingers slipped inside my mouth and I bit it as hard as I could. He howled, yelling at me, using words I'd never heard before. They were rough-sounding and raspy in his throat, and I knew he was no Brit. He was a German! He'd pulled his hand from my mouth and smacked me across the face, but I was already screaming. I've never made such a racket. I screamed at the top of my lungs, crying out for Daddy. Miles grabbed for his knife, but I managed to get one of my legs coiled up and kicked him with all my might and he fell right off the bed. I grabbed his knife then, fumbling on the floor for it because it was so dark, and then Daddy was in the room. I started sobbing when I saw him because I knew I was safe then.

"He's a German, Daddy!" I yelled quickly, reaching for the light on my night table, not caring about the blackout rules. I flicked the light on and saw my father standing in the doorway, his rifle at his side. Miles or whatever his name was pushed past him. He looked real frail, but he was strong and just bashed right through my poor father and turned left to take off down the hall. I watched Daddy raise the rifle to his shoulder, aiming down the hallway where I couldn't see, and I heard the pow of the gun and then the thud of the German dropping to the floor.

I couldn't breathe or speak. I just sat there in my bed, my mouth hanging about down to the mattress with shock. My father looked down the hallway a minute, then turned to me.

"Are you all right, Bess?" he asked me.

I managed to spit out that I was all right, and then Daddy turned and ran the other way, toward the guest room, and I knew he was going for the other man. He was going to kill them both.

Mama ran into my room and sat down on my bed and held me, and I cried in her arms like when I was a little girl with a skinned knee. She held me so tight, and I knew that no matter how many harsh words there are between us, no matter how often we disagree on things, nothing can kill the love we have for each other.

"Be careful, Caleb!" she called after my father, but she didn't let go of me. "My baby," she kept saying, rocking me, and I loved being rocked that way. Sometimes I think of myself as a woman, but right then, I was just a little girl. After a while, she asked me if he'd hurt me. She couldn't say the word *rape,* and I didn't want to hear her say it either. I told her I was all right, just scared. I couldn't tell her about the way he'd touched me. The thought of it still made me want to throw up. I wanted to heat up some water for a bath. But then I remembered the dead man in the hallway.

Mama and I sat there for what seemed a long time, listening for the crack of the rifle again, but we didn't hear it. Neither of us wanted to leave my room and face that dead German. We just sat still together, holding on to each other, waiting for whatever would come next.

After a long time, we heard my father's footsteps on the stairs. They were heavy and tired-sounding. He came into my room and sat down on the bed. He rubbed my head a little and asked me again if I was all right. Then he told us he'd lost the other man. He'd run off into the woods.

Daddy went over to the Coast Guard station and called the sheriff, since they have a special phone there. The sheriff came over and talked to me for a very short time because he wanted to get some men together to go out and look for the second man, Winston, although by this time we were pretty sure that wasn't his name. I was glad he didn't talk to me long, since I didn't want to have to give him details of what Miles had done to me, and I sure didn't want everybody in the Banks to know. I was embarrassed enough as it was.

We were all downstairs then, but all I could think about was the body up in our hallway. I hadn't looked toward it as I left my room for the stairs. The sheriff went to take a look at it. Daddy had shot the man in the back. That was not a good thing to do, and I was worried he might get in trouble, but the sheriff came back down, saying one of his men would be in later to take the body away and clean up the mess.

The sheriff got in touch with Mr. Hewitt and they did some checking into the ships that would have been sailing that night and there was no British trawler called the *Mirage*. The two men were probably saboteurs from one of the U-boats, the sheriff said, bluffing about their ship being sunk in order to get ashore. Daddy felt bad that he had fallen for their trick, but Mama said anyone would have, not to be so hard on himself.

Mama made me hot chocolate and I felt comforted by both my parents, like when I was sick and they took care of me. I finally got my bath and then we sat in the living room around the fireplace, Daddy only leaving my side to fetch more wood for the fire. It must have been just an hour later when the sheriff and one of the deputies came back in our house. They'd found the other man, they said. He hadn't gotten far from our house when something attacked him—probably a wild boar, from the look of his injuries. He had lost a lot of blood and was unconscious, and he'd been taken to the hospital in Norfolk.

"As soon as he wakes up," sheriff said, "he has a lot of questions to answer."

Then they went upstairs with Daddy to get rid of the dead German.

I knew he was dead and couldn't hurt me, and I knew the other man was far away and injured, but the thought of going back up to my room was scary to me. I felt like a baby. Mama knew, somehow. Maybe she knew how she would have felt at my age if such a thing had happened to her. She said I could sleep with her for the rest of the night, and that Daddy would sleep in my room. I was grateful to her.

It was strange sleeping with her. I did manage to sleep, but I'm not sure she did. I felt her petting my hair as I drifted off, and she was still there when I woke up in the morning, petting my hair and smiling at me. There were tears in her eyes. "My little girl," she said to me. "I wish I could have protected you."

I no longer felt that helpless kind of feeling from the night before, and I didn't like her being so close and so kind to me now. I sat up and turned away from her. "It was nothing, Mama," I said. "Really."

But I was very tired, more tired than I'd been in my whole life. Mama said I didn't need to go to school, and so I went back to bed, in my own room, not looking at the spot in the hallway where I was afraid I'd still see some blood. I slept most of the morning, and then had lunch, and now I'm writing this. And tonight I will see Sandy. I plan to go back to sleep now to make that time come quickly.

Chapter Twenty

SHORTY'S WAS OVERFLOWING WITH THE EVENING crowd when Clay stopped by to pick up Henry, and he had to park down the street instead of in the lot. He'd worked late, designing an addition for a house in Duck, a project he was excited about. The owners wanted something different and unique, and he'd actually lain awake the night before thinking about what he might create. It had been a while—eight months, to be exact—since he'd worked with any fervor on a project, and the excitement left him both relieved and guilty: Terri would never experience such joy in her work again.

Several people greeted him when he walked into the restaurant.

"Hey!" Kenny was seated at the counter, and he raised his mug of beer in the air. "Have a seat, Clay."

"Better not." Clay glanced toward the entrance to the back room. "I'm already late picking up Henry."

"Just for a minute," Kenny said. One of Shorty's thick, juicy burgers lay half eaten on Kenny's plate, and Clay was seduced. He ordered one for himself, then went into the back room to let Henry know he was there and make sure the old man had eaten. Returning to the main room, he took the empty seat next to his friend.

"I was in here for breakfast this morning and saw your new roommate again," Kenny said. "Man, that girl is hot."

"Housemate," Clay said.

"What?"

"Housemate, not roommate."

"Whatever. What's she like?"

Clay shrugged. "Hard to say." After a week and a half of sharing a house with Gina, he still knew little about her. "She's a teacher in Washington State," he said.

"I thought you said she was a lighthouse historian?"

"That's just her hobby. She really teaches junior-high science."

"Oh," Kenny looked dejected. "Probably one of those women who run the other way when they find out I don't have a college degree."

"I don't have a clue about that," Clay said. "All I know is, the only thing she seems to care about is the Kiss River lighthouse."

"Well, I can talk about the lighthouse," Kenny said.

"You can't talk to her about anything," Clay said with a laugh. "You had a chance with her on Saturday and you just sat there, stupefied."

Kenny laughed. "Yeah, well, I just needed to get over the shock of seeing someone like her in a place like this. I'm ready now. So, you going to set me up?"

Clay studied his friend. He knew women found Kenny attractive. He could seem like a real jerk sometimes, but he *was* smart—in his field, at least—and an all-around good guy who would give a stranger the shirt off his back. His ideas about women were a bit backward and heavy-handed, but maybe

Gina would like that. Who knew? She didn't seem drawn to Clay, so maybe Kenny would be more her type. Although, frankly, he doubted it.

"I'll check it out with her," he said, reaching for the beer the waitress had placed in front of him.

Kenny lifted his own beer again in a toast. "Awesome," he said.

The dark sky was shot through with color from the windows of the keeper's house by the time he got home. Both Lacey's and Gina's cars were in the parking lot, but inside the house, he found the kitchen empty except for Sasha, who leaped around his legs, whimpering as though he'd been afraid Clay was never coming home. The dishwasher was warm from having been recently run, and the aroma of tomato sauce was still in the air. Lacey and Gina had probably shared some pasta for dinner.

There was no sign of either woman now, though, and he figured they had gone up to their rooms early to read. The house was still and quiet, the only sound the clicking of Sasha's toenails on the kitchen floor and the alternating roar and whisper of the ocean through the open windows. A stack of mail rested on the porcelain-topped table. Lacey must have gone to their post office box. All bills, he noticed, thumbing through the stack. He was about to open the electric bill, when he spotted a mosquito on the wall above the oven. He smashed it with the unopened bill, then carefully peeled the envelope free and dropped it in the garbage. Noting the amount that he and Lacey owed the electric company, he groaned. Insane.

Sighing, he looked through the kitchen into the hallway, which glowed from the lights in all the other rooms. Every light in the damn house was on. It had become his job to turn them off in the evening. If Lacey had her way, they would burn all night long. He thought of taking the electric bill upstairs to her, tossing it on her bed and telling her they had to conserve. But then Kiss River would be dark and colorless when he arrived home each evening. He would pay the bill.

He took Sasha outside for a few minutes, letting the dog run on the beach until the mosquitoes drove them both inside. Back in the house, he began walking through the downstairs rooms, turning off the lights. When he reached the office, he was surprised to see Gina at the computer. She was reading e-mail, and she barely turned her head toward him when he walked into the room.

"Hi," he said, leaning against the desk. He nodded toward the monitor. "Any good mail?"

"Nothing special." Her voice sounded tight.

Maybe she has a lover, he thought. A painful situation she's run away from. They're trying to sort things out through e-mail. By the sound of her voice, it wasn't going too well.

"Did you want to check yours?" She glanced up at him quickly and he saw that her eyes were red. "I can get off."

"No, that's fine," he said, wondering if he should ask her what was wrong. It would seem like prying, though. "Where's Lacey?" he asked.

"Upstairs," she said, her gaze back on the monitor. She was scrolling through paragraph after paragraph of some long piece of e-mail, and she didn't look up at him as she spoke. "She's not alone," she added.

"Ah." He suddenly felt embarrassed, though whether *for* her sister or *by* his sister, he wasn't sure. "Is she with Josh?" he asked.

Gina shook her head. "No, not Josh. I don't remember his name. He has dark hair. He came over right after dinner and they went upstairs."

He sensed Gina's discomfort, as though she thought she might have been in the way when the man arrived and that's why he and Lacey had disappeared upstairs. He started to tell her that Lacey *always* disappeared upstairs with her male friends, but he didn't particularly want to give words to that thought.

"I wanted to ask you something," Clay said, looking for an excuse to stay in the room with her.

She couldn't seem to answer him. He saw a tear slip down her cheek.

"Gina?" He took a step closer. "What's wrong?"

She shook her head. "Nothing," she said, reaching for a tissue from the box on the desk.

"You're upset about something," he said.

"It's nothing," she repeated, wiping her eyes dry. She looked at him then. "What did you want to ask me?" she asked.

The time didn't seem right, but he'd already introduced the topic, so he might as well continue. "Do you remember my friend Kenny?" he asked. "I had lunch with him at Shorty's on Saturday and you waited on us?"

She nodded. "He was in again this morning," she said.

"Well." Clay squirmed a little. "He's interested in you. I'm supposed to check out whether you'd be interested in him."

She smiled at that, but there was still sadness at the corners of her mouth. "I'm not interested in anyone," she said.

"Okay," he said. "I'll let him down easy." He took a step toward the door, but stopped. "Are you sure you're all right?" he asked again.

"Yes. Oh—" she touched the printer to the right of the computer "—but could I use your printer?"

"Of course. Do you need some help with it?"

"No, I don't think so, thanks." She turned away from him, back to whatever had brought those tears to her eyes.

Upstairs, he heard laughter coming from behind the door to Lacey's room, and he closed his eyes against the sound. He walked into his room and lay down on the bed, Sasha jumping up to snuggle beside him.

God, Lacey was loose! He hated using that word to describe her, but there was no denying that it fit. She'd been that way as a teenager, but he'd assumed she'd outgrown it. Apparently not. He'd confronted her about her promiscuity once since they'd moved in together…and only once. She'd been more reassuring than indignant. She was hurting no one, she said, as if this might be his primary concern. She was careful about avoiding pregnancy and disease. So there was no need for him to worry about her, thank you very much.

He did not understand his sister. She was beautiful and bright. She could have been a veterinarian herself instead of an aide in her father's office. Yet, she had not even bothered with college.

In her senior year of high school, Alec had told her that Tom Nestor was her biological father. Clay remembered Lacey's shock and disbelief at that news. "Mom would *never* have done that!" she'd screamed. Clay had been stunned by the revelation himself, but it seemed to destroy something in his sister. Once she accepted the truth, however, she sought out Tom Nestor. He began teaching her stained glass, and Clay figured that it was her way of bonding with the crazy old man. Who could have known that she would become so absorbed by the craft, hungrily learning new skills, taking over her mother's place in Tom's studio? She was good at it. There was a market for her stuff, just as there had been for their mother's. So she didn't bother with college. She became the stained-glass expert in the area, a part-time aide in the

animal hospital and the local do-gooder, the person everyone turned to when they needed help. That was apparently
enough for her. That and her men. There were people who
were smart, brilliant even, but who possessed not a shred of
common sense, and he feared that described his sister.

Sasha lifted his head at the whisper of bare feet on the stairs,
and Clay listened as the sound faded into the room Gina was
renting.

"It's just Gina," Clay said, pulling Sasha's head down to his
side again.

Gina was alone, just as he was. And she seemed determined
to stay that way. Something had upset her tonight, but she
didn't want to share it with him. That much had been obvious. He didn't have whatever it took to draw someone out.
Terri had told him that more than once. "You get weird if I
talk about my feelings," she'd complained. "You don't know
how to comfort me." She'd added that she knew he couldn't
help it. He was male, and males were "disabled" in that way.
"I know it's not your fault," she'd said. "You're handicapped,
that's all."

She had been right. If only he had the chance to comfort
Terri now. If only he could see her again, hold her in his arms.
He would make up for all the times he'd turned away from
her when she'd needed him to listen to her. He would never
leave her alone with her feelings again. But second chances
were rare, and in this case, impossible.

He heard the door to his sister's room creak open, and
Lacey's laughter filled the hallway. He heard some murmured
words from her lover, then more laughter, and he buried his
head in Sasha's shoulder to block out the sound.

Chapter Twenty-One

IN THE PICTURE, THE LITTLE GIRL WORE A WHITE cotton shirt that was too big for her tiny frame. Her smooth skin was the color of caramels and her black hair was cropped very short. All the children at the orphanage had short hair to keep down the incidence of lice infestations. Gina lay on her bed in Bess's old room at the keeper's house, studying the picture, staring at the little girl as if she didn't already know her features by heart. The windows were open and a warm salty breeze filled the room, but Gina would not have noticed if snow had been blowing through the screen. She was focused on the two-month-old picture. How had Rani changed since then? How much sicker was she?

The first picture she'd seen of Rani had been of the child as an infant. A man had found her wrapped in a shirt, lying near the entrance to a building on a busy Hyderabad street. At first, he'd thought she was nothing more than a small, discarded pile of rags. The heart problem was discovered during a medical exam at the hospital before she was transferred to the orphanage, where they named the baby Rani. Gina learned that a single woman could adopt a child from India, and applied to adopt her. She thought she would be able to get Rani quickly because of the baby's urgent need for medical care. Yet the process dragged on. And on.

She did everything right. She'd moved obediently, if impatiently, through the tedious steps of the adoption process. There was the home study, the careful creation of a dossier, the interminable waiting. Finally, she'd received the referral. Rani would be hers. But there were still more months of waiting, and the occasional pictures of Rani sent to her from the orphanage were not enough. It had amazed her how attached she could become to a child she had never met. Her friends had not understood, but she belonged to a support group on the Internet filled with other parents adopting from India, and they had empathized easily with her bond to the little girl she'd never seen. They had all either endured the ordeal already or were going through it just as she was.

In April, she'd learned that the Indian court was finally about to grant her the guardianship order. She took time off from teaching, using her meager funds to fly to India, filled with excitement and every material thing she could possibly need for the little girl. Her friends had thrown her a shower, and she had with her a baby sling, packages of diapers, bottles, sippy cup, toys, picture books, little outfits, a pink and yellow blanket and some medicines her pediatrician had suggested. She'd been filled with the anticipatory thrill of discovery possessed by nearly every expectant mother.

Her plan was to spend the first three days in India at the orphanage, getting to know her new daughter and preparing with the Indian lawyer for the court hearing. On the fourth day, she would go to court to receive her guardianship order. She knew it might take more than one court date to receive the order, but after all the waiting she'd already endured, she could handle that. Then she would begin the preparations to take Rani home with her. She had already spoken to a pediatric cardiologist in Seattle who was ready to evaluate the little girl as soon as Gina brought her home.

The temperature outside had been ninety degrees and rising on her first day at the orphanage. Her driver dropped her off in front of the boxy, two-story building, and she had to step around a goat that was dining on leaves on the dirt path to get to the entrance. She had not anticipated the conditions she found inside. Most, although certainly not all, of the parents on the Internet support group who had visited the orphanages reported clean and caring conditions, and Gina had hoped Rani's orphanage would fall into that category. But it did not. The moment she stepped through the front door, she was greeted by the scent of urine and an ominous silence. She knew what that meant. "The bad orphanages," someone had told her, "are very quiet. The children have learned that crying is pointless because no one will respond to their tears. Making noise will only bring the ayah with her stick."

Rani's orphanage was bursting with children. There were sixty of them, infants to about twelve years of age, divided into four crowded rooms, where some of them slept on floor mats yellowed by urine. The little ones ran around naked, not even diapered, and Gina saw more than one pile of feces on the cold, tiled floor. The ayahs, those beautiful Muslim caretakers in their sapphire blue saris, seemed mostly kind and caring, yet overworked. There were not enough of them and too many children. They carried sticks to herd the children from one room to another, and although Gina did not witness any abuse, she knew corporal punishment was allowed in India and wondered if those sticks were used to hit as well as herd.

Flies were everywhere, and she batted them away from her

face as she waited in the sparsely furnished reception area. It was so hot. The large windows were wide open, but the air was still and suffocating. A portrait of Gandhi hung on one of the walls, but that was the only decoration. She watched a gecko crawl from one side of the room to the other while she waited, thinking about taking Rani away from this place as quickly as she could. She hoped the next day's court hearing would be sufficient to allow that to happen.

There was beauty in India; her driver that morning had taken her to the Golconda fort, from where she could look down on the city and the tombs of the Muslim rulers, and she'd been struck at finding such a stunning vista high above the crowded city. The culture was rich with history and ritual, and she was determined that Rani know about it. They would come back when she was older. They would make visits to India a part of their lives. Gina had made peace with the guilt she felt over stealing a child away from her culture, her roots. Yes, there was beauty in India, but there were no adoptive families available here for a damaged child. Especially not a damaged female child.

Finally, one of the ayahs came to the waiting area and led Gina into a small room, where three little girls were playing with blocks and dolls. Two of the girls scrambled around the room, but the tiniest remained seated on the floor, moving one of the dolls up and down with her arm.

"Rani," the ayah called to her.

Rani lifted her huge eyes to the ayah at the sound of her name, and Gina's heart twisted inside her chest. She felt tears fill her eyes and tried to prevent them from overflowing. She didn't want to frighten the little girl. Her daughter.

The ayah spoke to Rani in Telugu, and the child got slowly to her feet and toddled toward them. She was like a doll her-self, with dark eyes in a tiny, wheat-colored face. Gina could barely breathe. She squatted low to the floor, holding her arms out to the girl, who changed direction from the ayah to Gina, as though she knew that was where she belonged. Rani nearly melted into her arms. The other children looked up from their play, watching while Gina sat down on the floor and rocked her baby. Rani stared up at her with those huge eyes, her thumb in her mouth, and Gina could no longer stop her own tears. "Sweet little girl," she said as she rocked. "My sweet little baby."

Rani wore a loose diaper and a white cotton shirt, beneath which Gina could feel every one of her ribs. She was malnourished, she thought, but that might not be the fault of the orphanage. The heart problem could do that, just as it made her breathing so rapid. Gina could feel Rani's heart tapping against her ribs, and she held her tightly, as though she could keep that heart beating, keep the child alive until she could get her the surgery she needed. Rani didn't speak, but she listened attentively to every word Gina spoke, mesmerized by the sound of her voice, or perhaps by the English.

Gina spent three long and wonderful days with Rani, holding her as she slept, playing with her, showing her the picture books she'd brought along, feeding her, teaching her to drink from a sippy cup. Rani opened her mouth like a baby bird waiting to be fed. It took a while, but she finally got the hang of it, and although she didn't speak, she clung to Gina like a monkey.

Gina didn't want to leave the orphanage the night before her court date, but she had to return to her hotel. She'd been warned that the next day would be long and tiring, sitting for hours in the un-air-conditioned courthouse, waiting to receive her guardianship order. She tucked her daughter into bed and kissed her goodbye.

"I'll be back tomorrow," she promised, and she thought

for sure Rani understood what she was saying. Later, she was to hope Rani had no idea what those words had meant. She didn't want her child to think she had lied to her. Because she was not back the next day. That was the day everything changed.

Gina set Rani's picture back on the night table and picked up the sheet of paper on which she'd printed an e-mail sent to the Internet support group. She knew the woman who had written the e-mail. Gina had met her and her husband in the courthouse in Hyderabad, where they, too, had been waiting for the court order that would allow them to take their daughter home. Like Gina, they had gone back to the States empty-handed, and she knew from the information they'd shared in the support group that the last couple of months had been as torturous for them as they had been for her, as they waited and battled and hired attorneys and did all they could to get their daughter out of the orphanage. Tonight, though, she knew that couple was suffering even more.

"We are heartbroken and don't know where to turn," the wife had written. "We had not been able to get any information from the state orphanage, where Meena was moved in May, so we flew back to India last week. And there we were told they had no record of Meena ever being there. Neither does the original orphanage where we visited her. We *know* she was there, since that is where we spent time with her. Meena's existence has been expunged. It's as though we're the only people who know that she ever existed, because we held her and talked to her and loved her. And now we can't find her. I am sick over what might have happened to her."

Gina had never fully understood why Meena had been moved to the state orphanage, but she did know that no one wanted their child in that place. Might Rani be moved as well? Could she also disappear?

The e-mail had wiped from her mind her distress over the lost four hundred and ten dollars, as well as the unproductive conversation with Alec at the Sea Tern Inn, where she'd looked like an ignorant fool as she tried to answer his questions about the lighthouses in the Pacific Northwest. It even, if only for a moment, made her forget what he'd said about the missing panel and her fear that that very panel might turn out to be the part of the lens she needed.

Closing her eyes, she rested the e-mail on her chest. She used to be an active member of the Internet group, but she could no longer commiserate with those parents. She had become a silent lurker, reading their messages but never responding or posting any news of her own. She could no longer turn to them for advice or sympathy. She had taken a path they would never approve of, and she could not let them know.

And now it seemed that her only hope to get Rani lay in the secrets of Bess Poor's diary.

Chapter Twenty-Two

Saturday, April 11, 1942

I LOVE SANDY. I THOUGHT I DID BEFORE LAST night, but what I feel for him this morning goes a thousand times deeper.

First of all, all day yesterday planes were flying over the ocean. There's always some planes because of the bombing range not far from here, but this was different. I figured they were looking for the submarine that let off Miles and Winston. When I got out to the beach to be with Sandy last night, I asked him if that's what they were doing. He wasn't sure. He said the water out there is pretty murky, and unless the U-boat was on the surface or not far below it, it wouldn't be that easy to see. I wish those planes could find it and destroy it. I am getting pretty hard-hearted, I guess.

Then he gave me my birthday present! He pulled a little package wrapped in tissue paper from the shirt pocket of his uniform. I opened it up and inside was a beautiful ruby necklace! He put it on me, and I wished I'd had a mirror to look at it. I can only wear it with him, since Mama would be sure to notice and ask me where I got it. It's the most beautiful thing I own.

Then we got down to the serious business. Sandy knew that Daddy had killed one of the Germans the night before and that the second German had died the afternoon of my birthday without ever coming to. It wasn't so much the boar that killed him, Bud Hewitt told us, but that he must've fallen when the boar attacked him and split his head on a rock. Anyhow, I feel strange about it. I don't like taking pleasure in somebody dying. But if anybody deserved it, those German boys did.

So Sandy knew all about how they died, but what he didn't know, because Daddy wanted it kept real quiet, was what that Miles boy tried with me. I wanted Sandy to know, even though I wasn't going to tell him all the embarrassing details. We walked along the beach while he was on his patrol and I told him how I woke up, thinking he was touching me, and that it was really Miles. Sandy started cussing up a storm. "Bastard," he kept saying. "Damn lousy son of a bitch." I'd never heard words like those out of his mouth before, and I believe that if Miles and Winston, or whatever their names really are, had been there at that moment, Sandy could have killed them both with his bare hands. He was picking up pieces of driftwood and throwing them far out in the ocean, and I knew he was working off his anger.

After he was done cussing and throwing things, he sat me down on the beach and held me in his arms. "I wish I'd been there to protect you," he said. He had his arms wrapped tight around me and I could feel his cheek against my forehead. "It must have been so frightening," he said, and then I started crying. I ended up telling him *everything*. I couldn't even tell my own mother what that German did to me and I hadn't really intended to tell Sandy either. But with him holding me close, I knew I could tell him. I felt so safe talking to him. I could feel his whole body stiffen up as I spoke, like he was going to explode. I cried the whole time I talked. It was the first time I cried about what happened and I was amazed at all the tears I had inside me. I told him how I'd felt dirty afterward, how I scrubbed my skin raw in the bath basin, trying to get any hint of that boy's touch off me.

After I told him everything, he was quiet for a while. I finally had to ask him what he was thinking.

"Now I truly know I'm in love with you," he said. "I thought I was, but the way I feel right now, how I want to protect you, how I feel as bad for you as if something terrible had happened to me… Well, I think that means I love you."

"I love you, too," I said. I felt very happy. Strange how something good could come out of something so bad.

"Your first time needs to be with someone who loves you," he said. "Someone who will take care of you and never hurt you."

I'd never thought I'd be the kind of girl who would have sex at the age of (barely) fifteen. I thought only trampy girls did that sort of thing before they were married. But I love him so much that I wanted to do it with him right then and there!

"Do you think I'm too young?" I asked him.

He laughed a little. "Yes, you're way too young," he said. "But I want you. I want to erase those bad feelings you have from that German touching you. I want to make you feel wonderful about making love."

I have to admit, I wasn't sure what to do. To be honest, I don't really know how men and women have relations. I know the basics, of course, but that's about it.

"I don't know how," I said to him.

He laughed again, but not at me. "I do," he said. "Only one of us needs to know how."

I turned my head to kiss him, and immediately felt how hot and crazy he was with wanting to make love to me. He touched my breast, but it was through my jacket, so I could barely feel it, and I wanted to tear my jacket off to get him closer. All of a sudden, though, he let go of me.

"Not now," he said. "This isn't the right time or place. I have to finish my patrol, and I want you to have all my attention without me having one eye on the beach. And it's too cold out here. You'll catch your death. And timewise, it's all wrong. Too close to what happened to you with that German. I don't want what I do to you and what that son of a bitch did to you to be confused together in your mind."

I knew he was right, and I was grateful to him for stopping himself, even though I really wanted to do it *right then!* I kissed him, whispered "someday soon," and then I left him alone to finish his patrol.

I walked home through the dark feeling completely unafraid. The bad guys were dead, and I am in love with the world's most wonderful man.

Chapter Twenty-Three

GINA LEANED OVER WALTER LISCOTT'S SHOULDER to pour more coffee into the cup resting next to the chessboard. He'd add plenty of milk to it, but how these old guys could drink so much caffeinated coffee and not be climbing the walls, she didn't know. Come to think of it, Brian's and Henry's hands did tremble a bit as they moved the chess pieces around the board. She'd assumed it was old age, but maybe it was just Shorty's potent brew. Walter's hands, though, were still steady enough to carve his ducks.

Henry Hazelwood sat across the table from Walter, and Gina rested a hand on his shoulder. "You're coming over for dinner tonight, aren't you, Henry?" she asked. Henry came to the keeper's house for dinner, followed by an hour or so of gin rummy, every Wednesday night. Gina had begged out of the get-together the week before, her first Wednesday in the house, because she'd felt a bit intrusive. After living in the house for a week and a half, though, she knew she would be welcome.

"Sure am," the old man said. He was playing—and

beating—Walter, while Brian observed every move like a hawk. "You cooking?"

"As a matter of fact, I am," she said. "I'm going to make you some Indian food."

"Indian food!" Brian Cass said. "You making him buffalo meat, girlie?"

"Her name is *Gina*." Walter shook his head with his usual irritation, but Gina laughed.

"*East* Indian food, Brian," she said. "You know, from India."

"Too spicy for that old man." Brian pointed his crooked finger at Henry.

"I'll make it mild," she promised.

"I don't need it mild," Henry said, obviously annoyed with his friend. "I'll eat whatever you can dish up, honey."

"Gina!"

Gina turned at the sound of her name to see Brock waving to her from the pool table.

"Bring us a round?" he asked, pointing to the motley crew of his friends standing near him.

She nodded. "In a minute," she said. Her shift was ending, and she would give the order to the waitress who was taking her place. She'd tried to avoid waiting on Brock since the incident on Sunday. Without telling the other waitresses her suspicions, though, she could not avoid him completely. He'd come in yesterday sporting yet another tattoo, this one a finely detailed sea turtle on his back, a bit lower and to the left of the mermaid, and she wondered if he had used her money to pay for it.

She returned her attention to Henry, who was waiting for Walter to make a move on the chessboard.

"Clay asked me if I'd pick up some books for you at the

library on my way home today," she said. "He said you like mysteries, right?"

"Whodunits." Henry nodded. "I like that…uh…" He waved a finger in the air, trying to come up with a name.

"That A is for apple lady," Walter said.

"Right. That one." Henry nodded again.

"I know who you mean," Gina said, although she couldn't come up with the author's name off the top of her head either. "What letter are you up to?"

Henry laughed. "I jump around," he said. "But it doesn't matter. I can read the same one over again and not remember I read it the first time."

"All right." Gina squeezed his shoulder. "I'll get you a couple of those."

"Thank you." Henry smiled.

"You boys need anything else before I leave?" she asked.

"Your shift ending?" Walter looked up at her, his hand on his queen.

"Yes sir," she said. "And my feet are happy about it."

"Well, *we're* not happy about it," Brian said. "Nobody here can pour coffee the way you do."

She laughed. She never got a tip from any of them. As a matter of fact, she wasn't sure they even paid for all the coffee and occasional beer they drank, but they had definitely become her favorite customers. They'd grieved with her over the outcome of the talk she'd had with Alec on Monday, amazed that he could turn down the request of "such a bright and beautiful girl." Such sweet old guys. She wondered if they had been jerks when they were younger, like every other man she knew. Except, perhaps, for Clay, whose kindness toward his wife's grandfather was doing its best to redeem her faith in men.

She was taking off her apron in the main restaurant when Kenny Gallo walked in. Spotting her, he waved.

"Hey, Gina," he said, leaning on the counter near the cash register. "You just getting off?"

"Uh-huh." She folded her apron in half, then quarters, making sure her tips were tucked well inside the pocket.

"Well, have a drink with me," he said, pointing to an empty table. "Or a Coke, or coffee, or whatever you like."

"Thanks, Kenny," she said, "but I—" She noticed the embroidered name on the pocket of his green polo shirt. Gallo Maritime Construction. "Is that where you work?" she asked, pointing to his pocket

He glanced down at his shirt. "I own the place," he said, more than a little pride in his voice. He motioned toward the table again. "Come on," he said. "Just for a minute. I won't bite."

She nodded, then walked ahead of him to the empty table, guilty that her motivation for doing so rested in the lettering on his shirt and not the man himself.

"What sort of work does your company do?" she asked once they were seated and had ordered his beer and her Coke from one of her co-workers. The other waitresses were probably talking about them already. "I don't really know what maritime construction means. I assume you build ships?"

"Not build so much as repair," he said. "A couple other guys and me do most of the underwater stuff. Welding, cutting, inspection, that kind of thing."

"And you dive even on your time off, huh?" She smiled at him, remembering that he and Clay had explored the *Byron D. Benson* the previous weekend.

"Can't get enough of it." He grinned. He was cute, in a teddy-bear sort of way, with his full blond beard and laughing blue eyes. "That's why I'm just about deaf in one ear."

"I didn't know that," she said. "From diving?"

"Takes a toll after a while," he said.

Their drinks arrived, and Gina took a sip of her Coke while thinking through her next question. But he interrupted her train of thought.

"You really give this joint some class," he said.

She smiled. "Thank you," she said. "I like working here."

"A girl like you should be working at one of the high-end restaurants, though," he said.

Lay it on a little thicker, why don't you, she thought. "Thanks, but I feel at home in Shorty's."

"I'm not saying I want you to leave," Kenny said. "I'd miss seeing you here."

She smiled again, wondering how she could gracefully turn the conversation back to the subject that interested her most. She took another swallow of Coke.

"Does your company do any salvage work?" she asked.

He looked surprised by the sudden return to the previous topic, but shook his head. "No," he said. "Plenty others around here for that."

She toyed with the straw in her drink. "I'm very interested in salvaging the Fresnel lens from the Kiss River lighthouse," she said.

"Oh, yeah. Clay said you're a big fan of that lighthouse."

She nodded. "I am. And I'd like to get that lens on dry land and see it displayed somewhere."

"It's probably in so many pieces you could never find them all," he said.

"Well, then I'd like to see all the pieces displayed," she nearly snapped. *Settle down,* she told herself. *Slow and easy.*

"Won't work," he said.

"Why not?"

"They tried years ago but there were these protestors and such, who—"

"I know all about that," she said. "But as you pointed out, that was years ago. Maybe things would be different now."

"I doubt it."

"Well, let's pretend, just for the sake of argument, that things *are* different now. Hypothetically. What would it take to get the lens up? I mean…the mechanics of it. Do you know?"

"Sure, I know," he said. "First off, you'd have to find it. Or the pieces of it."

"I was wondering if a plane might be able to spot it."

"Possibly," he said. "Depending on, one, if any of the pieces are big enough to be seen from the air, and two, how deep the water is where it's at, and three, how clear the water is the day the plane is looking."

"Okay," she said. "Let's say all the conditions are right. And the plane finds it. Then how would the lens—or the pieces of the lens—be raised?"

"How much did that lens weigh, do you know?"

"Six thousand pounds," she said.

He nodded, thinking. "Well, you'd have to blow away the sand from around the pieces, then pass lifting slings underneath them and pull them up with a crane attached to a barge or a dragger."

"What's a dragger?" she asked.

"Fishing boat."

"Would the whole thing be a huge operation?" she asked.

"Not huge at all," he said. "I watched them raise a two-hundred-and-fifty-ton tug a couple years ago, south of here. A few pieces of glass would be a snap."

"Do you know anybody who'd be willing to fly over the area to see if they can spot the lens?"

Kenny grinned at her. "Do you ever talk about anything else?" he asked.

She shook her head with a smile. "Apparently not," she said.

"Well, I can't say Clay didn't warn me." Kenny took a long pull on his beer. "Clay and I have a buddy who flies tourists up and down the coast," he said. "I could talk to him. See what he'd charge to do the job for you. But, as I said, the conditions would have to be right for him to be able to see anything."

She tried not to let her excitement show. "I'd really appreciate that, Kenny," she said. "And thanks so much for the information. I've wondered how this could be done, and you had all the answers."

"Listen," he said. "Would you like to see a movie tonight? Or this weekend? Or ever?" He grinned his teddy-bear grin at her again.

She shook her head, the weight of her guilt on her shoulders. "Kenny," she said. "I'm sorry. I'm not interested in dating anyone. And I'd certainly understand if that changes your willingness to talk to your pilot friend."

"Do you have a boyfriend or something?" he asked. "You know, back in Washington or wherever you're from?"

"No." She shook her head again. "I'm just not into men these days."

His eyes widened. *"Oh,"* he said, and it took her a minute to understand his reaction.

She laughed. "No, that's not it," she said. "I'm not into women either. I just need some…time off from dating and… all of that. Haven't you ever taken time off from it?"

He shook his head with a laugh. "Not intentionally," he said.

"Well, I'm trying to be honest with you. And I understand if that means you might not want to help—"

"I'll talk to my buddy the pilot," he said. "No obligation."

Fiction was shelved in a small room at the side of the library, and when she stepped through the doorway, she was instantly surrounded by color. It was like being at the keeper's house. Stained glass hung in every window. Ignoring the books, she walked around the perimeter of the room, studying the panels. The stained glass was similar to Lacey's in its exquisite craftsmanship, but there were subtle differences she couldn't quite put her finger on. There were many panels of ethereal-looking women in long gowns that swirled around their legs. Simply stunning. It wasn't until she came to the last window that she noticed the small plaque on the wall: "Stained glass donated by Annie Chase O'Neill." Clay and Lacey's mother. What a talent. She shook her head, feeling sadness over the loss of a woman she had never known. How wonderful that Lacey had carried on her work with glass.

It was another minute before she remembered her reason for being in the room. She turned to the stacks, her gaze wandering over the spines. *H Is for Homicide*. She reached for the book, but stopped her hand in midair as she watched her skin turn blue and green and purple in the light from the window. She held her hand there, mesmerized, until another patron walked past her, looking at her as if she was quite odd. Smiling to herself, Gina lifted the book from the shelf.

Chapter Twenty-Four

"SO," CLAY SAID AS HE WALKED DOWN THE supermarket aisle next to Gina, "what do we need for this Indian feast?" He couldn't recall ever grocery shopping with Terri, and that struck him as both strange and sad. He was enjoying the sense of domesticity with Gina.

"Probably many things we can't find here," Gina said, stopping in front of the spices. She turned her head from side to side, surveying the possibilities, her hair shining in the overhead lights. "I'll just have to do my best."

"Well, since you're the only one of us who's ever eaten Indian food, you can fake it. We won't know the difference."

She reached for a jar of turmeric and put it in the shopping cart, then studied the rows of spices again. "These are so expensive," she said.

"Don't worry about that."

She glanced at him. "I'm not even paying for my share of the utilities, Clay. I win money and I lose it. You and Lacey—"

"You're cooking dinner for us." He touched her arm,

something he was aware he did often. "You've cooked dinner a few times already. More than we've cooked for you, that's for sure. So get what you need and don't worry about the price, okay?"

She shrugged and reached for another jar. "If you say so," she said. "Thank you."

He liked this side of her. Seeing her concentrate on something altogether different than the Fresnel lens was refreshing. For once, she didn't have the gloomy, desperate, "I need to raise the lens from the bottom of the ocean" look about her. "That girl has a one-track mind," Henry had said to Clay a couple of days ago on their drive home from Shorty's, and Clay knew he was right.

"I think this will do it," she said, putting another jar in the cart. She took a step back from the spices to scan the other products in the aisle. She was wearing a T-shirt he had not seen her in before, a royal-blue V-neck that gently hugged her breasts and made it hard for him to tear his eyes away from her. "Now we need some basmati rice and some chicken," she said.

"Three aisles down for the rice," he said, unsure if she would be able to find "basmati" rice there or not. He was not certain how it differed from the usual variety.

Clay pushed the cart as they walked toward the end of the aisle.

"Are you diving with Kenny this weekend?" she asked. The question sounded odd and out of the blue, but he supposed she was just making conversation.

"I hope so," he said. "We want to dive a U-boat that sunk off Nag's Head during the war."

"The *U-85*," Gina said, and he looked at her, amazed.

"How'd you know that?" he asked.

She smiled. "I told you. I'm an old history buff. I'm surprised you haven't dived it yet."

"I have. But not in a couple of years."

For a moment, she didn't speak. Then she said, "Maybe one of these days you could dive near the lighthouse and see if you could find the lens."

So much for his assumption that the lens was not on her mind this afternoon. He shrugged. "Maybe," he said. "Have you ever dived? You could go with me."

"I don't know how," she said.

"I could teach you. The lens can't be that deep."

She hesitated. "I think I'd panic, but thanks for the offer." They turned the corner to walk past the dairy case. "I had a talk with Kenny today," she said.

He felt a stab of jealousy. "Oh, yeah?"

"He was telling me that you two have a pilot friend who might be able to spot the lens from the air."

"He probably means Dave Spears."

"Kenny's going to ask him if he'd do it and what it would cost."

Clay turned the cart into the aisle containing rice and pasta and beans. If he talked to Dave himself, the pilot would probably do it for free.

"He might not be able to see anything, you know," he cautioned her. "It depends on how—"

"On the weather and the clarity of the water, and how big the pieces are, et cetera, et cetera," she said, reaching for a bag of rice. The store had basmati rice after all. "But one thing is certain."

"What's that?" he asked.

"He won't see it if he doesn't look for it."

"And if he finds it, then what?" Clay asked her.

"Then, at least we'll—"

"Gina?" It was a woman's voice, coming from behind them, and he and Gina turned around.

The young woman was very tall, with strawberry-blond hair in a bun on the top of her head and a nasty-looking sunburn on her face. She pushed a loaded shopping cart, a toddler in the seat.

"It *is* you," the woman said. "I thought, God, that woman looks like Gina, but I figured you couldn't possibly be in North Carolina."

He felt Gina stiffen at his side, but she smiled. "Hi, Emily," she said. "What are you doing here?"

"A friend of my cousin's has a house in Ocean Sands," she said. "We decided to come out here for a couple of weeks and visit the relatives. And how about you? What are you doing on this side of the country?" She shifted her gaze from Gina to Clay. "And who's this?" she added.

"This is a friend of mine, Clay O'Neill," Gina said. "Clay, this is Emily Parks. She and I teach at the same school."

"Ah," Clay said. "Nice to meet you. Small world, huh?"

"Merissa's getting huge." Gina ran her hand over the child's blond curls. "Hi, sweetie," she cooed in a voice that he had certainly never heard her use before. "Do you remember me, honey?" The little girl sucked her fingers, staring wordlessly at Gina.

"How's the adoption going?" Emily said, and for a moment Clay thought he must have misunderstood her.

Gina smiled, but there was ice there, the smile little more than a frozen, upturned line on her face. "Moving along," she said, then looked at her watch. "And speaking of moving along, I'm the cook tonight, so Clay and I had better get going."

"I guess I won't see you in the fall, then," Emily said, "Since you'll be—"

"I don't know yet," Gina interrupted her quickly, almost rudely. "Just taking things one day at a time." She waved at her friend. "Have a great vacation, Emily," she called over her shoulder as she stepped in front of Clay to grab the cart.

She started pushing the cart away from Emily Parks at a brisk pace and he followed, perplexed.

"Where's the chicken?" Gina peered down the aisle toward the deli case. Her hands were shaking on the bar of the cart.

"Adoption?" he asked.

She didn't even look at him. "I'm sorry, Clay. I don't mean to be rude, but I just don't want to talk about it." There were tears welling up in her dark eyes. He reached toward her to touch her arm again, but this time he felt her muscles stiffen beneath his fingers.

"Would you mind getting the chicken?" she asked. "A whole one, cut up. I'll get in line at the checkout."

Dinner that night was both exotic and delicious, and afterward, he and Lacey and Henry were able to persuade Gina to play a little gin rummy with them, but he could tell she was anxious to get to the office and her e-mail. She had been very quiet in the car on the way home from the grocery store, and he hadn't known what questions to ask or what to say to draw her out. He wished again that he possessed those skills. He studied her face while they played cards at the kitchen table, wondering, what adoption? Why was she so damn secretive? If she was not hiding in her room by the time he returned from taking Henry home, he was going to do his best to find out.

Chapter Twenty-Five

GINA HAD FELT CLAY STARING AT HER THE ENTIRE evening. She'd been relieved when Henry had pleaded exhaustion and the card game came to an end, and relieved, too, that Clay was now driving him home and Lacey had gone out and she had the house to herself. She'd wanted to get to her e-mail to read the latest news from the support group. It had become her only source of information about the adoptions in Hyderabad.

At some point, Clay was going to ask her again what Emily had meant about the adoption. She would have to make something up. Her isolation, the result of being honest with no one, was beginning to be unbearable, though. She had never been very good at keeping things to herself, and although she had become a master of it recently, she hated the way it shut her off from other people. Yet she did not see that she had much choice in the matter.

Bumping into Emily Parks in the grocery store had been a shock. Who would have guessed that, three thousand miles from home, she would meet one of her fellow teachers? All the teachers knew about the adoption plans, of course, but none of them knew the obstacles she was facing in bringing Rani home. She had wisely managed to keep that quiet. Even the two women she considered her closest friends did not know the magnitude of her problem.

Tonight, she had an e-mail from Denise, another mother who was trying to get her child out of the orphanage where Rani was living. It was a personal e-mail, as Denise's usually were, sent directly to Gina rather than to the support group as a whole. She and Denise had a bond. Denise had been at the orphanage the same time as Gina, but had stayed behind when the problems arose. She had the financial means to remain in Hyderabad, making sure her child had enough to eat and was receiving decent care until she was able to get her out. In Denise's e-mail messages, she always wrote "until I get her out." It was never a question of "if," but "when." Gina thought the woman was fooling herself. Things were only getting worse with the adoption fiasco in Hyderabad. But she was glad Denise was not giving up; she was Gina's one empathetic, English-speaking link to Rani.

Along with her e-mail this evening, Denise had sent a new picture of Rani. Gina stared at the photograph on her monitor. Rani looked even tinier than she'd been when Gina had visited her, more than two months ago. She wasn't smiling, but she was looking into the camera, every one of her long, dark eyelashes visible, and she was wearing one of the little dresses Gina had taken with her to the orphanage. She was still too tiny for the dress. A little doll of a child. An adorable waif.

Gina needed a print of the picture, something she could carry with her all the time. She checked to make sure there was paper in the printer, then clicked on the print command.

The printer had just started to produce the colored

photograph when she heard footsteps in the hallway outside the office. *Damn*. Clay was back from taking Henry home already. Poor timing. The printer was so slow.

Clay knocked on the open door, and she answered without turning around to look at him.

"That was a fast trip," she said, keeping her voice light.

Sasha trotted into the room and rested his heavy, dark head on her knee.

"Henry just wanted to go in and go to bed," Clay said. "He didn't need me to hang around."

She glanced over her shoulder at him. His gaze was on the monitor and the picture of Rani. She said nothing as the printer spit a duplicate of the photograph onto the desk.

Clay moved the chair from the drafting table and set it down next to her desk chair.

"Talk to me, Gina," he said, sitting down. "Who is this little girl?"

Gina touched the monitor lightly with her fingertips, but she hesitated only a minute. "This is Rani," she said. "She's my daughter. She's the child I'm in the process of adopting."

For a moment, Clay didn't speak. "You're adopting as a single parent?" he asked finally.

She nodded. "I wanted a child," she said. "I want *this* child."

"Where is she now?" he asked.

Gina leaned back in her chair but kept her eyes on the screen. It was easier to talk about this if she didn't have to look at him. She did not want to start crying again, as she had in the grocery store.

"She's in an orphanage in India," she said. "I went with one of my girlfriends to an orientation on foreign adoptions. She and her husband were planning to adopt, and he couldn't go that night, so I went with her." The meeting had been held in a church, and she remembered the photographs on the bulletin board, as well as the videos from the various orphanages. There had been no video of the orphanage Rani was in. Just one small picture, but that had been enough.

"There were several other single women there who were seriously considering adoption, and it started me thinking, 'I could do this.'" Gina nodded, remembering that epiphany. "And there were pictures of children." She felt herself smile. "There was a picture of the most beautiful baby I'd ever seen. All eyes. She was only two months old in the photograph. I fell instantly in love." She glanced at him. He was studying her intently, but she doubted he could possibly understand the depth of her feelings for the child in the picture.

"I asked about her," she continued. "Most of the other children were older, and I wondered why this beautiful baby hadn't been spoken for. It turns out she was sick. She was born with a heart deformity. She wasn't expected to live two years if she didn't have prompt surgery and treatment. So, of course, no one wanted her. But I did."

"You felt some kind of connection to her?" he asked.

She nodded. "On a lot of levels." She turned to him, and felt touched by how attentively he was looking at her. "I was born with heart problems myself," she said. "I had surgery when I was an infant and have never had a problem since. And…my mother had just died, right before I saw Rani's picture. Just a couple of weeks before. And I had no other family. But the real sign to me was that the baby's name was Rani, R-A-N-I, and my mother's name was Ronnie, R-O-N-N-I-E. Spelled differently, but pronounced the same. It seemed like it was meant to be."

Clay nodded. "I can understand that," he said. "So—" he looked back at the monitor again "—how old is she now? When do you get her?"

Gina wasn't sure how much to tell him, and she was surprised that what she had told him so far had been the truth. "It's a long process to adopt a child from India," she said. "First of all, only certain children can be released for foreign adoptions. They're the ones who have special medical needs, for the most part. Rani fit that bill without any problem, but she still needed to be formally evaluated. Then I had to go through a home study, which terrified me, because I'm single and I rent a town house. I don't own any property. But I passed. Then they had to check my finances, which was also scary. My divorce didn't leave me in the best of shape financially. But I guess they figured a teacher has job security these days. So, my dossier was okayed, and a couple of months ago, Rani was cleared by the agency for me to adopt her."

"Will you go to India to get her?" Clay asked.

"I already did, actually." She smiled weakly at him. "This is the hard part," she said. "I went to India in April to pick her up. There was one more step to go through, and that was to get a court order to release her to me. That shouldn't have been any problem at all. But while I was waiting for the hearing, the Indian government suddenly cracked down on all the orphanages in the area, because there were reports of black-market selling of children."

"Was that really happening?"

She nodded. "Yes. In some less scrupulous agencies, babies were being bought from poor parents or because they were girls, who were seen as more of a liability than an asset. I heard of cases where the Indian parents were paid about twenty dollars for their baby girl, while the adoptive family paid forty thousand. I'm not certain that the orphanage Rani is in is one of the good ones, frankly. I'd been told they were licensed, but who knows? And even if it was licensed, it didn't matter. All the orphanages had to go through a new licens-ing procedure before any of the children could be released."

"But your…Rani…needed urgent medical care," Clay in-sisted, and she loved the indignation in his voice.

She nodded. "You're thinking far too logically," she said with a rueful smile. "It's just not working that way. All adop-tions were frozen, regardless of the needs of the child. And I honestly understand that they had to do that to protect the majority of the children. But you're right that Rani was a special case. She needed surgery. I needed to get her home to Washington and onto my insurance policy so I could have that done for her. Even though the older Rani gets, the more risk there is that…" Gina shook her head, not wanting to finish the sentence. She looked at him. "She's sixteen months old and she only weighs thirteen pounds."

"Sixteen months!" Clay looked at the picture. "I don't know much about babies, but I would have said she was a lot younger than that."

Gina felt the tears she'd been fighting burn her eyes. "She's severely malnourished. When I was there, I brought food with me, because there just isn't enough for all those children, and her body doesn't seem to use it properly. I wanted to stay there with her until I could get her out, but I was out of money and had to get back to my job. I would go there now just to be with her and make sure she's all right, but I can't afford it. And they won't let her go. There's nothing I can do but wait and pray she holds on until she's released to me."

"Is the agency trying to get licensed?" Clay asked.

Gina sighed. It was such a complicated issue, so hard to explain. "Yes, but I'm not sure it will succeed. And that's not the only problem now," she said. She lifted the picture from the desk and stared at the little girl. "Since the whole adoption situation came to light in India, there's been a huge backlash against foreigners adopting Indian babies," she said. Then she looked at him. "For example, they're holding up the adoptions of the children who were going to couples who haven't been married long enough, in the opinion of one judge or another," she said. "So you can imagine how anxious they are to place a child with a single woman."

"Have you hired a lawyer?" he asked.

"Several. But it's useless." And she had no more money to pay a lawyer.

"What will you do now?"

"Wait and worry," she said. "That's all I can do." She had to look away from him then. She couldn't lie right to his face. "It's looking grim, though. Terrible things are happening."

"Like what?"

"I'm part of an Internet group of parents waiting for children from India. One couple has been told their child is gone. Just disappeared. They don't know if she died or was sold or moved or what. There's no record of her anywhere. Another couple went to stay in India until their daughter was released, and they found another child was in her place. They'd met their daughter before, so they knew what she looked like and acted like. This little girl was older, scrawnier and lighter-skinned. But the orphanage kept insisting it was the same child."

"Was there anything they could do?"

She shook her head. "They went to other orphanages searching for her, but they couldn't find her. You know…" She tipped her head back, looking blankly at the ceiling. "I think it's hard for people who haven't gone through this to understand how attached you can get to these children you don't really know. But I think it's like being pregnant. You start dreaming about that child, getting ready for her."

"And you've *met* Rani," Clay said. "Of course you're attached to her."

"I was even before I met her," she said. "But yes, once I held her in my arms…she came right to me. Maybe she goes to everyone, I don't know. But she just climbed right into my arms like she knew she belonged there."

"I'm sorry, Gina."

"The woman who took this picture of Rani has been in India for the past couple of months, so she can keep an eye on her little girl and bring food for her and play with her and make sure she's getting cared for while waiting for her to be released. But it could be months. It could be years. It could be never. That's the real fear we all have. Here's the e-mail I just got from her."

Gina used the mouse to click back to Denise's e-mail. "'I know you want the truth about how Rani is doing, dear Gina,'" she read from the screen in front of her. "'It's hard to tell you, but I would also want to know if I were in your position. She seems more isolated than when you were here. I always try to include her when I play with Sunil and the other children, but Rani has trouble keeping up with them because of her shortness of breath. I've advocated on your behalf to get her medical treatment, but you know how it is here. She is one of so many special-needs children. They can't possibly get as much help as they need.'"

Gina let out a sob. She lowered her head to her hands, and felt Clay's palm resting against her back, while Sasha prodded her temple with his nose. "I'd do anything to get her out of there," she said, lifting her head again. "Anything! I'd sell my soul. I'd sleep with the devil if it would make a difference. I'd…" Her voice trailed off, and Clay pulled a tissue from the box on the desk and pressed it into her hand.

"You know what amazes me?" he asked.

She shook her head, wiping the tears from her cheeks with the tissue.

"That you can spend even a second thinking about the Fresnel lens when you've got all of this going on in your life."

There wasn't a moment she didn't think of that lens. "Look at yourself," she said. "You work all hours of the day. Lacey said you didn't used to be that way. That it's your way of dealing with grief over your wife."

He sat back in his chair, his face suddenly unreadable, and she knew that she'd trod too hard on a place too tender. His obvious grief over the loss of his wife touched her. Their marriage must have been very strong.

"I'm sorry," she said.

"No, you're right." He shook his head. "I guess we're both escaping." He sighed, standing up. "If there's anything I can do to help, Gina, please let me know."

She looked up at him, at eyes that mirrored the sadness in her own.

"It helped just to be able to tell you," she said. And she meant it.

Chapter Twenty-Six

Tuesday, April 14, 1942

I AM SO MAD AND EMBARRASSED AND JUST PLAIN aggravated that I can hardly write this.

First, let me explain about what happened last night. I was on the beach with Sandy when we heard these BOOMS. By now, we surely know what that sound means. Another one of our ships had been attacked. But we couldn't see any light from a fire or anything, so we figured it had happened pretty far away. It wasn't until this morning that I learned what it was: one of our ships called the *Roper* sunk a U-boat! The *U-85*. Daddy was hip-hooraying over that news. Finally, we're fighting back. I don't feel nearly so scared now, because I'm sure this is just the start of the turning tide.

So I was by the lighthouse after school, raking up the twigs and leaves left over from winter, when Dennis Kittering came limping along. The school in High Point where he teaches is on a spring vacation, so he will be camping on the beach all week. He was whistling that "Perfidia" song.

"What's that song mean?" I asked him.

"What song?" He looked confused.

"That one you're whistling. 'Perfidia.'"

"I don't really know the words," he told me. "Just the tune."

"But what does Perfidia mean?" I asked him. "Is it a girl's name?"

"Ah." He smiled at me then, this smile he uses sometimes when I know he's feeling like he's better than me. "You have a dictionary, Bess. You look it up."

That annoyed me right there. We were off to our usual bad start. (I did look it up when I got in the house, though. It means "deliberate breach of faith or trust." I still don't know what that has to do with the song, though.)

Anyhow, then Dennis said, "It's such a beautiful day. How about we go up to the top of the lighthouse and look at the view?"

I'd taken him up last year when I first met him and he hadn't been up since, and while I felt sorry for him about that, I didn't want to take him up today. The truth is, I don't feel all that trusting of men these days, and I was not about to climb through that closed-up lighthouse with him. I said if he wanted to go up, he could go alone. He had my permission. But that obviously wasn't what he wanted. He said what he really wanted was to talk to me, that he was concerned about me. I immediately felt embarrassed, as I do anytime I think someone knows what happened to me in my bedroom with the German. People are always telling me they're sorry my family had to go through that ordeal, and I can't look them in the eye, wondering exactly how much they know. I said I didn't really have time to talk, but he somehow talked me into sitting on the bench near the lighthouse with him, and I got ready to accept his sympathy or whatever it was he was going to offer me. I did *not* expect him to say what he did, though.

"I'm aware that you're meeting a sandpounder on the beach at night," he said.

I was horrified!

"What makes you think that?" I asked him.

"I've seen you," he said. "Remember, I camp on the beach."

Thoughts were flying through my head. There were no lights on the beach now. Dennis could have been anywhere. He could have been a few feet from Sandy and me and we never would have known it. That thought made my skin crawl!

"The patroller and I are just friends," I said.

Dennis shook his head. "I believe you are far more than that," he said. "And I'm sure that since you're out there at all hours of the night, your parents have no idea."

I stood up then, feeling really angry and also scared that he planned to tell my parents what he knew. I couldn't bear the thought.

"You are nothing but a meddlesome snoop!" I said.

He grabbed my wrist, not hard, but tight enough to keep me from leaving.

"Don't run off," he said. "I'm not going to tell your parents, and I don't mean to embarrass you. I'm talking about this because I care about you. I'm worried about you. That's all. You're getting in over your head with an older man who—"

"He's younger than you," I said.

"He's what? Eighteen? Nineteen?"

"None of your business," I said.

"Boys that age are out for one thing, Bess," he said.

I figured he knew that because that's what *he'd* been out for at eighteen or nineteen.

"He's not like other boys," I said.

"Look, you're pretty and smart and I just worry that you could get hurt," he said. "I'd like you to seriously consider moving to High Point. You could live with me and my sister. I've already talked to her about it. I told her how smart you are, how your potential is getting wasted here and all. Do you think your parents would let you if I talked to them about how good it would be for you?"

I couldn't believe my ears. "You're crazy!" I told him.

"No funny business," he said. "As I said, I would talk to your parents about it. My sister and I have a little house, but it's nice. It belonged to my parents. You could attend a great Catholic school in our neighborhood. Your parents have to know you're getting a substandard education here."

"I've probably read more books than you have," I said.

He smiled at that. "Maybe you have," he said. "And that's exactly my point. You should be going to school somewhere where that brain of yours is appreciated. Where you can end up doing something more with your life than whatever sort of job a woman can get around here. Which isn't much, is it?"

He was talking about something that has truly been on my mind lately. I love it here. It's my home. As Daddy says, I have salt water in my veins. But not much is expected of the women here. My dream is that someday, when I'm older and when the war is over, I can move to Vermont with Sandy and go to college there and become a teacher.

"My parents would never let me leave here," I said.

"Are you sure about that?" Dennis asked me. "I know what happened at your house a few days ago."

I don't blush often, but I know my cheeks turned bright pink when he said that.

"Maybe a week ago, your parents wouldn't have given your safety here another thought. But now, I'm sure they'd love knowing that you were away from here, with all that's going on."

"It's getting better here now," I said. "That ship, the *Roper,* sunk a U-boat last night."

"We sunk it twice." Dennis had that look on his face I've learned means he's angry about something.

"What do you mean?" I asked.

"We sunk it, and all the men from the U-boat were in the water, begging to be picked up by the *Roper.* Instead of saving those men, the *Roper* bombed the damn submarine again. It was already sunk. All they did was kill a bunch of men begging for their lives in the ocean."

I honestly did not know that, but I couldn't get worked up about it like he was.

"Those Germans would've killed our men if they'd had the chance," I said.

"It wasn't honorable," Dennis said. "You don't kill a drowning man, even if he is the enemy."

I didn't want to talk about that anymore. I stood up.

"Well, back to our other subject," I said. "I'm not leaving Kiss River. And don't you dare say a word to my parents about the sandpounder, Dennis," I said. "Swear to me you won't mention anything about that to them."

"I wouldn't do that," he said. "But as an adult in your life, I need to do what I can to keep you safe. That's why I'm talking to you rather than to them. You're smart. *Act* smart."

I walked away from him, just bristling all over with anger, but knowing I'd better stay on Dennis's good side, anyhow. I can't take the chance that he'll tell Mama and Daddy what he knows. He made me feel about ten years old. I *will* act smarter though. I'll be far more careful that Dennis doesn't see me with Sandy from now on.

Chapter Twenty-Seven

"GINA?"

She thought she was dreaming. The voice came from far away. But then she heard the faint knocking sound and opened her eyes. Through her bedroom window, she saw the lighthouse, the white brick almost blinding in the early-morning sun, and she could hear the soft rhythmic lapping of a calm ocean.

The knocking came again. "Gina?" It was Clay, outside her door.

She looked at the clock radio. Six-thirty in the morning on her day off.

Sitting up, she brushed her hair back from her face. "Yes?" she answered.

"You need to get up, Gina," Clay said. He sounded as though his mouth was right against her door. "I spoke to my friend, Dave, after you and I talked last night. You know, the pilot. He offered—"

"You can come in," she said, suddenly wide-awake. She was still in her nighttime T-shirt, sitting up with the sheet to her waist, her hair a mess, but she didn't care. She wanted to hear what the pilot had said.

Clay opened the door. He kept one hand on the knob, looking a bit uncomfortable about being in her room. "He offered to fly us over Kiss River," he said.

"We can go *with* him?" She hadn't expected that. She'd thought the pilot would make his own search, if he was willing to do it at all. The thought of being in the plane with him was both exciting and unnerving. She was not a great flier.

"Right," Clay said. "First he said he could take us out tomorrow, but he called just a few minutes ago and said we should go now, that the conditions are perfect. You interested?"

"Absolutely!" she said, waving him out of her room so she could get up. "I'll be ready in two minutes."

"Bring a sweater," Clay said as he closed the door. "And sunglasses."

She tore off the old T-shirt and pulled on her shorts and a tank top. In the bathroom, she brushed her teeth and ran a comb ineffectively through her tangled hair. Grabbing a sweater, she then raced down the stairs to find Clay, Lacey and Sasha in the kitchen.

Clay laughed when she appeared in the doorway.

"Do I look that bad?" she said, trying to smooth her hair.

"I just never saw anybody move quite so fast," Clay said.

"Do you two want something to eat before you go?" Lacey had picked blueberries and was trying to wipe the stain from her fingers with a damp paper towel.

"No time," Clay said. "Dave said it's perfect right now. The water's really clear."

"Let's go, then." Gina headed for the door, but Lacey caught her arm.

"Clay told me about the little girl you're adopting," she said, her wide blue eyes full of genuine sympathy. "I'm so sorry."

"Thank you," Gina said.

"Come on," Clay was already out the door, and Gina nodded to Lacey.

"We can talk more about it later," she said.

The morning was warm and bright, the air unusually dry and filled with the scent of salt water and pine trees. In the parking lot, they climbed into Clay's Jeep.

"I hope you don't mind that I told Lacey," he said as she buckled her seat belt.

"Not at all," Gina answered. It had struck her as odd that it had been Clay she'd confided in instead of Lacey, but her talk with him the night before had left her feeling cleansed in a way, and less alone. She had no regrets.

Clay turned the Jeep around in the parking lot and headed down the narrow gravel lane toward the chain. Gina had her own key for the chain now, and she got out of the Jeep to unlock it and pull it aside.

"You can leave it unlocked," Clay called to her through his open window. "Lacey will be going to work soon."

In her two weeks in the Outer Banks, she had not seen a morning so sparkling clear. Once they reached the main road, she could see the individual needles of the loblolly pines crisply silhouetted against the vivid blue sky, and beams of sunlight pierced the forest.

"Do you like to fly?" Clay asked her as they drove south.

"I hate it," she said with a laugh. "And I don't like small planes. They make me feel claustrophobic."

"Uh," Clay laughed, "you shouldn't have that problem on this plane."

"Why not? Is it big?"

"You'll see."

She suddenly remembered there would be a fee for this flight. "I forgot to ask you how much this will cost," she said.

"Dave owes me a favor," Clay said.

She should have known Clay wouldn't let her pay.

"Thank you so much," she said.

He looked different this morning. The sunlight cut right through the pale blue of his eyes, made them look like jewels beneath his dark lashes and heavy eyebrows. His tanned skin was smooth over his high cheekbones and the sharp line of his jaw. She knew he didn't really look any different than he did any other day. The difference was in *her,* in how she was looking at him. She could not forget the way he had listened to her the night before, attentively and with compassion. The way he'd rested his hand on her back while she cried. And the way he had called his friend to arrange this flight of fancy for her. She glanced at him again. This morning, Clay was beautiful.

There was no airport, and that was Gina's first disconcerting surprise.

"It's just an airstrip," Clay said as he pulled into the small parking lot in Kill Devil Hills, near the memorial to the Wright brothers.

Her second surprise was the plane.

"Hey, Clay!" A skinny man with wind-tossed red hair walked across the tarmac toward them as they got out of the Jeep. A distance behind him stood a very small, bright-red airplane.

"Hi, Dave." Clay shook the man's hand. "This is Gina."

Dave grinned at her. "So you're the one who wants to find the old lens, huh?" He was so thin that she thought she could knock him over with the touch of a fingertip, and his blue polo shirt and khaki slacks looked too large for him. His voice was a deep surprise, though, and he spoke with that thick accent she'd come to recognize as the mark of an Outer Banks native.

She nodded at him, but her eyes were on the toylike plane. "There's no roof on that thing," she said.

Dave and Clay both laughed. "Some people would give their eyeteeth to fly in a Waco biplane," Dave said.

"Did it belong to the Wright brothers?" Gina tried to joke.

"I told you you wouldn't get that closed-in feeling in it," Clay said.

She rolled her eyes at him. "How old is it?" she asked.

"It's a replica," Clay reassured her. "It's only...what, Dave? Fifteen years old?"

"About that," Dave said.

"And where's the runway?" Gina asked.

"That's the airstrip," Dave said, motioning toward the narrow strip of macadam. She hadn't really understood what Clay had meant by "airstrip," and she cringed at the sight of it.

"Don't worry," Dave said. "It's plenty long enough for us."

"You don't have to go with us," Clay said. He sounded concerned about her reaction to the plane and the airstrip. "I can look for the lens for you."

"No," she said, getting a grip on her fears. "I'm going, too." She marched ahead of them toward the plane.

Dave reached into the front seat and lifted out two leather helmets and some other paraphernalia. "Well, I have to tell you," he said, handing one of the helmets to Gina, the other to Clay. "In all the times I've flown above Kiss River, I've never seen the lens. I *have* seen a bunch of stuff down there. Parts of the lighthouse, bricks and such, but never the lens. The water's right clear today, though, so we'll give it a shot."

"We should take a buoy with us in case we do find it," Clay said as he buckled the helmet beneath his chin.

"Already have one," Dave said. He turned to Gina. "You need some help with that?"

Her fingers shook as she tried to buckle the chin strap of the helmet. "I've got it," she said. "Listen, you won't do any loop-de-loops or anything, will you?" The little red plane looked like the type that might be used for aerobatics.

"Not if you don't want me to," Dave said.

"I don't. Please."

"I will do a hard bank, though, over the Kiss River area," he said, "so's you can get a good look at the water."

"You mean you'll tilt the plane?" she asked.

"That's right. So don't be scared when I do it. It's going to be fine, and we won't flip over or anything."

Clay was holding two sets of goggles in his hands. He handed one of them to Gina, and she pulled them down over the helmet and her sunglasses.

"And finally—" Dave handed her a large headset "—we can communicate through this intercom." He helped her fit the headset over her ears and arranged the microphone near her mouth. Until that moment, it hadn't occurred to her that they would not easily be able to communicate with one another in the air. In a little open plane like this one, it was sure to be noisy.

Clay opened the door to the front compartment. "I'll get in first," he said. "That way you'll have a better view of the coastline as we're flying north."

"Doesn't Dave fly up front?" She made no move toward the compartment.

Clay shook his head. "Nope. We do." He climbed into the passenger seat, then held out his hand to help her up. She settled into the admittedly comfortable leather seat and fastened her seat belt. A loud rush of static suddenly filled her headset. After a moment, there was a short pause in the static and she could hear Dave's voice.

"You two all buckled in up there?" he asked.

Clay raised his thumb in the air, and she did the same.

Dave taxied the plane to one end of the airstrip. The propeller began to spin right in front of Gina's face and the engine roared in her ears. Around their heads was a web of bars and wires that were probably very important but seemed terribly flimsy, and they began to vibrate from the buzz of the engine. Gina locked her damp hands together in her lap and drew in a long, shaky breath as the plane inched forward. No turning back now.

Dave gave the plane more power, and Gina felt her body forced back against her seat as they sped down the airstrip. It was nearly impossible to take in a breath, her lungs were so compressed, and she shut her eyes and swallowed hard. She knew the moment they were in the air, because her stomach dropped down to her feet.

"Open your eyes, Gina." Clay's voice came to her through the headset.

She forced her eyes open, and saw blue sky both above and below her as Dave turned the plane in the direction of the northern Outer Banks. The roar of the wind was deafening despite the headset, and the web of wires shook so violently she was certain they would snap from their bearings at any moment. Whether she survived this flight or not, it was going to be her last in a small plane.

Clay touched the back of her hand, rigid in her lap. "You all right?" he shouted into his microphone.

She nodded. Oh, what a wonderful liar she'd become.

He pointed toward the shoreline, and she looked down. The early-morning sun turned the sand into a broad strand of gold; the waves were white-tipped as they reached for shore. *It's beautiful,* she told herself. *Look at how beautiful it is.*

And it was. No one spoke, and the more she concentrated on the beauty below them, the more she felt herself relax. She began to recognize the areas they were flying over. There were the small cottages of Kitty Hawk and the beaches dotted with shell seekers and fishermen. She spotted the flat-roofed houses in Southern Shores. Then Duck came into view, followed by the long expanse of green that marked the wildlife reserve. Finally, she saw the white tower and the Kiss River promontory in the distance. The jagged line of bricks where the top of the lighthouse had been lopped off struck her anew from this height. The tower looked so fragile, like a small, broken toy, while the ocean was so expansive and powerful, that for the first time, she truly understood how the bricks and mortar—and the fragile glass lens—could have succumbed to the force of the sea.

"I'm dropping down a bit lower now," Dave said through the static as they neared the lighthouse.

Good. She wanted to go lower. She shifted her focus from the lighthouse to the sea. The water was calm and remarkably clear. The day she had walked through it in search of the lens, she had barely been able to see her hands beneath the surface. Today, though, the water was a bluish green, so translucent she could make out the ridges in the sand near the shore.

"Look at all that stuff!" Clay said, pointing, and she saw what he was talking about. There was a straight broad line of debris on the ocean bottom, as though the wind and sea had grabbed the top of the lighthouse and pulled it straight out into the ocean, dropping bits of it along the way. They were quickly past the line of debris, though, and Gina strained her neck to see behind her.

"I'm turning around," Dave said. "I'll come at it from the other side."

The plane tipped dramatically to the left, but Gina barely noticed. She wished that Dave could drop even closer to the water.

"Look there!" Clay suddenly called into his microphone.

Dave banked hard again, and looking nearly straight down from the plane, Gina could clearly see what had caught Clay's attention. Beneath the surface of the ocean, something captured the sunlight and sent it splintering into the water in shards of light.

"That has to be it," she said, although it was impossible to make out the shape of the object. But something was there. Something that glittered beneath the calm surface of the water.

"I think you're right, Gina," Dave said, and she jumped when he suddenly tossed a red buoy and chain from the plane. She watched it fall to the water, not far from the object. And then they were past it again.

"Ready to go back?" Dave asked through the intercom.

"Right," Clay said, and Gina held her thumb high in the air. She had found her lens.

Chapter Twenty-Eight

CLAY LEANED AGAINST HIS JEEP IN THE KISS RIVER parking lot, waiting for Kenny to arrive. They were going to dive the lens this afternoon, or at least they were going to try to, and he'd left Sasha in the house so the dog wouldn't follow them into the water. The more he thought about it, the less sure he was that what they had seen from the plane had actually been the lens. The image from fifty feet up was still with him: a large, shapeless object made of or containing glass or some other light-bending material. It could be pieces of the windows from the lantern room. Even so, even if the object was not the lens, he was determined that he would find what remained of that giant glass beehive today.

He eyed the gray sky. Gina had said it was sweet of him and Kenny to wait until she got home from work before diving the lens, so that she could be there. It may have been sweet, but it had also been stupid. Conditions had been much better earlier in the day for this. Now, at three-thirty, the clouds hung low above Kiss River, and the water visibility would be lousy, at best.

Gina had looked perplexed at first when he told her he'd wait until she had finished her shift before making the dive. "Why are you doing all this for me?" she'd asked him. "Taking me up in the plane. Diving to find the lens. Why?"

He'd told her that she'd made him curious about the condition of the lens himself, but the real reason was simply that it made him feel good to get his mind off his own problems for a while. Gina's genuinely happy smile was rare and wonderful. He would do anything he could to see it. Since there was no way he could help her get her baby girl from the Indian orphanage, this seemed the closest he could come to making her happy.

Kenny arrived, and by the time they had unloaded the diving gear and walked over to the lighthouse, Gina and Lacey were sitting on the tower's concrete steps, waiting for their arrival.

"Two very white women," Kenny said under his breath as they walked.

He was right. Both women were wearing bathing suits he recognized as Lacey's, and neither of them looked as though they'd ever seen the sun. Lacey, with her fair, freckled skin, always had to be cautious about how much sun she got, but Gina had the look of a woman who simply didn't care that her legs were the color of skim milk. They were beautiful legs all the same, not as toned as his sister's, but long and slender and thoroughly distracting. She had on a red tank suit that Lacey hadn't worn in years, not since their little sister told her it made her look like a giant bottle of ketchup because of her red hair. Lacey's suit today was green, and her hair was up in a long ponytail.

"Hey, girls," Kenny said as he and Clay reached the water churning around the base of the lighthouse.

"Hey, guys," Lacey said in return. "The ocean looks cloudy today. Are you going to be able to see anything?"

Clay climbed the stairs to get out of the water, setting his dive bag and tank in the open doorway leading into the tiled foyer. "We're sure going to try," he said.

"You two are looking mighty hot today," Kenny said, climbing the stairs to the foyer himself.

"It's not that bad," Gina said. "There's a nice breeze."

Clay grinned to himself at her intentional misunderstanding of Kenny's meaning.

Gina turned on the top step to watch Clay unzip his dive bag.

"Do you need a wet suit?" she asked. He and Kenny were wearing their bathing suits and T-shirts.

Clay nodded, pulling the light, short-sleeved suit from the bag. Gina watched as he unloaded his BCD and regulator and other paraphernalia. He raised his head to look at her. The red bathing suit dipped softly over her fair-skinned breasts.

"You two have sunscreen on, right?" he asked, shifting his gaze to his sister.

"Yes, Daddy," she said.

"I'll be happy to rub sunscreen on either of you," Kenny said, and Clay joined the women in rolling their eyes. He'd tried to fix Gina up with this bozo?

"Is that some kind of harness?" She pointed to the BCD, which was lying next to his bag on the top step.

"It's called a Buoyancy Compensation Device," he said. She watched while he put the BCD on his tank and attached the regulator. Then he reached into his dive bag again to extract an extra set of snorkeling gear and handed it to Gina.

"This is for you," he said. "Kenny's got a spare set for Lacey."

Lacey laughed at the look of surprise on Gina's face.

"What am I supposed to do with this?" Gina looked at the fins and mask and snorkel in her arms.

"You and I can watch from above," Lacey said.

"Though you may not be able to see anything today." Kenny handed Lacey her own set of fins.

"I have no idea how to use this thing." Gina held the snorkel in the air.

"Come on," Lacey said. "I'll teach you." She jumped from the side of the steps into knee-high water, her ponytail flying in the air. She looked like a little kid in a woman's body.

Gina hesitated, hugging the snorkeling gear to her chest.

"Go on," Clay said as he zipped up his wet suit. "You'll get the hang of it."

Gina stood up, descended the three steps and followed Lacey into the water.

Once Clay had hooked up the inflator hose to the BCD, he clipped the bright-yellow octopus to his vest. The octopus was used in case another diver was in trouble and needed to share his buddy's tank. But Clay had another plan for it today.

"If we find the lens," he said to Kenny, "I'd like Gina to be able to go down to see it."

Kenny looked up from his work on his own BCD. "She's never even used a snorkel before," he said.

"I know, but she really wants to see that thing. It might be her only chance."

Kenny hesitated a moment, then nodded. "All right. But let me be the one to take her down," he said, and Clay reluctantly agreed. He knew Kenny was making the suggestion not because he wanted to be close enough to Gina to share a tank of compressed air, but because he was the more experienced diver. It would be better if she was with him.

Clay moved to the bottom step of the tower and put on his

fins. Standing up, he let Kenny help him into his gear, then hooked the clasps together on the front of the BCD.

"Where's the buoy?" Kenny asked, looking past Clay to the ocean.

"Straight out and a little to the north," Clay said. He searched the water himself, but he couldn't see the buoy from where they stood.

Once they were backing into the water, though, he was able to spot the buoy over his shoulder. "Way out there." He pointed. "Must be about a hundred yards out."

"Man," Kenny shook his head. "Can't believe the storm whipped that thing way the hell out there."

"Well, the beach had a whole different configuration then," Clay said, letting the smooth surface of a wave pick him up and set him down on the sand again. "And if the lens is in pieces, as I suspect it is, it would've been easier for the waves to knock it around."

Once past the breakwater, he and Kenny lay on their backs and kicked out to where the women stood in chest-deep water, snorkels in their mouths.

"How's it going?" he asked as they neared them.

The women took out their mouthpieces, and he could see the look of accomplishment on Gina's face.

"It's fun," she said. Her eyes were hard to see behind the goggles, but she was smiling.

"Would you be comfortable in deep water, Gina?" He stood up.

"I can swim," she said. "But how deep are you talking about?"

"See the buoy out there?" He pointed toward it again and she turned to look at it. "I'm guessing it's about twenty feet deep, out that far."

"More or less," Kenny added.

"Gulp." Gina turned back to Clay, her smile sweet and sheepish.

"Get her one of the life vests from the back of my Jeep, Lace," he said.

"Good idea." Lacey caught the next wave and rode it into the beach.

"You won't be able to submerge with the vest on," he said to Gina, "but you'll feel a lot more secure while you're floating on the surface of the water."

"I haven't had a lot of experience with ocean swimming," she said, then added with a laugh, "None, in fact, except for that day I came out here looking for the lens. And there were barely any waves then."

"You know, that's been worrying me ever since you told me you did that," he said, feeling a little paternal. "Please don't do that again. Swim alone, I mean. It's dangerous, okay?"

She nodded. "Okay." Looking out toward the buoy again, she said, "What about sharks?"

He would have liked to reassure her that stumbling across a shark was an impossibility along this coastline, but a man had been killed by one just the previous summer, and there had been other sightings.

"Highly unlikely," Clay said.

"Except for the sand tiger sharks," Kenny added. "And they won't hurt you."

Lacey returned with the life vest and helped Gina put it on.

"We'll head out," Clay said. "You two have fun."

He and Kenny slipped beneath the surface of the water and began kicking in the direction of the buoy. Visibility was even worse than he'd thought, no better than six feet, and he tried to remember how close to the object Dave had managed to drop the buoy. Before he could replay the scene from the plane in his mind, though, he found himself face-to-face with a wall of algae and seaweed. He ran his hand over the wall and felt tiers of glass beneath his fingertips.

Kenny caught up to him, and Clay could see the awe in his friend's eyes behind the goggles. Turning on their dive lights, they moved back a few feet to get a good look at the object. It was enormous, dwarfing them. Somehow, even though he'd known its size and weight, he hadn't expected the lens to tower above him.

The lens was deep in the sand, perhaps four or five feet under, and resting at an angle so that the brass couplings cut across the glass prisms at a diagonal. He swam around the lens, touching it, wiping seaweed from the surface of the prisms until he could feel the smooth glass beneath his fingers. One panel of the lens was missing, but he seemed to recall that it had been missing even before the storm. The opening was large enough for him to swim into, and he was quickly cocooned inside the lens with a school of black-and-silver-striped spadefish. From what he could see—with the exception of the missing panel—the lens was entirely, incredibly, intact. He pictured the furious sea grabbing it from the lighthouse, tossing it on the waves as if it were a huge beach ball instead of three thousand pounds of glass, and dropping it to rest here, on this sandy bottom.

Kenny came into his field of vision. He had the underwater camera to his face and was snapping pictures. They would have something to show Gina.

Gina. He motioned to Kenny that he was ascending, then inflated his BCD and rose to the surface of the water. Kenny was quickly beside him, and they spotted Lacey and Gina treading water near the buoy.

"It's over here," Clay called to them, and the women swam toward him.

"You found it?" Gina asked once she'd reached him.

He nodded. "And it's in one piece, as far as I can tell. It's partially buried in the sand."

"It has a missing panel, though, right?" she asked.

"Just one," he said. "You want to see it?"

"How?" she asked.

"Kenny will take you down." He looked at his sister. "I can take you, Lace, if you like." Lacey had dived before, but she had never fallen in love with it, as he had.

She shook her head. "I'll stay up here with Gina's life vest," she said.

"But how would I breathe?" Gina asked.

Kenny unclipped the octopus from his BCD and showed her the regulator. "This is attached to my tank," he said.

Gina bit her lip, and Clay could see the war going on inside her.

"I want to," she said, "but I'm afraid I'll panic."

"You won't panic," Kenny said, moving close to her. "You'll hold on to my arm, and if you get the least bit scared, you just squeeze my arm and I'll bring you right back up, okay? It's not that deep."

"All right," she said. She took off the life vest and handed it to Lacey. Her teeth were chattering, but Clay thought it was more from nerves than from the cold. He would make sure she didn't stay down there long, no matter how much she loved it.

Kenny showed her how to use the regulator, and she put the mouthpiece in her mouth and practiced breathing for a minute or two, her hand wrapped around his wrist. She nodded when she felt ready, and in a moment, the three of them were under the water.

Gina did well. When they reached the lens, she let go of Kenny's arm to explore the glass with both hands, but Kenny was having none of that, and Clay was relieved when he took her hand and fastened it once more to his wrist. They ascended after a few minutes, Kenny calling for the ascent rather than Gina. Clay thought she could have stayed down there forever.

On the surface of the water, she was euphoric.

"How was it?" Lacey was now wearing the life vest, floating on the water as she waited for them.

"Incredible, Lacey!" Gina said as soon as the mouthpiece was out of her mouth. "Now I want to raise the light more than ever. It's in one piece! How can we let it just rot down there?"

"It won't rot," Kenny said. "It's glass."

"You know what I mean," Gina said. "It's the most beautiful thing I've ever seen."

Her wet hair was jet-black, and it was sleek and shimmering, the ends undulating above her shoulders in the water. The sun had turned her cheeks and forehead pink, and she could not seem to stop smiling.

It's not nearly as beautiful, Clay thought, *as the woman who wants it raised.*

Chapter Twenty-Nine

Saturday, April 18, 1942

I TOOK SOME GOODIES OVER TO THE COAST
Guard boys today. Sandy was there and he winked at me as I
was handing out the fudge I made this morning, but I knew
he wouldn't talk to me with everyone around. I talked to
Teddy Pearson and Ralph Salmon for a while, mostly about
Boston. They think I don't know anything because I haven't
ever lived in a big city. Jimmy Brown barely had a word to say
to me, as usual, but I don't care a bit about that these days. He
did take a piece of my fudge, though, and thanked me for it.

As I was leaving, Mr. Hewitt followed me outside. He asked
me how I was doing since that terrible night with the German
spies in our house, but I could tell he had something else on
his mind. Finally he told me, very quietly, looking over his
shoulder to make sure no one could hear him, that he needed
to talk to me about something serious. He would pick me up
along the Pole Road in an hour, he said, right at the entrance

to Kiss River. If anyone was there, he would drive right past me, and I should wait and he would return, but he would only pick me up when no one was around. No one must know we were meeting.

I could hardly speak as he said all this to me. I just kept nodding and nodding, wondering if he, like Dennis Kittering, knew about Sandy and me. If he did, I was going to be in a heap of trouble, but it would be even worse for Sandy. I went home, but didn't stop in the house before walking out to the road. I didn't want to have to explain to my parents where I was going.

Well, I don't think Mr. Hewitt knows a thing about Sandy and me. At least, that was not what he had on his mind. He picked me up on the Pole Road, which was, fortunately, deserted, and we drove north toward Corolla. Mr. Hewitt is someone I trust completely, so I did not feel afraid being with him. I just wished he'd get to his point, so that I could stop stewing. He was very quiet as he drove, though, looking around us as if he was afraid someone might see him with me. I decided I'd better keep quiet myself. Remember, right then, I didn't know if he was mad at me about Sandy or what. I had no idea what to say, anyway.

We drove all the way up the Pole Road, almost to Poyner's Hill, and he pulled the jeep off onto a little rutted trail leading into the woods, where it probably couldn't have been seen by anyone on the road. My heart started beating hard then, and I began to wonder if maybe Mr. Hewitt *was* planning to hurt me after all. Or, at the very least, yell his head off at me. But he just turned to me and smiled.

"You must be wondering what on earth I brought you out here for," he said.

I nodded, waiting for him to say something about Sandy.

"This is extremely serious business," he said, "and I need

your promise that whatever we talk about right now will be kept completely confidential. Completely secret," he added as if he was afraid I might not know what he meant by confidential.

I was confused, but I was pretty sure this wouldn't be about Sandy and me, so I relaxed a bit. "I won't breathe a word," I said. I crossed my heart and then felt stupid. That seemed like a little-girl thing to do.

"The German who was killed by the boar did not die right away," Mr. Hewitt said.

I nodded again. "I know that."

"But you think he stayed unconscious, don't you?" he asked.

"Didn't he?" That's what everybody had said. That he'd hit his head on a rock or something and never woke up.

Mr. Hewitt shook his head. "No, but it's important that people keep thinking that he did. Okay?"

Why, oh why, I kept wondering, was he telling me something no one else was supposed to know?????

"You mean, he was able to talk before he died?" I asked. "You could ask him questions?"

Mr. Hewitt nodded. "The authorities questioned him," he said. "Only a few people know about this. I'm the only person on the Outer Banks who does. And now you."

My eyes nearly popped out of my head. "Why me?" I asked.

"You'll understand in a minute. I just need to make you understand how important it is for you not to talk about this."

"Mr. Hewitt," I said, "I can keep a secret."

"Okay." He looked out the window behind us, and I started getting nervous again. "Okay. Here's what the German said. He said that he and the other men on the U-boats were getting classified information from someone in this area, someone onshore."

"Classified information about what?" I asked him. Even though I know everyone is supposed to be on the lookout for spies, Dennis had told me there was really no need for the Germans to get information about the merchant ships they were attacking. Nobody needed to tell the Germans where those ships would be or what they would be carrying or anything like that, because there were so many of them, just sitting out there on the ocean, ripe for the picking.

"We don't know, exactly," Mr. Hewitt said. "Our best guess is that someone here is helping the Germans plan to come ashore and sabotage our power plants and railroads and such. Maybe give them fake identification cards and money and that sort of thing."

"No one around here would do that," I said, shocked.

"Well, someone has, I'm afraid. They couldn't get any more information from the German sailor before he died. He just said they were supposed to meet up with the informer the day after they got to shore, but of course that never happened. Since they came ashore near Kiss River, our best guess is that the man—or maybe even the woman—they were supposed to meet is in that area."

I shook my head, sorting through everyone I knew who lived anywhere near Kiss River. "I can't imagine it," I said.

"I know. One thing I'm concerned about is that this person must be in a position to let the Germans land. It might be..." Mr. Hewitt seemed to have a hard time getting this part out, and I couldn't blame him. "It might be one of my men," he said.

"Someone in the Coast Guard?" I asked. It seemed crazy. Everyone I know in the Coast Guard is patriotic and working hard to protect the coastline. I keep thinking of how angry

Sandy would be if he thought for a minute one of his buddies would do something like that.

"It's a terrible thing to think about, isn't it?" Mr. Hewitt said. "But we have to face reality. Are you willing to help me?"

"How?" I asked, still confused.

"Through your friendship with the men at the Coast Guard station," he said. "They all like you. Most of them have crushes on you. They love it when you come around. You're the last person in the world they would suspect of being in cahoots with me. You're only fifteen, you're a girl. But you're smart as the dickens." He got a faraway look in his eyes. "Look, Bess, this is a huge thing I'm asking of you. I thought long and hard before asking you, too. I told the man who interviewed the German about you, and he said they would never ask a child to take on such a dangerous role. So they don't know I'm asking you to do any of this, and all you have to say is no, Bess, and I'll never ask you again. But the very fact that you're a fifteen-year-old girl is what makes the plan so perfect. If you do this, though, you will have to be extremely careful. Absolutely no one can know what you're doing."

It's hard to describe how I felt right then. *Honored* is the best word, I guess. Mr. Hewitt trusted me more than I ever would have imagined. He and I would be the only two people on the Outer Banks to know what was going on. Except for the culprit. I am certain it will turn out to be someone other than the Coast Guard boys, but who, I have no idea.

"I'll help any way I can," I said. "What should I do?"

"Just keep bringing goodies to the boys. Maybe more often than you are. Maybe just stop in to say hello now and again. See if you can—very carefully, mind you—find out if any of them might have relatives in Germany or if one of them suddenly seems to have a lot more money than he should."

"Why would he have more money?" I asked.

"Most likely he'll be getting paid by the Germans for his help."

Of course. I felt stupid for asking the question.

"You must tell no one what you're doing," Mr. Hewitt said again, just in case I didn't have the message yet. "Not even your parents. I'm sorry to put you in that position."

I told him I didn't mind. I had seen firsthand the death and destruction on the beach and I would do all I could to find the person who was helping the Germans make that happen.

I wanted to ask him if I could tell Sandy what I was up to. First of all, he could help. He knew the other men very well and might know who could possibly have some sympathy for the Germans. Plus, I was worried he would think I was flirting if I started spending more time with the other boys. But I caught myself just in time before I asked the question. If I asked if I could tell Sandy, Mr. Hewitt would guess about Sandy and me for sure.

"No one must suspect that you and I are talking about this," Mr. Hewitt said. "We have to work out a way of communicating so that no one can possibly know. Otherwise, the men will be careful what they say around you."

I thought for a moment, suddenly remembering the way my cousin Toria and I used to communicate when she lived nearer to Kiss River. I reached in my pocket and handed Mr. Hewitt the key to the lighthouse. "Here's what we can do," I said. "Once a week, or however often you think we should, I can leave you a note in the lantern room of the lighthouse, telling you anything I find out."

Mr. Hewitt frowned at the key. "Someone would see me

go up there, though," he said. "And your parents go into that room, I'm sure. They could find the note."

I had already figured this out, thanks to the system Toria and I had worked out. "I'll crumple up the note and tuck it in the brass coupling near the bottom of the lens, on the side closest to my house. That same night, you'll come after dark, let yourself into the lighthouse, get the note, and leave me another one if there's something you need me to know. How's that?"

He looked thoughtful. "You're sure your parents won't stumble over the note somehow?"

I shook my head. "We just need to be sure that you pick up your note the same night I put it there, and I'll be sure to pick up whatever note you leave for me first thing in the morning."

"Won't your parents suspect something if you go into the lighthouse before you go to school?"

"I don't think so. I'll try not to let them know, but even if they do see me, it wouldn't be that unusual."

"We need to do this more than once a week," Mr. Hewitt said. "At least twice. How about every Tuesday and Friday night. Will that work?"

I nodded. "But you have to promise you'll get that note every Tuesday and Friday night. Otherwise, if one of my parents finds it, I'd have to tell them what I was doing."

"No." He looked angry for a minute. "Under no circumstances do you tell them. You'll make something up to protect what we're doing. Your parents mustn't know." He shook his head. "They would kill me if they knew I was involving you in this."

"Well, just make sure we each get the notes when we say we will." I felt like I was suddenly the one giving the orders.

So, now I am working for the FBI, in a way! This is the

most important thing I've ever done in my life and I can't tell anyone. It's going to be hard to keep my mouth shut around Sandy, but I will.

Chapter Thirty

ALEC WOKE UP AT TEN MINUTES BEFORE midnight. He opened his eyes, and through the bedroom's wall of windows, he could see the triangle of moonlight shimmering on the sound, bright enough that he knew that was what had awakened him. Although the day had been cloudy, the night was beautiful, the half-moon surrounded by stars. An idea came to him, and he smiled to himself.

Rolling over, he gently shook his wife's shoulder. "Olivia?"

"Hmm?" she said. Slowly, she opened her eyes. "What's wrong?"

"Nothing's wrong," he said. "But it's beautiful out. I'm going to wake the kids up and take them to Jockey's Ridge."

"You're what?" She laughed, raising herself up on one elbow to get a better look at him.

"I used to do that all the time with Lacey and Clay when they were little," he said, missing those days all of a sudden. "Just a bit of an adventure."

She turned her head to look at the clock. "It's almost midnight," she said.

"On a Saturday night," he countered. "They can sleep in in the morning." He looked out the window again. "Look how clear it is."

Olivia rubbed her hands over her face as if trying to wipe away the sleep. "You'll never be able to wake Jack up," she said.

Jack was a deep sleeper and had been known to sleep through thunderstorms that kept everyone else in the house wide-awake.

"Bet I can," Alec said.

"And Jockey's Ridge is closed at dark," Olivia said.

"So?"

She smiled. "You're evil," she said. "You're going to teach your children to stray outside the law."

"So, you want to come be evil with us?"

She hesitated, but only for a moment. "Sure," she said, tossing off the covers. "I should be there to take the kids home when you get arrested."

"Great!" He was out of bed and heading for the closet. "I'll get Jack and you can get Maggie." He dressed quickly, then went to wake his son.

Jack was groggy and disgruntled as he opened his eyes. Alec was shaking the boy's arm, and when he saw the misery in his son's face, he felt a little guilty for waking him.

"I don't want to get up, Dad," Jack moaned, leaning against his father as Alec pulled him into a sitting position. That was the only way to wake him up in the morning for school, as well. Get him to sit up and keep him sitting. Otherwise, he would fall right back to sleep.

"You'll be happy you got up, Jack," Alec said. "I used to do this with Lacey and Clay all the time when they were your age. They didn't like getting up any more than you did, but I bet they'd tell you it was worth it."

Jack's weight grew even heavier against Alec's side.

"Come on, now," Alec said. "Do I have to carry you?"

Jack nodded, eyes shut, and Alec laughed. Jack was years beyond the carrying stage.

One hand on his son's shoulder, Alec reached toward the lamp on the night table and switched it on. The boy winced from the light, but it did the trick.

"Okay, okay," he said, rising to his feet. "I'm up."

"You can stay in your pj's," Alec said, knowing that Olivia wouldn't be crazy about that idea, but he was anxious to get on the road.

They met the women of the house in the kitchen, where Olivia was dropping a can of insect repellent into her rattan beach bag. Smart lady. He would have forgotten. Maggie had on shorts and a halter top, and she ran toward Alec to wrap her arms around his waist.

"You're the daddy with the best ideas!" She looked up at him, pure adoration in her eyes.

"I'm glad you think so, sweetie," he said. She was a lot like him, with a lanky body and more energy than she knew what to do with. Jack was more like Paul Macelli, his biological father. Smart and cerebral, with a touch of the poet in him.

"He's not dressed." Olivia looked disapprovingly at Jack's pajamas.

"At least he's up," Alec said.

Olivia relented with a smile. "Good point," she said, and Alec knew she had turned this night over to him.

In the garage, they piled into the van, his barefoot children buckled into the back seat and Olivia next to him in the front. Alec backed out of the driveway, then drove up the short street to Highway 12, where he turned right.

"You used to do this with Clay and Lacey?" Jack asked.

"Uh-huh." Their car was the only vehicle on the road. Alec liked that feeling of isolation.

"We should go get them," Jack said. "Take them with us."

"Yeah!" Maggie said. Both kids adored their older siblings.

"Kiss River's in the opposite direction," Alec said, although the idea was appealing. Lacey would be game, but he doubted Clay would want to get up in the middle of the night. Clay's joie de vivre had died with Terri, understandably so. It was hard enough for him to function during the day, much less at night.

"We might as well go get them," Olivia said. "If we're doing something this insane, we might as well do it all the way."

Grinning at being given permission, Alec turned the van around in a parking lot, and drove onto 12 again, this time in the direction of Kiss River. After a few miles, he noticed Jack in his rearview mirror, struggling to keep his eyes open, his head resting against the van window.

"We're almost to Kiss River, Jack," Alec said, and to his surprise, Jack opened his eyes and sat up straight.

They reached the unmarked road to Kiss River, and Alec turned the van into the dark, narrow tunnel formed by the trees. Not even the moonlight could reach this shrouded road.

"I always feel like I'm going to find a dead body on this road," Jack said. "It's so spooky."

"Or a witch," Maggie said.

"There's no such thing as witches," Jack informed his younger sister with disdain.

"There's no such thing as dead bodies, either," Maggie countered with the innocence of an overprotected child.

The truth was, Alec himself did not like driving down this road, not because of a fear of dead bodies or witches, but because of the memories. The aching uneasiness accompanied him anytime he came out here.

He had a key to the chain, and he handed it to Olivia, who got out to unlock the padlock. She looked cute in the headlights of the car, like a kid rather than a forty-nine-year-old physician. Her uncombed hair fell nearly to her shoulders and she wrinkled her nose at him as she struggled with the lock. Once she was in the van again, Alec drove onto the gravel road, and they bounced over the ruts and tree roots that were hard to avoid in the dark.

"Someone's up," Olivia said as they pulled into the parking lot.

Above the shrubs surrounding the lot, they could see that one of the upstairs lights was on in the keeper's house. Stained glass filled the upper half of the window and put a lump in Alec's throat. He should be used to Lacey's stained glass by now, but it still caused a visceral reaction in him, a combination of surprise and sadness, each time he saw it.

"Is that Lacey's room?" Maggie asked.

"I think it's the one Gina's renting," Alec said. He had frankly forgotten about the visitor.

"Who's Gina?" Jack asked.

"She's a woman who's renting a room from Lacey and Clay for a while," Alec said. He unfastened his seat belt. "I'll go get them. You guys can stay here."

He walked through the parking lot to the wide, sandy yard. The moon was so bright, it cast his shadow, long and lean, in the white sand as he walked toward the house. He didn't want to knock on the front door. Most likely, that would bring Gina downstairs, since she appeared to be the only person awake. Instead, he found some shells in the sand near the foundation of the house and stood below Clay's window, tossing the shells at the screen. "Clay?" he called in a voice barely louder than a whisper.

In a moment, he saw his son's face through the screen.

"Dad?" Clay asked. "What's going on?"

"I'm taking Jack and Maggie to Jockey's Ridge," he said. "They want you and Lace to come along."

Clay laughed. "You're nuts," he said.

"Come on. You can sleep late in the morning."

Clay hesitated a moment. "Can Gina come?" he asked.

"Of course," Alec said quickly, although the thought didn't please him. He'd wanted this to be a family outing. He understood, though, that they could not politely leave Gina alone in the keeper's house, especially when she was already awake. He still felt distrustful of her.

He walked back to the van. All the upstairs lights were on by the time he reached it, and the keeper's house glowed like a cathedral. In a few minutes, the three residents of the house arrived in the parking lot, and Jack and Maggie got out to let them climb into the rear bench seat. As they settled into the van, Alec overheard Lacey say to Gina, "I told you my father is not ordinary."

Gina said something back to Lacey, which he couldn't hear, but then she called out to him, "Thanks for inviting me, Dr. O'Neill."

"Call me Alec," he said. "And you're very welcome."

Everyone was quiet in the van on the drive to Jockey's Ridge. Alec felt the same sort of satisfaction he always did when he had his four children together. They were healthy and beautiful, if not perfectly happy. His *younger* two were happy, but they'd known nothing but joy in their lives so far. Even Jack, who knew that he was not Alec's biological son, seemed to feel he was lucky to have two fathers instead of one.

There were no cars, no people, in the parking lot near the dunes. They traipsed out across the sand, then began climbing the dunes in the eerie moonlight. Alec had not thought to bring a flashlight, but the moon was bright enough to allow them to see one another as they clambered through the sand. He could see well enough to know that Clay's gaze was on Gina as they climbed. And Gina's was on Jack and Maggie.

"Have you been up here before?" Olivia asked Gina when they'd reached the crest of the first dune. They would have to climb down the other side of this dune, then begin climbing up again to reach their goal, the peak of the largest dune.

"I've seen the dunes from the road, but haven't been up here," Gina said. She was a bit breathless, but then, so was Alec. She looked out toward the black ocean. "They didn't look this high from down there."

It took them ten minutes more to reach the crest of the tallest dune, and from there they could see the half disk of the moon reflected in both sound and ocean. But they were really here for the stars.

"Okay, Jack and Maggie," he said. "Make a bed for yourselves in the sand."

He listened as Lacey instructed her younger siblings in the fine art of flattening the sand on the angled dune top so that they could lie there comfortably, with nothing above them but sky. He and Olivia smoothed the sand for their own bed and lay down.

Alec put his arm around his wife. "Thanks for going along with this," he said.

"It was a great idea," she admitted. "Although I still have visions of the article in the newspaper, 'Olivia Simon, Director of Kill Devil Hills Emergency Room, Arrested on Jockey's Ridge.'"

Alec laughed, giving her shoulders a squeeze. Olivia had borne the brunt of a far more destructive article years earlier, and he knew she would forever feel a need to keep her reputation spotless.

"Look!" Lacey said suddenly.

From the corner of his eye, Alec saw his daughter raise her arm to point to the eastern sky.

"Oh, you guys missed it," Lacey said. "It was so—"

"There's another," Gina said, raising her own arm.

"I want to see!" Maggie complained. "I can't see any."

"Just keep watching, Mag," Clay said.

"I don't know where to look!"

"Relax," Alec said. "Let your eyes take in the whole sky instead of just focusing on one star."

They spotted a few more falling stars before they saw a large white-green ball of light shoot across the sky right above them, a long tail trailing behind it. It was the most extraordinary sight Alec had ever seen. He knew every one of them had seen it, as a collective gasp rose up from the dune.

"What was *that?*" Lacey asked in astonishment.

"A UFO!" Jack said excitedly.

"It was a fireball," Gina said. She sounded quite excited herself. "I've never seen one before, but that's what it was. Look." She pointed to the sky. "You can still see the tail."

She was right. The tail had grown fainter, but it still cut across the sky directly above them.

"What's a fireball?" Clay and Jack asked the question at the same moment.

"It's a meteor, but an enormous one," she said. "And very bright. You're supposed to report them when you see them because they're pretty rare."

"Should we report it?" Lacey asked.

"I think we can do it online," Gina said.

"Is the tail made from bits of the meteor coming off?" Jack's eyes were still on the tail, which was starting to lose its linear shape.

"Actually, no, although that's a good guess," Gina said. "It's just air molecules glowing from the fireball."

"Wow," Maggie said with reverence. "It's scary, though. Do shooting stars ever fall on the earth?"

Alec started to answer, but Gina beat him to it. "They sure do," she said. "But not often. Only somewhere between twenty and fifty a day."

"Fifty a day!" Jack said. "That's tons. How come we never see any?"

"It sounds like a lot, but think about it, Jack," Gina said. "Let's say fifty meteorites hit the earth every day. Where do you think they would fall? Think about the earth. About a globe. What does it look like?"

They were all lying down, and Gina's voice was disembodied, floating in the air. Alec had forgotten she was a teacher, but he heard the teacher in her now.

"It's round," Maggie said.

"And what's that round globe covered with?" Gina asked.

"Land and water," Jack said.

"Right. It's actually about two-thirds water," Gina said. "So what does that mean for the meteorites that are falling?"

"A bunch would just fall in the water," Maggie said, engaged.

"Right!" Gina said. "So, let's say two-thirds of the meteorites fall in the water. That leaves around sixteen or so to fall on the land. And picture that globe again. Is all the land populated?"

"You mean, have people on it?" Maggie asked.

"Right."

"No way," Jack said. "There's lots of places without any people."

"And lots of places with very few people," Gina added. "About one-fourth of the land is either uninhabited or not very inhabited. So, what does that mean for the meteorites?"

"We're down to twelve," Clay said.

"I don't get it." Maggie was confused.

Olivia answered her. "The meteorites that fall in those unpopulated areas will go unnoticed," she explained.

"Right," Gina said. "And about half those twelve meteorites will fall during the night, when they won't be seen."

"You could see a meteorite if it fell, though, because it's so bright," Jack argued.

"You would think so, Jack, but something happens to it when it reaches earth's atmosphere and it doesn't glow anymore," Gina said. "So when it falls, it actually looks something like a plain old rock."

"So, there's only six meteorites that fall on earth every day during daylight hours," Lacey said.

"Right," Gina said.

"That's still too many if they land on your head," Maggie pointed out, and Alec chuckled to himself.

"I don't think you have to worry about that, Maggie," Gina said.

They grew quiet again. She was a good teacher, Alec had to admit. His kids had hung on her every word.

Jack suddenly sat up. "Hey, Maggie," he said. "Let's roll down."

Maggie was instantly on her feet, tugging on Gina. "You do it, too," she said.

Gina laughed, and Alec was surprised when she lay down in the sand next to his children and started to roll with them. He sat up, watching them spin down the hill, and he could hear their laughter and his daughter's yelps even after he had lost sight of them in the darkness.

Clay was sitting up, too, watching, and Alec saw the small, sad smile on his son's lips, the telltale bobbing of the Adam's apple in his throat. Clay was so closed these days, so shut down, that it was impossible to know how to help him. They had both been widowed, but watching his child go through that experience was worse than going through it himself.

"Hey, Clay?" he asked softly.

Clay turned to look at him.

"You want to go windsurfing with me tomorrow if the wind's decent?"

It was a moment before Clay nodded. "Sounds good," he said.

"Hey!" Olivia leaned forward to call into the darkness. "Are you all right down there?"

There was no answer other than giggling. He could hear the three of them breathing hard, chatting and laughing, as they climbed up the dune again and settled back into their sandy beds.

All seven of them lay there, watching the stars awhile longer, until Olivia fell asleep in the crook of Alec's arm. He knew Jack and Maggie were asleep, as well. He wasn't sure about Lacey and Clay and Gina, but everyone was very still. He wanted to stay there with them until morning. His family, together, safe, under the night sky that put everything else, *everything,* in perspective. He wished he could say that to Clay. *Our lives are small—inconsequential—compared to all of this,* he would say. *We just have to make the most of what we're given.* But of course, he said nothing. It was a lesson Clay would have to learn on his own.

Chapter Thirty-One

CLAY MET HIS FATHER AT THE SOUND-SIDE beach at ten the following morning. A couple of other windsurfers were already there, but this was not one of the more popular beaches and it wouldn't get too crowded. Once they were on the water, the entire bay would be theirs, if they wanted it.

He hadn't windsurfed with his father since the summer before, when life had been so, so much simpler. September eleventh hadn't yet occurred. And on the more personal side, Terri had still been alive. God, he'd taken her for granted. He recalled windsurfing with his father, knowing that when he got home, Terri would have the house clean, the garden weeded, the dogs fed, and dinner on the table. He did his part, too, but she did more. He was coming to think women were more independent than men. The single women he knew were doing just fine, while he needed his sister to take care of him. No wonder Gina and Lacey were not interested in marriage.

"Great wind for July," his father said as he lifted the short-board and mast from the top of his van.

"Must be twenty miles per hour," Clay said, although to be honest, he had barely noticed the wind before that moment. Windsurfing was not the main reason he'd agreed to this outing today. He wanted time with his father in a way he'd never wanted it before.

"Thanks for joining us on the dunes last night," his father said as Clay pulled the boom and sail from the back of his Jeep.

"It was as good as I remembered from when we were kids," Clay said. He had felt full of Gina the night before. Watching her with his young siblings, listening to her laughter as she rolled down the dunes with them. It was a sound he had not heard often from her, part of a playful side he hoped he would see again.

"Jack and Maggie are in love with Gina," his father said as if reading his thoughts.

Clay lifted his board, holding on to the foot strap as he carried it across the sand to the water. "Yeah, she was good with them," he said over his shoulder.

Both men were quiet as they put together their windsurfers. It was too warm for wet suits, although his father sometimes wore one when the jellyfish were plentiful. But he was not wearing one today, and Clay had to admire his physique. His father was still thin, although he certainly had no appetite problem, and there was only a hint of extra padding around his middle. He wasn't as tanned as he'd been when Clay was growing up, but his skin was still a light golden-brown. Clay hoped he looked half that good when he was his father's age.

Out on the water, Clay felt himself relax as the task of sailing became his focus. They were both exceptional windsurfers. It was a silent sport when you were that good, and maybe that was why Clay liked it. No need to talk. Today, though, he *wanted* to talk to his father and he planned to do so when they were through on the sound.

They raced one another several times, out to a buoy and back to the beach, and Clay won three of the races, his father two. They were well matched. His father's energy faded before his did, though. Alec waited on the beach, while Clay chop-hopped for a while, using the waves as a ramp to launch himself into the air. In spite of the fact that he wanted some talking time with his dad, he couldn't resist the lure of the water.

After they had lifted their boards back onto their vehicles and loaded up their gear, Clay asked his father if he had time for lunch.

"Sure." His father looked pleased at the suggestion. "How about Shorty's?"

Gina would be working at Shorty's today, and given the nature of the conversation he hoped to have with his father, he didn't really want her around. Everyplace else, though, would be packed with tourists.

"All right," he said, wanting to see Gina as much as he wanted to avoid her.

When they'd returned home from the dunes the night before, Lacey had gone immediately to bed, but he and Gina had been hungry. He made scrambled eggs and grits and toast with marmalade, while she went online to find the site where she could report the observation of the fireball. Then they sat at the table to eat. He had ordered something for her from the Internet the day before, and he was tempted to tell her about it, but that would have spoiled the surprise. He wanted to be able to watch her face when she opened it, so with some effort he managed to keep his mouth shut. Sitting there with her, he'd felt tired and content, a quiet joy inside him that he could not remember experiencing in a long time, if ever. It had been so wonderful to find that lens for her and to see her pleasure in touching it.

Gina had sand in her long hair from rolling down the dune, and she apologized for grains of it falling on the table. Her hair was a disheveled mess, her skin pink from the afternoon in the water, and he thought she looked beautiful. They ate and chatted about Jack and Maggie and what it had been like growing up with Alec as a dad.

"He was the normal one," Clay had laughed. "It was my mother who was wacky."

In response to Gina's probing, he explained about his mother's refusal to wear a watch or have clocks in the house, her lack of rules for him and Lacey, her sense of spirit and fun. He'd talked on, trying to remember every eccentric and kooky thing his mother had done, using up more words in the space of an hour than he'd spoken in the entire eight months since Terri's death, not wanting the time with Gina to end. But the conversation was superficial, benign, focusing on facts rather than feelings. And when they said good-night to one another and went to their separate rooms, he had felt as though he had let something precious slip away from him.

As it turned out, of course, Gina was their waitress.

"I had trouble getting up for work this morning, thanks to you, Dr....Alec," she said, pouring coffee into the cups on their table. Her voice was chastising, but she was smiling. She did look a little tired this morning. Her eyes were puffy, probably from her slight sunburn as much as from lack of sleep, and that little touch of humanness in her, that one flaw in her otherwise perfect face, made Clay care about her more than he already did.

"Seems like you had fun, though," his father said.

"I still have sand in my hair," she said, running her free

hand through the perfectly clean-looking tresses. "Jack and Maggie are great."

"And you're a good teacher," his father said. "Maggie was still talking about meteorites and fireballs when she got up this morning."

"That was spectacular, wasn't it?" Gina rested the coffeepot on the table and pulled out her order pad. "Well, what can I get you two?" she asked.

They ordered sandwiches, then Clay watched his father's gaze follow Gina back to the kitchen.

Clay stirred cream into his coffee, not sure where to start this conversation.

"Last night on the dunes," his father said, starting it for him, "it became very clear to me that you really like Gina."

Clay took a sip of his coffee. What had he given away the night before? "Well, first of all, she has no interest in me or in any other man. And second of all..." He looked up at his father. "It's only been eight months."

His father nodded. "I know, Clay," he said, and there was so much sympathy in those words, so much understanding, that Clay felt tears fill his eyes. He blinked them back quickly.

"How long after Mom died did you start seeing Olivia?" he asked.

His father let out a long sigh, sitting back against the bench. He looked up at the ceiling for a moment, remembering. "We became friends in June," he said, "so that was about six months after your mom died. But we didn't get serious for another few months, mostly because I felt so guilty about it."

"You did?" Clay was surprised.

"Hell, yes."

Clay let out his breath. "That's how I'm feeling. It seems wrong that I could even look that way at another woman. I feel like I'm cheating on Terri."

His father smiled. "I remember that feeling very well. It goes away in time."

"I'm not sure I want it to go away. Or that I even…I don't know. That I deserve to have it go away. I wasn't the best husband." There. He'd said it. Then he realized how it must sound to his father. "I didn't cheat on her or anything like that. I just—"

"There are no perfect husbands," his father said. "Or wives, for that matter."

Gina picked that moment to reappear at their table to top off their coffee. "Sandwiches will be up in a minute," she said.

When she walked away again, his father leaned across the table toward him. "I understand how you feel," he said. "But you know, Olivia and I became friends first. I had no intention of it becoming anything more than that. I was still deeply in love with your mother. Our relationship had a natural progression as we got closer. So don't try to push romance. Just let yourself be friends with her. That way, your conscience can be perfectly clear."

His father had no reason to feel guilty, though. Clay didn't want to say that to him, didn't want to invite more questions, but his father seemed to read his mind.

"I felt particularly guilty because your mother asked me once to promise that if she died before I did, I wouldn't go out with anyone for a year," he said.

"She did?" It was unlike his mother to put a restriction on anyone.

His father nodded. "She was…I don't know…agitated about it, I guess would be the best way to describe it. And of course, I made the promise just to get her to chill out. So I had that weighing on my mind as I started falling for Olivia."

Clay stirred his coffee again. There was a lot he didn't know about his father. "It's good with you and Olivia, isn't it?" he asked.

"Wonderful."

"As good as it was with Mom?"

He watched his father's smile grow wistful. "Different, Clay," he said. "Just very different. But even if your mother had lived, my relationship with *her* would be different now than it was ten years ago. People grow and change and mature."

He looked up as Gina delivered their sandwiches.

"Can I get you two anything else?" she asked, hands on her hips.

"We're fine," Clay said. "Thanks."

Neither of them spoke until Gina had moved away from their table.

"I don't know that Gina's the one for you, though," his father said.

"Why do you say that?"

"Well, for one thing, she lives in Washington State, and I don't want you to move that far away."

"That's jumping the gun a bit, don't you think?" Clay laughed.

His father nodded. He took a bite of his sandwich and swallowed it before continuing. "Something's bothering me about her, and I'm having trouble putting my finger on it," he said. "I just don't understand why someone who calls herself a lighthouse historian wouldn't have known that the Kiss River light's been gone for ten years. Even as an amateur lighthouse aficionado, she would know that. And she didn't know the lens had a panel missing."

"Yes, she did."

"Before or after I mentioned it to her?" Alec asked.

Clay knew the answer to that question, but didn't want to

feed his father's suspicions. "I think she's had other things on her mind," he said, although he remained troubled by the subject himself. He could not forget her pronunciation of Fresnel. Still, he felt himself bristle at the implication. He thought of telling his father about finding the lens the day before, but he didn't want to test his ire right then. "She's trying to adopt a little girl from India," he said.

His father looked understandably surprised. "To raise alone?"

Clay nodded. "She went over there to pick the little girl up, but there was a sudden crackdown on adoptions and she had to leave her there until it's straightened out. The girl needs heart surgery or she's going to die. So, it's a big mess."

"That's terrible." His father frowned.

"I think the whole thing with the lens is her way of keeping her attention on something else while she's waiting. She'd go crazy, otherwise."

"Like you," his father said.

"What do you mean, like me?"

"You focus on your work," his father said. "But that's okay. Everybody has their own way of coping. I took the other tack. I wore my grief like a shroud, all the time. Do you remember? I took months off from work. I moped. I took endless pictures of the lighthouse because it reminded me of your mother. You, on the other hand, have lost yourself in your work, and even when you play, you play so hard it's like I can see you trying to keep yourself from thinking. On the sound today, you wanted to go faster, sail farther, catch more air. But you hide your sadness well, if that's your intention. No one would guess you're torn up inside. Unless they really know you. And I do, Clay."

Clay swallowed hard. He felt like a little kid, and didn't know how to respond.

"Just tell me one thing," his father said. "Try to be honest, okay?"

Clay nodded.

"Is it just her looks? Gina's?"

"Not at all," Clay said, although her looks certainly had something to do with his attraction to her. "It's…she's very smart, she's kind, she's interesting." The words sounded weak, but they were the truth.

"Then if you truly care about her, open up to her," his father said. "Let her know who you really are and see how she reacts to that. You're all closed up inside. I mean, this is the first time you've told me anything about how you're feeling, do you know that? You've always been…always kept things to yourself," he said. "But it's been almost impossible to get you to talk since Terri died. People care about you, Clay. They want to help you. Don't shut them out."

Clay tried to smile. "Okay," he said. The conversation had been his idea, but he'd had more than enough of it now. "Are you done with the lecture?"

His father sat back against the bench. "Done," he said.

"So." Clay blew out a long breath. "How do Jack and Maggie like day camp?"

Chapter Thirty-Two

Wednesday, April 29, 1942

I WONDER IF MR. HEWITT IS SORRY HE ASKED me to help him. We've exchanged notes three times and I have had nothing to report. (Mama, by the way, saw me go up to the top of the lighthouse before school and asked me why I did that. I said it was so beautiful out today that I just wanted to look at the ocean. I don't think she believed me. She says I am running wild, because I am hardly ever home.) I've left my notes for Mr. Hewitt right where I said, where the coupling is a little loose at the bottom of the Fresnel lens, and our system is working perfectly. I only wish I had something to report to him.

Anyhow, in the note I got from Mr. Hewitt this morning, he asked me if I'd try to have a talk with Mr. Sato. Here's what he wrote exactly. "Good morning, Bess. Since you know Moto Sato better than a lot of people around here, could you see if you can talk to him? Make it casual, of course. Just see if your intuition tells you something might be going on with him. There's a rumor that he's not really crippled. If you can get into his house, look for radio equipment. And check the exterior for antennas. See if you can catch him walking. Or speaking English. Or better yet, German."

I can't believe he asked me to do this! I don't know Mr. Sato at all. I've only waved to him a couple of times when I've gone past his house on the sound, and I haven't seen him in months, and I am sure he doesn't speak English and he's crippled as can be, so this assignment seems pretty impossible to me. Maybe Mr. Hewitt is giving up on me getting anything out of the boys at the Coast Guard, though.

I've spent *a lot* of time at the Coast Guard station. Someone donated them a pool table, and I've learned how to play pool. I go there after school. Mama and Daddy think I'm staying late at school to help Mrs. Cady organize some books, which I actually did do one day, but not every day. They would *really* think I'm running wild if they knew I was playing pool with a bunch of boys!

I wasn't sure how to spend so much time at the Coast Guard station without making Sandy wonder what I was doing there, so I am being careful to act like the tomboy I used to be instead of the young lady I am. I don't want him to think I'm flirting. He asked me why I'm there so much, and I told him I love playing pool. I hated lying to him!!!!!!!!! It's the only thing I've ever lied to him about. I wish so much that I could tell him what I'm doing. He could help me. I've asked Sandy if he minds that I'm at the Coast Guard station so much, and he says he doesn't. He trusts me. And that makes me feel even guiltier for lying to him.

I talk with the boys about the war, and Mr. Hewitt wrote in his first note to me that I am a great actress. No one would ever guess my real reason for being there, he wrote. The boys must think I am unbelievably curious about what is going on and their opinions about it. But Mr. Hewitt was right. They talk to me easily. I play dumb with them a lot, asking ignorant questions like why we're at war with Germans in the first place. And I pay attention to who answers me and if he says anything that sounds even slightly pro-German. So far, nobody's said anything to make me suspicious. When Sandy is around, though, I can't act that dumb. He knows better and would wonder what I'm up to.

A month ago, I would have been thrilled by the fact that I have now played pool four times with Jimmy Brown! What did I ever see in him? He looks like such a little boy, and he acts so immature, too. Ralph Salmon is probably the nicest of the boys, after Sandy. He's a softie. I can't forget how he threw up when he saw that dead man on the beach. But I am actually trying to spend more time with the boys I don't know well, Teddy Pearson, for example, and the other ones that keep more to themselves, because if anyone is guilty of treason, it would probably be one of them. Teddy is shy, though…or maybe he is keeping some secrets. I think he likes me, since he always asks to play pool with me, but it's hard to get him to talk.

While I was there yesterday, a report came in that two more ships had been sunk by the U-boats off the coast of Hatteras. All the boys got real quiet, an angry kind of quiet, I think. I could see both fear and fury in their eyes, and Teddy and Ralph didn't want to play any more pool. The note I left for Mr. Hewitt last night said that I thought his boys couldn't be more patriotic and dedicated to their jobs. And that's when he wrote back that I should talk to Mr. Sato. So, now I have to figure out how to see a man who never goes out of his house anymore. Good luck!

One person I have managed *not* to see lately is Dennis

Kittering. I am still annoyed with him for lecturing me about Sandy, but also I am afraid that he might somehow figure out that I am working for Mr. Hewitt. I wouldn't put it past Dennis to figure that out. That man has eyes in the back of his head.

Wednesday night at 10:00

Well, I talked with Mr. Sato, if you can call it that. Here is what I did: I went to his house over on the sound. His house is right above the water and although it's like any other sound-front cottage, it has a Japanese sort of look to it. It's hard to explain. There is a tall, skinny sculpture out front near the road that someone once told me is called a pagoda. It's almost as tall as me, and I bet it's the only one in all the Outer Banks. Probably all of North Carolina, for that matter. There are pots all around the deck of the house with these unusual plants in them. They look like bamboo, sort of. Anyhow, I felt right strange going up to that house. I was hoping his daughter-in-law would be there, because she could translate anything I said to Mr. Sato. She speaks Japanese. She studied it in college and that's where she met her husband, Mr. Sato's dead son.

I had a plan. First, I walked quietly around the front and sides of the house, looking for an antenna but not finding one. I couldn't see the back of the house, though, because it's on the water. Then I knocked on the door. There was no answer, but then I noticed Mr. Sato peeking out from behind the curtain in one of the front rooms. I realized that he was probably afraid someone might be coming to take him off to one of those internment camps. Even though I *was* there to see if he was a spy, I felt sorry for scaring him.

In a minute, he answered the door, probably feeling safe that it was just a local girl and not the sheriff.

He was in his wheelchair. He is a very cute old man. He smiled at me, nodding over and over again but saying nothing.

Well, I happen to know two phrases in German. My cousin Toria has a German grandma and I used to hear her say them. I don't know how to spell them, though. The first is "Vee gates?" which means something like "Hello, how are you?" The second is "Mock dee tore zu," which means "Close the door."

So, to test him, I said, "Vee gates?" when he opened the door.

He nodded at me like he might've understood me, but I don't know.

"Hello," he said back to me in English, but I figured that might just be the one word he knows.

"I was just wondering if I could use your telephone for a minute," I asked him. That was my plan. I knew they had telephones along that part of the sound, even though we don't have any less than a mile away.

His smile was an empty one, and I was pretty certain he didn't understand me. I peeked behind him to see if his daughter-in-law might be home, but was sure by this time that she wasn't. Her car wasn't there either.

I held my hand up to my ear as if I was holding a phone, and I pointed inside his house.

"Ah!" he said, nodding, and I knew he understood what I wanted. He motioned with his hand for me to come in, and he wheeled backward to let me past him.

It was the strangest thing, being in that house. I felt like I was in another country. There were these Japanese screens everywhere, and Japanese paintings on the wall (which I really liked!) and more of those bamboo plants and chairs with bamboo arms and legs. He wheeled ahead of me into the kitchen—he is pretty fast in that chair!—where the phone was, and I cranked up the operator and told her to hook me up to Trager's Store. I talked to Mr. Trager himself and asked him if he had Cheeri Oats in the store today, because sometimes he does and sometimes he doesn't. He knows that's my favorite cereal, so I thought it wouldn't seem too strange that I was asking about it. But I'm sure he was still surprised and confused by the call, since I could have just walked to the store from my house on such a nice day, but he told me, sure, he just got some more in, and to come on over and get it.

Mr. Sato wheeled ahead of me back to the front door, giving me just a slight chance to peer into a bedroom and a parlor kind of room before I reached the door. I saw a regular radio, like the kind we have, but I didn't see any radios that looked unusual. I didn't have much of a chance to look, really. When we got near the door, I said, "Mock dee tore zu," even though that means to close the door. I don't know how to say to open it! He just smiled and nodded at me like he'd done anytime I said something. I don't think he knew what I was saying. But then, my German is not very good.

I thanked him and said goodbye. Once I got outside, I looked back at his house, trying to see the rear of it so I could check for antennas, and I remembered how he had peeked out from behind the curtains. I should have paid better attention to how tall he'd seemed then. Was he in his wheelchair when he peeked out, or could he have been standing up? I think he'd been down pretty low, so he was probably in his chair.

Anyhow, I didn't have much of a conversation with him, and I don't really think much of Japs these days, but he seemed like a nice old man to me. I feel like I've failed in my assignment for Mr. Hewitt again. One more time, I have nothing helpful to report.

Chapter Thirty-Three

TUESDAY WAS OVERCAST AND STRANGELY COOL, but Gina didn't mind a bit because it made driving more pleasant. She still had no air-conditioning. Someone from the Pacific Northwest was not meant to live in this climate, she thought. Although the air today was still thick and difficult to pull into her lungs, the gray sky and misty haze reminded her of home.

It was late afternoon and her day off, but she was on her way to Shorty's nevertheless. Today was payday, and she needed her check. She'd told Clay she would save him a trip to the restaurant by taking Henry home, since she was going to be there anyway.

In her backpack, she had a few underwater pictures of the lens that Kenny had given her, and she wanted to show them to Walter and Brian. She had to figure out her next step. Her most extreme idea was to learn to dive. It had been wonderful underwater and the panic she'd expected hadn't set in at all. But she was afraid that diving would not be the solution to her dilemma. The lower part of the lens was buried deep in the sandy bottom of the ocean. And that was the part she needed to see.

The back room was filled with the usual crowd—plus one person she had not seen there before.

"Hey, Gina!" Lacey called when she walked into the room.

Gina turned to see Lacey at the pool table, a cue in her hand and Brock at her side. Lacey with Brock?

She walked over to them, unsure of what to say. She'd ignored Brock to the best of her ability since the incident with the raffle money. He continued to order her around as though she was his personal servant, and it took all her strength to serve him without saying a word. If she opened her mouth, though, she was afraid she'd create a scene.

"Hi, Lace," she said, keeping her voice casual. "Who's winning?"

Brock was bent over the pool table, his garish arms taut as he took aim with the cue.

"He is," Lacey whispered so as not to disturb his concentration.

Brock sunk a couple of balls in the corner pocket, then stood up. "Want to play the winner?" he asked Gina, and she shook her head.

"No, thanks," she said. "I'm just here to pick up Henry and take him home." She didn't mention her paycheck. She would not talk about money in front of Brock.

"I could take him home," Lacey offered.

Gina shook her head. "No, that's okay, thanks," she said. "You have a good game. See you tonight." She left the pool table, glad to get away from Brock and nursing an unwelcome sense of betrayal. Why would Lacey hang out with the guy who had, in all likelihood, stolen Gina's money?

Brian and Walter were deep in a game of chess, with Henry

watching every move. But Brian pulled his attention from the board as she neared them.

"Hello, girlie," he said. "Aren't you off today?"

"Yes, I sure am," she said, "but I had to come in for my paycheck, so I told Clay I'd give Henry a ride home." She was glad to see that Henry was not one of the players. She'd been afraid she would have to wait for the game to be over before being able to take him home. He and his buddies were notoriously slow chess players. They were in no hurry.

"Kenny said he was going to give you pictures of the Kiss River lens," Walter said.

"He did," she said. "Want to see?" She rested her backpack on the floor and reached into it to pull out the photographs, which she handed to Walter. He adjusted his glasses this way and that on his nose, finally taking them off altogether and holding the pictures close to his eyes.

"Well, isn't that something?" he said. "It looks like it's all in one piece and damn near covered with seaweed."

"You should show them pictures to Alec," Brian said. "Maybe if he sees it's in one piece, he'd give in."

"No, thanks," she said. She'd thought of that herself, but was frankly terrified of having Alec trip her up on her light-house facts again.

Henry looked up at her. "You ready to leave now?" he asked.

"Is that all right with you?"

He nodded, getting to his feet. "Let's hit the road," he said.

Henry put on his straw hat when he left the restaurant, but he took it off again as he got into her car. He was such a gentleman. But not much of a talker. She'd spent time with him at Shorty's and at the keeper's house, of course, but this was the first time she'd been completely alone with him. Henry was quiet in a shy sort of way. She apologized for the lack of air-conditioning, and he commented on the rattle that seemed worse every day, but that was about the extent of their conversation. The silence between them was not uncomfortable, though. Not in the least.

She had not been to his house before, and so once she was on Croatan Highway, he began giving her directions. From his description of turns, she guessed he lived near the sound.

"Do you live right on the water?" she asked.

He laughed. "Lit'rally," he said. "Wait till you see."

She turned onto a heavily wooded road and soon spotted a solitary house straight ahead of her. Driving closer, she saw that it was actually built *over* the water on stilts. A broad deck surrounded the house on the three sides that hung above the sound.

She started to pull into the short driveway. "What a fascinating—" She stopped her words as well as the car when she spotted the pagoda. It was to the side of the driveway and near the road, a tall, narrow stone structure. "You have a pagoda," she said.

"Yup," Henry said. "It came with the house."

Pressing the gas pedal again, she drove a little farther into the driveway and then turned off the ignition. "I'll walk you up to your door," she said.

"No need," Henry said, pushing the car door open.

"I'd like to," she said. "I'd like to see the view from your deck."

"Fine, then," he said. "I love that deck, that's for sure."

He beat her up the three stairs leading to the deck. "Come around the back, here," he said, pointing to the rear of the house.

She followed him around the back of the house. The sky above the sound was thick with haze, but she could still make out where the sun was burning behind the clouds. A few sailboats floated across the water in the fog. "You must have wonderful sunsets here," she said.

"Indeed." He nodded.

"How long have you lived in this house?" she asked.

"Since fifty-three," he said. "My wife and I had forty good years here. Raised our son in this house." He shook his head, more to himself than to her, and she imagined he was remembering two of the people he'd loved and lost. "Great place to raise a little tyke," he added. "That boy loved the water."

"Why do you think the people who owned it before you had a pagoda?" she probed.

"Oh, there was a Japanese man living here sometime before we moved in. It's one of them Oriental decorations. I decided just to leave it there. It's grown on me over the years."

She nodded. "Yes, it's very interesting." She pictured Bess walking around the house, looking for an antenna. "Doesn't it get lonely out here in the winter?" she asked. The way the house was situated, she wasn't able to see any other buildings along this stretch of the sound.

He laughed. "It's not near as lonely here as where *you're* living, honey," he said, alluding to the isolation of Kiss River. "At least I'm not that far from stores and such."

She started walking back toward the steps. "Can I do anything for you before I go?" she asked.

"No, I'm just fine," he said. "I'm going to have a crab or two for dinner and then go to bed."

"Okay." She left the deck and started walking down the driveway toward her car. "It's good to see you, Henry," she said, turning around to wave at him.

She watched him wave back as he walked into the apparently unlocked front door of his little house.

Backing out of the driveway, she took one last look at the pagoda and felt a chill. Moto Sato's house. How amazing.

★ ★ ★

Clay's Jeep was in the parking lot when she arrived at the keeper's house, and she was surprised to see it there, since he usually worked so late. But what surprised her even more was the heady pleasure she felt at knowing he was home.

Sasha greeted her as she got out of her car, and she and the dog walked together across the sand to the house. Clay was in the kitchen, taking a beer from the refrigerator, and a large pizza carton rested on the counter. The scent of pepperoni filled the air.

"What are you doing home?" she asked.

"I decided to duck out early," he said. "As it turned out, I could have picked up Henry. Sorry."

"I had to go to Shorty's anyway, so it was no problem," she said, slipping her backpack from her shoulders and dropping it on one of the kitchen chairs. She thought of telling him that she'd seen Lacey there, but decided against it. He would not want to hear about his sister with yet another man. Especially not one with tattoos covering two-thirds of his body.

"I have something for you." Clay twisted the cap off the beer and leaned against the counter.

"Pizza?"

"No. Well, yes, the pizza is for us for dinner. But that's not it." He pointed to a wrapped box on the porcelain-topped table. "That's for you," he said.

"What on earth?" She stared at the box.

"I saw it and had to get it for you," he said. "Go ahead. Open it."

Sitting down at the table, she pulled the box toward her. It was about the size and shape of a shoe box, wrapped in green paper and circled by a thin, wiry ribbon of gold stars. She tugged at the taped edges of the paper to unwrap it and discovered that it *was* a shoe box. Lifting off the top, she pushed aside the tissue paper and her mouth fell open. It was a Barbie doll, an *Indian* Barbie doll, complete with a bright-pink, gold-trimmed sari and a small black bindhi on her forehead. Gina looked up at Clay, speechless.

"It's for Rani," he said.

Instantly, she started to cry. They were strange tears, a mixture of joy and surprise and discouragement and hope. And gratitude. She tried to thank him, but the tears got in the way of her speech.

Clay sat down next to her, his hand on her arm. "I didn't give it to you to upset you," he said.

She pressed her own hand to her mouth, her eyes squeezed shut. "I...I'm overwhelmed. This was so incredibly sweet of you. So kind." She wiped the tears from her eyes with the back of her hand. "She's beautiful," she said, lifting the doll from the box. Sasha walked over to sniff the dark hair, and Gina touched the long, multicolored choli that hung over her shoulder, the tiny gold shoes. "Where did you ever find her?"

"Internet," he said.

Shaking her head, she leaned over and wrapped her arms around him, holding him close to her. She could smell the subtle scent of aftershave on his skin, a musky smell that made her want to stay there like that for a while, holding him. Suddenly, though, she felt overcome by a need to be alone. To think. Letting go of him, she stood up.

·"Thank you so much, Clay," she said, placing the doll back in the box and lifting it into her arms. "I think I'm going upstairs for a while."

He looked surprised. "Don't you want any pizza?" he asked.

"Maybe later," she said. "Thanks again."

In her room—*Bess's* room—she took the Barbie from the box and sat her up on the dresser, then climbed into bed, under the covers. She was not really a fan of Barbie dolls, but this one was special. She stared at it for a few minutes, then turned her head to the left to see the brick of the lighthouse, more gray than white against the darkening sky, and she started to cry all over again.

Get a grip, she told herself. That had to be her focus. The lighthouse. Her daughter. Not the man who cared enough to give her a gift, who validated her longing for her little girl in a way very few people had.

Chapter Thirty-Four

WORKING AT HIS OFFICE LATE THE FOLLOWING afternoon, Clay received a call from Gina.

"I'm at the service station near milepost three," she said. He could hear a whirring sound in the background.

"What happened?" he asked.

"When I went out to my car after work, it wouldn't start. I got them to tow me here."

Clay was frankly amazed that her car had made it all the way across the country. He wouldn't be surprised if the trip had been its last hurrah.

"I tried Lacey, but haven't been able to reach her," Gina continued. "Is there a chance you could pick me up on your way home from work? Would you mind?"

Clay looked at his calendar. He had planned to leave the office in thirty minutes for an appointment in Southern Shores.

"I can pick you up," he said, "but I need to make a stop on my way home to see a client. If you don't mind stopping off there with me, I could—"

"That would be fine," she said. "I'm sorry."

"See you soon," he said, then hung up the phone.

The night before had not gone as he'd hoped. Clay was certain Gina's enthralled reaction to the doll had been sincere, but he had not expected her to fall apart the way she did and then disappear upstairs for the rest of the night. He'd eaten the entire pizza by himself. When he went downstairs that morning, she had already left for work, and he'd felt enough concern for her that he called her at Shorty's. He worried that he had inadvertently done something to upset her, but she reassured him that she was fine.

"I'd just had a long day," she'd said. "I needed to crash."

Despite her denial, he couldn't help but feel that he'd made a mistake in giving her the Barbie doll.

He arrived at the service station and speculated with the guys working there about what might be the problem with Gina's car. He knew these guys, and although he thought they were honest and not likely to tack on extra charges just because Gina was female, it wouldn't hurt to have them know he was involved.

"Fix the air conditioner, too, while you're at it," he said, when they were about to leave.

"I can't afford it, Clay," Gina whispered to him.

"Fix it," he repeated to the attendant. Then to Gina, "I'll take care of it."

She was quiet as they walked back to his Jeep. Finally, she spoke. "You've done too much for me," she said.

"You need air-conditioning." He opened the door for her. "And I can afford it."

He noticed she was perspiring when he got into the driver's seat. The hazy cool air from the day before had given way to a brutal heat. "I don't mean to make you feel obligated to me in any way," he reassured her.

"I know," she said, her voice soft.

He asked her more questions about the rattle in her car, his mind clicking through the possibilities of how that sound might relate to the problem she was having with the car now. She suddenly interrupted him.

"There's Lacey!" she said, pointing past him to a strip of shops.

Clay turned to look.

"You missed her," she said. "She just went into a store with a guy."

He groaned. "Yet another one of Lacey's men," he said. "Was it Josh, I hope? Or at least someone you've seen her with before?"

"Nope. A new one," she said. "He looked like kind of an old guy. He had a ponytail and—"

Clay laughed, relieved. "That's Tom. Her father."

"Her… Oh! I forgot Alec is not her biological father."

"She spends a lot of time with Tom," he said. He felt nearly euphoric to know that Lacey was with Tom and not another nameless boyfriend.

Gina fiddled with the air-conditioning vent for a moment. "There's something I don't understand," she said. "You're older than she is, and Alec's *your* father, but—"

"My mother had a brief affair with Tom." Clay bit the words off. It was so hard to imagine his mother cheating on his father. Unbearable to think about, really. "My father needed to travel a lot in the early days of their marriage. My mother was young and vulnerable and I guess she felt neglected. But they had a strong marriage. They were able to work it out."

"That's good," Gina said. "I have a real problem with infidelity."

He thought he should ask her what she meant by that. The comment seemed like an invitation, but he couldn't make himself form the words to ask such a loaded, personal question, and an awkward silence stretched between them for a few minutes.

"What do you need to do for this client?" Gina asked as they neared Southern Shores.

"It's a couple, Joe and Fiona Reiker, who used to be friends with Terri and me," he said. He hadn't seen them since Terri's funeral. "They own an old cottage in Southern Shores and they want to bring it up to date a bit."

"May I come in with you? I'd like to watch you work."

"I don't know how exciting it will be," he said with a smile, "but of course you can come in. I wouldn't leave you in the car in this heat, anyway."

He pulled into the long driveway of the oceanfront cottage, which always looked a bit out of place tucked among the flat-roofed houses in Southern Shores. He'd had ideas for redesigning this cottage for years now, and he was pleased the Reikers finally wanted to do it.

Inside the cottage, Clay felt unexpectedly uncomfortable. It was strange to see Joe and Fiona without Terri's presence—and with Gina's. Fiona had been Terri's closest friend. She had probably grieved nearly as hard as he had over her loss. He introduced Gina to them, hoping they didn't think there was something going on between the two of them, that he'd been able to move on that quickly. He explained in far too much detail how Gina happened to be with him that evening, giving them more information than they could possibly want to know. But although Gina squirmed at the attention being given her, the explanation seemed to put Joe and Fiona's curiosity to rest. They showed him the house, and he took pictures and measurements and talked with them about the changes they wanted. It was a typical visit with a prospective client. No surprises, until they were about to walk out the door.

Gina hung back when Fiona gave him a long hug. "You know, Clay…" Fiona leaned away from him, but kept her hands on his arms. There were tears in her eyes. "We never talked about the baby."

"The baby?" He felt stupid. What was she talking about?

"You know. Learning that Terri was pregnant just days before she died," Fiona said. "I know that made it a double blow for you. I'm so sorry."

He kept his face impassive. "Thanks," he said with a curt nod that belied the sudden turmoil inside him.

His cheeks were burning by the time he and Gina reached his Jeep, and he thought he might be sick. He leaned against the driver's-side door, while Gina got in. *Terri had been pregnant.* When had she planned on telling him?

Whatever Gina might have thought of his reaction, she said nothing for the drive home. He barely remembered she was in the Jeep with him, as he tried to piece together all that had happened in those few days before Terri's death. She could have told him she was expecting triplets then, and he wouldn't have reacted. He'd had other things on his mind.

When they reached the chain across the dirt lane, he unbuckled his seat belt to get out and unlock it, but Gina already had her own key at the ready. She hopped out of the Jeep and unlocked the padlock, then got back into the car. He started driving again, avoiding the ruts in the road to the best of his ability.

"Something's bothering you," Gina said when they had come to a standstill in the parking lot.

"Not really." He felt himself shutting down, running away, and the feeling comforted him in its familiarity. *Open up to her,* his father had said. Then he heard Terri's words: *You're disabled. You can't help it. You're a guy.*

He turned off the engine, and the car quickly filled with heat. "Yes," he said, turning toward Gina. "Something's bothering me," he said.

"Do you want to talk about it?"

He sighed, rubbing his temple with his fingertips before he nodded. "Let's go up on the tower," he said.

The sky had turned a bruised purple color as they walked toward the lighthouse, but inside the tower, it was already night. They clutched the railing as they climbed the spiral staircase. Gina needed to stop on one of the landings to catch her breath, and he waited for her, leaning against the cool surface of the bricks. When they reached the top, he sat down next to her, wondering how he would start the conversation. But she made the first move for him.

"Something upset you at Joe and Fiona's," she said.

He looked out to sea. It was already too dark to see the buoy, but he knew the general location of the lens, and kept his gaze on the area.

"I didn't know Terri was pregnant." He blurted out the words.

"I thought that was it," she said. "I could see it in your face when Fiona said that about the baby. What a painful way to find out."

"Do you know how Terri died?" He glanced at Gina. Her cheeks were stained with purple shadows from the sky.

"Lacey told me she died in an accident," she said. "I didn't want to pry, though. Were you driving?"

He was confused, but only for a moment. "Oh, no," he said. "It wasn't that sort of accident."

She waited for him to speak again.

"She was a terrific wife," he said. "I was less than a terrific husband."

"Did you have an affair?" she asked, and he remembered her comment from a couple of hours earlier about having "a problem with infidelity."

"Yes," he said, then offered her a rueful smile. "But not the way you think. I had an affair with my search and rescue work and with my diving and windsurfing and architecture and with my big fat ego. I didn't give Terri the attention she needed. I took her for granted." He watched the lights of a ship move slowly across the horizon. "I wasn't the right husband for her, really," he said. "She needed someone who could talk to her about…you know the sort of guy women want. Men who can talk about their feelings. Men whose eyes don't glaze over when women talk about theirs. Men who can sit through a chick flick without falling asleep."

Gina laughed lightly. "That's what we have girlfriends for." She rested her hand on his back. "You know, you are one of the nicest men I've ever met," she said. "And you and Terri were together a long time. People tend to take each other for granted after a while. But you had a shared passion, right? The search and rescue work?"

Clay shook his head. "People thought we did, but that wasn't the truth. It was *my* passion. I started doing search and rescue right after I got out of college, about the same time we got married. Sasha was a natural, and I took seminars and really threw myself into learning search and rescue skills. Terri got into it mainly in self-defense. She knew if she didn't, she'd never see me. I was only thinking about myself."

"But she enjoyed it, didn't she?" Gina removed her hand from his back and he missed the feeling of it there. "I mean, once she got into it?"

"Not like I did."

"I think you're being too hard on yourself, Clay."

He was quiet for a moment. "I feel responsible for her death," he said, surprising himself. He had never spoken those words out loud before.

"Why?"

"Because…" He wasn't sure how to explain it. "I became reknowned as a dog trainer and it went to my head," he said. "The Discovery Channel wanted to film me for a show they were doing on search and rescue work, and I was so blown away by that fact, so damn puffed up about it, that I couldn't think about anything else. They were going to come on a Tuesday, right after Thanksgiving, to film me working with Sasha. But on Monday, I got a call that a building had collapsed in Florida and that Sasha and I were needed down there. I talked to the Discovery people, and they said that Tuesday was the only day they could be in the area to tape. They sounded like it was no big deal, that they would find another well-known trainer to film. I asked Terri if she would take my place in Florida with her dog, Raven. I knew she didn't really want to go. She liked the search and rescue training itself, I really believe that, but she would get extremely upset when she was at a site after a tragedy. She couldn't handle blood and gore and finding people dead instead of alive. She couldn't handle the human suffering." He remembered the nightmares Terri would have for weeks after a search. He remembered her telling him that she didn't want to do it anymore. "You don't really mean that," he'd said to her, ignoring her feelings because they didn't mesh with what he wanted her to feel.

"Terri said she would go," he told her. "I know I should have talked to her about it more. I knew she didn't really want to do it, but once she said yes, I just tuned her out. My ego had better things to do."

Gina was quiet, her hands folded and still on her bare knees, and he wondered what she was thinking.

"They came to do the taping," he continued, "but I got the call while they were setting up. The part of the building Terri and Raven had been in collapsed, and they'd been crushed."

"Oh, God," Gina said. "How terrible."

He was glad of the falling darkness, glad the emotion in his face would not be that visible to her.

"A couple of months later," he said, "I was cleaning up the files on her laptop computer and I came across an e-mail she'd written to a friend in Texas the day she left. She talked about how much she didn't want to go, how much she hated putting herself and Raven through it all. How she knew she would have nightmares afterward. But that she was glad she could do it for me, because…" He felt his voice starting to break and took in a deep breath. "Because she was so proud of me and so glad that I was finally getting the recognition I deserved."

"She didn't say anything in the e-mail to her friend about being pregnant?" Gina asked.

He shook his head. "She must have just found out. I know why she didn't tell me. She knew if she did, I would have stopped her from going to Florida in my place, and I'd miss out on being on the Discovery Channel."

"And you would have done that, wouldn't you? Gone in her place."

"Yes!" he said. He would give anything to have that chance all over again. To do things right this time. He was not a monster. He squeezed his eyes shut as Fiona's words about the baby came back to him. "I can't believe I was going to be a father."

"Is that something you wanted?"

He nodded. "We both did. We'd been trying, actually, but

it just wasn't happening." His voice caught in the back of his throat.

Gina turned to wrap her arms around him, and the gesture unleashed something in him and he began to cry. She rocked him ever so gently, half mother, half friend, one hundred percent confidante. After a while, he lifted his head from her shoulder and she loosened her grip on him. Only then did he see the tears in her own eyes.

He smiled, touching his fingers to her wet cheeks. "I'm sorry," he said. "I didn't mean to make you cry."

She smiled back. "It's all right," she said.

"No one knows that I sent Terri in my place," he said. "Except you. And I didn't mean to dump it all on you."

"That's all right," she said. "I'm glad you did."

"Let's go down," he said, standing. He held his hand out to her to help her up.

Carefully, silently, they made their way down the spiral staircase, then across the yard. At the door to the house, Gina touched his arm.

"Terri was wrong about one thing," she said.

"What's that?"

"You can, too, talk about your feelings."

Chapter Thirty-Five

GINA SAT CROSS-LEGGED ON HER BED IN HER robe, the Barbie doll in her hand. She'd opened both her windows wider, but still, the steamy heat of the night was barely broken by the ocean breeze. For once, she was not thinking about Rani or the lens. Out there on the lighthouse stairs, for just a moment, she had forgotten about her own pain and been caught up by Clay's. He'd lost his wife, his child. His future. The anguish in his voice was still with her. Hard to believe his wife had said he was unfeeling. She'd had him all wrong.

For the first time in years, she wanted to hold a man, to wrap her body around his. She wanted to awaken in the safety of his arms, a safety she had once imagined but never truly known and had given up on ever experiencing. In the room down the hall, she thought she might find it. She might find comfort, and she might be able to give it back.

Standing up, she tightened the belt of her robe over her T-shirt and opened the door to her room. The hallway was dark and silent, except for the ever-present whisper of ocean waves in the distance. *Courage,* she said to herself, taking a step forward. *The worst he can do is tell you to leave. You've had worse done to you before.*

She moved quietly down the hall, then knocked softly on Clay's door, not wanting Lacey to hear.

"Yes?"

"It's Gina, Clay," she said. "May I come in?"

He didn't answer immediately, and she bit her lip, waiting.

"Yes," he said.

She opened the door. The room was dark except for the rectangle of moonlight falling across his bed, and she could see that he was sitting up, bare-chested, leaning against the tall, wrought-iron headboard. He was covered only by a sheet, a light summer quilt folded at the foot of the bed. Sasha padded toward her to nestle his head beneath the curve of her palm.

"Is everything all right?" he asked.

Now that she was here, she felt embarrassed and awkward, inspired by one contemplative moment in her room that he had not been a part of. Maybe she had misunderstood what had happened on the lighthouse stairs. Maybe she'd mistaken his need for confession for a real intimacy between them. But now she was here. She just needed to blurt it out and take the consequences.

"I was wondering if I could get in bed with you?" she asked, her fingers deep in Sasha's fur.

He looked up at her, the moonlight playing in his pale eyes and on his lips. She saw the slightest hint of a smile there, and after a moment, he pulled back his sheet.

"Get in," he said, reaching for her hand.

She took his hand and slid beneath the sheet, and when she wrapped an arm across his chest and breathed in the salty scent of his skin, she started to cry. For what, exactly, she could not have said.

He wrapped both his arms around her then, holding her

the way she had held him earlier on the lighthouse stairs. She felt him stroke her hair, kiss her head.

"It's all right," he said, although he could not have known the source of her tears. "It's all right."

After a while, he drew away from her, gazing into her eyes. Lowering his lips to hers, he kissed her.

They moved deeper into the bed, and lying next to her, he tugged on the sash of her robe to open it, then reached inside to find her still well clothed in her nighttime T-shirt and shorts.

He laughed, pushing her away from him a bit to get a better look. "What do you have on here?" he asked, running his hand over the T-shirt where it covered her ribs.

"It's not too elegant, sorry," she said, giggling. "I didn't know I was going to be doing this tonight."

He lifted his hand slowly, then smoothed his fingers over the side of her breast through the shirt, one small touch that made her hungry for more. "I can tell this is the final layer, though," he said. His thumb grazed her nipple so softly it might have been a mistake, and she sucked in her breath. "Nothing under here but you," he said. "And you feel so good." He leaned over to kiss her again, one kiss that went on and on, and she felt her body open up to him.

It had been months for him, years for her. She had not known she would ever want this again, but she did. She'd forgotten how it felt to be undressed slowly by someone else, to be touched delicately, intimately, to be suckled by a lover who made her remember how connected her lips and her breasts, her neck and her earlobes all were to that place low in her belly that wanted him inside her. How could she have thought she would never want this again?

Once he *was* inside her, he moved slowly, saying her name,

and she wrapped her arms tightly around his shoulders, loving the closeness. Loving *him*.

There was no mistaking it when he came. Her husband had come so quietly that she was sometimes not sure, but Clay groaned loudly with release, his body rigid above hers. When he lay on top of her again, he was careful to keep his full weight from crushing her, and her eyes filled once more with sudden, unexpected tears.

They lay that way for a while without speaking. Then he rolled onto his side, his arm and leg still circling her, as if he was not quite ready to let her go. Lifting his head to look down at her, he ran his fingertip over her lips. "You didn't get a chance to come," he said. "I'm sorry. I couldn't hold off any longer."

She laughed quietly. "I'm glad you didn't, or you would have been holding off for a long, long time," she said. "It's not that easy for me. I've never come that way." The words embarrassed her, but it seemed a night for honesty.

"Ah," he said. "You should have told me."

"It's all right," she said. "It was wonderful anyway. Being close to you was all I wanted."

"Maybe so," he said, "but it's not all you're getting."

He kissed her gently, then moved down the bed until his head was between her legs. The first touch of his tongue made her catch her breath. The only man who had ever done this to her had been her husband, and then only a couple times. It took her "way too long," he had complained, and the more he complained, of course, the longer it took. But it didn't take her long tonight. Clay's mouth was magic.

Afterward, they lay together holding each other tightly, and his silence began to worry her. She knew it was possible to do things in the heat of passion that you would regret the moment that heat became lukewarm.

"Don't feel guilty about this, Clay," she said, her hand on his chest. "Please don't. I don't want you to feel—"

He leaned away from her and pressed two fingers to her lips. "I'm okay," he said. "Actually—" he gave a slight laugh "—I feel pretty good. I like how you were able to tell me what you needed."

She returned his smile, then snuggled up against him again. If this was a night for honesty, she had far more to tell him. Even so, she knew she would be leaving things out.

"You told me so much tonight out on the lighthouse," she said. "Now I'd like to tell you about me. Something I've been keeping from you. From everyone."

He smoothed her hair away from her damp forehead. "Okay," he said. "Tell me."

She pressed her lips to his shoulder. Where to begin?

"My mother," she said, "was adopted."

"Is that another reason you're interested in adopting a child?" he asked.

"Only in a small way," she said. "My mother was adopted as an infant, practically a newborn, and she was the only child of a couple who lived here in North Carolina."

"North Carolina?" he asked in surprise.

"Yes. Raleigh, I think. Anyhow, my mother didn't remember much about *her* adoptive mother because she died when my mother was very young. But her father was…not abusive, really, but I guess he sort of fell apart after his wife died. He moved them to Bellingham, for some reason I don't know. I guess he got a job there. I don't remember the sort of work he did, but it was a blue-collar job. He was an alcoholic and he gambled away his earnings. Although he himself wasn't abusive, some of his gambling buddies were, and he didn't do anything to protect my mother from them." She lifted her head to look at Clay, whose eyes were open, staring at the ceiling. "Are you following this?" she asked.

"Completely."

"Well, her father ignored her for the most part," she said, her head on his shoulder again. "He said she was in the way. So when my mother was seventeen, she got married to her high-school sweetheart, mostly to escape life with her father. But he was a drinker, too. That was all she knew, I guess. He wanted kids, and she had a couple of miscarriages, so he got fed up with her and divorced her." She was beginning to feel the old anger toward the entire masculine sex creeping in again, and she hugged Clay tighter.

"Then she was on her own for a few years," she continued, "working as a custodian in an elementary school, when she met a guy named Damon. They moved in together and she got pregnant and had me. They never married. Damon, who I don't remember at all, felt trapped by her and a baby, at least according to my mother. He took off when I was a year old, and he was killed when I was three in a motorcycle accident."

"I'm sorry," Clay said.

She shrugged away the sympathy. "My mother was wonderful," she said. "She took the place of two parents. She was still a custodian as I was growing up, in the same elementary school I went to, and the kids loved her. I never felt embarrassed that she was just a custodian. I didn't know any different, really. She was warm and friendly and funny. We lived in an apartment building that people would probably describe as seedy, but inside our apartment it was always clean and pretty. My mother would get fabric remnants and make nice curtains and things."

Gina took her hand from Clay's chest for a moment to hug herself. God, she missed her mother!

"You chilly?" Clay asked.

"No," she said, but she pulled herself closer to him. "My mom spent most of her time and energy on me. She never got married or really had a boyfriend after my father. She'd given up on men by the time I was in school."

"Understandably," Clay said.

"Right," Gina concurred. "So it was the two of us against the world, or at least that's how it felt. We were each other's best friends. And we were the only family either of us had. She pushed me in school. She didn't want me to end up like she did. She was so proud of me for becoming a teacher."

Clay was quiet, but she felt certain he was listening.

"I, um…I ended up marrying a guy I met in college," she said. "His name was Bruce, and he was wonderful, or so I thought. Even my mother, the man-hater, liked him. I trusted him completely. I was dying to start a family. That's all I've ever wanted. Family. I only had my mom, ever. That's one reason why I want Rani so badly. I'd like to think I'm going through with the adoption just to help her, but it's for me, too. I want her.

"We planned everything out, my husband and I. We decided to wait until we were thirty, when we'd be established in our careers and have some money put away. But then my mom got sick. That was two years ago. She was diagnosed with breast cancer that had already spread to her lungs. I knew she was dying."

Clay held her tighter and she pressed her lips to his neck. She could hear Sasha's gentle snoring in the corner of the room. "My husband and I talked about having her move in with us so we could take care of her. There were no other relatives, and I didn't want her to go into a nursing home. She was only fifty-seven. My husband was totally supportive of the idea. I thought I was so lucky to have found him. Then one day, one of my friends told me that she knew Bruce was having an affair with one of *her* friends, a woman I didn't know."

"Oh, shit," Clay said. "There's your problem with infidelity."

"Right. The woman had told my friend what a terrible wife I was, how I'd brought my mother to live with us and everything. She'd said, 'What twenty-eight-year-old man wants to live with his mother-in-law?' But Bruce had never told me that it bothered him, so how could I know? That's one reason why I admire you so much, Clay. The way you look after Henry."

Clay squeezed her hand where it rested on his chest.

"I felt like I was hearing about some other man when she told me all this about Bruce. It was so hard to imagine him having an affair to begin with, and saying that sort of thing was just so out of character. But it all turned out to be true." She remembered something else Bruce's lover had told her friend, something she couldn't share with Clay because the pain was still too great. The woman had said that Gina had never had an orgasm with Bruce, that she'd made him feel like "less of a man."

"So," she continued, "I confronted Bruce, and he said that he no longer loved me, but he hadn't known how to tell me that. He said the affair had been going on since the week after our wedding."

"Oh, Gina," Clay said.

"We split up, and that's when I decided I would be better off without a man in my life."

"I don't blame you a bit," he said.

"It got worse, though. It turned out that Bruce had bought all this stuff I didn't know about. He'd bought the other woman jewelry, taken her on expensive vacations when I thought he was out of town on business, et cetera, et cetera.

And half that debt became mine when we split up. I lost all my savings. I managed to pay off the debt before I applied to adopt Rani, but it left me broke."

"Couldn't your lawyer have spared you from that?"

"Unfortunately, no." No more than her lawyer had been able to help her get Rani out of India. "So, while all that was going on, my mother was having chemotherapy and getting sicker. I took a leave of absence from my job to take care of her. Hospice helped a lot, but I did most of it, and I felt…" She tried to remember the hodgepodge of feelings she'd experienced back then. "I felt miserable that I was going to lose her, but so glad I could be there for her. That I could be the one to take care of her."

"I love your attitude," Clay said, and Gina smiled. How could his wife have thought he wasn't a good listener?

"My mother had always had one wish," she said. "She wanted to find her birth parents. I made up my mind I was going to find them for her before she died. It seemed like a good chance that they'd still be alive."

"Did you find them?" Clay asked.

"Not exactly," she said. "I used one of those services on the Internet that can track down people for you, and I was able to find an original birth certificate for my mother. It named her parents as Elizabeth and Dennis Kittering." She stopped for a moment and lifted her head to look at him. "Do those names mean anything to you?" she asked.

Clay frowned. "No. Should they?"

"Probably not," she said, lowering her head to his chest again. "Anyway, I was able to find out that the last address for the Kitterings was in Charlotte, North Carolina. I hired someone to stay with my mother for a few days, and I flew there, to Charlotte. I went to the address I had for them. A woman lived there who turned out to be their grandniece.

She told me that Dennis had died a very long time ago and that Elizabeth had died ten years earlier." Gina had been so disappointed. Her fantasy of giving her mother the gift of her family before she died disintegrated. "I explained about my mother and asked her if she—the grandniece—could tell me about Dennis and Elizabeth so I'd have something to tell my mother. Like, for instance, why they had given her up for adoption."

"Was the niece shocked to know that her aunt and uncle had put a baby up for adoption?" Clay asked.

"No," Gina said. "She said that most people knew about it, although no one really knew why they did it. It wasn't really talked about. She said that she had saved a box of things belonging to Elizabeth and Dennis because she'd always thought she'd try to find that baby one day. But she never got around to it. She seemed glad to get rid of the box, and glad that my mother would have the things, but not particularly interested in pursuing any kind of relationship with us." Which had been fine with Gina. She hadn't really liked the woman.

"What was in the box?" Clay asked.

"A bunch of odds and ends. Some pins, a couple of books. An old pink diary and a ruby necklace." She lifted her hand, and the ruby ring on her finger caught the moonlight. "I had this made from the ruby," she said.

"Whose diary was it?" Clay asked.

"Elizabeth's," she said. "And it was a real treasure trove."

"In what way?"

"Well, I started reading it to my mother." They had moved a hospital bed into her mother's bedroom, and Gina had sat at the side of the bed, reading to her. Her mother's eyes would be closed, but she was listening. Sometimes she would ask Gina to repeat something she'd read. Gina took in a breath. "What we learned as we read the book was that Elizabeth had been the daughter of Caleb and Mary Poor. She grew up here, in this house. I'm a descendant. I'm Mary Poor's great-granddaughter."

For a moment, the room was very quiet, only the rumble of the ocean filling the air. She was not certain Clay had understood what she'd said, and she was about to repeat it when he suddenly let go of her and sat up.

"Gina." He was frowning at her, deep lines carved into his forehead. "Why didn't you tell us this?"

He was angry. She hadn't expected that, but perhaps she should have. "I came here just to see the lighthouse." She struggled to find the words to explain herself and her actions. "I didn't expect to meet anyone here. To make any friends. To get involved with people in any way. I wanted to keep my private life private. But I've come to care about you. To trust you. You're such a good person. And after you told me about Terri, I wanted to tell you the truth. I wanted you to know."

"It's just plain weird that you didn't tell us this," he said. "That you've been living in this house as though it meant nothing to you. That you've let us do things for you without telling us… It's…" He got up and pulled on his shorts, then sat down on the edge of the bed again, far from where she was lying. Gina wished she hadn't told him, or better yet, that she'd told him long ago. She felt the delicate thread of connection she'd had with him just moments ago slipping away from her.

"I never meant to—"

"Now I get why the lens is so important to you. It's part of your heritage. Why didn't you just say that in the first place? Why'd you give us that line about being a lighthouse historian? Which you're not, are you?"

She shook her head. "No."

"You've been manipulating Lacey and me. And trying to

manipulate my father, too. Man, he had you figured out right. I should have listened to him."

She wondered what Alec had said to him, but she didn't really care what his father thought about her. What mattered was what Clay was thinking.

"No, I didn't, Clay," she said. "At least, not intentionally." She knew even that was a lie.

"Why did you just sleep with me?" he asked. "You'd sleep with the devil to get Rani out of India. I haven't forgotten you said that. So you slept with me, hoping I'll persuade my father to help you raise the lens, right?"

"No, Clay." She grabbed her robe and put it on, getting out of the bed herself. "That's not it at all. I don't want you to say a word to your father about it, all right? That's not why I slept with you."

"Why then?" he demanded.

"Because I love you," she said, finding the truth after all. "I love you." More quietly this time. "I'm sorry that I hurt you by keeping the truth from you. I didn't intend that to happen. I've always been the one who got hurt in the past. I know what it feels like. I'm sorry if I've made you feel that way."

He turned away from her, facing the window. "Go back to your room, Gina," he said.

She didn't budge. "I know keeping that information from you was wrong," she said. "And I'm sorry. But please, Clay, don't make it be unforgivable."

"Get out," he said. "Maybe we can talk about it tomorrow. Right now, I'm too pissed off."

"All right," she said. "But think about this. Think about if you're trying to find a reason not to love me. If you think you're honoring Terri somehow by not living your own life."

He didn't turn around, and she feared she had pushed too

far in saying that to him. Before he could answer her, she left his room and went back to her own.

Crawling into her own bed, she fought back tears. She hadn't expected his anger, but he certainly had a right to it. She'd always thought of men as the deceptive gender, but who was the deceptive one now? She couldn't help it. She wouldn't have told her own beloved mother what she was up to.

Just moments earlier, he'd been touching her, loving her. She shivered with the memory of his hands on her body, and she could still smell the salty scent of his skin like an aura around her. Rolling onto her side, she stared out at the ruins of the lighthouse, barely visible in the soft light of the night sky.

Her mother had made her read the diary to her over and over again, holding on to the past she had never known. After her mother died, Gina had tucked the diary away with the other things belonging to her mother that she'd wanted to save. The small, pink book would always be linked to her mother's final weeks in her mind, and she needed no reminder of that painful time.

But two months ago, she'd brought the diary out again, needing to reread it. She'd needed to pursue the secrets it held.

Chapter Thirty-Six

Thursday, May 7, 1942

LAST NIGHT WAS THE BEST NIGHT OF MY ENTIRE
life. It's amazing that with all that's happened in the past few
weeks I can say that, but it truly was. I snuck out as usual
and was walking through the woods to be with Sandy when
he suddenly appeared in front of me. He told me he was not
on duty tonight, that Teddy Pearson was, and that he had a
plan. He held my hand as we walked through the woods,
across the Pole Road and on out to the sound, and we finally
reached the rickety old pier west of Kiss River. There was a
small motorboat there, which he had borrowed from a friend.
I have to say, I know more about motorboats than he does,
but I let him think he was doing a good job as we sailed into
the sound. There was a full moon last night, and the weather
is really warming up. It was beautiful out there, and the jellyfish were lighting up like they do sometimes. That shocked

Sandy. He'd never seen anything like it. I think it just made the night that much more spectacular.

For the first time ever, we talked about the future. Sandy wants to be a mechanical engineer, he said, working on ships. He's really gotten to like the Banks and the sea. I'm proud of him for letting it seep into his bones when he'd hated it so much when he first got here. After he gets out of the Coast Guard, he wants to go to college. He asked me what I want to do after I graduate and I said I want to go to college, too. I told him I want to be a teacher. He said maybe we could go to the same school, and then get married and live back here in the Banks. He said all that! I was floating, as you can imagine, and not just because I was in a boat.

We talked about having children. We both want to have three. Both of us are only children, and we don't want any of our children to ever have that alone feeling.

Then Sandy told me that he needed to talk to me about something serious. I couldn't imagine how anything could be more serious than marriage and children! But I said, okay, what is it? He admitted that it bothers him how much attention I am giving to the other boys, as well as how much attention I'm getting back from them.

He said, "I've tried not to be jealous, but I don't understand why you started spending so much time with all of them, especially Ralph and Jimmy and Ted. I'm not accusing you of anything. Just confused." He was hurt, I could tell.

I was afraid, but knew I absolutely *had* to tell him. I said, "I'll tell you the real reason why, but only if you swear you won't tell anyone. Not a soul."

He looked very confused. "What are you talking about?" he asked.

"Swear to me. No matter what I tell you, you'll keep it to yourself."

"I swear it," he said. He looked real serious.

So then I told him everything. I said how Mr. Hewitt took me up near Poyner's Hill to talk to me. I told him, "Mr. Hewitt said the German who was hurt by the boar told the sheriff that…"

"He was killed before he could tell the sheriff anything," Sandy said before I could finish my sentence.

"No," I said, "he wasn't. And he told the man who questioned him that someone in the Banks was in cahoots with the Germans, giving them information or whatever and maybe helping them sneak onshore to blow things up."

Sandy looked shocked. "That's ridiculous. Who would do something like that?"

"First he thought it might be one of the Coast Guard, since they'd have that information. Now I'm not sure what he's thinking."

Sandy looked as angry as I've ever seen him. "How could Bud think it would be one of us?" he asked me. "He knows us better than that. I don't even think a one of us has any German blood in him. Except Jimmy Brown."

That was a surprise! "Jimmy Brown is German?" I asked.

"Yes, but keep that to yourself, all right?" He still looked a little angry and I was afraid it was with me. "He changed his name when the war started. Brown was really spelled B-r-a-u-n. That's the way the Germans spell it. But that just shows how much he didn't want to be associated with the Germans. He hates them."

So Jimmy was German! There were a million questions I wanted to ask Sandy, such as was Jimmy born in the United States, did he have relatives still in Germany. Finally, I thought I had something important to put in a note to Mr. Hewitt. But now I realize that I would be double-crossing Sandy if I told him. So I'll have to look further into Jimmy myself before I say anything to Mr. Hewitt.

"Does Mr. Hewitt know about Jimmy's name?" I asked.

"It's none of Bud's business," Sandy said. "Jimmy would never do anything to hurt America." Suddenly, he pounded his fist on the side of the boat. "I just can't believe Bud would put you in such a dangerous position. You have to stop this spying or whatever it is you're doing right now."

I ignored what he said, starting to wish I hadn't told him.

"I saw Mr. Sato," I said. "Mr. Hewitt suspected he might be helping the Germans somehow."

"What do you mean, you saw him?"

"I went to his house and pretended I needed to use his phone."

"And what if Moto Sato had been a spy and you were in his house? He could've hit you over the head with something and no one would ever have known what happened to you."

"I'm sure he's not a spy," I said. "He's just a crippled old man. He doesn't understand English at all. And I tried some German on him. He didn't understand that either."

Sandy raised his eyebrows. "You speak German?"

"Just two sentences," I said. "But he didn't understand them."

Sandy shook his head. "Bess, you are the sweetest girl. And you're kind and beautiful. But you are still really young and you can be pretty naive sometimes."

That made me mad, but I didn't say anything. I hate that word *naive*.

"Let's not talk about this now," I said. I had to change the subject, because Sandy and I had been feeling so good about each other a few minutes ago and I'd ruined it by bringing up all this talk about spying.

He was still upset, I could tell, but at least it wasn't because he was jealous. I was a little worried he might say something to Mr. Hewitt, but I tried to put that out of my mind. He would get himself in trouble as much as me if he told Mr. Hewitt we were close enough that I'd confided such a big secret to him.

He finally relaxed, and we turned off the motor and pulled the cushions from the seats of the boat onto the floor and got comfortable, lying next to each other, looking up at the beautiful stars. I knew what was going to happen. This was the right time and the right place. I can't put the details here, of course. I'll just repeat—it was the most wonderful night of my life. I *was* a little afraid of getting pregnant, but Sandy said we could practice withdrawal and that I wouldn't get pregnant that way. I think that was hard for him to do, and I felt really cared about that he did it.

Then came the one bad part of the night. We were just floating in the boat when we heard some noises from shore. Our boat had drifted down the sound a ways, and now we were straight out from Mr. Sato's house. We heard some whoops and yelling, and saw some boys running around the house. Their feet were pounding on the deck.

"What's going on there?" Sandy asked me, like I might have the answer.

We soon found out. The boys disappeared, and then we noticed fire around the bottom of the house. Those boys must've poured gasoline around the house and set it on fire! Before I could say a word, Sandy started the boat up and we zipped over to the beach near the house.

"We have to get Mr. Sato and his daughter-in-law out!" I said, jumping from the boat.

Sandy was already ahead of me. I noticed that the daughter-in-law's car was not in the driveway. There's a rumor she has a boyfriend, so I figured she was with him.

Sandy jumped right over the flames and into the front door, and I followed him. Inside, we found Mr. Sato unconscious on the floor near his bed. It was real smoky in there and it looked like he was trying to get to his wheelchair when the smoke got him. Sandy and I were both choking. I was scared we would all be trapped inside the house.

I was worried Mr. Sato might already be dead. "Help me carry him," Sandy said. He got Mr. Sato's arms and shoulders, and I took his legs and we carted him into the living room, Sandy and me coughing and hacking and Mr. Sato quiet as a dead man. He was very light, but my arms were still shaking like he weighed a ton. The flames were too high by the front door for us to get out that way, so we carted him through the kitchen to the back door that led out onto the deck. We were able to get outside there, but the deck was on fire and there was nowhere for us to go but over the railing. We had to throw Mr. Sato into the water first and then quick jumped in ourselves to hold him up. Not even the water woke him up and I was sure then that he was dead. Sandy and I swam to the beach, dragging him all the way, trying to keep his head out of the water. Then we lifted him and carried him to the front of his yard where he'd be safe from the flames.

Mr. Sato was still unconscious, but Sandy felt his pulse and said he was alive. Then he started groaning a bit, and I know Sandy and I were both thinking the same thing, that we couldn't stay there with him. We couldn't take the risk of being seen together, by him or anyone else.

Sandy turned to me. "You go home," he said. "I'll make sure the sheriff knows Mr. Sato's house is on fire. Don't tell anyone what we did or that we were even out here."

I sure knew better than to tell anyone! I ran all the way home and snuck in the house, hoping the dip in the sound had washed the smell of smoke off me, and went to bed. It was a long time before I fell asleep. I kept remembering how strong and good Sandy was, caring about an old Japanese man enough to risk his own life to save him.

This morning over breakfast, Mama told me about the fire at Mr Sato's and how half the house was destroyed but he somehow managed to get out just in time. I pretended like this was all news to me. Mama doesn't know anything about my life. She doesn't know I'm a lifesaver, the owner of a beautiful ruby necklace, and no longer a virgin. And I think I'd better keep it that way!

Chapter Thirty-Seven

CLAY HEARD LACEY AND GINA TALKING IN THE kitchen as he and Sasha walked downstairs the morning after he'd banished Gina from his room. There was animation in their conversation, or at least, in his sister's voice, and he guessed that Gina had told her about her relationship to the Poors. He hoped that was all she had told her.

He still felt burned by the night before, by the secrets that Gina had kept from both him and his sister. What was her game? Her reticence to share her connection to Kiss River still did not make sense to him.

He should not have invited her into his bedroom, and certainly should not have made love to her, although he was finding that hard to regret despite the guilt that still teased him—and the realization this morning that, as far as he knew, they had used no form of birth control. She'd said she loved him, and he wanted to believe her; her actions toward him had grown loving indeed. Yet she'd withheld so much from him.

"Morning." He walked past the table to the back door to let Sasha out.

"Isn't it cool?" Lacey said, as he stood at the screen door waiting for Sasha to return. "About Gina being Mary Poor's great-granddaughter?"

"Very cool," he said without turning around. The flat tone of his voice didn't even seem to register on his sister's radar. She continued talking to Gina. "Mary never told me much about her daughter," she said. "Although I do remember her saying something about her running wild, and she didn't want me to turn out that way."

"Yes," Gina said, "she was a little adventurous."

He thought he could feel Gina's eyes burning a hole in his back.

"So, tell me more about your relationship with Mary," Gina said to Lacey.

Lacey laughed. "We smoked together a lot," she said. "She always wanted a cigarette. I started to feel like her drug dealer. She couldn't get them anyplace else, I don't think. She told me about how great my mother was and everything. She gave me lots of old-lady type advice. You know, be a good person, be honest, save yourself for marriage—"

"Smoke like a chimney," Clay interrupted her as Sasha ran past him into the room, ready for his breakfast.

Lacey leaned back to look at him as he scooped kibble into Sasha's bowl. "You really got up on the wrong side of the bed this morning, didn't you?" she asked.

He set the bowl on the floor for Sasha, not bothering to respond to his sister's question, and she returned her attention to Gina.

"You look like her," Lacey said, tilting her head to study their houseguest. "I mean, she was ancient and you're certainly not, but I can see her in the way your nose is shaped, and your eyes are the same shape, too, even though they're a different color."

Clay nearly laughed. He'd only seen Mary Poor once or twice, but Gina looked nothing like the old woman.

"Really?" Gina said. "I resemble my mother, so maybe I did get the genes from that side of the family."

Clay dropped two pieces of bread in the toaster and poured himself a cup of coffee, which he promptly dropped on the floor, sending coffee and shards of the ceramic mug in all directions.

"Damn it!" he said.

"What's going on with you?" Lacey sounded exasperated as she got up to reach for the paper towels.

"He's angry that I didn't tell both of you sooner," Gina said. "I should have, I know, and I'm sorry. I'm a private person. With the adoption and all, I've just had so much on my mind."

"Of course you do," Lacey said, helping him mop up the mess, and Clay wondered why his sister had been the child to inherit one hundred percent of their mother's kind tolerance.

Standing up from the floor with the pieces of mug in his hands, he looked at Gina and saw the hurt in her eyes. He remembered her tenderness from the night before. The way she'd listened to him on the lighthouse. Why should she have confided in him before last night? He certainly had not confided in her. He held her gaze now, the hard core inside him melting.

Tossing the mug into the trash can beneath the sink, he suddenly remembered that her car was in the shop.

"Do you need a ride to work?" he asked.

"I'm taking today off," she said. "I've decided to call your father just one last time. I'll tell him my connection to Kiss River. Maybe now that we know exactly where the lens is and that it's in one piece…" Her voice faded. "I have to give it one more try." She looked at Lacey. "Does he wear down eventually or does he just get more stubborn?"

"I'll talk to him for you," Lacey said.

"No, don't." Clay poured himself a fresh cup of coffee and sat down at the table across from Gina. "I'll call him," he said. He looked across the table at her, at the gratitude in her face. He wanted to reach over and touch her hand, take her back up to his room and make love to her again. And tell her that he loved her, too.

He left his office at eleven-thirty and drove to the Beacon Animal Hospital. Two men and three women sat in the waiting room, along with one crated cat, one lethargic white German shepherd and a golden retriever puppy with a serious-looking scratch on his nose.

The receptionist was new, someone he didn't recognize.

"I'm Clay O'Neill," he said to her. "Would you ask my father if he has time to have lunch with me today?"

"I'd know who you were without you saying a word," she said. "You sure got his eyes, didn't you?" She left her desk without waiting for his response and went through the door to the rear of the hospital. She returned a moment later.

"He said to give him fifteen minutes," she said.

"Thanks." He sat down next to the woman with the golden retriever, and the puppy immediately jumped from her lap into his.

"What happened to his nose?" He stroked the pup's silky head.

"We're down here on vacation," the woman explained, "and my daughter brought her cat. Rudy got a bit too close, I'm afraid."

"Ah," Clay said. He held the puppy's head between his hands as he looked into the brown eyes. "No more cats for you," he said. It was a nice pup and it would grow into a good dog. He already had that goofy golden retriever personality, but there was a sharpness in his eyes, an alertness Clay had learned to recognize. A year ago, he would have talked to the woman about training this handsome pup in search and rescue work. He wouldn't have been able to help himself. He might have performed a few evaluative tests with him right there, checking the dog's sensitivity to sight and sound. Goldens could be good at search and rescue. What they lacked in nose, they made up for in obedience and willingness to please. But he was no longer a dog trainer, and when the vet tech called the woman into the examining room, he looked away without even watching the puppy's gait.

In twenty minutes, Alec came into the waiting room.

"How about Sam and Omie's?" Alec suggested.

Sam and Omie's was every bit as old and nearly as casual as Shorty's, and it was much closer to the animal hospital. But Clay knew his father's real motivation for selecting it.

"You're in the mood for soft-shelled crabs, huh?" he asked.

"How'd you guess?" His father smiled at him as they headed out the door.

They took Alec's car, heading south along the beach road.

"Henry's birthday party's this Saturday, isn't it?" his father asked as he drove.

"Uh-huh." Clay had nearly forgotten and was grateful for his father's reminder. He'd planned the surprise party for Henry's eightieth birthday months ago. It would be held in Shorty's back room, and as far as he knew, everyone was managing to keep it a secret.

"How are you going to get him to Shorty's?" his father asked.

"I'll tell him that Lacey and I are taking him out to dinner," Clay said. "He'll know something's up when we take him to

Shorty's, since I'm sure he'd expect us to take him someplace fancier, but I think he'll still be surprised. Hope so, anyway."

They talked about one of Clay's projects for the rest of the drive, and he knew that his father was wondering what was really behind this request for lunch. Neither of them addressed that question, though, until they were sitting in one of the booths at the crowded restaurant and had ordered their soup.

"You seem…" Alec said, "I don't know…a little preoccupied, I guess. Is everything all right?"

Clay hadn't realized that his mood was that obvious. "Well," he said, "I have some interesting news."

"What's that?"

"It turns out that Gina is related to the Poors."

He saw his father's instant look of distrust. "How so?" he asked.

Clay repeated much of what Gina had told him the night before, about her mother being adopted and her deathbed wish to learn about her roots, and about the box of effects she had received from the grandniece, along with the diary.

"Have you seen the diary?" his father asked.

"No. I don't think she has it with her. At least she didn't mention it."

His father folded his arms across his chest, lips in a tight line. Finally, he spoke. "I know you like her, Clay, so I'll just say this once. I promise. But I have to say it."

Clay waited, knowing he couldn't stop him.

"Could she have made this up—this relationship to the Poors—as a way to up the ante?" he asked. "You know, make our hearts bleed for her about her long-lost family roots so we'll help her raise the lens?"

Clay sighed. "Dad, I believe her. She's not a lighthouse historian. She admitted that. Her connection to the Poors has been her real motivation all along."

"Then why the hell didn't she just say that?"

Clay hated the deep crease between his father's eyebrows as much as he hated the logic of his words.

"I think she just never expected to get to know people here. She thought she'd show up, see the lighthouse, visit the place where her grandparents lived, and go back to Washington. She didn't want to have to explain the whole thing with people who meant nothing to her. She didn't expect to make friends with Lacey and me. Or to have us...me...begin to mean something to her." God, he hoped he wasn't kidding himself about this.

"You're in love with her, aren't you?" his father said.

Clay nodded. "It's your fault," he said, half smiling. "You said to open up to her."

His father returned the smile. "And you did?"

Clay nodded. "She was great," he said, remembering the night before in his bedroom. "She was wonderful."

"Is the feeling mutual?"

"I think so."

His father sighed, then sat back as the waitress placed their bowls of soup in front of them. When she walked away, he leaned forward again and looked Clay squarely in the eye.

"I'll think about the lens, Clay," he said. "I will give it some very, very serious thought."

Chapter Thirty-Eight

Saturday, May 9, 1942

ALL OF A SUDDEN, EVERYTHING IS GOING WRONG.

This morning, I was late getting up and I didn't have time to go up to the lantern room to find the note Mr. Hewitt always leaves me on Friday nights because I had to help Mama with the baking and she would've been suspicious. I was real quick in my trip to the Coast Guard station with the pies and cookies because I needed to get that note before anyone else did. So when I got home, I went directly to the lantern room, and you can imagine how shocked I was to find Daddy there! I was afraid he might've found the note. I got ready to be asked a million questions, but then I saw Mr. Hewitt's note wedged into the coupling where it always was. What a relief! Daddy was only up there to clean the windows.

When he saw me, he put down the sponge he was using. "Guess what, Bessie?" he said to me. "They caught a spy!"

My first thought was Jimmy Brown, of course, because in

the note I left Mr. Hewitt last night, I'd told him about Jimmy changing his name. But that wasn't it at all.

"Who?" I said. I was trying not to sound all that interested because I didn't want to make him suspicious.

"Moto Sato, that's who!" Daddy said. "Bud Hewitt was just over here to tell us."

I was dumbfounded, but Daddy didn't seem to notice. He just kept on talking. "Everybody's suspected he was up to something, but nobody wanted to believe it because he seemed like such a nice old man who just liked to spend his days fishing in the sound."

I started stammering, I had a billion questions to ask. I was so confused!

"You know, he didn't burn up in that fire at his house," Daddy said, like this was news.

"Right, I know that," I answered.

"Well, when the sheriff got to his house, Mr. Sato was sitting up by the road, soaking wet. What do you think of that?"

I wasn't sure what Daddy was trying to say. I wondered if he knew what Sandy and I had done and was trying to trip me up. Maybe Mr. Sato had been more awake than we'd thought, and he told the sheriff we'd saved him. I clamped my mouth shut, afraid I was going to stick my foot in it if I said another word.

"So, they knew then that he wasn't crippled at all. That wheelchair of his was still in his bedroom. He must've run through the house and outside, jumped into the sound, swam to land and walked across his yard to the road. A crippled man couldn't have done all that. He couldn't give any other explanation for how he came to be there."

"Maybe someone saved him and left him there in his yard," I said.

"Then why didn't he say so?"

I didn't know how to answer that. "Why do they think he's a spy?" I asked.

"Because he's been faking being a crippled man all this time. Probably been stealing out to the beach at night, sending messages to the subs. They found a burned-out radio of some sort in his house."

It's just a regular old radio! I wanted to scream.

"He's *still* faking it, Bud told me," Daddy went on. "He pretended he couldn't walk when they tried to get him in the sheriff's car."

That old man can't walk worth a damn. I started to cry. I grabbed the chammy and went around to the other side of the lens, pretending to help with the windows, but the first thing I did over there was pull Mr. Hewitt's note out of the coupling and stuff it in the pocket of my dungarees. "So, what will happen to him?" I asked. I hoped he couldn't tell I was crying from the sound of my voice.

"Bud said he'd be questioned. If they can find some evidence on him, he'll be arrested. Otherwise, they'll just send him to one of them internment camps. His daughter-in-law was screaming and crying when they carted him away, but they'll be questioning her, too. She might have something to do with this. She was married to a Jap herself, after all."

Well, I knew I had to talk to Sandy right away. We needed to come clean, even though it would mean…well, I wasn't sure what it would mean. He might just get some kind of warning, but I would be locked in my room for life. It didn't matter. We couldn't let an innocent man get sent away.

I helped with the windows for a while so as not to make Daddy think I was up to something. Then I left the lighthouse and ran all the way back to the Coast Guard station, stopping only to read the note from Mr. Hewitt.

He wrote:

Bess, thank you for the information on Jimmy's last name. I don't think he's the one, though. I don't really blame him for changing his name, do you? It turns out, Mr. Sato managed to get out of his burning house without his wheelchair, so our suspicions about him might be correct after all. This is not a certainty, though, so please continue your good work and our exchange of notes, at least until I tell you otherwise.

"Oh, what a mess!" I thought when I read that note. He wasn't even going to bother talking to Jimmy now that he thought he had his spy.

Once I got to the Coast Guard station, I realized I had no idea what to do. I wasn't supposed to talk to Mr. Hewitt because people would get suspicious. I couldn't talk to Sandy for the same reason. Anyhow, it turned out that Mr. Hewitt and a bunch of the boys had gone to the scene of a sunken ship down to Oregon Inlet. Fortunately, Sandy was one of the boys left behind, along with Jimmy and Teddy and a few others. He hadn't been around when I'd brought the pies over earlier. He looked at me when I walked in, and I knew he was upset, too. I could tell by the look in his eyes. I didn't know how I was going to get to talk to him, but he solved the problem.

"Bess," he said, "I'm so glad you're here! I want to make some of that fudge you and your mama make, but I don't know how."

"Do you have the ingredients?" I asked. It was like we were talking in a secret code.

"Sure do," he said. "In the kitchen." He nodded toward the kitchen, and I followed him in there. I was afraid some of the other boys would want to come with us, but no one did.

Once in the kitchen, he grabbed my arm. "You heard?" he asked me.

"Yes. We need to tell Bud we saved him."

"We can't do that," Sandy said.

"We have to," I said. "I know we'll get in trouble, and probably lots of it, but we can't let Mr. Sato get sent to one of those camps or worse."

"He'd be better off in a camp than out here where people want to burn his house down."

"But they think he's a spy. They might torture him. Or kill him, even." I really don't know how a spy would be treated, but I know it wouldn't be good.

"Bess, listen to me," he said. "We can't tell anyone we were there together."

"Then I'll say I was there alone," I said. "I'll leave you out of it." I felt like crying again.

"And why will you say you were there?" Sandy asked me. "And exactly how did a pip-squeak like you manage to cart a full-grown man through the house, over the deck railing and through the water to the yard?"

I knew he was right, although I really resented being called a pip-squeak! I'm nearly as tall as he is.

"Then you say *you* did it alone," I said.

"Sure," he said. "I'll say I was just out wandering around on my night off, and for no good reason I crossed the island to the sound and noticed Sato's house was on fire and saved him."

I looked down at my shoes. "Sandy, isn't a man's life worth us getting in trouble for being together?" For some reason, I started thinking of what Dennis Kittering would say about all this. He hated those internment camps. He would be proud of me for sticking up for Mr. Sato.

"Look," Sandy said. "Let's not do anything about this right now, all right? Let's give it a few days and see what happens."

I could tell I wasn't going to be able to persuade him.

Suddenly, though, I had an idea. I would watch Jimmy Brown on his patrol tonight. Maybe I would see something suspicious. The way to free Mr. Sato would be to find the real spy.

"Okay," I said, "but I won't be able to sneak out to see you tonight. I'm sorry."

"You're not upset about the other night, are you?" he asked. "About what we did?" He was whispering in case anyone could hear him. "You know I love you, Bess."

How I loved hearing those words from him! I told him I wasn't upset about it, but that I *was* upset about this whole Mr. Sato mess and we would have to talk about it again in a day or so.

"Why can't you come out tonight, then?" he asked.

"I'm just tired," I said. "I need a good night's sleep."

He seemed to believe me, although I've never needed a good night's sleep before. But I was glad he didn't ask me any more questions.

I left the Coast Guard station feeling happy he said he loved me and sad he would not tell Mr. Hewitt that we'd gotten Mr. Sato out of his house. I think he'll come around, though. He just needs a day or two to think about it. And maybe he's right to wait. If I can find something out about Jimmy tonight, then we won't have to ever tell.

Chapter Thirty-Nine

SHORTY'S WAS BUSY ON FRIDAY MORNING, AND Gina hoped Clay would decide to stop in for lunch so she could talk with him a bit. Or at least look at him. She'd awakened in his bed with him that morning, and she'd simply watched him sleep for a few minutes before she got up. His face had looked peaceful, with none of the anguish that had troubled him the night before, and watching him had filled her up in a way that was both unfamiliar and comforting.

Last night, when Clay took her to get her car, he told her that Alec had said he would think about helping her raise the lens. Or at least, he would think about not standing in her way. That was more than she'd dared hope for. What had Clay told his father? Had he talked to him about his feelings for her? She knew he had them, even if she also knew those feelings were tinged with guilt that only time could erase. He had told his father about her connection to the Poors, that much she knew. "I told him about the diary and that you're Mary Poor's great-granddaughter," he'd said. "And that you're not a lighthouse historian."

"What did he say to that?" she'd asked him.

"He said, 'No kidding.'" Gina had winced, but Clay'd laughed. "It's not a big deal," he said. "I think he understands now why you lied."

She'd slept with him the entire night, and they'd made love again, interrupted only by Lacey knocking on Clay's door, wanting to be sure he was all right. Gina and Clay had started laughing, and they could hear Lacey gasp.

"I'm sorry!" Lacey had said. "Just ignore me. You guys have fun."

"We just made her day," Clay said. "She's wanted this from the moment you arrived here."

Gina remembered back to that evening, three weeks earlier, when she'd arrived at Kiss River to see the lens. She had barely noticed Clay then. Becoming involved with a man had been the last thing on her mind.

Clay grew quiet, the laughter of a few minutes earlier quickly fading. Gina tipped her head up to look at his face. His mouth was a flat line, his gaze on his dresser, where she knew there was a picture of Terri and her dog. The room was too dark for him to have been able to make out their features, but he stared in the direction of the photograph nevertheless.

"What are you thinking?" she asked, lowering her head to his shoulder again.

He sighed, turning away from the dresser. "Nothing," he said.

"Is that what you used to tell Terri when she'd ask you what was wrong?" She hoped she was not slugging him below the belt, using one of his confidences against him.

He gave her what could only be described as a dirty look, but then he started talking.

"I've had some moments of happiness lately," he said. "Like with you tonight. Laughing with you. Making love to you.

And then I suddenly remember Terri and…I hate myself for being able to laugh again. I don't feel as though I deserve to be happy."

"You do, Clay," she said.

"I'm so damn pissed off at myself for sending her down there in my place," he said angrily. "And I'm pissed off at that building for collapsing. And at the forces of the universe for taking her and our baby away."

Gina bit her lip. She had asked him to tell her; now she had to listen. "You miss her," she said.

He laughed, a short, bitter sound. "I *don't* miss her anymore, and I feel worst of all about that. What kind of a son of a bitch *am* I? The scary thing is, I get it now. I can see how I shut her out. I finally got it the other night when I told you everything. *That's* what I should have been doing with her all along. Talking to her about everything on my mind. We would have had a better marriage."

She didn't feel threatened by his talking about how he could have improved his marriage to Terri. Instead, she relished his words. He was being honest with her, a gift she'd never before received from a man.

"I remember when Bruce left me," she said. "I wanted to have a fast-forward button. You know, so I could just fast-forward a year or two and skip over all the pain."

"Exactly."

"Doesn't work that way," she said.

"I know." He turned to look at her. "You're so amazing," he said. "I feel like I can tell you anything."

"You can," she said, wishing she could tell *him* everything as well. It was her turn to feel guilty. He had forgiven her for withholding information from him. She knew that was more than she deserved.

Clay did not show up at Shorty's during the lunch hour. Instead, Olivia Simon did. Gina didn't recognize her at first.

The woman standing inside the front door looked vaguely familiar, but Gina took her to be just another Shorty's customer. She had only seen Olivia twice before, and one of those times had been at night on the dunes.

Olivia stood near the cash register, refusing the seat one of the other waitresses offered her. Instead, she caught Gina's eye and motioned to her to come over.

"Hi, Gina," she said. She must have seen the blank look in Gina's eyes, because she offered her name. "Olivia Simon. Clay and Lacey's stepmother," she said.

"Oh, Olivia, of course!" Gina said. "I'm sorry. I didn't recognize you out of context."

"That happens to me all the time," Olivia said. "I see people in the E.R., and then I see them later on the street and I don't have a clue who they are." She was so pretty. She had the loveliest green eyes and her skin was flawless.

"What can I do for you?" Gina moved out of the way of a customer wanting to pay his check.

Olivia looked past her toward the crowded tables. "I can see you're very busy," she said, "but I wanted to stop by and give you these." She held out a grocery bag. Peering inside, Gina saw several cassette tapes.

"What's this?" she asked.

"Alec told me that you're a descendant of Mary Poor, right?"

"Her great-granddaughter, yes."

"Well, my ex-husband, Paul, taped several interviews with her long ago. The plan had been to put together a booklet about the Kiss River light in order to generate funding to save the lighthouse. But the storm destroyed the lighthouse before the booklet was ever created, and after that, of course, it wasn't needed. I've hung on to these tapes, although I don't really know why. I guess you're the reason." She smiled. "I thought you might like to have them. To hear your great-grandmother's voice."

Gina was touched. "That's so nice of you," she said. She had no tape recorder, but Lacey or Clay probably did. "I'll listen to them and get them back to you."

"No, they're yours to keep." Olivia pushed the bag toward her. "I have no need for them." She looked toward the back room. "I'll stop in to say hi to Henry," she said. "Then I have to get back to the E.R."

There were no other cars in the parking lot at the keeper's house when Gina arrived home that afternoon. Inside the house, she poured herself a Coke, then carried it into the office to connect to the Internet and check her e-mail. Once online, her fingers automatically hit the right keys to take her to the parents' support group.

She noticed immediately that there were three times as many messages from the group as usual, and she saw the subject line repeated over and over again, in capital letters, with three exclamation points that marked the alarm of the parents. HYDERABAD CHILDREN MOVED TO STATE ORPHANAGE!!!

God, no. "Rani," she said out loud. *"Rani."*

She began reading the messages. As part of the crackdown on the private orphanages, many of the children were being moved to the state orphanage, a place known to be even more institutional than Rani's current home. There would be crowds of children, with too little food perhaps, and not enough staff to give them proper care. A quiet, ailing wisp of a child like Rani would not stand a chance there. Gina plowed through the messages from the panicked parents, trying to see if Rani's orphanage was one of those whose children had been moved, but she saw no mention of it. She didn't dare write the question to the group. They would ask her why she had disappeared. Better to stay quiet.

She logged off the Internet and picked up the phone on the desk, extracting her address book from her backpack at the same time. Her hand shook as she paged through the book for the phone number she needed, and she hoped it would be a while before Clay and Lacey got their phone bill. A call to India was not cheap.

She recognized the taped outgoing message from Mrs. King. Gina had never met the woman, although she'd spoken to her on the phone several times. Certainly "Mrs. King" was an alias, and Gina was not sure if she was Indian or not. Her accent was faintly British. Her ethnicity didn't matter, though. Her power did.

"Leave a message after the tone," Mrs. King said.

"Hello, Mrs. King." Gina heard the quaver in her voice. "I'm calling to let you know that I'll have the money for you very soon. Very soon." She shut her eyes. Would she? The panic rose up in her again. "Please, please make sure that Rani is not moved from her orphanage. I understand children are being moved to the state orphanage, and I'm sure you know that with her…special needs…that would be a terrible thing for her. Please do what you can to keep her where she is." It was possible, she knew, that Rani's orphanage might be shut down. "Or if she *has* to leave there, please be sure she goes someplace where she'll be safe. I'll have the money for you very soon. I promise."

She was barely able to put the phone back in its cradle, her hand was trembling so badly. She connected to the Internet and the support group again, reading and rereading the messages. There were other parents who had quietly dropped out of the support group as well; she had not been the only one. She wondered if they, too, lurked in the background, reading these messages in a panic as they struggled to pull their funds together. One hundred thousand dollars. That's what Mrs. King demanded to get Rani safely out of India. Was that the same amount other parents were being asked to pay?

The parents who still participated in the support group, who were either as frightened as she was right now, or content in the knowledge that their promised child was safe in another part of the country, all knew about Mrs. King. Everyone did, and most of those parents understood desperation, but they were not the type to go outside legal channels to get their children. They warned one another against resorting to the use of "baby brokers," which is what they called Mrs. King.

They're fools, Gina thought. *They'll obey all the rules and end up with dead children.*

After she logged off the Internet, she sat very still in the desk chair. She felt frozen there, uncertain what to do next. What *could* she do? How much time did Alec need to "think about it"? Even if he agreed to help her, how long would it take to raise the lens? And even if the lens were raised and she could examine it, then what?

She stood up quickly to stop her thoughts from racing. One step at a time. She should watch TV, or read a book, or do something to get her mind off the news from the support group. Then she remembered the tapes.

She opened one of the desk drawers, then another and another, and finally found what she was looking for: a cassette player.

Upstairs, she lay down on her bed and put in the tape marked "1." The first voice she heard was that of a man. Olivia's ex-husband, probably.

"Just begin anywhere," the man said.

It was a moment before the woman spoke. Her voice quivered with age.

"The Kiss River lighthouse was illuminated for the first time the night my husband Caleb's father was born," she said.

Gina pressed her fist to her mouth. It was her great-grandmother speaking. Bess's mother. How strange to hear her like this, across the years. She listened as the old woman described her life at the lighthouse, her life in this house. She talked about the incident with the two Germans who had pretended to be stranded Englishmen to get ashore, and she had some of the details wrong. Wrong enough that Gina smiled, listening to her. She wondered how many of the other details on these tapes were inaccurate. It didn't matter though. It was a pleasure just to hear her speak, to know that she was, in some long-lost way, her family.

Finally, Mary Poor spoke about her daughter, Elizabeth.

"She was a wild girl," Mary Poor said. "One of them girls who's always out looking for trouble. She found it, too, I'm afraid. She found it more often than not."

Chapter Forty

Sunday, May 10, 1942, 4:00 a.m.

MY HEART IS BROKEN IN A MILLION PIECES AND I don't know what to do, besides cry. Which I am doing right now and may do for the rest of my life. And the one person I've turned to with my problems for the last month and a half is someone I can never go to with a problem again.

Last night, I spied on Jimmy Brown, as I'd planned to do. I rode my bicycle to the beach about two miles north of Kiss River, where I knew his patrol would be. I was really scared, because the trail out to the beach there was not familiar to me and it was pitch-black out. I had a flashlight with me, but that just made it spookier, because it lit up the deep, dark trees as I rode. I could hardly breathe, I was so nervous. I'm not usually afraid of the dark or the woods. After all, I've been sneaking through woods by myself every night to see Sandy. But this was different, because I just didn't know where that trail was going to turn or where the ruts would be or who or what might come running out of those trees.

I could tell when I got real close to the beach from the way the waves sounded, and I left my bike in the woods and turned off my flashlight and walked as quietly as I could toward the beach. I didn't see him at first, but I huddled down in the brush to wait, figuring he was walking up and down the beach and would show up soon. After a while, he did. He was on horseback, just slowly clip-clopping along the sand. When he'd ride out of my sight, I'd walk out on the beach and watch him from behind a dune. There was just enough of a moon so that I could see him and his horse. I wasn't sure what I was looking for. If he left his post on the beach, I guess that would be something suspicious. If he allowed someone to come out of the water onto shore, I would know for sure. That's what I expected to happen, I guess. But although I watched him for over three hours, absolutely nothing unusual occurred and I was getting very tired, not to mention bored.

I started back to Kiss River, and when I was close, I got the idea that I could see Sandy after all. I no longer felt that tired, and I thought it would be real fun to surprise him, since he wasn't expecting me to come see him last night. So I left my bike by the lighthouse and started walking through woods that are more familiar to me and much less scary. I don't even use my flashlight in those woods, I know them so well, but I carry it with me just in case. I was almost to the beach when I saw a light shining ahead and to the right of me, through the trees. I couldn't imagine what it was. Nobody was supposed to be on the beach at night, and certainly not with a light. I stood stock-still on the path for a minute, watching to see if the light was blinking, like they do with Morse code, but it was just a small, steady beam of light. Sandy has a powerful flashlight, but he almost never uses it now that lights onshore are forbidden. Then I remembered the murderer, someone I haven't thought about in weeks. My imagination started going wild. What if the murderer had killed Sandy and was holding the light on his body while he stole things from him or something?

Anyhow, I walked real quietly down the path, although I don't know how necessary it was for me to be quiet, since the ocean was rough and loud last night. I climbed up in my tree. I haven't been up there since the night I met Sandy, but last night I thought I'd better hide up there and see what was going on before going straight out onto the beach.

What I saw is still burned into my head. There was Sandy, pointing his flashlight out to sea. Not blinking it or anything. Just pointing it straight out. I thought maybe he was looking at something in the waves, but I must've known that wasn't it, because I didn't climb down the tree and go running out to him. I just sat and watched. I was remembering the time those Germans came onshore at Kiss River, when I held the flashlight steady so my father knew which way to go as he towed them in.

After a few minutes, I saw something on the waves, and Sandy turned his flashlight off. Sure enough, it was a dinghy, like the one those Germans had been in, only this one had a small motor on it. I thought maybe this one had survivors from a torpedoed merchant ship, but I couldn't see any flames out on the horizon or smell the burning smell that always blows onshore after a ship's been hit.

Sandy ran forward to help the men in the boat. There was just enough of a moon that I could see there were two of them. And then the thing happened that has changed everything. I heard Sandy call out to them, "Vee gates!" I was sure I'd misunderstood him. After all, the waves were crashing on the beach between me and him. But then I heard them talk back to him in very fast German, and I thought that Sandy wouldn't possibly be able to understand what they were saying. But I was wrong. He started talking to them in German! The words came out of his mouth almost as fast as theirs did. When the men got out of the boat, I saw their German uniforms. They huddled with Sandy on the beach and talked quietly then, and Sandy handed them something in a big envelope, along with a bag of some kind.

I couldn't believe what I was seeing! I felt angry and hurt and just plain crazy. I got down from my tree and turned my flashlight right on the three of them. They turned to look at me, though I know they couldn't make out who I was because of the flashlight being in their eyes.

"Go, go!" Sandy yelled at them, and the men scrambled back into their boat and set out over the waves again. He turned to look at me. "Who's there?" he asked.

I turned the flashlight on my own face, and he laughed, but there was no mistaking the nervousness in the way he did it.

"Bess!" he said. "I'm glad to see it's only you. You scared me there for a minute." He looked just like a little boy getting caught by his mother for doing something bad.

I was thinking about the day I'd told him I knew a couple of phrases in German. He'd never said a word to me then about knowing a couple himself. A lot more than a couple, actually. Then I remembered how Sandy hated it when anyone called Germans Krauts. No wonder he'd been so upset when he heard that Mr. Hewitt had asked me to help him find the traitor. Well, I'd found him now. I started to get weepy as I walked toward him, because all my hopes and dreams were falling apart.

"What are you doing here?" he asked me. "I thought you were going to stay home tonight."

"It doesn't matter what I'm doing here," I said. "What were you just doing with those Germans?"

"Those guys?" He looked out to sea, where the dinghy had already disappeared in the darkness. "They weren't Germans."

"Don't lie to me, Sandy," I said. "I saw their uniforms. I heard you talking in German to them. I saw you give them something."

Sandy rubbed his hands over his eyes. I wanted him to tell me I had misunderstood what I'd just seen. Instead he said, "You should never have spied on me." His voice was not loud, but it was very, very angry. He didn't sound nervous at all now, and I suddenly felt afraid of him. I felt like I didn't know him, like he was a stranger. He could kill me out here in the dark. I backed away from him a step or two, but he grabbed my arm.

"Have you been suspecting me of something?" he asked. "Is that why you snuck out here tonight? After lying to me about being tired?"

He'd asked me so many questions all at once that I didn't know where to begin to answer them. Besides, I didn't owe him any explanations.

"I'm glad I came out here," I said. "I've discovered the truth about my boyfriend. He's a goddamn spy." I was trying to get my arm away from him, but he held it tight. I was truly scared, and what I really wanted to say was, "Please don't hurt me," but I didn't want to sound that weak and afraid.

"Don't you dare say a word to Bud about this," he said. His face was so close to mine that I could feel his breath against my cheek. "Don't say a word to anyone."

"Why are you doing this?" I asked. I was crying, I think. He was hurting my arm, but my heart was hurting even worse.

"For money, why else?" he said. "I'm getting millions from

the Germans for what I'm doing," he said. "I am going to be a very, very wealthy man."

He sounded so greedy. I suddenly remembered the night he told me about how poor his family was, how he never got toys at Christmastime and how sometimes they didn't have much to eat. A lot of money could make someone like that crazy.

He twisted my arm harder. "Swear to me you won't say anything to anyone about this," he said.

I know I should have just agreed to what he was asking, but I couldn't. "I'm not going to stand by and watch while American seamen are being killed right and left," I said.

The next thing I knew, he had me pinned to the ground, my arm twisted behind me so hard I thought it was going to pop out of my shoulder. "Remember that man you found murdered right here on this beach?" he asked me.

I nodded.

"Well, he was the last person who snooped on me," he said.

I could hardly breathe. "You killed him?" I asked.

"If you tell anyone, *anyone,* what you saw tonight, you'll pay for it. And so will your parents, do you hear me? You may be willing to put your own life at risk for some stupid desire to serve your country, but are you willing to risk the lives of the people you love?"

I loved you, is what I wanted to say, and I started crying harder.

"Are you?" he asked me again. His knee was digging into my stomach. I shook my head no.

He let go of my arm then, but still kept me pinned to the ground. "Look, Bess," he said. He sounded more like the Sandy I knew then. "You're in a lot of danger now. You need to leave here. Leave the Outer Banks. Get as far away as you can. And never talk to a soul about this."

"You still care about me," I said. I couldn't help myself. I felt joyous that he cared what happened to me, even if he was turning out to be traitorous scum.

"You're misunderstanding me," he said. "All I'm saying is that, if you want to stay safe, if you want your family to be safe, you'd better go away."

"I thought you loved me," I said.

He laughed at me. "You're just a kid," he said.

"But you said…"

"Something you should know about men," he told me. "They'll say anything to get what they want from you."

He let go of me all of a sudden, and I jumped to my feet and ran back toward the woods. I cut myself running through the brush in the dark, and I didn't care. Behind him, he called out to me, "Not a word to anyone!"

So now I am home, up in my room, still shaking from what happened on the beach. I've been crying so hard, my throat hurts. I keep thinking crazy things, like maybe that man who just warned me and called me a kid wasn't really Sandy? It sure didn't sound like Sandy. I have never heard him sound so mean and angry and nasty. I didn't think he had that side to him. But I know it *was* Sandy. And now I have to figure out what to do. I keep picturing my parents sleeping down the hall from me, peaceful and not having any notion of the danger I've put them in. If anything happened to them, I would never forgive myself. I keep hearing that song playing over and over in my head. "Perfidia." I finally understand what it means. The last line is "Perfidious one, goodbye." I hated that song before I even knew what it meant. Now I hate it even more.

Oh, dear God! I fell asleep after I wrote that last line. Don't ask me how I managed to do that, but I did. And I had a terrible, terrible dream. Sandy came to my house. He came inside and I met him in the living room. He said he was sorry, that he loved me and never meant to hurt me. He asked me for a cup of tea, which I didn't even think about being a strange request. When I came back with the tea, I could hear screams from upstairs. I ran up the stairs and found Sandy beating my parents with a big club. There was blood everywhere and they were dead. I woke myself up screaming. I know what I have to do now. I am not going to think about another thing today. Just what I have to do.

Chapter Forty-One

GINA LEFT WORK AND DROVE STRAIGHT HOME in her rattle-free, air-conditioned car. She'd thought of stopping off at Henry's, where she knew Clay was doing some repair work on the house that had seen both fire and flood, but she was anxious to check the online support group to see if there was any more news about moving the children to the state institution.

She was surprised to see Lacey's car in the parking lot of the keeper's house; Lacey usually tutored kids on Saturday afternoons. There was also a truck in the lot, and at first Gina thought it was Kenny's. It was dark red, just like Kenny's, but this truck was dented and muddy, while Kenny took great care of his. Another of Lacey's boyfriends, Gina thought as she got out of her car.

There was no sign of Lacey or her guest when Gina walked into the house. Sasha greeted her merrily and accompanied her into the office, but before Gina was able to log onto the Internet, a short, piercing scream rang out from upstairs. Gina's hands froze on the keyboard, and Sasha lifted his head and looked toward the living room, waiting, as she was, for the sound to come again. Were Lacey and her friend just fooling around? But the scream was quickly followed by shouting, and Sasha got to his feet, a growl rising from deep in his chest.

Gina stood up, too, her hand on the dog's head, and walked through the living room to the foot of the stairs.

"Lacey?" she called up to the second story.

She heard a thud, the sound of something—or someone—falling on the floor above her head. A door opened, then slammed shut, and Gina stood frozen at the bottom of the stairs, unsure whether she should go up to Lacey's room or call the police. Sasha put his front paws on the bottom step and Gina instinctively curled her fingers around his collar.

Suddenly, Brock Jensen appeared in the upstairs hallway. Sasha barked as Brock bolted down the stairs, running past Gina without even seeming to notice her or the barking retriever she was keeping in check. He practically flew out the front door.

It was Brock's truck, of course. She remembered seeing it in the parking lot at Shorty's. Letting go of Sasha's collar, she rushed up the stairs to Lacey's room, afraid of what she might find. In the hallway, she knocked quickly on the door, then pushed it open without waiting for a response.

"I'm all right," Lacey said quickly. She was on the floor, leaning against her dresser, her eyes open but narrowed in pain. A dark bruise was already forming on her cheek and she was rubbing her jaw. She had on her denim shorts, but nothing else, and her long red hair rested on her breasts. Sasha nearly jumped into her lap, and she hugged the dog close to her.

Gina dropped quickly to Lacey's side. "What happened?" she asked, smoothing the hair back from Lacey's face so she could get a good look at the bruise. "Are you sure you're all right?"

"What a pig." Lacey choked out the words. She tried to get to her feet, leaning on both Gina and the dog, but flopped down on the floor again. "Could you hand me my bra, please?" she asked.

Gina retrieved the bra from the footboard of the bed and helped her into it, fastening it for her against her back.

Lacey tried to get up again, and this time she managed to get over to the bed, where she sat down on the edge of the mattress. She looked up at Gina.

"Is my face a mess?" she asked. Her right cheek was already starting to swell.

"We should put some ice on it," Gina said. "But first we need to call the police."

Lacey shook her head. "Don't bother. I invited him up here. They're not going to do anything."

"What happened?" Gina asked again, sitting down next to her on the bed.

Lacey shrugged. "He wanted to have sex again, and I didn't. What I really wanted was to talk about what happened to your raffle money."

"Oh, no, Lacey." Gina felt an irrational twinge of responsibility for what had occurred in this room. "Is that why you've been hanging out with him?"

Lacey shrugged. "Doesn't matter," she said. "He got testy when I asked him about the money. He was already pissed because I wouldn't sleep with him again. I asked him to leave, and he smacked me." She pressed her fingertips gingerly to her jaw. "Is it black and blue?" she asked.

"It's getting there," Gina said. Lacey's fair skin was rapidly growing purple on the entire right side of her face, and the bruise hurt just to look at.

Lacey turned her head to the right, then the left, as if try-ing to work a kink out of her neck. "I have to make up some excuse for why I'm bruised or Clay will give me a hard time," she said. "That's the only bad thing about living with him. He still sees me as his little sister."

"He loves you," Gina said. "He just wants to protect you."

"I know."

"Lacey..." Gina hesitated, not sure if her opinion would be welcome right now. Sometimes it was easy for her to forget she was only a guest in this house. She'd come to care deeply for Lacey, but damned if she understood her. "I worry that you're playing with fire with some of the guys you go out with," she said carefully. "You barely know Brock, and ev-eryone thinks he's a little strange. Who knows what he could have done to you. He could have killed you."

"I know him." Lacey looked defensive as she reached for her T-shirt where it lay on her pillow. "He goes to the same Al-Anon meeting I do. I wanted to try to get close to him. You know, to figure out if he took your money or not."

"The money's not that important," Gina said, but she knew this was not the time to argue with Lacey about her behavior with men. "I'll get some ice." She stood up and headed for the hallway.

On the stairs, Gina discovered that her knees were shaking. Too much adrenaline. She could still hear that scream, the way it cut through the still air of the house. In the kitchen, she filled a plastic bag with ice, and she was tying a twist tie around the top of the bag when Clay opened the screen door and walked into the kitchen.

He wrapped his arms around her, and she dropped the bag on the counter to return his hug.

"Are you trembling?" he asked.

"I'm okay," she said. "But Lacey fell and hit the side of her

face. I'm getting her some ice." She let go of him to turn back
to the counter, hating that she was lying to him again.

"Lacey fell?" he asked. "What happened? Where is she?"

"She's in her bedroom. She tripped on the rug in there and
hit her cheek on the dresser."

"Ouch." He winced, seeming to buy the story. He reached
into the drawer where they kept the dish towels. "Here. Wrap
this around the bag."

He put his arm around her as they walked up the stairs
together. "Is there any new information on Rani today?" he
asked.

"I haven't checked my e-mail yet," she said, touched that
he cared enough to ask.

Lacey was still sitting on the edge of her bed. She'd put on
her T-shirt, and the bruise was already a few shades darker
than it had been when Gina had left her to go downstairs.

"Looks painful," Clay said, sitting down next to his sister
as Gina handed Lacey the bag of ice and the dish towel.

"I'm so clumsy sometimes," Lacey said. "I walked right into
the edge of my door."

Gina cringed.

"Oh, yeah?" Clay looked at Gina, then back at his sister.
"Was that before or after you tripped on the rug and crashed
into your dresser?"

Lacey looked confused. "What?"

"I told him how you tripped," Gina said.

"Oh." Lacey seemed to deflate, sinking lower into the bed.
She knew the jig was up.

Clay folded his arms across his chest. "All right, girls," he
said, suddenly all business. "How about the truth. One of your
asshole boyfriends smacked you, didn't he?"

"Don't worry," Lacey said. "I won't be seeing him again."

"No, but you'll see some other asshole," Clay said, his voice rising. "And maybe that one will finish the job."

"Will you two please get out of here and leave me alone?" Lacey said.

Clay ignored her plea. He leaned over and touched her cheek, pressing lightly against the bruise, then running his fingertip down to her jaw. "Are you sure nothing's broken?" he asked. "This looks pretty bad."

"I'm fine," she said. "Goodbye."

Clay stood up and held his hand out to Gina. "Come on," he said. "We're not wanted here."

As soon as they had closed Lacey's door and stood together in the hallway, Gina turned to him. "I'm sorry I lied," she said. "She didn't want you to know, and I didn't know what—"

"It's all right," he said, running his hand over her arm. "You were caught in the middle. She really got slugged, though. That was no little slap across the face."

"I know."

"Do you know who the guy was?"

"Brock. You know the guy—"

"Brock Jensen?" There was fire in Clay's eyes now that he could attach a face to his sister's abuser.

"Yes. I think she wanted to find out if he took my—"

"I'll see you later." He turned toward the stairs, then shot down them every bit as fast as Brock had earlier.

"Clay!" she called after him. "Don't do anything crazy."

But he was already out the front door. She sat down on the top step, wondering what she should do. Should she follow him to Shorty's, which was undoubtedly where he was going? Should she call the police and tell them they'd better get over there? Or was she simply making too much of the whole situation. Brock probably wouldn't be at Shorty's anyway, and

Clay would be fine once he'd gunned his Jeep all the way to the restaurant and gotten some of his steam blown off.

Instead of taking either course, she walked downstairs and into the office, to see if she could learn anything new about her daughter's fate.

Chapter Forty-Two

CLAY SPOTTED THE BANGED-UP RED TRUCK IN Shorty's parking lot. He pulled into the empty space next to the truck and got out of his Jeep, then headed for the front door. He was wired, his hands already balled into fists. He had never felt quite like this before. He'd sat in the courtroom during the trial of his mother's killer, watching the murderer sit stone-faced next to his attorney. He'd been on search and rescue teams hunting for the bodies of brutalized children. But he'd honestly never felt this keen-edged rage before.

"Hey, Clay!" Kenny was at the bar, but Clay walked right past him without a word on his way to the back room.

"Afternoon, Clay," Walter Liscott called out from the chess table, and Clay ignored him as well. He looked toward the pool table. Brock was turned away from him, leaning over to make a shot, the tattoos on his back nearly visible beneath his thin white T-shirt. Clay walked over and touched his shoulder.

"Hey, I'm setting up a shot here," Brock said without turning around.

"Turn around, you son of a bitch," Clay said.

Brock straightened up slowly, then turned to face him.

Clay pulled back his arm, then let it fly, his fist connecting dead center with Brock's face. He heard the *crack*. It was a great sound.

Brock put a hand over his bloodied nose. "What the hell are you doing, dude?" he asked.

"How do you like it?" Clay said, punching him again. He had never hit anyone in his life, and it felt good. Too good. He hit him one more time. "Now you know how my sister felt," he said.

"Your sister's a whore," Brock was stupid enough to say.

"And you're a freak." Clay pushed him until Brock was half lying on the pool table, and then he pummeled him hard, his fists smashing into his face and body over and over again. He was vaguely aware of people around him, some shouting, others cheering. Someone told him to cool it, and he could feel Kenny's ineffectual attempts to drag him from the table. Even old Brian Cass was trying to pull him away from his target, but he could not be stopped. Blood was flowing, flying. His hands were covered with it, and he didn't know or care whether it was Brock's blood or his own. One thing he did know, though. One thing crept into his awareness and made him fight with even greater fury: He was not only beating up Brock. He was beating up the building that had collapsed on his wife and unborn child, and the sloppy construction workers who'd put that building up in the first place, and on his overinflated ego that had led him to send Terri in his place. He was beating up on God.

Chapter Forty-Three

THE CALL FROM THE EMERGENCY ROOM CAME at six o'clock in the evening. Alec was swimming with Jack and Maggie in the sound behind their house when he heard his cell phone ringing on the deck. He waded through the water as quickly as he could, but by the time he'd run up the beach to the deck, he was too late. Olivia had left a message, though.

"If you can find someone to watch the kids," she'd said, "please come to the E.R. Nothing too serious, so don't panic."

Nothing *too* serious? He tried to call her back, but was told she was with a patient. He called the kids out of the water and told them to get dressed quickly. Then he phoned the mother of one of Jack's friends to see if she could watch Jack and Maggie for a while. She agreed, and within minutes he had dropped them off at her house and was on his way to the E.R.

He didn't like being called to the emergency room for any reason. Even though ten years had passed, being in the E.R. always brought back the memory of the night Annie had died

there. And right now, he didn't know how worried he should
be. "Don't panic," Olivia had said. She didn't say, "Don't
worry."

He arrived at the emergency room to find that the waiting
area had been transformed into Shorty's back room. Kenny
Gallo was there, along with Walter Liscott in his wheelchair
and Brian Cass and a few others. There were a couple of cops,
guys he knew well. One of them, Pete Myron, had obviously
been keeping an eye out for Alec and approached him quickly
when he walked into the room.

"What's going on?" Alec asked him.

Pete took him out of the waiting room and into the back
hallway, near the treatment area.

"Do you know Brock Jensen?" Pete asked.

It took him a moment to realize who Pete was talking
about. "The guy with the tattoos?" he asked.

"That's him. Apparently, he beat up your daughter," he
said.

Alec thought of Maggie, safe at their neighbor's house, and
then realized that Pete was talking about Lacey.

"Where is she?" He peered behind Pete's head, trying to
see into the main treatment area. "Is she all right?"

"She's at home," Pete said. "We sent someone over to check
on her. She's fine, except for a few bruises. But Jensen is a
mess. He's being stitched up right now. Clay broke a finger."

"Clay?" He was confused. "What do you mean?"

"Clay found Jensen at Shorty's and beat him to a pulp."

"Clay?" Alec found this hard to believe. Clay was no wimp,
but he was definitely a pacifist. He hated violence. More im-
portantly, he held the concept of revenge in disdain. Even at
Zachary Pointer's trial, while listening to witnesses describe
how the man had shot Annie, Clay kept saying, "I won't support the death penalty for him. I just won't."

"Lacey's not pressing charges," Pete said. "And Brock's wisely not pressing charges, either. So there's not much for us to do."

"Where is Clay?" Alec asked. He had many more questions, but figured it was time he started asking them of his son.

"In there." Pete pointed behind him at the treatment room. "He's with your wife."

Olivia was sitting at Clay's side, wrapping a bandage around his finger, when Alec found them in the third curtained compartment of the treatment area. Clay had a nasty-looking cut high on his cheekbone and a swollen lip, but otherwise he seemed to be all right. He looked up when Alec opened the curtain.

"Hi, Dad," he said simply, as if this sort of thing occurred every day.

"What the hell happened?" Alec asked.

Olivia didn't take her eyes off her work. "Just your usual barroom brawl," she said.

Clay looked reluctant to speak. He sighed, sounding tired. "Brock Jensen was at the keeper's house with Lacey," he said.

"What do you mean, he was with her?" Alec could not picture his daughter with Shorty's tattooed wonder. "He didn't rape her, did he?" Alec asked.

Clay looked away from him, avoiding the question. "He hit her," he said. "When I found out, I went to Shorty's and…." He looked up at Alec, a sheepish half grin on his face. "Doesn't sound like me, does it?" he asked.

No, it sure didn't. "Why did he hit Lacey? Did he force his way into the house or—"

"I'm sure she invited him, Dad," Clay interrupted him. "She's not terribly…discriminating."

He didn't want to hear that. He'd seen hints of Lacey's

promiscuity, things he'd ignored. Things he wished he could continue to ignore.

"You didn't answer my question about rape," he said.

Clay looked annoyed, but Alec had the feeling it was actually Lacey he was annoyed with. "As far as I know," he said, "anything that happened between them was consensual."

Olivia had finished bandaging Clay's finger and was now examining the cut on his cheek.

"Do I need stitches?" Clay asked her.

She shook her head. "A butterfly will do," she said, selecting one of the small bandages from the metal tray at her side.

"How bad is Brock beaten up?" Alec addressed the question to his wife.

"Broken nose, a fair share of contusions." Olivia was using her flat, reasonable doctor's voice. "And he'll probably need some plastic surgery on his cheek."

He had to stop himself from smiling. He couldn't help it. He was a gentle man, the father of a gentle son. And yet he couldn't help feeling a primitive sense of masculine pride that his son had defended his daughter and come out the winner.

Clay suddenly sat up straighter, his gaze falling somewhere behind Alec's head, and Alec turned to see Gina stepping through the curtains. She was instantly at Clay's side.

"Are you all right?" she asked, real concern in her voice. She touched his swollen lip in a way that told Alec the two of them had moved beyond friendship to something more.

Clay took her hand. "I'm fine," he said. "Is Lacey with you?"

"She wouldn't come," she said. "I don't think she wants anyone to see her face. Although it doesn't look that bad," she added quickly, as if wanting to allay Alec's fears. "And the policewoman was still there with her."

"I'm going over to see her." Alec pulled his car keys from his jeans pocket.

"Don't, Dad," Clay said.

"Why not?"

"Just…give her some space. Talk to her on the phone."

"And I'd like to talk to you, too," Olivia said to Alec. She had pressed the butterfly bandage to Clay's cheek and now stood up.

He rested his hand on her back. "As soon as you get home," he said.

He and Olivia waited until Jack and Maggie were in bed that evening. They sat on the glider on the screened porch, listening to the rippling waves of the sound lap at the narrow beach behind their house. He held her hand on his thigh. Both of them had spoken to Lacey, who insisted she was fine, that they were making a big deal out of nothing and it was ridiculous that Clay and Brock had both needed some serious medical treatment because she'd received "one little smack." He'd wanted to see her face for himself, but she was adamant that he not come to the keeper's house. He would see her on Monday, anyway, when she came to work at the animal hospital.

"You wanted to talk about Lacey?" he asked Olivia.

"Yes, but first I want to talk about Gina."

"What about her?"

"Have you decided what to do about the lens?"

"I haven't given it much thought."

"You told Clay you'd think about it, though."

This was going to be one of those nagging talks, he knew. One of those "you're doing everything wrong" talks. They were rare for Olivia. Very rare. For that reason, he'd learned to pay attention to what she said, no matter how irritating the conversation might be. She was usually right.

"And I will," he said. "Think about it."

"If it's true that Gina is related to the Poors, then you really should help her raise the lens. It obviously has sentimental value to her. For whatever reason, the lighthouse seems to have become her link to her relatives. Clay said she has no family. That's why she's trying so hard to adopt that little girl in India. She wants to give her a family and create a family for herself."

Alec stiffened. "If the lens has sentimental value to her, why didn't she just say that in the first place? Why did she give us the song and dance about being a lighthouse historian?"

Olivia was quiet, and he figured she had no answer to that question. The gentle splashing of water against the sand filled the silence.

"Alec, honey." She turned in the glider until she was facing him. "I need to say something to you and I'm afraid to say it."

"Afraid?" He couldn't imagine where this was going.

"Just...let me just talk for a minute, okay? Don't say anything back. Let me just talk."

He nodded.

She held both his hands in her lap. He wanted to wrap his arms around her. He hated that she felt fear in talking to him. He didn't think she ever had before.

"Years ago," she began, "you were desperate to save the lighthouse. And the reason you were so desperate was because it reminded you of Annie. It's where the two of you met. It's where you spent time together. You both loved it. It had so much meaning for you. I understand that."

He nodded again.

"Now, though, you are equally as desperate to leave the lens where it is, at the bottom of the ocean, for the same reason."

"What do you mean?"

She pressed a finger to his lips. "Shh," she said. "Let me finish. The lighthouse *still* reminds you of Annie, and no longer in a good way. Once you learned the truth about her, you wanted to bury everything that reminded you of her."

She was right. He hated the lighthouse he had once held so warmly in his heart.

"Either way, sweetie," Olivia continued, "whether you wanted to save the lighthouse, or want to let the lens stay in the sea, either way, your decisions are still based on your feelings for Annie. It's a piece of glass, Alec." She squeezed his hands hard. "You're giving it so much power over you. A piece of glass."

He opened his mouth to speak, although he wasn't yet sure what he would say.

"I'm not through." She interrupted him before he could utter a word, and he saw tears in her eyes as she locked her fingers in his. "I love you so much. These past ten years have been the best of my life, by far. But…please don't get angry with me when I say this. I feel very strongly that you *must* tell Clay and Lacey the truth about Annie."

He could no longer be silent. "Why should I?" he asked. "They have absolutely no need to know. Why should I ruin the image they have of their mother? Lacey knows Tom is her father. That's all she needs to know."

"You're still protecting Annie's memory," she said. "It doesn't deserve that protection. And it's harmed your children."

He was beginning to get angry. "This is a little self-serving of you, don't you think?" he asked.

She started to cry. "I'm worried about Lacey," she said, removing one of her hands from his to wipe her eyes. "It's creepy, don't you think? That she'd take someone like that guy home with her? And to the keeper's house?"

He knew what she was thinking, because he shared the thought. Annie used to do that. Take men to the keeper's house when Mary Poor lived there. Annie would sleep with anyone who came along. She'd slept with Alec within minutes of meeting him. She was always hungry to give pleasure rather than receive it. Always taking care of other people. But Lacey didn't know about that.

"I didn't think promiscuity is inherited," he said to Olivia.

"That's what's so spooky about it," Olivia said. "But we have to face facts, Alec. Lacey's always had a string of boyfriends. No one special. She's...she's Annie all over again. She looks identical to her. She didn't go to college, just like Annie."

"Annie went to college."

"But never got a degree," Olivia countered. "Lacey's made stained glass her career, just like her mother did, even though she used to talk about being a veterinarian like you when she was younger. You and I both know she had real interest in animals, and she had the brains to do it if she wanted to. But she put that interest completely aside and lost herself in the stained-glass studio."

He knew that Olivia understood the obsession to emulate Annie O'Neill better than he did. Long ago, struggling with envy and confusion, Olivia had suffered from that obsession herself.

"She's the community do-gooder, just like Annie was," Olivia said. She gripped both his hands again. "Alec, she needs to know," she said. "And *you* need to let go of that attachment you have to the light, whether it's positive or negative. Either way, Annie is still running your life."

Alec was quiet for a long time. He knew Olivia was right, on all counts, whether he wanted to admit it or not.

"I'm just not ready to ruin Clay and Lacey's image of their mother," he said finally. "I'm sorry, Olivia, but I can't do it. But you're right about the lens. I'll call Clay and tell him I'll do anything I can to help raise it."

Chapter Forty-Four

Monday, May 11, 1942

WHAT HAVE I DONE???? WAS IT THE RIGHT THING to do? I am not certain I'll ever have the answers to that question. All I know is that I feel terribly sick. I threw up all last night, and now I'm lying here in this strange bedroom in a strange house in a strange town, and I can hear Dennis and his sister, SueAnn, talking in the living room, although I don't know what they're saying. I'm sure they're talking about me, though. SueAnn was shocked when I arrived, that I know, but she's been kind to me, and she's the one who brought the chicken rice soup that's getting cold on the night table next to me. I can't eat yet. I can't imagine ever wanting to eat again, actually.

One thing I didn't know about Dennis is how extremely Catholic he is. I mean, I knew he wore that scapular thing, and I knew he always went to the Catholic service up in Corolla, but I had no idea what a big part of his life religion is.

SueAnn is the same way. She's a nurse at a Catholic hospital. There are little statues of Jesus and Mary all over this house, and pictures of Jesus with his heart showing. I feel like I'm in a whole other country.

So much has happened, although it's only been a little more than a day since I last wrote in this diary. Yesterday morning, after I woke up from the hideous dream about Sandy clubbing my parents to death, I went out to the beach to where Dennis was camping. I told him I wanted to take him up on his offer to go away with him to High Point. He looked surprised, to say the least. He asked me why I'd changed my mind, and when could he talk to my parents about it. I said I would only come on the condition he *never* talked to my parents about it and that we never came back to the Outer Banks. He said he couldn't do that, couldn't just take me away without letting them know. I started to cry, or maybe I already was crying. But I really started sobbing then, and he could tell that I was in a panic. He kept asking me, "What's wrong? Are you in some kind of trouble?"

He probably thought I was pregnant, the way I was carrying on. (I just realized I'd better hide my diary here even better than I hid it at home.)

"I found out something about the war, something that puts me and my family in danger unless I go away," I said.

He frowned at me. "What could you possibly have found out that would—"

I interrupted him. "It doesn't matter. And I can't tell you. Please don't ever ask me again. Just let me go away with you."

He stared at me a long time, then he finally nodded. "All right," he said.

"And you promise me we won't come back here? That you'll find someplace else to camp out on the weekends?"

He nodded again. "I have a feeling if I came back here,

I'd get arrested," he said. He sounded like he was talking to himself. Then he asked me, "When can you go?"

"Tonight," I said. "I'll sneak out and meet you on the Pole Road. Okay?"

"All right," he said.

I had something else to do before I could leave. I needed to somehow get the message to Mr. Hewitt that Sandy was the traitor he was looking for. I was so upset about this. How could I turn Sandy in? I kept remembering all the loving things he'd said to me over the past few weeks. I remembered that beautiful night in the boat. Was he really just using me? I couldn't believe it. But the horrid way he'd treated me the night before made me know he was not the man I thought he was. And I couldn't let them keep on thinking that Mr. Sato was the spy when it was really Sandy. Still, I couldn't go over to the Coast Guard station to tell Mr. Hewitt. First of all, Sandy would see me and know what I was up to. Second of all, Mr. Hewitt would be angry that I tried to talk to him in front of the boys.

I also couldn't leave him a note on the lens, because it was only Sunday, and he wouldn't be checking for my next note until Tuesday night. That left three days for my parents to go up to the lens and find the note. So I did something that may work but may not work. I went up to the lantern room with the ruby necklace Sandy gave me. A ruby is one of the few things that can cut glass. For a moment, I wondered if maybe he'd given me a fake ruby. I was about to find out. Right where I usually stuck the note for Mr. Hewitt, I carved Sandy's name. His real name, of course, which I have now cut from the early pages of this diary with a razor blade, in case anyone finds this book and learns who the traitor is and turns him in and gets me and my family in trouble with the Germans. I am so scared. I hope I'm thinking straight!

The truth is, I don't know if Mr. Hewitt will see the carved name or not. Part of me hopes he never does. Part of me can't believe Sandy could be evil. I did my halfhearted best to let Mr. Hewitt know. Whether that works or not is up to fate, I guess.

I left a note for Mama and Daddy. I told them I was going someplace where I could get a better education and someday go to college and become a teacher. They think I am running wild. I will let them think that this is part of it. So I didn't even write that I loved them or that I would miss them, and both those things are very, very true. I did write that I would be safe, though. I just had to add that because I couldn't stand the thought of them worrying about me.

I didn't talk the whole drive to High Point. It took forever, and I felt sicker with every mile. Once we got to this house, where Dennis lives with SueAnn, I threw up the entire night. I was just so scared at what I had done. Leaving home, turning in Sandy, everything. I took only my diary, some clothes and the ruby necklace, which I now know is real. How could a man who gave me a real ruby necklace ever hurt me??? I just don't understand.

Dennis and SueAnn both know how sick with worry I am, and they are not pressuring me to tell them anything. I'm grateful for that. SueAnn is the kindest person. She said to me, "You just let us take care of you, honey." So that is what I'm going to do. I can't think of any other choice I have, anyway.

Chapter Forty-Five

GINA HAD NEVER SEEN SHORTY'S PARKING LOT so empty. Apparently, everyone invited to Henry's eightieth birthday party had heeded the warning to leave their cars around the corner so that the guest of honor's suspicions would not be aroused. She parked close to the side door, however. She'd had enough trouble with the twenty uncooperative balloons in her car already. She did not want to risk losing any of them on a long walk from the street.

It was going to be a struggle to shift her mind from thoughts of Rani to this party. She had not heard back from Mrs. King, in spite of leaving the woman another message on her answering machine. But this afternoon, she'd received an e-mail from her friend Denise, in Hyderabad.

"The children are still here," Denise had written in her e-mail. "But I know they may be moved to the state orphanage any day. Rani remembers you. She keeps asking where 'Mommy' is. One of the new ayahs speaks English, and so she translates for me. I've told her to explain to Rani that you are waiting for her, and that you think about her every single day."

Every single minute. Gina had cried when she read the message, first, with relief that Rani had not been moved and that Denise was still there to keep an eye on her, and second, over Rani remembering her as her mommy. This was so unfair. So cruel to both child and mother.

She turned her focus to extracting the balloons from her car, and she was soon walking toward the side door of the restaurant, holding tight to the long ribbons. Once in the back room, she let them go, and a couple of the early guests began arranging them so that they were spaced evenly against the wooden ceiling.

It was six-thirty and the back room was already filling up with partyers. The room was closed to the public for the evening, but it hardly mattered because most of the back-room regulars had been invited—with the exception of a couple of pool players who had been good friends with Brock. A game of pool was already under way, and a couple of guys were throwing darts that she hoped would not puncture any of the balloons. Walter and Brian were engaged in a game of chess, which they promised to abandon as soon as Henry arrived. The table with the chessboard had been shoved to the far end of the room, and small square tables, complete with green linen cloths and simple floral centerpieces, had been brought in for the party. The tables were set as elegantly as was possible at Shorty's, and the chef was making stuffed flounder and pasta primavera for a crowd.

"Gina!"

Gina turned at the sound of her name to see Maggie O'Neill running toward her from the side door. She bent over to receive the hug Maggie apparently intended to give her.

"Hi, Maggie," Gina said, delighted by the enthusiastic

greeting. They had met only once, that night on the dunes, and she was surprised at being recognized by the girl, much less hugged. The rest of the O'Neill family was walking toward her, and Gina held her hand out to Alec.

"Thanks so much, Alec," she said. She had not spoken to him since he'd changed his mind about helping her raise the lens. It had amazed her how quickly things started to happen after he made a few phone calls to the right people. That man had clout. She wished he had used it a month ago, when she'd first asked, but at least it was forthcoming now. There was more money than was necessary to accomplish the task. Not only had the lighthouse association come through, but the tourist bureau, a few of the banks, and Dillard Realty as well.

"You're welcome," Alec said. "When is it going to happen?"

"Monday, weather permitting."

"Will it be going to the Graveyard of the Atlantic Museum?" he asked.

"I've asked the lighthouse association to see if they can find a place for it up here, somewhere in the northern beaches, if at all possible. Otherwise, yes, it will go there."

"What time is Henry coming?" Olivia asked, and Gina glanced at her watch.

"In ten minutes," she said. "Clay and Lacey should have picked him up by now, and they're bringing him over, ostensibly for a birthday dinner with just the three of them." She turned to the crowd. "Listen up everybody!" she said loudly. The chatter in the room quieted down and people stopped what they were doing to look at her. "They should be here around seven," she said. "Lacey is supposed to come in first to let us know they're here, and then we'll get ready to shout 'surprise.' All right?"

The guests nodded as they returned to their games and conversations.

"How is Lacey doing?" Olivia asked her.

"She's fine," Gina said. "Still a little black and blue, but not in any pain." She knew that Lacey had been afraid to come to Shorty's tonight in case Brock showed up. But Brock had left town, it seemed, probably to find himself a good plastic surgeon to fix that face of his. The night before, Gina had given Lacey the massage she'd promised her on her birthday. Lacey had needed it. The muscles in her shoulders had felt like knotted ropes beneath Gina's hands. The incident with Brock had taken something out of her, and Gina thought that was probably for the best. Lacey needed to be shaken up a little.

The other person who was a bit nervous about tonight was Clay. This would be the first time that she and Clay would be together as a couple in front of Henry, and he was worried about how the old man would react to the realization that his granddaughter's widower had moved on.

"Why don't you talk to him about it?" she'd suggested when he told her his concern, but she knew that was hard for Clay to do. Even if he *did* talk to Henry, the old man would most likely respond with little more than a grunt. If ever there were two men more suited to one another with regard to communication, it was Clay and Henry. Clay could talk to *her,* though, and that was all that mattered. They'd grown closer in the last few days, and they'd slept together every night in his bed, since it was a queen-size and hers was a double. They were using condoms now, of course, neither of them able to believe they hadn't given birth control a thought that first night. But she had her period now, as she'd expected. She was not good at getting pregnant.

They didn't talk about the future, and that was a relief to her. She didn't want to think about the fact that she was due back at her teaching job in a month. It was hardly her priority at the moment.

"There's Lace," Alec said as Lacey walked through the door from the main room of the restaurant. The bruises on her face were still there, though barely noticeable in the back room's dim light. Gina watched Lacey's eyes dart to the pool table, and she could see the relief in her face when she realized that Brock was not present.

Lacey gave her younger brother and sister quick hugs, then came over to where Gina was talking to Alec and Olivia.

"We're a little early, sorry," she said to Gina. "I told them I needed to run ahead of them to use the rest room, but they should be in here any second."

"Everybody!" Gina said again, clapping her hands together, reminding herself—and probably everyone else in the room— of the fact that she was a teacher. "Be quiet now. Clay's bringing Henry in."

A hush fell through the room, just in time. Gina could hear the two men on the other side of the door leading from the main restaurant into the back room.

"What's this door doing closed?" Henry was saying. People in the back room chuckled softly to themselves. Henry opened the door and walked in, Clay right behind him.

"Surprise!" The sound was loud, with Maggie's voice rising above the rest. "Surprise, surprise, surprise!" she said, hopping up and down.

Henry grabbed his chest as if he was going to keel over, but he was laughing. "What on earth?" he asked as people began to sing. Gina couldn't help the wide smile that spread across her face. The dapper old man looked so pleased. He stood arrow straight as they sang. His narrow tie lay neatly against his pressed white shirt, and he held his straw fedora in front of him.

The party was a great success. Gina helped another waitress with the serving, and she liked the comfortable feeling of having something concrete to do. When she was not running around with trays of food, she was with Clay, whose finger was still splinted and whose face still bore the scrapes and bruises from defending his sister's honor. Clay held her hand and was affectionate with her despite Henry's presence. And Henry noticed. He spotted Clay stealing a kiss from Gina and she heard the old man say to him, "You still have great taste in women." *Bless him,* Gina thought as she walked out of the room to get another tray of food. With just a few words, Henry had done his best to put Clay at ease.

After dinner, Henry opened the cards and gifts people had brought for him. He had nearly finished, when there was a sudden *thud* in the back of the room, and everyone looked in the direction of the sound.

"Walter!" Brian stood up, walking quickly around the table at which he'd been seated with his friend, and only then did Gina see that Walter had fallen forward out of his chair and lay crumpled on the floor. She got up from her own seat next to Clay and ran toward him, but Olivia and Alec were there first. Everyone backed away a bit, silent and shocked, as Olivia and Alec stretched Walter out on the floor. Olivia checked his neck for a pulse, shaking her head at her husband.

"I'll do the compressions," Alec said, quickly unbuttoning the old man's shirt.

"Call an ambulance!" Gina shouted over her shoulder, to no one in particular.

"Is he dead?" Maggie was standing at her side, and Gina put an arm around the girl, thinking through how to answer her, but Lacey appeared next to them before she could say a word.

"Come on, Jack and Maggie," Lacey said, exchanging a knowing glance with Gina. "Let's go outside for a while."

"What's Mom doing to him?" Maggie asked as she followed her older sister to the side door. Lacey held the screen door open, letting her younger siblings walk out ahead of her, and Gina didn't hear her answer.

The sounds were terrible. Gina could hear Olivia's breath pouring into Walter's lungs, and Alec grunted as he pressed down on the man's chest. Murmured conversations filled the room, but there was no sound from Walter at all.

Henry had moved over to the table where Walter had been sitting, and he and Brian sat next to each other quietly. They were looking into the air, not at the scene on the floor, and Gina wondered what they were thinking. Walter and Brian and Henry were all fixtures in the back room. It was hard to imagine the place without any one of them.

Come on, Walter, she thought to herself.

Clay moved close to the threesome on the floor. "Can I take over for one of you?" he asked Alec and Olivia.

"We're okay," Alec said, pressing down on Walter's frail-looking breastbone, and Clay stood to one side, waiting to see if he was needed.

Minutes passed. Finally the sound of a siren could be heard in the distance, and just as the medics raced into the room, Walter sputtered, coughed and started to breathe on his own. The people in the room let out their own breath in a collective sigh of cautious relief. Olivia sat back on her heels, her face damp and white. Alec put his hand on the back of her neck, beneath her hair, and pulled her toward him to give her a kiss on the side of the head, and the simple gesture touched someplace deep inside Gina and made her throat tighten up.

The medics lifted Walter onto a stretcher and took him out the side door to the ambulance. Olivia said she would follow in her car, while Alec drove Jack and Maggie back to their house.

"I'm taking Henry home," Clay said to Gina, once his father and stepmother had left. "And I'll probably stay with him awhile."

She nodded. "I think he's more upset than he looks."

Clay squeezed her shoulders. "I think we all are," he said. "Come over to his house when you're done here, if you like."

"I will," she said.

Slowly, and far more quietly than when they'd arrived, people left the restaurant. Gina and the other waitress stayed behind to clean up. The silence in the room was overwhelming with everyone gone. The balloons had congregated in four places on the ceiling, probably because of the location of the air-conditioning vents, and the neatly arranged tables had been shoved this way and that to make room for the medics and their stretcher. Walter's wheelchair was still at the table where he'd been sitting, a half-carved decoy lying near it on the floor. She had never seen the chair without the old man in it, and it looked sad and strange.

"You go on," the other waitress said to her as she started to clean up.

"Oh, no," Gina said. "I can't leave this mess for—"

"Go." The waitress pushed her physically toward the side door. "You need to go be with your loved ones."

Gina thanked her, then walked outside to her car. *Your loved ones.* The words made her smile, and she turned the key in the ignition and headed over to Henry's.

Chapter Forty-Six

Monday, June 8, 1942

I'VE BEEN HERE A MONTH NOW AND HIGH POINT still feels strange and too big to me. Dennis and SueAnn laugh when I say that, because I guess High Point isn't very big at all compared to a lot of other cities, but every place is bigger than Kiss River.

Dennis's house is really old, but he takes good care of it. He doesn't have a lot of money, though. I am trying to help out. Yesterday, I painted the bathroom.

Dennis got me into school here, pulling some strings, I think, because he is not my legal guardian. School is almost over for the year already. The other kids are nice, but I don't really have any friends yet. I am so different from everyone. Some of them make fun of the way I talk, but I know they're only teasing me. At least I hope they are. I honestly never realized how different I speak from everyone else. I am supposed to be a high-school freshman, but I am way behind what they are learning. I know what Dennis meant now about needing to get a better education than I could get in Kiss River. I am used to all different ages being in one classroom, but here I am with a lot of kids my own age. Dennis is tutoring me at night so I can keep up. He gave me the choice of working extra hard so I could stay with the other freshmen or going back a year or two. I sure don't want to do that. I will have to go to summer school, and then I should be caught up enough and I won't feel so panicky next year when I'm a sophomore.

I have to go to church with them every Sunday. It's part of the rules of living here. The only big rule, really, besides going to school. I actually like church, even though I am still confused about when you're supposed to stand up and kneel and all, and I'm amazed Dennis and SueAnn can figure that out since I don't see the rhyme or reason to it. I also don't have any idea what the priest is saying because it's all in Latin, but since I am learning Latin in school, I guess I will understand some of it in time.

I also have a library card here, and the library is amazing! I go there after school some days and Dennis has to bring a crowbar to pry me out of there. He laughed the first time he picked me up and saw all the books in my arms! "You don't have to bring the whole library home at one time," he told me. "The books will still be here tomorrow."

I feel sorry for the kids I went to school with in the Banks. They don't know any better. They don't know what they're missing. But then, they also are with their families, and I know I will probably never be with mine again.

Dennis is much kinder than I ever realized. I even told him about Sandy turning on me, although I said nothing about him being a spy, of course, only about him being a traitor to me. Dennis could have said, "I told you so," but instead he held me while I cried about Sandy, and SueAnn got tears in her eyes and smoothed my hair. They did ask me if that was the reason I wanted to run away from Kiss River. I told them it wasn't, but that I couldn't tell anyone the real reason, and they have not said a word about it since. I wonder what they think that reason is, but it doesn't seem to matter to them. They both care a lot about the world and making it better, and I think they've taken me on as a project. That's okay. I feel so lucky to be here with both of them. Otherwise, where would I have gone?

I miss home. I miss my parents, and I would give anything to watch the stars from the gallery with my father or even to have Mama holler at me right now. When the war is over, I will try to go back to see them. I hate that they are worried about me. But I'm still glad I did what I did. I know they're safe, even if they are probably very upset over the way I left. Of course, I wonder all the time if Mr. Hewitt found and understood my carving on the lens.

Here at the Kitterings', I have become a paper reader. The newspaper here in High Point is amazing! Living in Kiss River, you had to keep reminding yourself that there were things happening in other places. This newspaper tells you not just about the rest of America, but the whole world, and Dennis loves that I'm reading it. He talks to me about the articles. But he doesn't know what I'm really looking for, which is an article about the capture of a traitor in the Coast Guard. I read nearly every word in the paper looking for that news, and so far I have not seen it. I am afraid to see it, for so many reasons. If he's caught, would he think I had turned him in somehow after all and then would he send someone to harm my parents? That horrible dream I had is still fresh in my mind every time I close my eyes. Or maybe Mr. Hewitt didn't find a note from me and never bothered to look close enough at the lens to see his name. Or maybe he knew I'd run away and didn't even bother to look for a note. The way I chose to get the message to him seems sillier by the day, and the less sure I am that he saw it. I am ashamed to admit it, but I am relieved every time I read the paper and don't see Sandy's name there. Love is such a crazy thing. How can I still love someone who hurt me so badly? How can I want him to be safe even when he was doing something so terrible and costing Americans their lives? And what about Mr. Sato? Sandy was willing to let him go to prison or an internment camp, when *he* was actually the one doing the spying.

I can wear my ruby necklace here, and I do wear it every day. At first I thought I should throw it away or at least give it away because it came from a man who turned out to be a cruel and horrible liar. But I decided to keep it. Everybody has good in them, I figure, and I'll wear it to remember whatever good parts there were of Sandy.

Chapter Forty-Seven

THE WEATHER WAS HOT, SULTRY AND HAZY ON Monday morning, and Gina was up early, out on the beach with Clay and Sasha. They stood in the water a few yards east of the lighthouse, the water splashing nearly up to their thighs. With any luck at all, today she would learn the identity of her grandfather, a man who, as long as he had not been arrested as a spy, might very well now have an estate worth millions. One hundred thousand dollars would be nothing to him. She had to guard her motivation closely, though. It was the lens she cared about, she told herself, over and over so she would start to believe it. The salvaging of the lens.

"I don't like the look of those waves," Clay said. He stood with his hands on his hips, staring at the water. The weather would be a factor in being able to raise the lens, and Gina had been encouraged by the absence of rain that morning. But Clay was right. The waves seemed to be growing wilder as they watched. The buoy, though, was still a distance beyond the breakwater.

"It's not that bad out where the lens is, though," she said.

Clay shrugged. "It'll be up to the barge operator." He looked at his watch. "They're due here at ten, right?"

"Right."

"Maybe it will settle down by then."

"If they can't do it today, will they do it tomorrow?"

"I would hope so," Clay said. "I guess it depends on what other obligations the barge operator has."

"We're visiting Walter tomorrow, though," she said.

He gave her a slightly patronizing smile as he put his arm around her. "That's tomorrow evening," he said. "Try to relax, okay?"

Walter had suffered a heart attack the night of Henry's birthday party, but he was recovering well in the hospital in Elizabeth City. You wouldn't know he was recovering at all, though, by the way Henry and Brian were grieving. They sat glumly hunched over the chessboard at Shorty's, barely talking. The men had been a threesome for so many years. They'd grown old together, and Henry and Brian must have been feeling their own mortality as much as they were missing their old buddy.

"Hey, you two!"

They turned to see Kenny walking toward them, and Sasha looked like a dolphin as he leaped through the water to reach him.

"I talked to Smitty, the guy who owns the barge," Kenny said as he neared them. "He wanted me to come check out the conditions up here." He looked at the waves. "Whoa. Not looking too good for a salvage operation."

"But underwater, where the lens is, wouldn't it be calm?" Gina asked, still clinging to her optimism.

"Maybe, maybe not," Kenny said. He was going to be one of the divers doing the underwater work. "If the barge is bobbing up and down, the lens will be bobbing up and down too when the crane lifts it up. Not a good thing."

Gina didn't respond. She wanted a miracle to occur. She wanted the waves to suddenly flatten and the sea to grow calm.

"I'm afraid this isn't going to happen today," Kenny told her. "I don't want to get that barge out here and then have it turn around and go back. That would jack the price tag up considerably."

Clay squeezed the back of her neck, the same gesture she'd seen Alec do to Olivia, and she leaned against him, giving in. She would have to wait one more day.

Worse news faced Gina inside the house. Logging on to the Internet, she found a long e-mail from Denise, and it contained the words she had been dreading: Rani and Denise's daughter, Sunil, had been moved to the state institution on Thursday night, when their orphanage abruptly and chaotically shut its doors.

I wish I could tell you everything is fine, Gina, Denise wrote. *And if you ever prefer that I do that, just let me know. But even in that short couple of days we got to know each other, I realized you are not the kind of person to hide from the truth.*

The main problem with the state orphanage where our girls are now is that it is so institutional. The ayahs are overworked and just don't seem to have the same warmth about them that we all got used to. The physical space is even grimier, if you can imagine that, and both our girls were infested with lice within a day.

A big problem now is that I can't see Rani as much as I used to. She is in a different part of the orphanage from Sunil, and I've only been over to her part of the place a couple of times. She was weepy when I was there, but it may just be that she needed her nap. I have spoken with the director of this place, making sure they know that Rani needs special medical care, so maybe that will help.

I am getting the usual runaround from the courts, and the negative attitude toward foreign adoptions seems worse than ever. Can you tell I'm getting depressed? I can only imagine how you must feel, so many miles from your beautiful daughter. I will try to see her again tomorrow, Gina. Maybe they will let me take Sunil over to that part of the orphanage to visit with her.

The situation was getting worse and worse. Gina printed Denise's message and carried it outside to Clay, where he was working on repairing the roof of the old outhouse.

He stopped his work to read the e-mail. He was shirtless and beautiful as he stood next to the ancient privy. The dappled shade from the trees sent patches of light across the face she had grown to love. God, it felt good to have someone to share this e-mail with!

Shaking his head as he read, he reached out to pull her to him.

"It seems criminal," he said into her hair. "Aren't there authorities over there who can do something about this?"

She was accustomed to such questions. She used to ask them herself.

"Some of the authorities are the cause of it," she said, drawing away from him. "I'm so afraid she's going to die, Clay. If she does I'll feel so guilty."

"Why guilty?" he asked. "You've said there's nothing you can do."

"But I'll always wonder if there was something more I could have done," she said.

She was trying, though. She looked at the ocean, at the place where the waves billowed above the lens. She was trying everything she knew to try.

Chapter Forty-Eight

Tuesday, July 7, 1942

I AM FIFTEEN AND I AM PREGNANT. THERE. I'VE put it down in writing. I think up until now I haven't really believed it, but when I read those words back to myself, I have to admit they're the truth.

With everything that's happened, I didn't realize I'd missed a period until two days ago, when I woke up in the middle of the night and suddenly remembered I'd brought no sanitary napkins with me and that I'd better get out and buy some. And then I realized I've been here two months and haven't needed any, and I began to panic. I told SueAnn, who I can talk to about that sort of thing, and she immediately took me to her doctor. He did a test on me that we won't know the result of yet, but he felt inside me and said I am definitely pregnant. I thought I would cry when I heard the news, but I just went sort of still and stared at the ceiling above the examining table, pretending he had made a mistake and it wasn't true.

When we got home, SueAnn told Dennis, which was horribly embarrassing to me, but he just got very quiet and serious and said we would work this out somehow. That's when I started crying. He could've yelled and said he'd warned me and what a tramp I am and all of that, but he didn't say anything of the sort. And neither did SueAnn. Both of them being so Catholic and all, I felt like a terrible, sinful person. I heard the two of them talking till very late last night. I heard them mention my name a few times, but their voices were low. This morning, Dennis told me what they'd decided to do. He didn't have to tell me I have no choice in the matter. I already know that.

First, he said, he would arrange to have a priest talk to me. I need to confess what I'd done and promise never to sin that way again. Even though, Dennis added, he knows that Sandy "used me and discarded me," I am still not completely innocent. He is right. I most certainly am not. I feel like a stupid girl who has messed up her life. The thought of talking to a priest about that sort of thing is horrid, though. But I will do it.

Then Dennis said, "You and I will get married."

I must have looked shocked out of my mind, and he raised his hand to keep me from saying anything, not that I could have.

"You can't walk around pregnant out of wedlock," he said. "And I don't know if you noticed this, but I love you."

I was still speechless. I used to think Dennis loved me when he would talk to me at Kiss River, but since we've been here, he's treated me more like a kid sister or even a daughter than a girlfriend. Now I know he has been avoiding treating me like a girl he's interested in, not wanting to scare me off. The funny thing is, when he said he loved me, I got tears in my eyes and I realized that I love him back. Not the way I loved Sandy, not like a girl should love a man she's going to marry, but I love him for all he's done for me. He wasn't the man I'd ever expected myself to marry, but he was right that I couldn't be pregnant and unmarried or I'd be scorned by everyone in High Point.

"That is too much for me to ask from you," I said.

"Well, it comes with a price," he said. "I can't raise another man's child, especially not a man like Sandy. When you have the baby, you'll have to adopt it out."

Without thinking, I placed my hands on my stomach as if I was protecting the baby inside me, holding on to it. I hate the way Sandy treated me, and I hate how he's hurt his own country, but deep in my heart I still love him. Is that crazy? He is a cowardly, money-hungry traitor. How can I still go weak in the knees when I think about him? The baby inside me is his, but is it the child of the gentle man who loved me so sweetly, or of the vicious criminal who caused the deaths of hundreds of good men out of greed? What I knew right then was that I couldn't go through this alone. I could go home to Kiss River, possibly putting myself and my family in danger and then having to face my parents with what I'd done, but *that* would be a fate worse than death. If Sandy was still there and not arrested, I could confront him and tell him he was about to be a father, but I don't think I could survive him being mean to me again, especially now. I need to stay here, and I need Dennis's help. I will marry him, and I will give this baby up, when the time comes. Right now, thinking about that actually sounds like a relief. I know I look like a woman, not a girl. I can pass for much older than I am. But I *am* a girl, and I'm afraid of being pregnant and I can't imagine being a mother. *Damn.* I have really messed up my life.

Chapter Forty-Nine

IT WAS TURNING INTO THE SORT OF WEEK THAT made the tourists wish they'd stayed home. Rain pelted the van as Alec drove through the outskirts of Elizabeth City, and although the trip had not been that long, he'd be glad when they reached their destination of the hospital. He felt like the chaperon on a field trip.

Brian Cass sat in the front passenger seat, but he'd been twisted around beneath the seat belt the entire time so that he could talk with Henry Hazelwood, who sat behind Alec. In the rear of the van, Gina and Clay sat holding hands like two teenagers. Gina was sullen, probably upset at the delay the weather was causing in raising the lens. It was obvious to Alec that Clay had become her support, her best friend and her lover. He was worried, though, about his son's heart. Gina's home and work were three thousand miles away, and Alec still nursed the suspicion that she was using Clay to get that lens raised. Clay refused to talk to him about it. "I'm taking things one day at a time," he'd said.

Alec recognized the wisdom in that approach. Maybe Gina

was simply helping Clay in the transition from inconsolable widower to a living, breathing male again, and he would be able to move on easily when she left. Yet he couldn't help but worry.

In spite of his concerns, Alec was growing to like Gina. He still didn't understand why she'd felt the need to lie about her connection to the Poors, but he was trying hard to overlook it. He'd seen her at work in Shorty's, and he liked the way she treated her customers with a pleasant deference that was neither cloying nor insincere. She wasn't provocative with the male customers the way some of the other waitresses were. With her beauty, she attracted a lot of attention. Men turned their heads to follow her when she walked past them, their forks forgotten halfway to their mouths. She had to be used to it. She dealt with the men easily, with just the right mix of appreciation and gentle condescension, and he could tell they respected her for it. He particularly liked the kindness she'd shown Henry and Brian since Walter's heart attack. And his two youngest children, although they'd only met her a couple of times, talked about her constantly, as though they knew her well. So, he was ready to forgive her sullenness right now.

"Is this it?" Henry asked. In his rearview mirror, Alec could see Henry peering through the rain at the large building they were passing.

Brian scoffed. "That's not it, old man," he said.

"Not yet, Henry," Alec said with a smile. He wondered if he and his friends would talk to each other like these guys did when they were old. "It's a couple more blocks."

"That *does* look like a hospital," Gina piped up from the rear of the van, and Alec knew she was saying that in Henry's defense.

Alec had spoken with Walter's two sons, both of whom had arrived from Colorado shortly after their father's heart attack.

They were flying back today, so Walter would be alone again. It seemed like the right time to visit him.

They finally reached the hospital, and Alec pulled under the portico to let everyone out before he went to park the car. He caught up with them in the large waiting area on the first floor, where the four of them sat across from one another in the upholstered chairs.

"He's on the second floor," Alec said, waiting for them to stand up again. They paraded toward the elevators.

"I hate this place," Brian said with a shudder as the elevator door closed on them, and Alec recalled that Brian's wife had died here only a couple of years earlier.

They found Walter sitting up in bed, the wires of a monitor running beneath his blue-and-white hospital gown to his chest.

"Well, look at this!" he said, smiling broadly. "I must be dying for you all to come way out here to see me."

Gina moved forward to kiss him on the cheek, but the rest of them surrounded the bed in an awkward circle.

"You look really good," Alec said. He did. His color was far better than it had been the last time he'd seen him, when he was being carried out of Shorty's, that was for sure.

"I understand you and the missus saved my life." Walter reached a hand toward Alec.

Alec took his hand, and the elderly man held it more than shook it. "I'm just glad we were there," he said. It had been something, working together on a patient with Olivia. He'd been aware of both the depth of her skill and her trust in his.

"Thank you," Walter said. "And tell your wife thank you from me, too, okay?"

"I'll do that," Alec said.

Walter turned to Henry. "Sorry I ruined your party, Henry," he said.

"You always did like being the center of attention," Henry said, and everyone chuckled.

"You were out for a while," Brian said with his usual lack of tact. "Hope it didn't kill none of your brain cells, or you'll be a lousy chess player."

"My brain cells are just fine, you old son of a bitch," Walter laughed. "So don't think you're going to have an advantage on me when I get outta here, 'cause it ain't going to happen."

Walter told them that he'd be going into an in-patient rehab program straight from the cardiac unit, and that he planned to do everything he was instructed to do to get home quickly. They chatted a while longer, then said their goodbyes and filed out of the room. All the way down in the elevator and across the waiting area, they talked about how good he looked, and Alec could see the unspoken relief in Brian's and Henry's eyes.

The rain had stopped, although the air was still thick with it, and the drive back to the Outer Banks was not as grueling. He dropped Brian and Henry off at Shorty's and then drove Gina and Clay to the keeper's house.

"Whose car is that?" Alec asked as he pulled into the parking lot. Lacey's car was there, along with Gina's car and Clay's Jeep. But a fourth car, an old, amazingly well-preserved woody, was parked next to the Jeep.

"Very cool!" Clay was out of the van as soon as Alec brought it to a stop. He and and Gina joined him next to the car. It was an aquamarine-colored Mercury station wagon, and the wood siding was in remarkable condition. Alec ran his hand over it. The last place he'd bring a car like this would be the beach, with the humid, salty air.

"I know whose car it is," Gina said. "It belongs to a guy who comes into Shorty's sometimes. I don't know his name, though."

"Why would he be here?" Alec asked.

Neither Gina nor Clay was quick to answer. Clay looked toward the keeper's house. "My best guess is that he's visiting your daughter." There was disdain in his voice.

Alec remembered the chartreuse discoloration on his daughter's cheek, still visible that morning at the animal hospital, a week and a half after Brock had hit her. Was the woody's owner another potential abuser?

"At least this one has good taste in cars," Clay said.

"Seriously, Clay," Alec said. "Is she…is she taking care of herself?"

Clay glanced at Gina, then at the keeper's house again. "Dad, I don't know what it is with Lacey," he said. "She tries so hard to be like Mom, but…I'm sorry, Dad. She's got this slut routine going on that I just don't get."

Alec dropped his hand from the smooth wood of the car. Olivia was right. It was time to tell them, whether he wanted it to be or not.

"I need to talk to you, Clay," he said. "To you and Lacey."

Clay frowned at his serious tone. "What about?"

"I'll tell you when I have you both together. And I'd like that to be right now." He turned to Gina and rested his hand on her arm. "Gina, I have to ask you to excuse us for a while. Would you mind?"

"Of course not," she said. "I need to make a run to the grocery store, anyway. I just have to go into the house for a minute to get my backpack."

"That's fine, thank you," Alec said. "While you're in there, would you please tell Lacey I need to talk to her?"

"She might be busy, Dad," Clay said.

"I don't care what she's doing." He knew he sounded angry. He *was* angry, but more with himself than with his daughter. "I need to talk to her *now*."

"I'll get her, then," Clay said, obviously wanting to spare Gina from having to interrupt whatever Lacey was up to.

Alec followed them into the house, his own pace slow. How was he going to tell them? The words would come, he reassured himself as he waited for them in the living room. He would find a way.

Gina left for the grocery store, and a moment later, Lacey appeared in the room. "Are you all right, Dad?" she asked. She looked worried, and he realized he might have given them the impression he was ill. She walked over to him and hugged his arm to her. "What's wrong?" she asked.

Strangely, he felt himself tear up. Lacey's concern, her little-girl hugging of his arm, touched his heart. She looked so much like Annie. And he was about to change her world. Hers and Clay's.

"I'm fine," he assured them, "but there's something I should have told you long ago, and I want to tell you now, okay?" He looked from Clay to Lacey and back again, as if asking for permission. They offered small, apprehensive nods in unison.

"Let's sit down, then."

He sat on one end of the sofa with Lacey at the other, while Clay sat on the ottoman, leaning his elbows on his knees.

"Your mom was a wonderful person, as both of you know," he began. "She was an incredible mother. But she was troubled, too."

"About what?" Lacey asked.

"She was…promiscuous," he said.

"You mean, before she was married, right?" Lacey asked.

He shook his head. "I mean, throughout her entire adult life."

"Mom?" Clay asked in disbelief.

Lacey wore a deep frown. "Are you saying…more than just with Tom?" she asked.

Alec nodded. "Yes, hon. I'm sorry to have to tell you this about her. I never wanted to, but—"

"She cheated on you?" Lacey asked.

He nodded again. He heard the man upstairs moving around, using the bathroom.

"Did you know about it?"

"Not at the time, no. I didn't learn about it until after she died. Mary Poor told me. Your mother used to bring men out here to the keeper's house."

"Jesus." Clay exhaled the word.

"I don't think Mary's memory was that good," Lacey said.

As proof, he could tell them about Annie's affair with Olivia's husband, Paul, but that would be unwise. They saw Paul from time to time, when he came to visit Jack.

"I believed her," Alec said. "There were many, many clues that I missed. Obviously, Mom had a need that couldn't be met in our marriage. That I couldn't meet."

Lacey began to cry. Alec moved over to put his arm around her, but she shrugged him away, much as she had as a teenager.

"Why are you telling us this now?" Clay asked.

Alec looked down at the old, worn floor for a moment, remembering the terrible day in this house when he'd learned the truth about his wife. "Because I see Lacey following in her footsteps, and it worries me." He looked directly at his daughter. She'd grown pale, the yellowish bruise the only color in her face. "I'm worried about you, Lace," he said.

Lacey looked up at him. "Are you making this up because you think *I'm* promiscuous and that by telling me a story like this I'll stop?"

He shook his head. "I'm not making it up, Lacey. Believe me, I wish I were. I know it seems unbelievable. But what's really unbelievable is watching you turn into her right before

my eyes. All the good parts as well as the bad. You're Lacey
O'Neill, honey. Not Annie."

Lacey stood up. She scooted past Clay, then ran to the
stairs, her bare feet slapping lightly on the wooden floor. Alec
sighed. He knew she wasn't going upstairs to throw her lover
out. She was going there for comfort.

"Dad," Clay said. He ran his fingers through his dark hair.
"I just...I wish we didn't know. I wish *you* didn't know."

"I had to tell you," Alec said.

Clay nodded. "I'm sorry. What that must have been like
for you...to discover..." He shook his head. "Man."

Alec stood up and nodded toward the second story. "Keep
an eye on her, okay?" he asked. "She's built her life around
her mother being the great Saint Anne."

Clay walked him as far as the back door, and he continued
the rest of the way to his car. He still didn't know if he'd
done the right thing or not. Olivia would say he had. But he
couldn't forget the pain in Lacey's face. With a few words,
he'd hurt her. He only hoped those words would stop her
from hurting herself.

Chapter Fifty

Saturday, August 15, 1942

TODAY, DENNIS AND I WERE MARRIED. Nothing has changed except that I am now Mrs. Dennis Kittering. Elizabeth Kittering. Not a name I'd ever expected to have. If anyone had told me a year ago that I'd be married to the schoolteacher who camped on the beach on weekends, I would have laughed in their face! I'm not laughing now.

We were married in the rectory at St. Mary's, by the priest who told me the only way to atone for my sin would be to convert to Catholicism, and I am doing that, although not with my whole heart. I'm just doing it to get the priest off my back and to make things easier for Dennis, since I know he could only imagine being married to a Catholic. SueAnn was there, and a lady from the rectory, and that was it. Just a quiet, simple exchange of vows.

This was not what I'd expected for my wedding day, that is for sure, but it's me who messed everything up, so now I guess that's my payment. Or penance, as the priest would say. "For your penance, say five Hail Marys and have a small, peculiar wedding." Of course, we are not taking a honeymoon. We are not even sharing a bedroom. Dennis told me that he loves me, but he knows I don't feel the same about him and that we don't have to sleep together until I'm ready. I do love him, although I didn't tell him that, since it's not the sort of love he means when he says it to me and I don't want to give him false hope. But I know marriages used to be arranged all the time and they worked out even if the two people didn't start out loving each other, so I'm hoping this one will work, too. It has to, because Dennis doesn't believe in divorce. Not that I do either. I guess I am glad to be married, actually, since it will soon be very obvious that I'm pregnant. It's best I have this ring on my finger.

Of course, the whole point of Dennis begging me to move here was so I could get a better education, and now here I am, not able to go to school in the fall. He is going to teach me himself. He'll bring books home for me and tell me what books to get from the library and have me study by myself during the day. I like this plan, although I will feel even lonelier here than I already do, not being able to make friends at school. But that is hardly Dennis's fault. I have only myself to blame for my predicament.

I wonder if I'll ever see Mama and Daddy again. I already feel so different from the girl I was a few months ago. I'm afraid of all the questions they'd ask me if I go back to visit and afraid of getting Dennis in trouble. It might be better if I never go back, although I get a heartache when I think about that.

If I was still in Kiss River and they discovered I was pregnant, I know what would happen. After I got the tar beat out of me by Daddy (That's just an expression. He wouldn't ever lay a hand on me, but the words he'd chew me out with would feel like it all the same), I would have to drop out of school and live with Mama and Daddy. I'd have the baby right there, in the house, and be one more Banks girl who just becomes a mother and nothing else. It is better for me here, I keep telling myself. Yet, if I still lived at Kiss River there'd be a chance I might at least see Sandy every once in a while. If he didn't get picked up by the FBI, that is. And although I know that seeing him is the wrong thing to wish for, I can't help it. I miss him, at least the Sandy I knew before that night that changed everything.

Some pain goes on and on. I can hardly remember what he looks like now. I keep trying to get his image in my head, but I can only see around the edges of it. I can't really make him out at all. But I can remember him holding me, and us walking the beach on his patrol, and a lot of times at night I cry myself to sleep thinking about him, hearing those ugly words he said to me the last time I saw him. Tonight will be one of those nights, because whatever hope I still had that I might someday see him again, that some miracle might happen to make things go back the way they were, is gone.

Yours in heartache,
Mrs. Dennis Kittering.

Chapter Fifty-One

CLAY WAS GLAD GINA WAS NOT YET HOME FROM the store. He sat in the living room after his father left, Sasha's head on his knee, staring into space. He needed some time to think, to absorb all his father had told him, and to come to grips with the anger that now tarnished the feelings of love and loss he had for his mother. He wished Lacey would kick her damn boyfriend out so that he could talk to her about what they had learned. She was the only person who could share his sense of horror and betrayal. He had a feeling, though, that she felt it even more deeply than he did.

The phone rang, jarring him out of his lethargy, and he went into the kitchen to answer it.

"Miss Gina Higgins, please." The caller was a woman with a vague, possibly British accent, and he realized that this was the first call Gina had received since living in the keeper's house.

"She's not here right now," he said. "Can I give her a message?"

The woman hesitated a moment. "Yes. This is Mrs. King.

Tell her that, given how complicated matters have become over here now, the price has risen to two hundred thousand dollars. Tell her I'm sorry, but everything's become much more difficult."

What was she talking about?

"Where is 'over here'?" he asked. He was afraid he knew, and afraid, as well, that he knew what the money was for.

"I'm calling from Hyderabad," the woman said. "Be sure to give her the message." She hung up the phone abruptly, and Clay was left with the sound of the dial tone in his ear.

When Gina arrived home with her load of groceries, he was waiting for her in the kitchen.

"Did things go all right with your father?" She set the three overstuffed bags down on the counter and bent over to nuzzle Sasha.

"You had a call," he said from his seat at the table. He'd been sitting there as numbly as he'd been sitting in the living room, and he didn't make a move to help her with the groceries.

Gina's hands froze on Sasha's neck. "A call?"

"From a Mrs. King."

She stood up, reaching into one of the grocery bags to extract a box of cereal. "What did she say?" she asked.

"That the price has gone up to two hundred thousand dollars because it's more complicated 'over there' now."

Gina set the box of cereal down and leaned stiffly against the counter, her back to him. She pressed her fist against her mouth.

"You want to tell me what's going on?" he asked. "Who is Mrs. King? Are you paying some sort of bribe? And with what money?" The questions poured out of him quickly. His temper felt very short. On this day of revelations, he was sick of being lied to.

Gina turned and walked toward him, lowering herself into one of the chairs at the table. She covered her eyes with her hand and cried silently, her shoulders shaking, and he had to fight the urge to comfort her.

"I want the truth, Gina," he said.

She nodded, dropping her hand from her face. "Yes," she said. "I know. And I'm sorry, Clay. I'm so sorry. But I just couldn't tell you this."

"I thought I was supposed to be the one with the communication problems," he said.

She ignored the comment; he wasn't sure she had even heard it. "Mrs. King has gotten other children out of the orphanages in Hyderabad," she said. "She gets paid a lot of money for doing it, but she succeeds. How she avoids getting arrested, I don't know. And I don't know what she does with the money. She pays bribes, I'm sure. She probably buys off judges and attorneys and orphanage staff and who knows who else. I don't care." Her hand trembled as she pressed her fingers against her temple. "I just want my baby," she said. "She's dying. One of these days, it's going to be too late to save her."

"Why didn't you tell me this?"

"If you were going to pay someone an illegal fee for saving your child's life, would you tell anyone?" she asked.

I would tell you, he thought, but he wasn't sure that was the truth.

"I'm not a bad person, Clay," she said. "I'm not a criminal. I don't even jaywalk. But I can't see any other way to get Rani out of there."

"Where do you intend to get two hundred thousand dollars?" he asked.

"I..." She sighed, then looked at him with those dark eyes

he had come to love. "I'd like to read you some of Elizabeth Poor's diary, all right?"

He was perplexed. "That's going to tell me where you're getting the money?" he asked.

She nodded.

"How? Did she bury diamonds in the sand behind the privy or something?"

"Actually, it *is* something like that." She stood up. "I'll be right back."

She went upstairs, and he put away the groceries, trying to muster up a good self-righteous anger at her for keeping this from him, but he found he couldn't. They were not married, not committed to a future with each other. She didn't owe him anything.

She reappeared in the kitchen, a small, pink diary in her hand. "Could we sit on the lighthouse stairs?" she asked, glancing toward the hallway. "In case Lacey comes down?"

They were quiet as they walked out to the lighthouse and climbed the tall spiral staircase. The top step was still wet from that afternoon's rain, and they had nothing to dry it with before sitting down. They brushed the water off with their hands as best they could, and Clay felt the dampness seep through his shorts as he sat down.

Gina began to read to him from the diary. It was strange to listen to the tale, to hear about a world that had existed so long ago, right here on the land and in the house where he was living. He was shocked when Gina read about Bess's discovery that the Coast Guard boy, Sandy, was the spy. But when she read the part about Bess carving his real name into the prism of the lens, he felt his anger rise.

"*That's* why you want the lens?" he asked. "All this crap about… Gina! *Damn it*. Why didn't you tell me any of this?

Why didn't you tell me your grandfather's name will be on the lens?"

"I'm sorry." She was crying, wiping tears from her cheeks with her fingers. "I'm so sorry, Clay. But I just couldn't tell you."

"I don't get it," Clay said. "What does a name on the lens have to do with getting the money?"

"He was being paid for spying, remember?" She held up the open diary. "My grandfather has money. He was probably wealthy, while my mother—his daughter—had absolutely nothing."

He heard a rare sort of anger in her voice. She was making so little sense that it frightened him. "But he was probably arrested," he said.

"I don't think so," she said. "Bess still loved him, so she made a very weak attempt to turn him in when she carved his name into the lens. She knew it was unlikely Bud Hewitt would even notice the name. And she read the newspapers all the time, and never saw a word about him being captured."

"It could have been kept very quiet," Clay said. "And in any case, he sounds like a cruel, traitorous psychopath, not the sort who's going to just hand two hundred thousand dollars over to you."

"Then I'll…" There was desperation in her eyes. "Then I'll blackmail him with the diary."

"This is ludicrous, Gina, don't you see that?" he said. "Even if he wasn't caught, he's probably dead."

"I know." She brushed a tear from her cheek. "But the diary should give me proof that I have a right to some of his estate."

Suddenly, he felt very sorry for her. Her love for a child had turned her into a desperate and thoroughly irrational woman.

He doubted, though, that she was the first woman to suffer that fate. He pulled her to him, and she seemed surprised.

"You're not mad at me?" she asked.

"I am royally pissed off at you," he said. "But it's obvious to me that you're not thinking clearly. Your love for Rani has made you a little crazy. You've lost sight of what's right and wrong, and pinned all your hopes on a pipe dream."

"Don't say that, Clay, please." Her voice broke. "There's nowhere else for me to turn. I couldn't get the money anywhere else. I tried to borrow it, but my credit is terrible because of my ex-husband's debt." She leaned back to look at him, her features contorted by her tears. "*This* is why I didn't want to tell you," she said. "I didn't want to hear you say that I'm crazy or that this plan can't possibly work."

"It's not just that you've picked a hopeless way to get the money," he said, "but that you're paying off a...baby broker, or whatever she is, to begin with."

"I don't know what else to do," she repeated.

He pulled her close again, thoughtful for a moment. "You know," he said, "it's possible that Henry or Brian or Walter might know who Sandy was."

"Why would they know that?" She sniffled against his shoulder.

"They were all in the Coast Guard here," he said.

"They were?"

"That's how they became buddies," he said. "I'm not sure if it was during World War II, though, but we can ask them. Of course, they won't know the name Sandy, but maybe they would remember who patrolled that beach."

She tipped her head back to look at the sky, and he smoothed his hand across her wet cheek. "Only if we can't find out from the lens," she said. "With any luck, we'll be able to see it tomorrow. I don't want to involve any more people than I have to in this."

"All right," he said.

She leaned her head against his shoulder again. "I know you're mad at me, Clay," she said, "but I just want to thank you for not being madder. I wouldn't blame you."

"I think your plan is nuts," he said, "but I also know how crazy a person can get when they feel like they're losing someone they love."

"Thank you," she said. Then she raised her head to look at him. "Is your father okay?"

It was Clay's turn to sigh. "He told us some things that were a bit hard to hear," he said.

"Can you tell me?" she asked.

He felt torn, hesitant to speak the words out loud, but he wanted her to know. "He told us that Lacey is apparently taking after our mother, who was...well, I guess she cheated on him throughout their marriage."

"Oh, no," Gina said.

"Not that Lacey's cheating on anyone," Clay continued. "But my mother apparently had a series of lovers, my father being just one of them. And she would bring them here, to the keeper's house. Mary Poor, your great-grandmother, knew all about it, I guess."

"She did? She was so strict with her own daughter."

"Well, not with my mother, apparently."

"I'm sorry, Clay. That must have been so terrible for you to hear."

He shook his head, still incredulous. "It's like I have to adjust to a whole new world," he said. "It's as though I just found out that I'd been lied to all my life about the stars being three-dimensional objects in the sky, when they're really just dots painted on a dome."

"Did your father have a clue that was going on?" Gina asked.

"He didn't find out until after she died. He thought she was a saint, just like everyone else did. Can you imagine how he felt?" He ached for his father. "Why do people have to betray each other?"

"They don't," she said. She turned to him, taking his hands. "Clay, I have no idea what will happen between you and me. Whether we have a future or not. I don't know and you don't know." Her voice was strong now, the tears gone. "But I am through with lying and with keeping things from you, I promise you that."

He squeezed her hands, and asked her the question that had been on his mind since she'd first told him how desperate she was to get Rani. "How would you feel if someone else was able to adopt Rani?" he asked. "Maybe an Indian couple, so they wouldn't be subject to the problems you're dealing with."

She stiffened in his arms, and it was a moment before she answered. "If they would get her the surgery she needs right away…" She spoke slowly. "And if they were the sort of people who would…" She started to cry again, shaking her head. "But she's my *baby,* Clay," she said. "She's my *daughter.*"

Chapter Fifty-Two

"AH, THIS TWINKIE'S GONNA BE NOTHIN' TO LIFT."

Gina sat on the edge of the barge, listening to the barge captain, or operator, or whatever he was called, talking to Kenny about raising the lens. It was the third time she'd heard him call the lens a "twinkie," and she assumed he was referring to the fact that, compared to the sort of things he usually had to retrieve from the ocean bottom, the lens was relatively light.

She'd awakened that morning to the sound of voices slipping through the window of Clay's bedroom. Peering outside, she saw Kenny standing in the knee-high water east of the lighthouse. He was wearing a short-sleeved wet suit and shouting something to a man who stood on a small, yellow-rimmed barge floating near the buoy. The early-morning sun tinted the entire scene with gold, and the sea was like glass. The crane rising from the middle of the barge looked like a giant, amber-colored insect standing upright on its hind legs.

Gina awakened Clay, then dressed quickly in Lacey's red bathing suit and rushed out to the beach.

She and Clay had to swim out to the barge, climbing up the ladder attached to the rear of the floating deck. The barge was much larger than it had looked from the window of Clay's room, and Gina felt dwarfed by the crane. On the deck, a short distance away from the crane, sat a square framework of wood timbers, perhaps a foot high.

"The crane will put the lens down on top of that set of timbers there," Kenny explained, pointing to the box. He was on the barge now as well, perspiring in his wet suit; the morning was very warm. "Then we'll transport it to Hatteras to get it cleaned up."

Kenny explained the entire process to them in great detail. They would use a water jet to blow the sand away from the bottom of the lens, he said. Then they'd put lifting straps beneath it, attach the straps to the cable coming from the crane, and that would be it. "A snap," Kenny said.

She and Clay watched as Kenny and the other diver climbed down the ladder and into the water, carrying hoses and other paraphernalia needed to prepare the lens to be raised. Although the water was fairly clear today, she would not be able to see what was going on beneath the surface, since the barge was anchored a distance from the lens to prevent the crane from swinging the lens onto its side as it raised it into the air. Gina kept glancing at the framework of timbers where the lens would be brought to rest. If the bottom of the lens was too deep inside that network of timbers, she would not be able to see what she needed to see.

"You excited?" Clay asked her.

She was chewing on her lower lip. "What do you think?" she asked. "I can't wait to get a look at that twinkie."

She knew that Clay was curious to see what, if anything, they would find, regardless of how harebrained her scheme seemed to him. He'd talked about searching the Internet once they had the name of the spy. Maybe they would be able to find out if he had been caught. Or if he was still alive, maybe they could find an address for him.

She'd been feeling embarrassed for the past two days, ever since telling Clay her plan. She could see why he thought the scheme seemed crazy. It *was* crazy. But it was the only course of action that she had been able to see. It was the only course of action she could see even now.

She'd had no word from Denise in three days, and that raised her anxiety level even higher. Denise used the computer in her hotel for her e-mail, and sometimes those computers were down. Gina hoped that was the reason for Denise's silence, and that it was not an indication of something more ominous.

Lacey had wanted to join them on the barge, but one of the other vet techs was out sick, and she'd had no choice but to go in to work. Gina was glad. It was going to be hard enough for her and Clay to examine the lens without arousing suspicion from the diver and barge operator and Kenny. It would have been just about impossible with Lacey there.

Lacey had been very quiet since Alec told her the truth about her mother on Tuesday. She was nearly impossible to engage in conversation. Gina and Clay decided the best approach was to leave her alone rather than press her to talk. "She'll talk when she's ready," Clay had said. But it was hard to watch Lacey's sparkling personality slip into something dark and brooding.

A half hour passed. Gina knew her skin was starting to sunburn. She hadn't given a thought to sunscreen. She didn't care, though. Clay rubbed her back as she closed her eyes, trying to breathe evenly, patiently, in an attempt to still her nerves.

Finally, Kenny reappeared on the surface of the water and gave the guy operating the crane the thumbs-up sign. Slowly, with a grinding, whirring sound, the cable attached to the arm of the crane began to rise, dragging seaweed with it. In less than a minute, the giant, algae-covered beehive broke the surface of the water. It rose into the air, a series of waterfalls pouring from the tiers of glass.

Gina and Clay stood well out of the way as the crane lifted the lens high into the air, then turned and began lowering it into the timber frame.

"It's on an angle," Clay said to her.

She had already noticed that fact, and it was good news. The lens was not upright, but rather lying nearly on its side in the cradle of straps. If it was still on its side when the crane let it down on the frame of timbers, she and Clay would be able to see the prisms at the bottom of the lens with relative ease.

A couple of workers from the barge guided the lens into the frame, laying it almost on its side, in the same position it had been in in the cradle.

Gina and Clay walked toward the lens, ignoring the crane operator's pleas to keep their distance.

"This is the bottom," Gina said, her hands already feeling the prisms beneath her palms. *Don't let the name have been on the missing panel,* she thought. She scraped at the algae-covered prisms with her fingernails, while Clay used a rag he found on the deck of the barge.

"Gina!" Clay suddenly called from the other side of the lens. "I've got it! I can see a couple of letters."

Quickly, she circled the lens to see him holding the grubby rag in his hand, a look of shocked disbelief on his face.

She followed his gaze to the prism. The glass was nearly clean, and the etched name was more vivid for the green algae held deep in its crevices: Walter Liscott.

Chapter Fifty-Three

SITTING NEXT TO CLAY IN THE WAITING ROOM of the rehab center, Gina played with the clasp on her backpack. It had been mere hours since they'd seen the name on the lens, and Clay had wanted to wait a day before they went to Elizabeth City to talk to Walter, but Gina could not have put it off another minute. She had to confront the man who had betrayed Bess Poor and his country.

"How long do you think his exercise session lasts?" Gina asked, looking at her watch. They'd been waiting forty minutes already.

"Has to be over soon," Clay said. Then he sighed. "You know, Gina, Walter's a really nice guy."

"So was my husband," Gina said. "And Sandy-slash-Walter was extremely nice to Bess, too, before he turned on her."

"That was sixty years ago." Clay took her hand. "People can change a lot in sixty years. I know you're hoping he's some sort of multimillionaire, but Walter doesn't have any money socked away. I'm sure of it. If he ever received it, he spent it long ago. He lives in a little bungalow."

She feared he was right. Frankly, she no longer knew what she hoped to discover by speaking with Walter. She was having a difficult time reconciling the kind old man she'd come to care about with the traitorous Coast Guard patrolman who had turned on Bess so cruelly. But she'd had trouble reconciling the fact that Bruce had changed so radically, too. She wondered if Clay was destined to change, as well.

She squeezed Clay's hand. "I'll be gentle with him," she said. "I promise." She knew Clay was afraid that confronting Walter might cause him to suffer another heart attack.

It was a few more minutes before Walter wheeled himself into the waiting room.

"Well, it's nice to see you two," he said, a broad smile on his face. "I sure do miss home. I miss Shorty's. Not a soul to play chess with here."

"Is there someplace private we can go, Walter?" Gina asked him. There were other people in the waiting room and this was not going to be the sort of conversation that should be overheard.

He lost his smile. "Is everything all right?" he asked. "Everybody all right?" He probably thought something terrible had happened to Brian or Henry.

"Everyone's fine," Clay reassured him. "Gina and I just need to talk to you for a few minutes."

"We can go to my room." Walter pointed toward the hallway behind them. "I have a roommate, but he's getting PT right now, so it'll be private, at least for a while."

They followed him down the long corridor to his room. There was only one chair, and Gina sat down on it, clutching her backpack in her lap, while Clay sat on the edge of Walter's unmade bed.

Walter looked from one of them to the other from his wheelchair. "What's on your minds?" he asked.

Gina glanced at Clay. Now that she was face-to-face with Walter, she was unsure where or how to begin.

"We wanted to talk to you about when you were in the Coast Guard," Clay said.

Walter wore a look of confused surprise. "You do?" he asked. "I wasn't in all that long. Henry and Brian could tell you more than I could."

"Walter," Gina said suddenly, "you're my grandfather."

"I'm *what?*" Walter laughed.

Gina reached into the backpack and pulled out the pink diary.

"This is the diary Bess Poor kept the year she was fifteen," she said.

The color drained from Walter's face and he stared at the book. Then he shook his head. *"Bess,"* he said, more to himself than to either of them. He pointed to the diary. "What does she say in there?" he asked.

"She talks about falling in love with you. With Sandy."

He chuckled. "Sandy. Haven't heard that name in a long time. She sure was the only person in the world who ever called me that."

"She adored you," Gina said.

"And I adored her, too." Walter looked suddenly somber and sad. "I worry her life didn't turn out too well."

Gina felt angry and had to struggle to control her voice. "And whose fault was that? You sent her away from her home. Were you ever caught? Were you paid millions of dollars by the Germans?" The words spilled over each other as she rushed to get them out.

Walter looked dumbfounded. Finally, he spoke. "Maybe I should see that diary," he said.

She pictured him ripping the pages out, tearing them up

before she could do a thing about it. She should have made a copy of the book.

"She tells about you spying for the Germans, Walter," Clay said, his voice much calmer than Gina's. "Don't worry. We're not going to tell anyone. It's water under the bridge. We just wanted to know if it's the truth."

Walter suddenly laughed. "Is that what you two are worried about?" he asked.

Neither she nor Clay said a word, and Walter sobered at the serious expressions on their faces.

"Well," he said. "I can see I have some explaining to do." He looked at Gina. "But what's this about you being my granddaughter?"

"Bess was pregnant when she left Kiss River," she said. She felt like adding, *Withdrawal is a lousy method of birth control,* but managed to bite her tongue.

"Oh no." Walter turned away from them, staring blankly out the window. "For many, many years, I didn't know where she had gone," he said. "Her parents didn't know, either. No one did."

"Did you care where she went?"

"Yes, I cared." He faced Gina, sounding a bit defensive. "It wasn't easy for me to let her go."

"Let her?" Gina asked. "You *sent* her." She was not doing a good job of treating him gently, and Clay leaned forward to wrap his hand around her wrist.

"Take it easy," he admonished her.

Walter looked down at his lap, where his hands lay still, one resting upon the other. "Listen to me, you two," he said. "I...I was never really in the Coast Guard."

"What do you mean?" Clay asked.

"I was actually working for the FBI as a double agent."

Gina frowned. "I don't understand," she said.

"We had some intelligence that German saboteurs were planning to come ashore," Walter said. "The FBI sent a fellow to the area to gather information, but he got himself murdered, probably because he spoke German with a terrible accent and they grew suspicious of him. That's when they sent me. German was my first language, since my parents were both born in Germany."

"You never told Bess that," Gina said.

"Of course not," Walter said. "There was plenty I didn't tell her. My job was to make the Germans think I was working for them while I was really working for the government. Bud Hewitt, the chief warrant officer, didn't even know. It would have compromised the entire mission if anyone knew. Ultimately, we were able to prevent the subs from landing any saboteurs along the coast there."

"You told Bess they were paying you millions," Gina said.

"Millions?" Walter laughed. "The only money I got was my paycheck. If I *did* tell her that, it was because it was the only thing I could think of to say at the time. When Bess realized I was in cahoots with the Germans, I panicked. I didn't dare tell her the truth. She was in real danger. She could have been killed by the Germans or…well, it wouldn't have been the first time an American was killed to protect a mission. I'd put her in danger by falling in love with her." There was a sheen of tears in his eyes. "I sent her away, *scared* her away, because I loved her. I told her I killed the fellow on the beach. I hate that she left thinking the worst of me. I know it must have been very painful for her. But now, to find out she was pregnant!"

He mistook Gina's numb silence as disbelief. Wheeling over to the night table, he fumbled in the drawer for a set of keys and he handed them to her.

"In my house, in the file cabinet in the den, there is a file labeled Personal," he said. "In it, you'll find a quiet little letter signed by J. Edgar Hoover, commending me for my service to the United States government in 1942."

Clay slowly shook his head, stunned. "Holy shit, Walter," he said.

Walter looked at Gina. "Now, please," he said. "Tell me about you and how you came to be my granddaughter."

Suddenly, she saw her mother in his eyes and in the shape of his mouth. She felt herself starting to tear up, and she looked down at the diary. There was so much to tell. She hardly knew where to begin.

"Bess gave her baby—*your* baby—up for adoption," she said, leaning forward to press the keys back into his hand. Settling deeper into the chair, she prepared herself to tell him the story, from start to finish, forgetting for just a moment about money and Rani and India. For the first time in her life, she had a grandfather.

Chapter Fifty-Four

Monday, February 8, 1943

FOUR DAYS AGO ON FEBRUARY 4, I HAD A BABY girl at the hospital where SueAnn works. I came home today, glad to get away from all the happiness and sounds of crying babies that filled that place, while my arms were empty. I didn't even see her. I wanted to. Even though I knew it would be hard, and I would have to hand her over to the nurse to take her away forever, I still wanted to see her and look in her face. I wanted to see Sandy in her, because his face is so lost to me now, and I wanted that little reminder of him. But if I'd seen him there, I would never have been able to let her go. Maybe they knew that. Maybe that is why the nurses wouldn't let me see her.

I had a very difficult time giving birth to the baby. I honestly don't remember very much of it. They kept me asleep, or nearly asleep, most of the time, and when I was awake, I kept calling out for Mama. They told me I may not ever be able to have another child. Something about my uterus. Right now I don't care. I am fifteen. I don't want a child. Except maybe the one I just gave away.

The priest took her away. She is going to a "good Catholic couple," he said. She will have a good life. I asked him if the couple went to our church, if I might get to see her from time to time, but he said, "Certainly not," as though I'd asked the most stupid question in the world.

Dennis is being real kind to me, even more than usual. SueAnn told him some women get very sad (melancholy was the word she used) after they have a baby, even if they don't have to give that baby up. I think that's what's happening to me. I just want to sleep. I want to wake up and have this whole year erased from my life and my heart.

Chapter Fifty-Five

A PALL HAD SETTLED OVER THE KEEPER'S HOUSE. Clay was living with two pensive, tearful women. One felt as though she had lost her child, the other her mother. He had never seen his sister like this, so quiet, so withdrawn. "I don't know who I am anymore," she told him, and he understood. She had wanted so much to be like their mother, to keep Annie alive in that way. She had not realized exactly how much like her mother she had become, in both good ways and bad.

And Gina was bereft. There was no other word for it. She contacted a group of physicians who volunteered their time and skill to help children in other countries and begged them to take on Rani's case. She told him it was not the first time she'd called that organization, but it was the first time she'd sobbed into the phone while talking to the woman who was their liaison. The woman told her how sorry she was, but "there are just too many children. We wish we could help them all, but we can't. And especially not a child in an orphanage, where she is unlikely to get the sort of aftercare that is so necessary to her recovery."

In bed at night, Clay held Gina close to him and let her cry. She slept poorly, tossing and turning and keeping him awake much of the night. She offered to sleep in her own room, but he wanted her with him, and he knew that was what she wanted—what she *needed*—as well.

Lying there awake at night, a plan began to take shape in his mind. He thought about it for a day or two and talked it over with his father, who gave him compassionate, if reluctant, support. He had decided not to tell Alec the real reason behind Gina's desire to raise the lens. He would tell him in time, but right now, he needed his father on his side, and that information would only increase Alec's already conflicted feelings about Gina.

On Saturday night, Clay sat with her on the top step of the lighthouse, watching the stars and fighting off the mosquitoes, and he told her what he wanted to do.

"I don't have two hundred thousand dollars for you to give Mrs. King," he said. "And I think you know that I wouldn't give it to her if I did. But I *do* have enough money to take us both to India, and to let us stay there and take care of Rani while you—while *we*—fight the system."

She looked at him, wide-eyed. "Why would you do that for a child you don't know, much less love?" she asked.

He rested his hand on her cheek and kissed her, the woman who had given him back his life.

"Because I love *you*," he said. "That's why."

Chapter Fifty-Six

Monday, May 17, 1943

TODAY I UNDERSTAND THE MEANING OF THE word *ambivalence*. I've heard it before, of course, and read it in books and had some knowledge of what it meant, but I never realized that it perfectly describes what I am feeling.

This will be the last time I write in my diary. Or at least, in this diary. My life has changed, and I need to put all that has happened to me in the last year behind me. Often, when I write in this book, I read back over what I wrote in the past and it keeps it alive for me. I can remember every moment. I want to stop remembering. I want to look toward the future and not back at the past, because the past makes me feel sad and regretful.

Last night, Dennis and I made love for the first time. I cried for an hour afterward, not even sure why I was crying, and he held me close to him and told me everything would be all right, that he would take care of me forever. I think I was crying because I knew I had to give up the past. I suppose somewhere in my heart I've been hoping I could return to Kiss River to see my parents and to get back that future Sandy and I had talked about, that I could get back to *Sandy*. I keep thinking about certain things, like how strange it is that I used the ruby necklace he gave me as a tool to turn him in. And here's another thing I thought of: he told me that he was the one who murdered that man I found on the beach, because the man was snooping on him. But unless I am going completely crazy, Sandy had not even arrived in Kiss River when that man was murdered. See how I can go round and round about this? It is so hard for me to let go.

But last night, I finally did make myself let go of Sandy and my parents and the past. I am with Dennis now. If there is a better man in the world, I don't know who he is. And so I am going to do my darnedest to be happy with him, and to make him happy, too.

I am ambivalent about it all. I left Mr. Hewitt the etched message in the Fresnel lens in an ambivalent way, wanting to do my duty to my country by turning Sandy in, yet not wanting to see him hurt. I gave up my baby with ambivalence. I move through my days with ambivalence, not really caring that I excel in school, doing so mainly to please Dennis. It's time for all that to change. It's time that I moved forward with certainty. And that is why, dear diary, I am putting you away for all time. Thank you for being there for me. I have needed your complete acceptance of me, with my warts and all. Thank you thank you thank you. And goodbye.

Chapter Fifty-Seven

IT WAS A CARAVAN THAT MADE ITS WAY TO Norfolk and the airport the second week of August. Gina and Clay rode in Alec's van with him and Olivia, Jack and Maggie. Lacey followed behind, transporting Walter, Henry and Brian in her car and Walter's wheelchair in her trunk. No one wanted to miss saying goodbye and good luck to Gina and Clay as they embarked on the first leg of their long journey to Hyderabad.

Gina worried they were taking too many things with them. The waitresses and some of the customers at Shorty's had given her a baby shower, and she had toys and clothing for Rani, as well as a diaper bag and a stroller, which she hoped would be allowed on the plane. All the gifts were borne of a certain optimism on the part of her friends, and Gina prayed that their optimism would be rewarded. Rani was still at the state orphanage, becoming more withdrawn by the day, according to Denise's latest e-mail. For whatever reason, Mrs. King had dropped the price of her bribe down to a hundred thousand dollars again, but even if Gina had the money, she knew that she wouldn't pay it. They would fight through legal channels now, difficult and frustrating though she knew that would be. Now, she would not be doing it alone. She *had* gotten a bit crazy these last few months and she owed her newfound sanity to the man sitting next to her. Clay seemed to think it was the other way around, though, as he thanked her regularly for making him care about living again.

They arrived at the airport very early, not only to allow enough time for the security check, but to have a meal together, all ten of them. They sat around two pushed-together tables in the airport restaurant. Everyone was talking at once, but Gina's eyes were on Maggie. At Maggie's request, Gina had made her a copy of one of Rani's pictures, and the girl had it propped up against her water glass where she could see it easily. Gina was touched. She looked around the table at the people she cared about, and who cared about her. This was the world she wanted to bring Rani home to.

She didn't know what the future held. Bellingham seemed very far away, and she had already told the superintendent of her school she was taking a leave of absence. She would have quit altogether, but she needed the insurance to cover Rani's surgery when she brought her home. What she would do for a paycheck, though, she had no idea. She would figure that out when she needed to. Right now, the only thing on her mind was getting her daughter.

By the time she and Clay—and Rani, for they were both determined not to leave Hyderabad without her—returned from India, the lens would be on public display. People would admire it in awe, that nearly perfect glass shell. A few very observant people might notice the faint etching of a name on one of the prisms and wonder how and why it came to be there. They would probably think it was the work of Walter Liscott himself, the prank of a young boy, perhaps, who wanted to leave his name there for all time. They would never guess that it had been the ambivalent etching of a heartbroken fifteen-year-old girl.

The search for the lens itself may have been misguided; it had certainly failed at giving her the answers she had hoped for. But as Gina looked around the table at people she had come to care about, she knew that she *had* found what she had been looking for: a family.

★ ★ ★ ★ ★

Acknowledgments

I RESEARCHED MANY TOPICS WHILE WRITING *Kiss River,* including life in the Outer Banks both past and present, foreign adoption, scuba diving, the plight of Japanese Americans during World War II and the impact of that war along the Atlantic coast, and of course one of my favorite topics, the North Carolina lighthouses. I have many people to thank for their help in writing *Kiss River.* Kathy Birnbaum, Dixie Browning, Jim Bunch, Lloyd Childers, Janet Ha, Linda Lewis, Rob Lopresti, Tony Moyer, Frank Newman, Dallas Patterson and Sharon Van Epps were all generous in sharing their expertise with me. Fellow authors Emilie Richards and Patricia McLinn were my partners in critiquing and brainstorming as well as in feasting on delicious meals each time we got together. I am grateful, too, for the support of my former agent Ginger Barber of the William Morris Agency and my editors Amy Moore-Benson and Miranda Stecyk at MIRA Books.

I hope you'll visit my website at www.dianechamberlain.com.

Turn the page for an exclusive preview of

HER MOTHER'S SHADOW

the compelling novel from
Diane Chamberlain

available soon!

Her Mother's Shadow

by

Diane Chamberlain

Christmas 1990

There was cheer in the house in the heart of Manteo. From the outside, the large two-story frame building that served as the battered women's shelter was nondescript. There were no Christmas lights hanging from the eaves, not even a wreath on the door, as if the people who ran the house were afraid to draw attention to it, and Lacey supposed they were. Cruel men had put the women and children here, the sort of men she had no experience with and found hard to imagine. But she could see the fear in the women's faces and knew those men existed. More than that, she did not really want to know.

Although there was no sign of the season outside the house, inside was another story. Fresh garlands decorated the railing that led up to the bedrooms, and branches of holly were piled on top of the huge old mantel. The scent of pine was so strong it had seared Lacey's nostrils when she first walked inside. A huge tree stood in the corner of the living room, decorated with white lights and colored glass balls and topped by one of her mother's stained-glass angels. The tree was alive, and Lacey did not need to ask if that was her mother's doing. Of course it was. Annie O'Neill always insisted on live trees. They had one at home, and Lacey knew both trees would be taken inland, away from the sandy soil of the Outer Banks, to be planted once the Christmas season was over.

She had not wanted to come to the battered women's shelter tonight. She'd wanted to stay home and listen to her new CDs and try on her new jeans with the rivets down the sides. She'd wanted to talk on the phone to her best friend, Jessica, to compare the gifts they'd received and decide what movie they would see the following afternoon. But her mother had insisted.

"You have so much," she'd said to Lacey the week before. "You will have already opened your presents and had Christmas dinner with me and Daddy and Clay. These women and their children will have nothing. *Less* than nothing. They'll have *fear* for Christmas, Lacey." Her mother spoke with great drama, the way she always did. "Their families will be torn apart," her mother continued. "Serving them dinner, singing a few carols with them—that's the least we can do, don't you think?"

Now, standing behind the long tables and dishing out Christmas dinner to the women and children, Lacey was glad she had come. At thirteen, she was certainly the youngest of the volunteers, and she felt proud of herself, proud of her kindness and generosity. She was just like her mother, whom all the other volunteers turned to for direction. Annie O'Neill was the most important person in the room. The tree in the corner probably wouldn't exist if it weren't for her mother. The weighted-down buffet tables would probably hold half as much food. Maybe the entire shelter would not be here if it weren't for Annie. Lacey wasn't sure about that, but it seemed a real possibility to her.

She smiled at the women as she spooned green beans onto their plates. Six women, some of them still bearing the bruises that had sent them to the shelter, and more than a dozen children filed past the tables, balancing real china plates. Her mother had insisted that all the volunteers bring their good china for the women and their children to use. "They can't eat Christmas dinner off paper plates," Lacey had heard her say to one of the volunteers a few weeks before. At the time, she thought her mother was just being silly, but now she could see how much the beautiful plates and the cloth napkins and the glittery lights from the tree meant to these women. They needed every speck of beauty and warmth they could get right now.

Outside, a cold rain beat against the house's wood siding and thrummed steadily against the windows. It had rained all day, a cold and icy rain, and she and her mother had skidded a couple of times as they drove to Manteo.

"Remember how it snowed on Christmas last year?" her mother had said as Lacey complained about the rain. "Let's just pretend this is snow."

Her mother was an excellent pretender. She could make any situation fun by twisting it around so that it was better than it really was. Lacey was too old for that sort of pretending, but her mother could always charm her into just about anything. So, they'd talked about how beautiful the snow-covered scenery was as they passed it, how the house tops were thick with white batting and how the whitecaps on the ocean to their left were really an icy concoction of snow and froth. The dunes at Jockey's Ridge were barely visible through the rain, but her mother said they looked like smooth white moutains rising up from the earth. They pretended the raindrops falling against the windshield of the car were really snowflakes. Lacey had to put her fingers in her ears to block out the pounding of the rain in order to really imagine that, but then she could see it—wipers collecting the snow and brushing it from the car. It fluttered past the passenger-side window like puffs of white feathers.

"The first Noel..." Her mother began to sing now as she used salad tongs to set a small pile of greens on the plate of a young girl, and the other volunteers joined in the carol. It took Lacey a bashful minute or two to join in herself, and the beaten-looking women standing in line took even longer, but soon, nearly everyone was singing. The smiles in the room, some of them self-conscious and timid, others filled with gratitude, caused Lacey to blink back tears that been brought on her so quickly, she had not been prepared for them.

A tall woman smiled at Lacey from across the table, nudging her son to hold his plate out for some green beans. The woman was singing "Oh Christmas Tree" along with the group, but her doe-eyed son was silent, his lips pressed so tightly together that it looked as though no song would ever again emerge from between them. He was shorter than Lacey but probably around her age, and she smiled at him as she spooned the beans onto his plate. He looked at her briefly, but then his gaze was caught by something behind her, and his mouth suddenly popped open in surprise. Or maybe, she wondered later, in fear. His mother had stopped singing, too. She dropped the good china plate filled with turkey and mashed potatoes, and it clattered to the floor as she stared past the volunteers toward the door of the room. Lacey was afraid to turn around to see what had put such fear in the woman's eyes. One by one, though, the women and children and volunteers did turn, and the singing stopped. By the time Lacey could force her own body to turn around, the only sound remaining in the room was the beating of the rain on the windows.

A huge man stood in the doorway of the room. He was not fat, but his bulk seemed to fill every inch of the doorway from jamb to jamb. His big green pea coat was sopping wet, his brown hair was plastered to his forehead and his eyes were glassy beneath heavy brows. Held between his two pale, thick, shivering hands was a gun.

No one screamed, as if the screams had already been beaten out of these women. But there were whispered gasps—"Oh, my God" and "Who is he?"—as the women quietly grabbed their children and pulled them beneath the tables or into the hallway. Lacey felt frozen in place, the spoonful of green beans suspended in the air. The tall woman who'd dropped her plate seemed paralyzed, as well. The doe-eyed boy at her side said, "Daddy," and made a move toward the man, but the woman caught his shoulder and held him fast, her knuckles white against the navy blue of his sweatshirt.

Lacey's mother suddenly took the spoon from her hands and gave Lacey a sharp shove. "Get into the hall," she said. Lacey started to back away from the table toward the hallway, but when she saw that her mother wasn't moving with her, she grabbed the sleeve of her blouse.

"You come, too," she said, trying to match the calmness in her mother's voice but failing miserably. Her mother caught her hand and freed it from her sleeve.

"Go!" she said, sharply now, and Lacey backed slowly toward the hallway, unable to move any faster or to take her eyes off the man.

In the hallway, a woman put an arm around her, pulling her close. Lacey could still see part of the room from where she stood. Her mother, the tall woman and her son remained near the tables, staring toward the doorway, which was out of Lacey's line of sight. Behind her, she could hear a woman's voice speaking with a quiet urgency into the phone. "Come quickly," she was saying. "He has a gun."

The man came into Lacey's line of sight as he moved forward into the room. The woman grabbed the doe-eyed boy, pulling him behind her.

"Zachary," the woman said. She was trying to sound calm, Lacey thought, but there was a quiver in her voice. "Zachary. I'm sorry we left. Don't hurt us. Please."

"Whore!" the man yelled at his wife. His arms were stretched out in front of him and the gun bobbed and jerked in his trembling hands. "Slut!"

Lacey's mother moved in front of the woman and her child,

facing the man, her arms out at her sides as though she could protect them more efficiently that way.

"Please put the gun away, sir," she said. "It's Christmas." She probably sounded very composed to everyone else in the room, but Lacey knew her well enough to hear the tremulous tone behind the words.

"Bitch!" the man said. He raised the gun quickly, squeezing his eyes together as he pulled back on the trigger. The blast was loud, splitting apart the hushed silence in the room, and the women finally started to scream. Lacey's eyes were on her mother, who looked simply surprised, her deep blue eyes wide, her mouth open as if she'd been about to speak. The tiniest fleck of red appeared in the white fabric of her blouse, just over her left breast. Then she fell to the floor, slowly, as if she were melting.

The man fell to the floor, too. He dropped the gun and lowered his face to his hands, sobbing. One of the volunteers ran into the room from the hallway. She grabbed the gun from the floor and held it on him, but the big man no longer looked like a threat, just weak and tired and wet.

Lacey broke free from the woman holding her and ran to her mother, dropping to her knees next to her. Her mother's eyes were closed. She was unconscious, but not dead. Surely not dead. The bullet must have only nicked her, since the amount of blood on her blouse was no more than the prick of a thorn would produce on a fingertip.

"Mom!" Lacey tried to wake her up. *"Mom!"* She turned her head toward the man, who still sat crumpled up on the floor. "Why did you *do* that?" she hollered, but he didn't lift his head to answer her.

Women crowded around her and her mother. One of them knelt next to Lacey, holding her mother's wrist in her fingers.

"She's alive," the woman said.

"Of course she's alive," Lacey snapped, angry that the woman had implied anything else was possible. The sound of sirens mixed with the pounding of the rain. "Her body just needs rest from being so scared." She could hear her mother's voice in her own; that was just the sort of thing Annie O'Neill would say.

Somehow, she didn't need to look to know that the woman the man had meant to kill was huddled in the corner, her arms around her son. She could hear her speaking, saying over and over again into the pine-scented air of the room, "I'm so sorry. I'm so sorry," and another woman was telling her, "It's not your fault, dear. You were right to come here to get away from him." But it *was* her fault. If she and her son hadn't come here, this crazy man wouldn't have run in and shot her mother.

The room suddenly filled with men and women wearing uniforms. They blurred in front of Lacey's eyes, and their voices were loud and barking. Someone was trying to drag her away from her mother, but she remained on the floor, unwilling to be budged more than a few feet. She watched as a man tore open her mother's blouse and cut her bra, exposing her left breast for all the world to see. There was a dimple in that breast. Just a trace of blood and a small dimple, and that gave Lacey hope. She'd had far worse injuries falling off her bike.

She stood up to be able to see better, and the woman who had tried to pull her away wrapped her arms around her from behind, crossing them over her chest and shoulders, as though afraid she might try to run to her mother's side again. That was exactly what she wanted to do, but she felt immobilized by shock as much as by the heavy arms across her chest. She watched as the people in uniform lifted her mother onto a stretcher and wheeled her from the room. The man was already gone, and she realized the police had taken him away and she hadn't even noticed.

Lacey tugged at the woman's arms. "I want to go with her," she said.

"I'll drive you," the woman said. "We can follow the ambulance. You don't want to be in there with her."

"Yes, I *do!*" Lacey said, but the woman held her fast.

Diane Chamberlain

Giving in, she let the woman lead her out the front door of the house, and she turned to watch them load her mother into the ambulance. Something cool touched her nose and her cheeks and her lips, and she turned her face toward the dark sky. Only then did she realize it was snowing.

Diane Chamberlain

GETS TO THE **HEART** OF THE STORY

THE LOST DAUGHTER
By telling the truth she'll lose her
daughter. By living a lie, she'll
lose herself.

THE BAY AT MIDNIGHT
All children make mistakes.
But some mistakes are deadly.

BEFORE THE STORM
Your little boy has been accused
of murder. Would you stop at
nothing to protect him?

SECRETS SHE LEFT BEHIND
She almost killed her brother.
Her punishment is just beginning.

BREAKING THE SILENCE
Your husband commits suicide.
Your daughter won't speak.
Do you want to know the truth?

Diane Chamberlain

Diane Chamberlain

GETS TO THE **HEART** OF THE STORY

THE LIES WE TOLD

How far would you go to
protect your sister?

THE MIDWIFE'S CONFESSION

Only you know a terrible truth.
Can you keep a secret?

THE SHADOW WIFE

You're pregnant by your best friend's
husband. Can you live with
the guilt?

KEEPER OF THE LIGHT

Your husband's mistress is dead.
Would you walk in her shoes
to get him back?

THE GOOD FATHER

Would you abandon your little
daughter to give her a better life?

A little girl, all alone, with a note that reads 'Please look after me'. What would you do?

Four years ago, nineteen-year-old Travis Brown made a choice: to raise his newborn daughter on his own. So far he's kept her safe, but now he's lost his job, his home and the money in his wallet is all he has.

As things spiral out of control Travis is offered a lifeline. A one-time offer to commit a crime for his daughter's sake. Even if it means leaving her behind. Even if it means losing her.

What would a good father do?

'What was so extraordinary about her? What did she have that I'm so horribly deficient in?'

As your husband grieves his mistress, you find yourself falling for the family she left behind, but they don't really know you.

You can go back to the husband who loves you second best or be content to live as a pale imitation of another woman.

Two paths, two lies.
Which way would you turn?

www.mirabooks.co.uk

M243_KOTL

You have a choice—
But can you live with it?

Your best friend has suffered a devastating brain injury. Alone and grieving, you turn to the only person who understands the pain.

Her husband.

When Joelle discovers she's carrying Liam's baby, she's torn between grief and unexpected joy. How can she share her secret?

Tell him and face a lifetime of guilt or lie and deny her unborn baby a father?

www.mirabooks.co.uk

One tragic secret
Four lives changed forever
Only you know
Can you keep a secret?

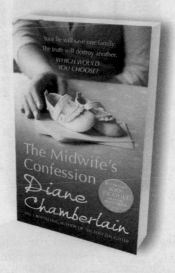

I don't know how to tell you what I did…

An unfinished letter was hidden amongst Tara and
Emerson's best friend's things after her suicide.

Noelle was the woman they entrusted to deliver their
precious babies into the world, a beloved friend.
Her suicide shocked them both. But the legacy
revealed in her letter could destroy them.

www.mirabooks.co.uk

**Why aren't you scared?
Because you said you wouldn't
hurt us if we were good**

An ordinary schoolday in March, snowflakes falling,
classroom freezing, kids squealing with delight,
locker doors slamming. Then the shooting started.
No one dared take one breath…

He's holding a gun to your child's head.
For each wrong answer he will shoot a child.

Who would take a gun into a school and
start shooting?
Who would the innocent victims be?

I think it might be my son.

www.mirabooks.co.uk